SAFE STATES

DON TRUMBULL

SAFE STATES
PREPARE ✦ ORGANIZE ✦ UNITE

Cover Design by the Kuhn Design Group
Cover photo by Molostock / Freepik

ISBN: 978-1-7330972-0-8 (EBook)
978-1-7330972-1-5 (paperback/print)
978-1-7330972-2-2 (Hardcover/reserved)

Version: 001.19

CONTENTS

★ ★ ★

THE SAFE STATE EFFECT

In the beginning there were two Americas. There were two truths and the people were divided, but then something strange occurred. A deadly threat was revealed and the entrenched powers couldn't tell us why it had been obscured. SAFE STATES is the story of our greatest victory. It uncovers the secret of our survival and it unites the people to defend life, liberty, and freedom. The truth is extraordinary.

Herein, we observe the catastrophic difference between an America that defends its people and an America that defends its politicians and rulers. Will we become a socialist nation? Will climate change take us out before we go green? What about our grids, and will they be attacked because it's the only way to win a war? These are the key questions, but only one of them is unspoken. For the reasonable and clear minded, the epiphany is now discoverable. This story is real.

Open borders, bribery, deception, critical mass; we're all familiar with the terrible consequences that are approaching, but what if there was something much worse, and what if we couldn't see it? What if our deception went much deeper, and what if our political establishment—through various methods—sabotaged the American people so that our families couldn't survive a new war strategy that was now firmly in place, well underway, and expected? What if there was a simple countermeasure—but we didn't know?

Where climate change is now the principal justification for an emergency transformation of America into a more restricted, regulated, and controlled nation; what if there was another existential threat that required every home, neighborhood, and community in America to immediately secure a backup survival infrastructure and a local civil defense?

What if today's experts believed that an EMP weapon was the most likely nuclear device to be used on America, and what if they believed an EMP attack was impending? What if this anticipated weapon produced a long-term event where all supply chains, electronics, communications, and modern-day vehicles were suddenly rendered inoperative from coast to coast? Worse yet, what if there was an effective low-cost countermeasure that preserved the people's critical technology—and what if certain forces were keeping it concealed?

Nearly unimaginable, we find the deception to be familiar, but to substantiate the claim of gross negligence, willful abandonment, and even political sabotage, we need to delve deeper into the details. We need to refine our questions. We need to get to the core.

What if North Korea could win the war with one EMP detonation? What if North Korea already had the weapon, and what if many of our experts believed that an EMP device is likely contained within one of their two satellites currently orbiting from the southern hemisphere? What if North Korea and Iran were immune to the deterrent of mutually assured destruction? Does the bank robber mentality apply? As long as they win, are the consequences secondary?

A new war winning strategy that exploits our Achilles Heel; as the intended victims we have to assume both North Korea and Iran are taking advantage of our divided government. Our critical infrastructures have never been hardened, and they can't be hardened without a government that's united in defending the people over advancing its rule. Worse yet, our government and our military have defended their critical infrastructures from EMP, and it's highly appropriate, but a conundrum exists. We've been left out. We've been told other things. We're the intended victims, we're still undefended, and our entrenched powers have boxed us in.

As reasonable people, we find that our instincts support a general warning. We can confirm the visible consequences of a divided America, but is this really life and death, mortal sabotage—politics with no remorse? How could it be true? How can we prove this hypothesis?

With an astute review of the congressional reports on EMP, we can validate the threat as catastrophic and nation ending. Our government and military have defended their continuity from EMP, but if we look closely at the National Infrastructure Protection Plan (NIPP); we find that it has never been implemented, and we find a stark omission.

At first look, we see a comprehensive framework that identifies the key "critical risk" sectors of our civilian infrastructures, assigns controlling agencies for each, and establishes a set of emergency goals to harden these critical infrastructures for the purposes of national security. A lifesaving plan, if implemented as intended it would prevent a catastrophic grid down event from ever occurring in America, but is it a Trojan Horse with respect to EMP, N. Korea, and Iran? Would it defend the private sector from a high altitude EMP? Would the hardened grids have access to a mobilized workforce, or would they fail because the people are trapped on foot with no working cars, no communication devices, and no working technology?

It is here where we find a catastrophic gap in NIPP's plan to harden. No established goals to mitigate the private sector risk to EMP. No reference to a community shielding plan that would protect our private transportation, our personal electronics, our communication devices, and our ability to organize, unite, and survive. Given this stark omission, we find no alternative plan to distribute food to the stranded populace of every town, nationwide. We find no workforce to operate the hardened grids, the public water and sewer systems, or the national supply chain. With respect to EMP, we find 300 million people trapped with no hope because NIPP was only designed for solar flare/CME and cyberwarfare. With respect to EMP, we find NIPP has been forced to accept defeat.

Moreover, we find the fingerprints of a catastrophic threat being suppressed, underreported, and minimized by the entrenched powers. As long as we don't know, there's no reason to defend.

It is here where we can make the additional conclusion that no defensive solutions to the people's EMP vulnerability—or solar flare vulnerability—will be instituted from the top-down. The facts are the facts, and for all journalists in pursuit of the truth, consider the observable.

The *National Infrastructure Protection Plan* only defends the private sector from a catastrophic solar flare/CME (E3) event, and because our cars and autonomous electronics will not be destroyed from a solar flare/CME (E3) event, the plan to secure America works well for this type of threat. But not with a man-made, high altitude EMP (E1/E2/E3) event. Even if the grids were hardened in accordance with the *NIPP* plan, the private sector would still be trapped on foot without cars and electronics. While waiting for outside help, they'd never receive it, they'd suffer and starve, and hundreds of millions would perish.

Furthermore, our enemies can now win the war with one high-altitude nuclear detonation (HEMP). MAD may not work. Our establishment politicians are behaving dangerously and irrationally. The only way to survive is to shield our private technology on-site, and within our communities and states so that we have a backup infrastructure of food, water, communication, and transportation. The countermeasure presented herein is both sufficient and achievable—it has been omitted from NIPP—and it has been routinely silenced under the threat of political retribution.

Given these discernible conditions we find the underlying consequences of our political division to be far worse than anything we've contemplated before. Status quo ensures that the American people will suffer and die and that our freedom will be destroyed by our radicalized enemies. Our Achilles Heel is undefended. Our adversaries will eventually take advantage. It could happen at any second, so how do we respond? How do we defend our families from a terrible suffering and death, and can a story help us see the life God wants us to fight for now?

This is our true story. This is America, and this is where Safe States begins. So, what do we do? And what would happen if the people suddenly learned the truth?

What if we had a President that wasn't afraid, and what if he told us we needed to defend our homes, communities, and states before it was too late? Would every state defend its people, or would some states refuse and say the President was lying? What if we were attacked? Who would live and who would die? How many SAFE states would it take to defend our borders, maintain our freedom, and save the undefended?

An extraordinary scenario; SAFE STATES is a hybrid novel that reveals why we need to unite at the instinctual level. Engineered for the reasonable minds, its sole purpose is to merge the observable with the hidden so that we can see and assess what we didn't know. It is not politically correct, nor is it comfortable; however, it is steeped in American values, Christian values, and the conventional morals we all learned as children and strive to follow. It depicts good versus evil, love and forgiveness, suffering, and hope.

Ahead, we'll find a terrible new reality that is dangerous to write, read, and acknowledge. It is for all Americans. All conservatives, liberals, and independents who aren't afraid; this is the story of our victory and our death. It describes how we can survive, and it reveals the core consequence of our divided nation and divided government. Where radical policies and green "New Deals" use temptation and deceit to exploit the people, this is the "Real Deal" and it is both horrific and lifesaving.

We're not supposed to know, but in this novel, we see how the patriots started a peaceful movement that defended half the people's food, water, and technology. One America survives—or everybody dies, and our freedom gets taken. The clock is ticking. SAFE STATES or no defense. Our future starts here.

CHAPTER 1

A TERRIBLE WAR

On Day 402 the story of America is beginning to unfold. To all patriots; prepare your souls. Remember everything. Embrace your freedom. See what you have earned.

On Day 1 a single nuclear weapon was detonated over the Continental United States and the electromagnetic pulse destroyed our electronics, our critical infrastructures, and our supply chains. We know the weapon came from an altitude and trajectory consistent with two North Korean satellites orbiting from the southern hemisphere. The method of airspace intrusion, the true aggressors, and the sequence of events are still in question.

Recently, additional facts have been confirmed. One minute before the satellite detonation a weather balloon delivered a smaller EMP over the southeastern portion of the United States. Two minutes later; a civilian aircraft detonated a nuclear weapon fifty miles downwind from the city of Jerusalem. As of last month we've learned the following. The Korean peninsula is now entirely controlled by the regime of North Korea. Iran and Saudi Arabia are at war. China and the United States are now engaged in conventional warfare. Russian interests have become uncertain, mutually assured destruction still exists, and the Islamic state has a flourishing army that's spreading everywhere, including here.

The world is at war and it's complicated. We were attacked by a foreign aggressor. We were attacked from within. We were attacked by a united force that wanted us dead because we were the holders of a freedom that couldn't be re-written, corrupted, or overcome. Within milliseconds, Americans were trapped on foot with no food, no water, and no cars. Power grids were destroyed. Communications stopped. From coast to coast—a total blackout occurred—and then it got worse. The undefended states suffered and starved. Safe States had a backup. Remember what happened then?

Before the attack, twenty-three states implemented an emergency countermeasure system that protected the essential equipment needed for long-term survival in all zones. With Alaska and Hawaii unaffected by the threat of EMP, America had a backup on the mainland, but twenty-five states refused under the claim that the Safe States were anti-American, racist, and radical. Remember how we felt? Remember what it was like after the attack? Remember all the good people who were trapped, hunted, and killed?

Today, we've seen the ramifications of our past fulfilled. We struggle with our forgiveness and we thank God for the circumstances that kept us from falling into their new world. We were saved, and we were saved a thousand times over, but this was an unthinkable battle and we all wonder. The details must be incredible. Is it a miracle?

Battered, but alive, we survived the EMP, but how we survived the internal war and the invasion of foreign troops is still a mystery. We heard the rumors and random reports. Our radios told us bits and pieces. They controlled the seaports. They were recruiting by force. They had slaves, and they were using people as a food source to feed their growing armies. We heard about territories lost and territories gained, but no back-story, no details.

Without our grids and technology we've been isolated from our real-time history and we've all had to speculate and wonder. The wait is over. The Press is back. The facts are remarkable.

Today, and for the first time, we'll see the terrible war that broke our hearts, broke our nation, and failed to break our freedom. We'll see our purpose. We'll experience the battle between the Safe States and the evil forces entrenched within the undefended states along our western coast. From the cockpit of an airplane and from the boots on the ground; we'll see how the patriots suffered. We'll see how they were trapped, and we'll relive the horrors faced by our fellow Americans.

Anne Wilkes brings us the astonishing new details. From the eyes of the heroes themselves, she delivers our history as if it were a movie on the big screen. Released in print—and for all to read—it begins from the back seat of a semi truck in Kalispell, MT.

"Anne, there's a pillow and blanket behind your seat. Hell, there's a bed back there if you want to sleep. We've got a good fourteen hours, minimum. It's a comfortable ride, shouldn't be too bad. Seat belts are behind the arm rest, there."

Sweat dripping off his forehead, Ken moved the pillow and pointed. "Those are the air controls. Two minutes and we'll have 'em on."

"Thanks Ken. What's this?" Anne held up a small box with her name on it.

"It's the meds and some notes from your doctor. I put the icepack in the cooler next to your seat."

"Nice." Anne opened up the cooler and looked in. "Thanks Ken."

From the driver's side, radio in hand, Jim climbed up the two steps of the semitruck's cab and he swung into his seat using the handrail. He held the radio up, and in a silent "I'm-waiting-for-this" signal, he closed the door, put his seat belt on and started the engine.

"We're dying here," Ken said, sweat dripping off his nose. "Let's pop the brake and roll."

"Yep. On standby with the colonel, give it a second."

Parked at the loading dock, the asphalt was getting hotter and the air was still. Sweat pooling on the two passengers inside, Jim appeared unaffected.

"Anne," he said turning around. "It's a pleasure to meet you." Jim set the radio down and extended his hand. "You comfortable?"

"Yep, I'm good."

Droplets rolling off her forehead, Anne shook his hand and smiled. "Sorry for the wet handshake. A little hot back here."

"Yeah, I know. It's like a sauna. You guys look like you've been swimming.

I'll turn on the AC." Jim flipped the switch and then he threw a towel over to Ken. "You're drenched."

Wiping his head, Ken laughed. "He's been in the snow too long. He's still cold. Your fan speed is on that big dial there in the center. Crank it all the way and it'll work good."

While waiting for the green light by the colonel, the cool air didn't take long and the high temperature in the cab started to drop slowly. Suddenly, a voice came over the radio.

"Jim, I'm up. You still with me?"

He picked up the handset. "I'm with you colonel. We're good to go. We've got two runners, and we've got our 'one extra' on board."

"Roger. You're cleared. Let her roll. Remember, she's just like a boat on a trailer, but longer. You'll do fine. You guys got some pointers, right?"

"Yeah, we got some pointers. We did parking lot practice and we're ready. We'll get her there."

"Excellent. How's your ride-along?"

"Doctor says she's fine. She's got a cast on her left arm, a few stitches. No worries."

"That's good. I'll pass it on. And she's earned this, Jim. Give her the scoop, and get her here safe."

"Roger colonel. Will do."

While handing him his reading glasses, Ken held up the Dispatch paperwork and tapped his finger on the highlighted portion.

"Release shows our ETA at Salt Lake City: 2230, local. Checkpoint is Overland, and we're on time. I'm guessing we'll see you around midnight."

"Sounds good, Jim. Girls are settled in and I've got Ralph. You're cleared. Smooth sailing."

"Roger. We're cleared. See you soon."

Jim handed the radio over to Ken and then he reached forward and flipped the truck's running lights switch to "on." He opened up his door, unbuckled his seat belt, and stepped out onto the ramp. Grabbing the handrail, he leaned out as far as he could, and with his arm rolling, he signaled the two security vehicles behind them that it was time to go. He then swung back in, closed the door and put his seatbelt on. Cinching it tight, he nodded to Ken and pulled the shift lever into Drive.

"Here we go," he said giving it some gas. "Let's see how this works."

With a smooth roll out, the semitruck full of essential equipment pulled away from its loading dock at the Kalispell, Montana airport. Operating under the command of the U.S Army, this was a military transport mission, but for Ken and Jim, it was the last leg of a long path to their new homes and new life. Idaho was still two years out from the new power grid, and like most, both men had families with a new purpose.

What they'd salvaged from their homes over the last two weeks had been shuttled to Montana in the back of their two pickup trucks and everything remaining they were able to sell. They made two trips, and as of last night—everything important was on board. They were leaving Idaho behind, and once again, life was changing.

"Big flippin' truck," Ken said pointing his finger straight ahead.

"No kidding." Jim watched his finger and he reduced his turn radius abruptly. He wasn't used to the mirror yet and the inches mattered.

"That was close." Shaking his head, he accelerated out of the turn and looked over to Ken. "The pointing helps. I need to go wider on the right turns."

From behind, Anne was studying the two men and she was planning her strategy. She'd spent the last month tracking them down and they were her final interview. They were the key to the story and she'd envisioned all sorts of characters, but this was interesting.

Obviously, there was a strong bond and they were highly secure in what they were doing. They communicated well, and while much of it was abbreviated, and even supplemented with hand gestures, they appeared to anticipate and predict one another effectively. There was a unique honesty with both men, and she could sense an underlying strength. It felt good, and the more she observed, the more her assumptions were confirmed. *This is big, Anne. This is perfect.*

She'd risked her life to get here, and she almost died, but she didn't. She was here. It was really happening and it was the story of a lifetime, but she needed to get a grip on how to proceed. *Clear your mind. Forget about everything else and focus. Just breathe.*

Resting her cast on the center console, she leaned forward. "Are you saying you learned how to drive this truck in a parking lot?"

"Yep." Jim was nodding. "We know enough to get started, and we'll learn the rest as we go. It's not that difficult."

"Really? It looks high-tech. Is it hard to drive?"

"No. It's got an automatic transmission and it's actually pretty easy. Most of the cool stuff is for military use and we'll learn that later. Steering wheel, brake, and gas pedal. It's all we need for today. And it is fun. If you didn't have a cast you could drive."

Anne held up her arm and laughed. "Damn cast."

Appearing in his driver-side mirror, Jim watched one of the two heavily armed security vehicles that were trailing behind begin to pass and then take the lead. In another twenty-mile's or so, they'd be entering unsecured territory and the extra security was a comforting sight. There were several high-risk areas along the path, but they'd all been cleared, and if they needed it—they had the muscle. With firepower in front, and behind, Jim could feel his heartbeat slow. With a nod to Ken, he turned to Anne.

"So we've been briefed on what you're looking for." Coming out of a wide turn and now on the on-ramp heading south, he started to accelerate. "We're all in, but we're not exactly sure what your mission is."

From the passenger side, Ken swiveled his seat towards the center console and crossed his leg to get comfortable. "We're at your disposal, but what's the premise of your story? What do you need?"

"The details."

Her official response wouldn't cut it, so she went with her gut. "Like when Moses parted the waters. Was it divine intervention or was it a fluke? Same thing with us. Nobody knows for sure, but something happened here and America wants the details."

Scooting to the edge of her seat, she leaned forward. "I'm getting close, guys. The gaps are filling in and the story's led me here. You're it, and whatever happened up here, I want to document it carefully."

"It needs to be documented."

"It does, Ken. And there's something I want to tell you both, but I can't talk about it yet. We'll get there, but I need to hear your stories first. Raw details. From the beginning. What do you think?"

Both were nodding and Jim responded. "Somebody needs to thread the needle, Anne. You fought hard to get here. We've got the details, and I'm glad you're on it. I'm glad you made it."

"Me too, Jim."

Wiping the sweat off her forehead, she pulled out a binder of official documents and it was filled with yellow sticky notes. "So, I've got tons of info on you two, and I've talked with my dad and the colonel, but I'm still confused. The sequence of events is strange. The timing is strange—and I've got questions."

Driven by the lure of a mysterious history, Anne was on a mission to bring clarity to the masses. Her travels throughout the Safe states had armed her with a unique awareness, and she had a knowledge that most didn't have. Where the communication infrastructures were still rudimentary, and where the collective pulse of a new America was difficult to discern, Anne was resolving the ambiguity by inspecting all quadrants of the United States that were in controlled territory. She was connecting the dots by hand, and her research was bearing fruit. Her project was nearly completed, and she'd examined all locations—except for here.

The Northwest region was her final component. With the record reflecting Ken and Jim's vital roles in securing the western borders with Washington State and Oregon, Anne knew there was a story that few knew. Both men were on the front lines, and one got trapped behind. This was the unimaginable, and well aware of the documented horrors, she was about to hear the story of true evil, and she'd hear it from the two people who were there.

With the brutal facts approaching, she wanted to clear the air so that nothing would be held back. She wanted all personal barriers removed from the interview. She wanted the whole truth—and she wanted it told from the heart. Where an immense suffering had occurred, and where the unedited version was urgently required, this was the golden opportunity and it had to be maximized. She'd set the tone, and she'd lay the foundation. It was a split-second decision and she needed to open the door, so she did.

For the very first time, she described her brutal assault in Montana to others. It was a horrific event and it was only three weeks old, but she didn't hold back and she was proud of herself. She let it rip, and her words came out with confidence. Both her strengths and her weaknesses were revealed, and with conviction she found solace in talking it out. She'd fought for her life and she'd won. There was a new wisdom, but she'd also been scarred irreparably and both Ken and Jim had the same affliction. Offering a unique empathy, it became obvious they were well equipped to help her deal with the experience.

Anne was relieved. Over the last week she'd felt a cloud and it was getting thicker, but now it was gone. She wasn't alone and she was thankful for the unplanned ice-breaker. The vibe was good and it was time to begin. It was perfect, and she dove in.

"So, I need you both to confide in me, and I'd like to start at the very beginning. Are you ready?"

Jim nodded. "Yes."

Ken nodded. "Yeah, fire away."

Anne set her pen down on the notepad and looked up. "So much has happened—tragedy after tragedy. Refugee camps, starvation, Americans killing Americans. In just one year ..." She picked up her pen and drew the number "1" at the top of her page.

"The story of America hasn't been told yet. Nobody knows it. The horrors are terrible and the victories are amazing. They happened everywhere, and they happened here."

Eyes wide, she looked at Ken. "We'd never imagined this could happen—and then it did—and it all happened in one split second. It was supposed to kill us all, but it didn't. Why? Why were we ready for the attack? Why did we suddenly have a backup plan, and why did the others say no?"

Still resting her wounded arm on the center console, Anne scooted in closer with her notepad. "We all want to know why, and the "why" is difficult, but the how is telling, so let's begin there. That Pulse attack took us all down, but then the Safe states got back up. The deeper you lived in SafePort territory, the better your odds, but if you lived in the Border States—those odds were much different. These were the front lines, and this is where evil threatened us all."

She drew a line at the top of the page and then she wrote "Day One" in big letters.

"Guys, I want to know what happened up here. You both fought evil, and you did it in a unique way. I mean, honestly, we wouldn't be here if you'd failed." Setting her pen down, she sighed.

"Jim, I want to start with you."

Catching her eyes in the rearview mirror, he cinched up his seat belt.

"You were airborne when the weapons hit, weren't you?"

"Yes, I was."

Wrapped in rubber bands, she grabbed a manila file folder from her bag and held it up so that Jim could see it. "Just so you know, what I have in this file is a bunch of factual snapshots. Most of it makes no sense and it doesn't explain how A leads to B. I mean, hundreds of airliners came crashing down, but yours didn't. Both of you live in Idaho, and yet you both flew to Seattle on the day of the attack. From the very first day, astonishing events were taking place, but we have no back-story and we have no details. Just snapshots."

Setting the file down, she wiped her forehead again. "Jim, I have an idea. I think it's the best way to go, and it's a lot better than just asking you a series of questions."

"You want me to tell the story don't you?"

"Yes. I want you to sit back and let your mind go. Keep us on the road, but tell me the story of Day One. Everything, Jim. The details, your perceptions, and even your thoughts."

Sweat flowing, she thought about turning her AC to the highest setting, but she'd wait. "From the very beginning, Jim. What was it like leaving your home that morning? You live in Sandpoint, Idaho, right?"

"Yep. Right on the river."

"So, the EMP hit us at 1:33 pm PDT. Do you remember the hours just before?"

"I do. Just not sure where to start, Anne. A lot happened on that day."

Once again, he cinched up his seatbelt. "I can remember waking up and I can remember walking out onto the deck with my first cup of coffee. In hindsight, it's crystal clear. I do remember my thoughts."

"Well then, take me through your day and include them all. Your thoughts are essential here, and you'd be surprised at what I've found. Let it flow, Jim. And tell me about the morning. Keep it going. First cup of coffee, and then go from there. Most say the day was 'odd.' How'd you feel? Take me to your deck on that morning."

"Well if you want the visual, it was an amazing place. Not because it was fancy or plush or anything. It was just a cabin in the woods and it was on a river, but for me, I guess I'd say everything seemed extra good. That's how I remember it anyway. It was odd, but it was also a great day, and then everything changed."

Grabbing his water bottle, he took a swig. He cleared his throat. "I'm pretty sure I remember it all, Anne. Everything."

CHAPTER 2

THE BEGINNING

Saturday Morning: 0600 Hours PDT
Sandpoint, Idaho

He'd lived all over the world and he'd been to many places, but in northern Idaho during summer he'd found no place more peaceful. This was his preferred world, and like now, it was at its best in the moments just after sunrise. It was here, from the bird's eye perch of his home's elevated wooden deck, where Jim found his life to be most authentic, and most agreeable. It was safe, and when he needed it, this was his shelter from the hectic world. Most of all, this is where he'd staked out his claim. It was a front row seat, and if the world went bad he had a lifetime pass. He had food, water, and a home. He had the American dream. He had sanctuary.

Jim loved his job, and when it called him away, he'd complete his mission and then he'd circle-back and come home. He'd found the good life and he knew what it was. It was here, and it was with his wife and three dogs. No matter where he was, he could bring it with him and it was always there. He'd pursued happiness, and he'd found it. For Jim, it was here—and it was everywhere—and the scales of life were well balanced.

Today, duty called and he'd depart soon, but for now—none of it mattered. It was early Saturday morning and nature was waking up. With his coffee cup full, he'd watch the world rise from his favorite chair on the back deck. There was no better place to be and the view was spectacular. It was his time to burn and he'd earned it, so he set an alarm for thirty minutes on his watch. Only then, and at the sound of the beep would he let his mind focus on work, and for now there were personal tasks that needed his attention.

There was a Sunday project to plan and this was precisely where he'd scheduled himself to plan it. It was a no brainer, and his confidence was high. He'd fly airplanes and then he'd be home by dinner. Tomorrow, the sprinkler repair project would commence and then by noon it would be completed. It'll be easy. He still had thirty minutes to plan his attack, and he only needed ten. Another sip of his coffee and life was good.

Both humble and strong-willed, Jim was a healthy man with a "can-do" personality. While he looked intimidating, he wasn't. He was wise, accommodating, and measured.

Contorted and reaching behind, he flipped the lever and reclined his chair two notches. "There we go," he said scanning the view.

This was where he contemplated. Whether it was fun or just another task—and especially if it was a challenge—this is where he'd go, and this was where he'd plan. The stage of nature had a beneficial effect, and for Jim it was a strategic advantage. It was calming, and out here, it was always there.

The sprawling deck at the back of his home provided for a stunning view to the west. From here, he could see the property's private lagoon below and he could see a good ten-mile stretch of the river valley to the south. Everything was perfect and the setting was most appropriate for the commencement of a Saturday morning daydream. With his stopwatch clicking, the destination was set and he let his mind go.

He planned and he re-planned his moves. Step by step, he visualized his attack. It was his third attempt at repair—and the yard was beginning to suffer. Tomorrow, the leak would be found, and he'd find it using simple deductions. He had all the information he needed. There was only one area he hadn't explored, and it had to be there. One or two more holes and he couldn't stop now. Tomorrow he'd win. He'd win and it'd be an easy fix. Couple of hours. Maybe a few.

Well aware of his over-positive attitude, under the surface he'd apply the appropriate time adjustments when necessary, but he routinely kept them to himself. For Jim, the covert system worked well, and when safe and suitable he'd merge his challenges with optimism. His wife, however, found it to be a grueling exercise of constant correction. In Sarah's mind, Jim was famous for his gross underestimations of project timing, and she reveled in catching his mistakes. To recalibrate his schedule was a win, so if it took longer, she was happy.

The end result was balance. Optimized reason; and it worked best when he was right. Oftentimes, he was, and for the sprinkler project, he'd keep the adjustments to himself. He'd give his wife all the available ammo—and he'd let her do her thing. Tomorrow, he'd plan for a full day, but if he fell short of his two-hour estimate, it would be Sarah who was smiling.

Another sip, his eyes began to wander. He wanted his attention to stray, but he'd keep the turmoil out of it. If he wasn't careful, it would slip in and he could only imagine what kind of stories might be on the news when he got home later today. He'd catch up later. He'd think about something else, and he yawned and stretched his arms out wide. Look at that, he thought. The sunlight was orange across the river and he could see the rays hitting the water.

The mountain sunrise brought new scenes daily, and with his eyes on target he let everything stack up in the queue—and he gazed. Today was a unique blend of colors and the orange rays forming along the river valley took priority. This was an amazing sight and it was worthy of distraction. With a quick glance to his wrist, he saw he still had plenty of time, and it felt good. Let it go, he thought, and he did. His eyes went back to the show— and he relaxed. Sprinkler's a done deal. Sarah's not awake yet. Have another sip. Soak it in.

Jim and his wife had been married for ten years now. Each had lost family members to a drunk driver, and a little over a decade ago it was a chance meeting that brought them together. Once in despair, they were now happy. Genuine and contagious, it was an observable joy and Jim sought nothing in life that he didn't already have. He'd seen the good and the bad, and he'd earned the skills to find solace. He had love, he had peace, and his freedom was well defended. He was an American, and around here, freedom reigned.

Jim had clarity, and while much of the world was acting strangely, he'd found peace through self-responsibility. Terrible things were happening and a dangerous change was underway. Patriots were under attack, deception was rampant, and hate was spreading like a wildfire. The American people were divided, but he had balance, he had hope, and he had a defense that protected everything. He was thinking about it now—and he wasn't supposed to be. Another sip of his coffee and he scanned the river.

With a flip of the switch, Jim was feeling energized and he was ready for the day. He looked forward to the Sunday project and he could already feel the triumph of conquering the sprinkler leak that had been plaguing them for well over a month. The birds were awake and the sun was up, and with another glance at his wrist, he saw that he still had fifteen minutes left before he had to leave for the airport. Keep it going, Jim. You'll see Paul today. Beautiful day for a flight. It'll be smooth. You'll see Ken.

Lost in his thoughts, Sarah opened the back door. Like a freight train, three dogs came running out onto the deck.

"Morning hun," she yelled, closing the door behind her.

Bella was the oldest dog and she walked slow and steady. Ralph, the youngest and largest of the bunch was a Great Pyrenees, and at a 150 pounds of two-year-old puppy—he was unsteady, overconfident, and he had no fear. Deck shaking, the three dogs swarmed, and the slobber and chaos were headed straight for Jim.

Max, short for Maxine, was a female German shepherd. She was the middle child, and at all times, she was Jim's shadow when he was home. It was Jim who'd take her on walks, and it was Jim who'd take her on car rides. When he was home, Maxine was happy, but when he'd leave her behind she was sad. She knew the routine, and she knew that Jim was leaving the house without her. The ritual was occurring now. Maxine wanted to go, and with her head in his lap—she was sad.

Still in her PJs and half asleep, Sarah was on a mission and she'd rounded up the four humming bird feeders that needed fresh nectar. Balancing them in her hands, she opened the back door and called for the dogs to follow her inside. These were the rules, and like a traffic cop, she snapped her fingers and rolled her arm.

"Inside—now!" she commanded. "Come on. Inside! Inside!"

She was the law, and the dogs obeyed—except for Ralphy. He wasn't ready, and for him, relaxing on the deck with Jim suited him better. In blatant defiance of her commands, he stretched out his body, and then with a deep breath and a big sigh, boldly remained at his favorite spot on the deck. It was a bad move.

Sarah looked at Jim. He was an innocent bystander—and Ralph was on his own. Her arms braced firmly on her hips, Sarah marched toward the giant white puppy and the correction was about to commence.

Confident in his choice, Ralph rolled over on his back and with his paws in the air he opted for the tactic that used to work, but for some reason wasn't producing the same results anymore. Jim laughed, and while Sarah's hand headed straight for his collar—before she got half way, Ralph jumped to all fours and he ran for the door. Her finger pointing and snapping; she restated her commands and she used a firm and demanding tone.

Already inside, ears up and worried, Ralphy looked back at Sarah and she threw up her hands. Turning around, she looked at Jim. "Sweetest boy. He's learning."

Closing the door, she remained outside so that she could say goodbye. Leaning against the rail, Jim smiled, and he was going tell her when he'd be home, but then she spoke.

"Be extra careful today," she said with her stern voice. "Promise me. Be safe. And I love you. Don't forget the lunch I made for you and your bro. It's in the fridge."

Sarah kissed him and then she pointed her finger towards the kitchen. "Don't forget it! Have a good flight."

Smiling, Jim nodded. He downed the last sip of his coffee and they both walked inside.

"You get in the shower and I'll be home for dinner." Jim closed the back door and headed for the refrigerator. "Thanks for the lunch, hon. I love ya!"

He was in a good mood and he was looking forward to seeing Paul. He'd fly his boss to Seattle, and then on his way back he'd fly his brother to his home in Eastern Washington near the town of Chelan. It was lunch with Paul, drop him off, fly back empty, and he'd be home early. Not a bad day, he thought pulling out the soft-case cooler from the kitchen refrigerator.

It was stuffed with Sarah's catering and it felt substantial. With Maxine glued to his side, he set the cooler next to his flight bag and it was time to leave. He bent down, he gave Bella and Ralph a pet, and then he grabbed his flight bag and threw it over his shoulder. The departure routine had commenced, and everybody knew what it meant, but Maxine still had hope.

"Love ya, honey," he yelled passing the stairway to the loft. "See you for dinner."

Strapping his flight bag and a cooler full of food, he and Max made their way toward the front door. The moment had come and it was time to say goodbye to his sad dog. With an extra hug, he told her to sit and then he closed the door and left her behind. He was off. The official departure into the realm of another world had begun. He was happy and it was a good day.

For Jim, it was the trek out of his long winding driveway that seemed to initiate the shift from safety and peace—to chaos and danger. Now in his truck and headed for the transition, crossing through the driveway gate was very similar to the feeling he'd get when descending into the clouds and dodging the storms to make a landing.

He loved to fly in all conditions and navigating through the thunderstorms came with the territory. It was simple. If you were on the other side of the gate—or if you were flying from the good into the bad—you just needed to be careful or the cruel world would bite you. Jim had thirty years in the air, and with a life full of lessons, he knew it could bite hard. Now at a hundred feet and approaching fast, the gate at the end of the driveway marked the border between smooth and bumpy, peaceful and cruel. Each had their place and each had their benefits, but you had to be vigilant and cautious.

With a canopy of dense trees, the long driveway was carved out of the woods and the road felt like a secret tunnel that was hollowed out and hidden from the rest of the world. This was home, and this was where he and his wife lived a good life that was surrounded by nature. Leaving it, just like this morning's trip and all trips prior, was predictably bittersweet. He loved his job. For every assignment that took him away, he was excited to leave, he was excited to fulfill the mission, and he was excited to come home.

Today, like all the rest, he was off to have an adventure. It couldn't be better. Chalk it up to the morning sun or anticipation of seeing his brother, but for some reason his trek out of the driveway seemed extra special. It was a beautiful day and he started whistling as he made the right turn out of his driveway. Today's airport was 40 miles away, and he'd find the company King Air waiting for his arrival.

With two miles of slow, bad road behind him, the dirt path from his driveway to the paved county road was riddled with bumps that felt like a continuous cattle guard crossing if you didn't know how to drive it. There goes the wash job, he thought shaking his head. Looking in his driver side mirror, he could see the thick tunnels of dirt vortices swirling behind him and the dust covering the rear half was all new.

Now on the pavement, the tactical bump avoiding s-turn driving course was over and it was time to sit back and enjoy the drive. Dog gone it, he thought with another glance at the mirror. Why do we even wash 'em out here?

Now on the move and cruising at a good clip down the freeway, he reviewed his task for the day while nursing his coffee and listening to the radio. Today, he'd be the facilitator in charge who'd maximize the company flight schedule and efficiency. The mission couldn't be any better. He'd fly his boss from Coeur d'Alene, Idaho, to Everett, Washington, and then on the return leg he'd fly his brother to Chelan. After some lunch with Paul, he'd fly the King Air back to Coeur d'Alene and then he'd drive home. With both his brother and Ken in Seattle on business, the timing worked out perfectly and it was the luck of the draw.

He'd heard from Dispatch yesterday, and when they told him Paul was scheduled on the return leg, for Jim it was a slam dunk. He'd assign the flight to himself, and he did it with the click of a mouse. He was the Chief Pilot for U.S. SKYJET, and the only person, other than his boss, with the power to do so.

Still whistling, Jim was excited to see his brother and he was anxious to catch up. He forged south on the highway and as he neared the city of Coeur D'Alene, he weaved his way through the traffic and headed for the town's airport. He knew that his favorite aircraft, King Air N77TL was waiting patiently. At SKYJET she was called Tango Lima, which represented the last two letters of her call sign, and she'd been with the company since day one.

Pulling into the airport, he headed for the Fixed Base Operator that managed the hangar where the company King Air was temporarily being stored. The FBO catered to general aviation and it served as the primary passenger terminal for private flyers.

Ken, who was the owner of the company and Jim's one-way passenger for today's trip, preferred this facility as it was the closest to his home in Idaho.

Specifically, he felt they were doing a good job and Jim agreed. Pulling into their parking lot, he'd worked close with the company and there were some minor issues, but they were willing to adapt, and they did. So far, U.S SKY-JET liked their attention to customer procedures.

Just this year he'd established the contract authorizing the FBO to handle limited maintenance on several of the company's aircraft. Now an approved vendor, as the Chief Pilot Jim liked the new official arrangement. Things always went smoother when everybody was trained on the same page. It was standardization, and it was another good way to start the day.

Having called in his fuel request from home, the aircraft should be ready and waiting with full fuel. On his first leg to Paine Field airport he had zero passengers in the back—and on his return leg from the Seattle area his passenger load didn't matter. It was simple. All tanks were topped off to the brim. Fuel was cheaper out here, and for the company's sake, it was best to take advantage when able.

It was time for work and Jim straightened his tie. He opened the truck door, and when he did he could feel the heat rushing in. It was supposed to be 85 degrees and he was sure that it was almost there. With his truck locked, he headed for the lobby and he could see that the King Air was already fueled and waiting for him on the ramp. The door was closed, it was chalked, and there were four orange cones. Good job, guys. Way to go.

With his flight bag slung over one shoulder and his soft-case cooler slung over the other, Jim walked through the double entry doors at the FBO's front entrance. Cindy, who was manning the morning shift at the dispatch desk, saw him enter, and then she headed for her desk.

As Jim arrived on the other side, she placed a large yellow envelope on top of the counter in front of him. A new employee, she was learning the basics, but he could tell she was starting to learn his routine. She asked all the right questions and that was good.

"Ken's here," she said sliding him the yellow trip folder. "Think he's in back, or maybe he's at the aircraft now. Is the aircraft in the hangar tonight?"

"Yep. Out and back today."

Jim signed the fuel ticket and then he placed his copy in the folder. "Shooting for 1600 on the return, so we'll see you around then. If you see Ken again, tell him I'm in the briefing room."

With his bags re-slung, he grabbed the trip folder and smiled. "Have a good one, Cindy."

"You too! It's a beauty out there. Enjoy!"

Firmly entrenched in flight mode, Jim walked toward the briefing room to perform his pre-flight paperwork. The FBO's briefing room was where everything in the proposed flight came together. From start to finish, with the most current available information on weather, airport status, and all the other pertinent details, every step of the flight was assessed and planned.

Much like his deck at home, this was where he planned everything flight related. It was a ritual and every pilot had his own way of doing it, but in the end, and with standardized procedures—everything got done the SKY-JET way. Company rules wouldn't be complete until the trip folder was signed and the request for a Flight Release was sent to the Flight Operations department. It was then, and only then, where the flight would be officially approved and released, or unapproved—and delayed.

Coincidently, Jim, in addition to serving as the Pilot in Command on today's flight, was also the CP, and designated as an Operational Control manager for the company. This meant he was approved for issuing a company Flight Release, with the exception of those flights—like today's flight—in which he also served as the Pilot in Command. As a result, today's flight would be approved by someone other than Jim. Knowing his boss well, he he knew exactly who that would be.

Once the flight crew initiated a request for a Flight Release, the request was immediately forwarded via fax and email to all Operational Control managers of the company. The technology used in the system was simple, but the comprehensive methodology was impressive. The company system in use today was a byproduct of industry expertise at its best. Blessed by the FAA and designated as SKYOPS, its standards became the model for integrating on-demand air carrier safety checks with FAA oversight. In the name of safety, it merged technology with accountability by requiring an approved Operational Control manager's hands-on review and decision before any aircraft performed any flight operation.

Among the many checks and balances, the system handled all real-time flight release requests from the company pilots. Upon submittal for a Flight Release, the request was immediately sent to the Flight Operations department via the pilot's cell phone or computer. The Operational Control managers of the Flight Operations department would then receive the request for release via their personal cell phones or computers, review all relevant information, and then immediately either approve and release the flight—or not approve. It worked beautifully and most importantly—the FAA loved it.

A safety system of checks and balances, SKYOPS ensured the airworthiness of everything. Aircraft, crew, route, schedule, and customer service. Company aircraft didn't move an inch unless SKYOPS approved it to do so, and when it did—it moved safely. It allowed for expansion, and it optimized customer service. It was how Ken built his reputation, and his reputation was special.

Ken had a style, and Jim liked it. He was a good boss, he could perform a thousand things at once, and he could do it very well. In Jim's book, he was a good pilot, and he was smart enough to know his limits. He'd sacrificed his love of flying, and he did it for the good of the company.

U.S. SKYJET was now a highly successful operation—and it was Ken's leadership and sacrifice that made it happen. Fifteen years ago, Jim was the first pilot he'd hired, and in the beginning it was Ken and Jim flying the King Air. Then it got bigger and he had to replace himself. He had to grow the business and he had to focus on safety. Suddenly, he had jets and crews based in all parts of the world and everything had to run flawlessly. Ken made it happen, and from the beginning Jim watched him do it. He pulled it off, and Jim trusted him implicitly.

Using his phone, the morning's preflight paperwork was done and the request for a Flight Release was in the system. Loaded with his gear and a coffee thermos that needed to be filled, he turned the corner from the briefing room into the hall. Inches from running head-on into Ken, he heard the words he'd expected. "Release approved. See you out there."

Dodging the incursion, Jim reached out and patted him on the shoulder as he passed by. "Morning, Ken. Thermos duty. Two minutes."

Upon his arrival at the plane, Jim was happy with what he saw. Ken had already thrown his briefcase on the left side captain's seat signifying this would be his seat for the leg to Seattle. He was the boss—and it looked like the boss wanted to fly. This first leg to Seattle was dispatched as a company flight, and thereby operated under the less stringent noncommercial part of the regulations. Ken would fly, and Jim would act as the nonfunctioning check pilot. He'd make sure he was following the rules.

Years ago, it was Ken who was the check pilot—and now the tables were turned. The morning was getting better and better, and now he and his boss were about to have a lot of fun flying in the airplane that started it all. With a busy flight schedule and a company that was growing, the two flying together was increasingly unusual, and for Jim, it was another bonus to a good day.

Walking up the King Air's passenger stairs, Ken entered the cabin. He closed and latched the cabin door and then he walked up the center aisle towards the cockpit and slid into the captain's seat. "What a great day," he said buckling into his shoulder harness. "I've been looking forward to this all week."

"What's the occasion?"

"Samantha. She's flying into Seattle today." Getting organized, he plugged in his headset.

"I'm headed straight for the airport when you drop me off. Meetings on Monday, but we'll get the rest of the weekend in Seattle and then on Tuesday she's coming home with me. It's a good day, Jim!"

Ken looked at his watch and then he picked up the checklist. "We're a little late. Let's roll. I'm flying."

He began his checklist flows and his old rituals came back to life like they'd never been gone. With all pre-start items completed, he fired up both engines and then he swiftly procured his taxi clearance. Like a man on a bicycle who didn't forget, Ken taxied the King Air toward the runway in use and he followed the company SOP's flawlessly. With almost two-years out of the cockpit, things were coming back nicely. Jim was watching his boss do what he did well, and he envied the back-in-the-saddle feeling.

Taxiing toward the runway ahead, both engines purred with an eager anticipation of power and thrust. At the hold short line, it was time to roll, and Jim watched as the boss ran the show.

Ready for departure, Ken pushed the little red button on his control yoke and called the tower for his takeoff clearance.

"Coeur d'Alene TOWER, King Air 77TL is at ALPHA 1, Runway 34 Left, ready for takeoff."

"King Air 77TL, winds light and variable. Cleared for takeoff Runway 34 Left, Fly Runway heading. Climb and maintain 6000 feet. Contact Departure 123.75."

Ken responded. "King Air 77TL is cleared for takeoff, Runway 34 Left. Runway heading to 6000. Departure 123.75."

Takeoff clearance in hand, he slowly advanced the throttles and released the brakes. In one fluid motion he rolled onto the runway and he headed for the centerline. With the nose-wheel locked on the white line, he increased the engines' thrust to the predetermined takeoff power setting. The aircraft rolled down the runway and the thrust and speed increased with every second.

Ken was back in the groove. Accelerating rapidly and approaching his rotation speed, he added the required back pressure on the yoke and the nose of the King Air rose up and the wheels left the ground. They were off and the engines howled with the sound of horsepower. Ken raised the landing gear and "Tango Lima" climbed straight ahead and rapidly.

"Smooth, Ken. She's awesome, isn't she?"

Before he could respond, Coeur d'Alene Tower came over the radio and announced updated instructions. "King Air 77TL; turn left heading 300 and climb to Flight Level 190, contact Departure and good morning."

Ken replied. "Roger, King Air 77TL, left turn heading 300 and that's up to Flight Level 190. Contact Departure. Good morning."

With his new course and altitude set—he flipped the frequency selector on the radio to the Departure Control and then turned to Jim.

"Yeah, she's awesome." His eyes gleaming, he could feel the bond with the airplane rekindling. "Just like I remember. Oops, forgot my check-in."

Smooth as can be, and with only a little roughness on the edges, Ken made his check-in with Departure Control, and then he turned on the autopilot and took his hands and feet off the controls.

"This is nice, Jim! I miss it!" Ken had a full blown smile and his eyes said it all. He was happy.

"She's a peach," he said giving a loving pat on the instrument panel and nodding. Tango Lima was the first aircraft he'd ever purchased and he started the company with this aircraft alone. She was important. She was nothing but good, and she'd seen it all.

Over the many years, both men had developed an elevated affection for the airplane known as Tango Lima. Each considered himself to be her gallant protector, and for Jim, this morning's flight seemed extra special. A pause in the cockpit chatter occurred, and as the climbed to the assigned altitude there was a silent moment where they both soaked it in. As they headed towards the Pacific Northwest, the view was crystal clear and the ride was smooth. It seemed notable—and it felt more important than it should—but it did.

"You know that training slot is still open, right?" Jim threw out a nudge, but he knew it was a long shot. "I can hold it for another month, and I can even drag my feet if you want me to."

Nodding, he looked at Ken and he added the sales pitch. "That Challenger in Scottsdale needs a second captain soon. With Bob's retirement looming—why hire another when it could be you? It's only one trip a month. An occasional hop to Hawaii. It could be the perfect fit."

Shaking his head, Ken smiled. "This could be the year, but I just don't know."

He went silent for a moment and then he continued. "If I were to pull back from the desk, lots would have to happen. Allan's sharp, and he's ready to be the DO, but let's put on ice for a couple weeks. Keep it open for now."

Allan was SKYJET's Assistant DO. Ken had filled the director of operation's position for the company from day one and he was more than ready to retire from his fulltime duties. The FAA's requirement was that all Air Carrier DO's be appropriately qualified to serve, and with Allan's experience at both the airlines and the FAA, he had all the right stuff to hop in at any time. All he needed now was for Ken to hand over the reins, and this in itself seemed to be a slow process.

Now at its cruising altitude of 19,000 feet and approximately 25 minutes from its destination airport in Everett, Washington; the King Air was making good time and it had a groundspeed of 240 knots. The airport at Paine Field was 25 miles north of downtown Seattle, and it worked better than landing at Boeing Field, or SeaTac. SKYJET still had a maintenance base at Paine Field, and for Seattle trips—landing in Everett was the preferred choice.

Currently, they were flying over the eastern portion of Washington State and the area below was a dry, barren, and inhospitable land. When compared to the western slopes of the Cascade Mountain range—which was just ahead—the terrain would change dramatically with endless trees, wetlands, and greenery. The border of Eastern Washington and Western Washington was officially defined by the Cascade Mountain range, and these mountains, to include Mt. Rainier were approaching rapidly.

Over the years, Ken and Jim had become good friends and they were on the same page when it came to integrity, politics, and family safety. They used the remaining minutes of cruise flight to talk strategy regarding their personal departure from the company, and their involvement in other pursuits. Both were approaching the retirement decade, and if they wanted out—they needed to implement their replacements soon.

"King Air 77TL, descend to One-Six thousand. Contact Seattle Approach on 124.5."

"Down to One-Six thousand. Approach 124.5—King Air 77TL," Ken replied.

Switching to the Approach frequency, he checked in with the new controller and initiated the descent to 16,000 feet. The entire flight had been unusually smooth. It was clear blue every direction, and the high-pressure, late-August weather system was locked in for the rest of the month. Around here, it was the best time of year, and soon the weather in Seattle would change to rain. All points east of the Cascades would get cold and snowy. Summer had a short window, but when it was here, it was beautiful.

In his day, Ken was a master of this particular airplane. Even now, he was maneuvering the flow of throttle, pitch, and trim like it was extension of his body. The turns, climbs, level-offs and rollouts were all crisp, clean, and keenly anticipated.

Jim sat back, and he watched as Ken worked to get his advanced skills back. His attention to the company's Standard Operating Procedures was right on the money. It was both men who'd developed, drafted, and implemented the SOPs for each aircraft in SKYJET's fleet—and Tango Lima was the first. With the exception of a few minor misses, Ken had it pegged like he did it every day.

"There she is," he said pulling out the checklist. Paine Field was coming into view, and for Ken it was a known point on the far horizon.

"In and out for you. I'm stuck till Monday." Running through the checklist, he got ready for his upcoming descent into the Seattle airspace.

"If it weren't for the meeting, I'd grab Samantha and we'd go back to Idaho today. We've got her for three whole weeks, and then she goes back to finish her internship. She's excited Jim. She says she needs to get home and 'breathe' as she called it. Guess there's just no place like home." Ken finished his checklist items and he was ready for the approach.

With the airport in sight, he had a strategy in mind and he wanted to maximize his stick time and capitalize on some much needed recurrent training in the airplane. With a mental flick of a switch, he turned on his "A" game, squeezed the push-to talk-button and contacted Seattle Approach with his request.

"Seattle Approach, King Air 77TL has Paine Field Airport in sight with information Bravo. If you can fit us in today, we'd like to request vectors for the ILS 16 Right approach to a full stop."

"Roger, King Air 77TL. We can do that. Descend to 3000 feet and fly heading 350."

"Down to 3000—Heading 350. King Air 77TL." Ken's wish was being fulfilled.

"Ah, yes," Jim snickered. "The old-fashioned autopilot approach. Getting your money's worth."

"I am," he responded. "Refreshed the old memory with the Operators Manual this morning. Think I'm feeling pretty good, but we'll see."

Ken had requested the precision instrument approach into Paine Field to capitalize on a training event. The weather was beautiful, the wind was calm, and the visual approach to Runway 16 Right was in use. He certainly didn't need the approach and he could hand fly it in his sleep, however, flying the King Air's antiquated and user unfriendly autopilot in the coupled approach mode was a skill easily lost in this aircraft—and Ken wouldn't have it. In the King Air, it was every pilot's weak link and it required steady practice to remain proficient. It was a unique and not so pretty sight to behold. The last time he'd flown Tango Lima was two years ago and he was determined to make the most of it. There was only one way to do this, and he'd have to beat the autopilot.

Jim was a Check Airmen for the company and had been for ten years now. He'd flown with and trained many pilots in his time, and in his humble opinion it was only the exceptional pilots who continually challenged themselves. Ken was one of these, and in honor of his impending humility, he wouldn't let the opportunity pass to inflict more pressure. He folded out a clean sheet of paper from his yellow legal pad and clicked open his pen with intensity. "I'll just make some notes as we go along," he said smiling. He clicked his pen a few more times.

Ken nodded. "This could get ugly, so get ready."

It was years ago that both men had worked together in developing the Standard Operating Procedures for the King Air's coupled autopilot approach, and due to the system's poor design, it was a challenge to establish standardized procedures that were straightforward and uncomplicated. As a result, the adopted company procedures weren't pretty—but they were the best they could do with what they had to work with. The procedures were demanding on the pilot and the system inherently required significant pilot input throughout various stages of the approach.

What made the coupled autopilot approach truly ugly was the awkward positioning of multiple displays in the cockpit that required the flying pilot to hunch over, lean over, and stretch out to push the buttons and turn the knobs. Sometimes this was required just to read what the screen was displaying.

If everything was performed in the correct sequence and at the right time, however, the autopilot would "capture" the approach signals emanating from the ground—lock on and fly the aircraft down to its published minimums. It was a bad design. On top of everything else, the buttons and knobs were tiny and foolishly positioned way too close to each other. Add some bumps, and the challenge increased tenfold. Add an emergency while flying single pilot in bad weather—you better know your stuff.

Ken wanted his skills to come back, and he knew they were there, but he had to find the rust and he had to polish it off. He had a thousand things on his mind, but when he flew the approach everything else faded away. He felt clear, and his instincts took full control. He had what he wanted. He'd mastered the autopilot and his landing was right on target.

"Nice job," Jim said, closing his notepad.

"Sure feels good. Other than picking up Sam, best part of the day—guaranteed!"

Ken was taxiing the King Air to the FBO on the east side of the airport near the control tower. It was at this executive hangar where SKYJET began its operations with this airplane fifteen years ago. Five years ago, SKYJET's Principle Base of Operations was moved from this building to Scottsdale Arizona as the company began to grow. It was always a good, but strange feeling when they'd visit. They knew every inch of the hangar, but the faces had changed and everything seemed different.

"Check out the staging over there by the old tower," Ken said putting on his sunglasses. "Looks like three, maybe four C130s? Not sure what's behind them. Looks like transport vehicles."

"It's a National Guard exercise," Jim replied.

"They've been flying in and out of here a lot over the last couple months. This is the airport where our Challenger got delayed 4 hours last week because they closed things up without notice. It was an unscheduled event. Seattle crew told me they were offloading modular containers and heavy equipment right on the taxiways. What training events are so important that they require an unscheduled airport closure?"

Venting, Jim had a good reason. "That cost us a lot of money last week."

"Yep, it sure did," Ken said nodding as he taxied to a full stop on the tarmac in front of the FBO. He powered off the avionics and shut down the King Air's two engines. "My ride's here. She's all yours, bud. Got to go." He took off his shoulder harness and powered up his phone.

On quick-time, Ken slid out of the captain's seat and stood in the center aisle behind Jim while he gathered his briefcase and tote bag. "I forgot to tell you. Paul called dispatch and said his son was going home with him on today's flight. I had Scheduling add him for you on the manifest. Reapproving the new release now," he said, holding his cell phone out and pushing the "Send" button.

"Also, I told Paul that his flight home is on us today. I put a note in the Trip Folder." Seemingly distracted, Ken departed from his double-time and Jim was watching him stare out the side window. Curious, he wondered why, and then he saw Ken break the gaze and grab his bags.

"I'm out of here buddy—have a good flight home." Expecting him to move, he was still standing there, motionless.

"You feel okay?"

Unsure about his answer, Ken shook his head. "I don't know. I mean, yeah, I'm fine. But it's weird. Don't get trapped here, Jim. Something is off."

His eyes sincere, Ken nodded and then he turned and walked quickly out of the airplane. It was strange, and Jim wondered if he was feeling sick. His face was pale, and he was way too serious. It was non-standard. It was odd.

Jim checked the time and it was 11:45. Anytime now, he thought. Still worried about Ken he gathered his stuff and prepared for the slide over to the left seat. From the copilot seat on the right side, he slid his left leg over the center console and then, with a shift in weight, he sat down on the captain's seat.

With his right leg the last remaining appendage that needed to be pulled over, just as he did, he immediately stopped and froze. With the center console supporting his leg, he thought about Ken's words. Don't get trapped here. Something is off. He knew Ken was stressed, but he had to consider the source and his little voice was telling him to listen. He saw Ken's eyes when he said it and he was dead serious. He didn't like the premise, but he brought his leg over and he could feel the pressure. Dog gone it, he thought. What is this?

For no good reason, he had the urge to go quick. As in now. As in get your brother and nephew on board and fly home. It was wrong, and it was uncalled for. It was out-of-place, and he didn't like it one bit.

CHAPTER 3

OUT OF THE BLUE

Jim had the aircraft ready to roll and all he had to do was get his brother and nephew inside and close the doors. He looked at his watch and he could feel his stomach churning. He was anxious and it was concerning. He didn't know why, but he needed to call Sarah and he needed to check in.

Grabbing the phone, he pulled the sun visor down, and still, with the bright sunlight he could barely see the numbers on the touch screen. Suddenly, he found the right spot. He was hunched over and contorted, and then from behind, his brother Paul tapped him on the shoulder.

Stowing the phone, he raised his head. "Hey! Glad you're here. You ready?"

"Yep. But John's with me. It was a last minute thing. Are we good?"

"Yeah, we're good. What's up with John?"

Standing in the center aisle, Paul smiled. "Not sure, but I'm glad he's going. He called last night at the hotel and said he wanted to catch a ride and go home for a few days. Definitely out of the blue, but it works for me."

Seeing the lobby doors open, he paused. "Here he is now. Are we ready?"

"Yep. Let's go. I'll get us out of here and we can talk in the air."

Talking on his phone, John walked up the King Air's air-stair and he stuck his head in the passenger cabin. Formally known as little Johnny, he was Jim's little nephew who wasn't a small boy anymore. He'd grown up, and at six-foot-four, he had the mind of a scholar and he could take on a bear.

"Hey bud. Hop aboard," Jim said waving him in. "I'll batten down the hatches."

Out of his seat and headed for the cabin door, Jim stopped and shook John's hand. "Good to see you, dude. We've got sandwiches on board if you're hungry."

Talking to someone important on his phone, John nodded to his uncle and then he mouthed the word "yes" as Jim walked by.

While Jim focused on the preflight inspection, the two passengers took their preferred seats in the King Air and they got settled in. Paul climbed in the copilot's seat on the right side and he plugged in his personal headset that Jim had given him last year for his birthday. Jim had been working him hard over the last few years on the idea of going in together on the purchase of a floatplane. The headset was one of many hooks he'd used to entice him on the idea—and they were all working. Paul was now a Private Pilot, and he'd just gotten his floatplane rating.

He'd been hooked for months and he planned on broaching the subject with Jim today. He'd brought his "for-sale" folder and he had three spec sheets on three floatplanes that were among his top picks. Like a little kid, Paul couldn't wait to show him what he had—and he couldn't wait to tell him what he was thinking.

John, still busy on his phone, had the entire cabin to himself and he'd chosen the rear forward-facing seat. The passenger cabin of Tango Lima was configured for five executive passengers and two pilots. The seating arrangement behind the cockpit consisted of four large executive style seats that faced each other, and then behind this section there was a jump seat that was smaller, but still better than the airlines.

In the passenger cabin there were two opposing seats on the left and two on the right, and the cabin had a center aisle. Both opposing seats on each side of the aircraft had a fold out table positioned between them, and when extended, the King Air's cabin could be transformed into an effective conference room in the sky. For most, it was a great place to have a meal, work on the laptop, or play cards.

John's favorite seat faced forward, and it was located in the rear and on the right side of the aircraft. He was still on his phone, and as Jim finished securing the luggage in the back of the plane, he overheard some key points of the conversation. It was slightly familiar and it was slightly obvious. For some reason, there was an unhappy girlfriend on the other end, and it was clear that John was doing his best.

At a faster than normal pace, Jim performed his final walk around inspection of the airplane and then came back around in a big circle to the left. He walked up the air stair of the main cabin door and then closed it behind him. The door latch required a firm grip and a solid turn. Confirmation that the door was securely closed was obtained visually through several access points along the closed and latched door. He checked each one and then moved on. He walked up the center aisle and then he stopped just short of his nephew.

When flying the public and all non-company passengers, it was now that Jim would perform his verbal safety brief and educate the passengers on all emergency exits and safety procedures used in the aircraft. Jim had flown his brother and nephew in Tango Lima many times, and over the years John had learned his way around the airplane.

Fascinated by the mechanics, while growing up, Jim had watched him take it on himself to learn about the aerodynamics of the airplane and the systems that were on board. He was always asking questions, and he was always asking questions that were complex, exceedingly smart, and highly astute. He was a natural, and Jim had always been certain that he'd pursue flight school, but he was wrong. John loved the law better and he was just like his dad.

Putting his hand on his shoulder, Jim asked him if he wanted the safety briefing.

"I'm good, Jim. Let's go. Ding the cabin chimes when you're ready for lunch."

"Okay. I will. Here we go."

Jim patted his nephew's shoulder and then he walked into the cockpit and buckled in. Following a quick seat adjustment, he ran through the Before Start checklist, and then he used it to tap his brother's left knee.

"I'm going to run us through an accelerated departure. Things will go fast, and I'll tell you why later."

He knew he didn't have a good explanation for the double-time departure, but he'd work on his excuses in the air. Doesn't matter now, he thought. Just get out of here. It's Ken's fault.

He took a deep breath and then chuckled about his previous thoughts. He wouldn't get stuck and they wouldn't close the airport. Even if they did, who cares? He put it out of his mind and he engaged the starter on the number 1 engine. The propeller spun via the starter only, and as it spun faster and faster, Jim watched and waited for just the right point where he could add fuel. With the push of a lever he gave her the juice, and then wooooof! With a puff and a howl the left engine had ignition and it quickly assumed its steady state low idle speed.

The King Air was a twin-engine aircraft and it had two little jet engines; each connected to a propeller and located on each wing. The turbine engines are what made it reliable and the King Air was a capable airplane. It was pressurized, radar equipped, and suitable for all-weather operations. King Air 77TL was a rock solid corporate workhorse with healthy, strong engines. Under a 1000 horses each, they were small, but they did the job nicely for 5 passengers—and they did it in style.

He fired up the number 2 engine on the right side, and then with both engines running he flipped the avionics master-switch to "on." This switch turned on the onboard avionics and both headsets were now active.

"You with me?"

Paul nodded as he searched for his boom mike that was folded under his chin. He swung it up and placed it in front of his mouth.

"Loud and clear," he said. Paul's fingers were fumbling near the edge of his seat and he was obviously reaching for something in his file.

Stashed between the co-pilot seat and the center console, with his left hand, he had two fingers on the spec-sheet and he squeezed tight. He didn't want to wait and it was time to tease Jim. This was the sale sheet he'd been eying for weeks, and it had a photo of the floatplane he liked best. With absolutely no patience, he pulled it out of the folder and with his two fingers he handed it to Jim.

"Look what I brought. This is my favorite, but we've got some contenders here. When we get some time. There's four or five in here."

Somewhat distracted, Jim responded. "Awesome, Paul. We'll make some time."

With the checklist complete, he set it on his lap and then he handed the sale sheet back to his brother. "That one looks nice, but let me get us out of here first and then we'll take a look."

Jim turned around. "You ready, John?" With two thumbs up, he pushed the little red button and called Ground Control for his clearance.

It was 12:45 PDT and the King Air was ready to roll. With his taxi clearance in hand, Jim released the brakes and the aircraft began the long taxi toward the departure end of Runway 34 Left on the other side of the airport. The winds had switched since landing, and now they'd be taking off to the north.

Jim knew the airport like the back of his hand, and he proceeded to the runway at a taxi speed slightly faster than normal. With all pre-take-off checks complete, he had the aircraft ready for departure as the King Air came to a stop at the runway's hold-short line.

The tower frequency was crowded with arrivals. With his annoying thoughts telling him go fast, it was eating at him and his patience was wearing thin. It didn't belong, it was unsafe and it was all wrong. As he waited for his opening on the radio, he started to question whether he should takeoff at all.

Suddenly, a split-second pause occurred and he took his shot. "Paine Tower, King Air 77TL is at ALPHA 9. Runway 34 Left. Ready for takeoff."

The tower responded. "King Air 77TL. After departure; fly Runway Heading. Climb to 3000 feet—and contact Departure on 125.9. Clear for takeoff Runway 34 Left."

He had his clearance and he released the brakes. "Roger. King Air 77TL is cleared for takeoff Runway 34 Left. Runway Heading up to 3000 feet. Departure is 125.9."

His response to the tower signified his receipt of the official clearance, and with a correct read-back, it consummated the takeoff agreement between Paine Tower and the pilot-in-command. The King Air rolled onto the runway centerline and with its throttles advancing it rapidly began to accelerate to its flying speed. Suddenly, the nose wheel lifted off and then the main gear followed. Tango Lima was airborne.

Feeling the unwanted pressure starting to release, Jim retracted the landing gear and then he completed the after takeoff checks. He shook his head, and he was perturbed. They were off the ground and that was all it took.

Tango Lima climbed rapidly and straight ahead to the north. Flying on the runway heading of 340 degrees and at climb airspeed of 140 knots, the moment was over and he'd deal with it later. In accordance with the takeoff clearance from the tower, Jim reduced the power and leveled off at 3000 feet.

The anxious "get out of here now" feeling was simply and probably, in Jim's analytical mind, a culmination of unique events and sensations. Perhaps it was just the power of suggestion, and regardless, it's still a good morning. Whatever it was, it's over. *Everything's fine now.*

"King Air 77 Tango Lima. Turn right and fly Heading 140 degrees. Contact Seattle Departure on 125.9."

The tower's radio call focused Jim's attention on the present. While banking the airplane to the right, he responded to the controller.

"Roger. Right turn Heading 140. Departure 125.9. King Air 77TL."

Jim rolled out on his assigned heading of 140 degrees and activated the new frequency of 125.9 for his check-in with Departure Control.

"Seattle Departure. King Air 77TL is with you at 3000. Heading 140 degrees."

"Roger King Air 77TL. Seattle Departure. Climb and maintain One-Six thousand. Join Victor 120 and I'll get you Direct Chelan Airport as soon as I can."

"That's up to One-Six thousand. Join Victor 120. King Air 77TL." Jim responded and then complied with the instructions.

Cleared to climb, he raised the nose and added the requisite power to establish a normal climb speed up to their assigned altitude. Tango Lima was now flying up and away, on its final trek out of the fishbowl metropolis that was corralled by the Puget Sound to the west and the Cascade Mountain Range to the east. The city of Seattle and all of the Pacific Northwest cities on its outskirts could be easily seen, and the visibility was about as far as the human eye could muster on a clear day. Soon, the high-density populations beneath them would fade away and the rugged terrain would take over.

Both Lake Chelan and its municipal airport were located on the eastern slopes of the Cascade Mountains and it was deep within the Wenatchee National Forest. The area was much like Switzerland, and with rugged terrain and alpine forests in every direction—it was a tourist hot-spot. Lake

Chelan was a deep glacial lake with a smorgasbord of desirable real estate on its eastern shorelines. It was a top contender for Washington State's most preferred location, and it had enticed many to the area.

Paul and his wife Lisa owned a Bed and Breakfast in the small town of Chelan, and recently, they'd purchased a new home that was on the lake and several miles from town. Starting his career as an attorney in Seattle, Paul switched gears fifteen years ago and he'd made the right choice. Focusing his talents on a specialty niche, he'd capitalized on the real estate market and he'd carved out his own success.

He'd worked hard and he was a smart businessman. When it all came together, Paul and his family moved to Lake Chelan and ever since he'd been commuting to his office in Seattle twice a week. It was four hours each way in a car—or thirty minutes by air. He was ready to slow down, and if he bought an airplane—he could. Big decisions were afoot.

Now approaching the western peaks of the Cascades, Paul seemed mesmerized by the rugged terrain below. He spotted a remote lake in the gorge between two mountain peaks ahead and he'd never noticed it before. Two months ago Paul had passed the FAA check ride and was a newly rated private pilot with a floatplane rating. He had a folder full of planes for sale, and now, with the remote lake below, he had the perfect spot to let his mind take a test-flight.

He focused his eyes on the terrain and then he quickly realized he'd never have enough power to make it out of that little lake. Now fully engrossed, the realities didn't matter and his daydream stare out the cockpit window was the perfect palate for his mind to exploit. With the dark blue lake becoming his scene of choice, he shuffled through the many reasons why he wanted to buy an airplane.

The floatplanes he'd selected for today's in-flight review were way out of the price range discussed by him and his brother last year. Paul's recent financial success allowed for a much nicer airplane than the 50/50 split on an old Cessna 172 on floats. The original idea was based on an older airplane, and an older and cheaper one was likely more in line with what he knew his brother was thinking. He'd heard Jim mention early retirement from U.S SKYJET, and he knew there'd be no extra money to throw at airplanes.

With a nod to himself, the fundamental premise of his upcoming in-flight presentation was confirmed. He'd buy the aircraft. It'd be a nice one, and he'd have Jim manage the operational side in exchange for his personal use. It was the perfect plan. Both he and his brother lived on the water and they were less than two hundred miles apart. The plan would work well for everybody, and he was pretty sure he'd already made the decision. He hadn't told anybody yet, but Jim would like it, and with Jim on board, he could easily sell the idea to his wife.

Entrenched in his gaze out the side window, he imagined himself floating in his brand new airplane on the remote lake below. He was a pro at turning fantasy into reality, and he used his skills to concoct an imaginary point of view that was elevated and circling around him. Like a silent helicopter doing a news story on his brand new airplane. There he was, standing on the front of the airplane's left float and the aircraft was drifting in the sunny blue water of the remote lake.

He imagined that it was a clockwise aerial flyby, seeing the top of the airplane's fuselage, its wings sporting a brand new paint job of glossy white with dark red and grey pinstripes. It was his favorite paint scheme and it was a beautiful daydream. God willing, it was one that could someday come true. He enjoyed the adventure of pursuing dreams, and he knew what it took to make them real. For Paul, it was a good day. He hadn't felt this way in a long time, and he felt excited.

Flying level, they were now at the cruising altitude of 16,000 feet. The Cascade Range was just below, and Jim suspected that at any moment now, Departure Control would call with their Direct to Clearance to the Chelan Airport.

He entered the navigation data into the onboard GPS, and he included the current assigned heading of 140 degrees and the upcoming merger with Victor 120. The onboard equipment knew exactly where Jim wanted it to go, and exactly how he wanted to get there. With the GPS unit tied directly to the aircraft's autopilot, all it took was a push of a button and the autopilot would fly the aircraft wherever it was told to go.

He configured the GPS so that it was primed and ready for Seattle Departure's Direct to Chelan clearance. Upon receipt, and a far cry from the chaotic coupled autopilot approach flown this morning with Ken, all he had to do was reach out to the unit mounted directly in the center stack of the cockpit instrument panel, press the "Direct To" button, and then press "Enter."

Paul, having completed his analysis, snapped out of his prolific daydream and turned to Jim. "When's lunch?"

"Few minutes works for me. Let's make our turn and then I want to see what you have in that folder there." He glanced to the right and in his peripheral he saw John. He had a half-eaten sandwich in his hand and his mouth was full.

"I knew I smelled something." Jim pointed to the back.

Paul turned and he looked at his son. "Good man. Smells good!"

"It's awesome Dad.Roast beef, turkey … little plates of everything."

Besides his half-eaten sandwich, John had a platter full of personalized ingredients sitting on the passenger cabin table in front of him. He was hungry and his appetite had just arrived. He'd been under more stress than usual and he seemed to be feeling a little bit better now that he was headed home. He had some big decisions to make and home seemed like the right place to be. He couldn't wait to surprise his mom and his stomach started to grumble from hunger the minute the main wheels lifted off the ground.

This time around, John gathered his lunch items on a plate and he prepared two more for his dad and Jim so that he could hand them forward when they were ready. He settled back into his chair and opened a bag of corn chips that he'd found in the cabin's snack drawer. The stress of life seemed to be slipping away and he found himself staring out the window and wondering about new things.

John was feeling a relief that he wasn't expecting, and now that he was headed for home, things were becoming a bit clearer. Perhaps the city wasn't where he wanted to be after all. He ate another corn chip and a half smile began to form. He was about to make a big decision, and it was turning out to be an important day.

"King Air 77TL. Seattle Departure. Cleared direct Chelan Airport. Contact Seattle Center on 119.3. Have a good flight."

The clearance was here and Jim responded. "King Air 77TL is cleared to Chelan Airport. That's Center on 119.3. We'll see ya!"

He pushed the two buttons on the GPS. The aircraft banked slightly to the left and then it rolled out on its final course of 059 degrees. With Tango

Lima heading straight for the Chelan Airport, Jim flipped to the new frequency for his check-in with Seattle Center.

"Seattle Center, King Air 77TL is with you at One-Six thousand—Direct Chelan Airport. Good afternoon."

With lunch sounding good, he glanced to the GPS display on the center instrument panel to his right. The display was configured to tell the pilot all relevant stats associated with the flight as programmed. Jim poked at his brother with his pen and then pointed to the display's eighteen-minute ETA. Paul started to speak but was interrupted by Seattle Center's reply to Jim's check in.

"King Air 77TL. Seattle Center. Good afternoon."

"Time flies," he said, smiling at Paul. "Let's eat. Let's look at some of those contenders. If we need to, we'll finish talking on the ground."

With his right hand, Paul gave his thumbs up and nodded. "Okay," he said, turning to his son. "Ding, ding ..."

John, who'd been briefed on the upcoming sales pitch proposal his dad was about to make to his uncle, was now sitting sidesaddle on the forward rear facing seat and he was eagerly leaning in behind his dad so he could overhear the conversation. As Paul turned around, John caught his father's eyes, heard the "ding, ding," and looked back with raised eyebrows. He was clueless, but then it clicked.

"Sorry guys," he said, hopping out of his seat. John walked over to the table where he'd made two customized lunch platters for his dad and uncle.

"Wasn't sure if you wanted these now, or on the ground."

Jim reached over to the cabin chime switch and he started dinging it on and off for a good five-seconds. "We're ready John. What's the hold-up?"

Smiling, he reached for both plates, and as he prepared for the two handed delivery, something happened before his hands got there. There was an instantaneous jolt, and suddenly, John dropped to the floor. There was a loud snapping sound and it was accompanied by an ear piercing decompression wave that flooded the airplane. John was in shock, and he could see Jim's hands immediately go for the controls. This was an emergency, and something was wrong.

On the floor, John was on both knees in the center aisle of the aircraft. He wasn't sure if he had been forced down or if he just dove down. From the sound he'd heard, he knew that the aircraft autopilot had disconnected at the same time that the pressure bump occurred. He'd heard the manual disconnect and he was familiar with how it sounded from flying with his uncle as a kid.

He could remember. His Uncle Jim was always cursing the disconnect switch in the King Air because of its location on the center console. Passengers, like John as a clumsy kid, would always snag it with their shoe strings or pants legs when climbing in and out of the copilot seat during cruise flight. It was a "clunking" sound, and John recognized it now. He looked forward toward the cockpit. He could see that Jim had his hands on the controls and he was flying the airplane. They weren't going down, but what happened?

John stood up and he walked to the forward seat just behind his dad. "What the hell, Dad?"

"Don't know yet." Paul grabbed his arm and he tightening his shoulder harness. "Just buckle up."

Jim had the airplane under control, and as far as he could tell at this point the situation was not dire. She was flying and he had flight control and thrust. The immediate problem was that all systems were down, the instrument panel was dark, and so was the annunciator panel. There were no Master Warnings, no caution lights, and no clues to the cause. It was clear the airplane was experiencing multiple failures, but he'd never seen this combination before. The totality was extreme. Both generators were out and so was the battery, or were they? He needed to think.

Jim needed to make critical decisions and take several actions before even getting to the emergency checklist. First up was the new destination.

"It's back to Paine Field," he said, banking the aircraft back to the west.

"Sorry guys! No doubt we've got us a problem here. I hate to say it, but I don't quite have a handle on this yet. She's flying, but we need to get her on the ground."

Jim was running his fingers along the circuit breaker panel looking for clues. "We'll need a full service airport and Chelan has nothing, so it's simple." He looked at his brother.

"What we're going to do here is we're going to make a nice flight back to Paine Field, and we're going to work things out along the way. Paul, I'm putting you to work. Starting now, we're a crew. There's something funky here, and I'd like you to fly her for a few minutes. When we get to the western side of those hills up there, I'll drop us down to some better air."

Jim grabbed the checklist and then looked back to Paul. "So if you're ready, here we go. It's your airplane."

"Okay. My airplane."

Paul took the controls and he flew in the direction Jim was pointing. Their new course was a U-Turn and now Paul was headed straight for the fishbowl metropolis they'd just departed. He flew the airplane straight and level and he was feather light on the controls. Maybe something was hanging by a thread and he didn't want to break anything. He'd never experienced a real emergency before and he was scared. The airplane was flying, but in his mind he didn't know for how long and he was sure that something was definitely broken. He knew there was a pressure bounce, but he thought he'd heard a loud snapping sound and it almost felt like the airplane had hit something. Paul could feel the thin air. His imagination was running wild and his heart was pumping fast.

"Shouldn't we descend, Jim? Should we put our oxygen masks on? We did lose our pressurization, right?" His brother going through the checklist, Paul wanted to help, but he could see Jim shaking his head.

"We're okay for now. We'll get down in a minute."

He was perplexed, but he'd give Paul a quick rundown on the plan. "So this is where we're at. We're going to make a safe landing, and we're going to be fine, but so far—this is what I'm seeing. We've lost pretty much everything. We have no power—as in zero. No avionics, no AC or DC instruments and no generators. We've got nothing, and the hot battery bus is dead too. This is all wrong, and this shouldn't be happening."

Jim chuckled, and then he shook his head. "So we're not going to touch a thing. We're going to fly her back to Paine Field and then we'll land safely and we'll let the mechanics figure it out."

He looked at Paul first, and then back at John. "Sound like a plan?"

Both men nodded, and then Jim nodded back. "Okay. I've got the airplane. We'll get down to some better air. Looks like 340 on the heading, and we'll fly over that low ridge."

Using his fluid filled compass that was mounted on the dash, Jim flew the new course and descended. Shaking his head, he felt like he was forgetting something.

"This is odd, Paul. Really odd."

"Great," he said, wiping the sweat from his hands onto his pants. "Just get on the ground."

Paul was confident in his brother's skills and he knew they were safe with Jim at the controls. The floatplane however, was quickly transforming into a bad idea. He was a nervous wreck and his mind was drawing a blank. What if this happened with Lisa on board? Drawing a blank didn't bode well with the current plan. Maybe he didn't want to be a pilot after all.

The mountain ridges were now behind them and Tango Lima continued its descent back into the Pacific Northwest. Jim reached up to the cockpit sun visor on the captain's side and positioned it so that the self-contained backup compass could be seen in the bright sunlight. Jim could see 50 miles ahead and didn't need the compass for anything, but it was working, and that was good. He was now focused on what he had, and when he called Seattle Approach on the cell phone, if they told him to fly a heading—he could.

"Okay Paul, so our Pitot-Static system is working fine. Airspeed, Altitude, Turn and Bank, and we've got a working compass up here on the dash. All these are all working. She's flying, and I've got engine thrust, so that's great. We just don't have the juice for our electronics. For the life of me, I don't know why we lost everything. Without any other symptoms, we should have the entire battery buss, but we don't have anything."

Confused, Jim talked it through. "Where's our battery? In the event of a total electrical failure, such as ours, usually—scratch that—in all cases, the aircraft battery power is all that remains for the pilot to manage an emergency landing. We should have our battery. And if we did, I'd simply reduce the electrical load, I'd abandon the non-essentials, and we'd have a short time to use our navigation instruments and our radios." He paused and scratched his head.

"So then we lost it immediately, right?" Paul was trying to understand. "Does that mean the battery was never charging and it was just dead?"

"Nope. If the battery started to discharge, we'd know. There was no Master Warning. No circuit breakers have popped. We had both generators, both inverters, and we had a fully functioning battery buss, but now they're all inoperative. They failed instantly, and they all failed at the same time. Can't wait to hear what maintenance says. It's something strange."

With no easy answers, Jim didn't like the piling on of multiple failures. Without some understanding of which system had failed and then subsequently caused the chain reaction of other failures, he didn't want to start troubleshooting beyond what the emergency checklist contemplated.

The most applicable procedure that was somewhat similar to their current condition was the emergency procedure for "Dual Generator Failure." In big bold letters, this procedure stated, in part, "… land as soon as practical, and expect the battery to be the only remaining source of electrical power." King Air 77TL had no electrical power, but fortunately, she had two strong engines and Jim could see the ground.

Thanking his lucky stars, they had a simple plan. Fly back to Paine Field and pump the landing gear down manually. They'd do a flyby with the tower for confirmation that the gear was down and locked, and then they'd land soft and uneventful.

Thank God, he thought. The good visibility was precisely why the emergency wasn't life-threatening, and today he'd be able to land the airplane safely. Had this been in the soup with low visibility and no instruments, it'd be a whole different game and it'd be dangerous as hell. The Pacific Northwest was notorious for its low clouds and fog, but today it was a clear summer day.

"Grab my phone, John. It's in my flight bag behind my seat."

Scanning the instrument panel for more clues, Jim needed to explain the evolving plan to his passengers. "When we get up here another 20 miles or so, I'll call the tower for a landing clearance. We'll stay clear of the Seattle airspace for now, but we'll use the phone for our communications. When it's time to land, we'll be cranking the gear down manually on this one. I know you've both wanted to see it, so today you will."

Flying at 8,000 feet and still descending, with the west side of the Cascade Range behind them, Jim was visually circumventing the controlled airspace around Seattle due to their inability to communicate with Seattle Approach. Now on a more westerly course of 320 degrees, all three occupants could see Paine Field's runways on the far horizon. The landscape ahead was engulfed within a hazy afternoon sky and the cities below were beginning to come into view. Like defeated sailors returning to port, they each stared out the windows, and all three were re-planning their day.

"Kind of ironic," Jim said, half chuckling. "This morning, I was in a big rush to get us out of there. Now we're going back. It's very weird."

Curious, Paul was about to ask him why, but then he caught sight of something outside the window. "What is that?" he said, pointing left.

John yelled from the back, "That's an airplane!"

Stunned, all three went silent as their eyes found the target. Ahead, and over the highly populated city below, a large airliner was rapidly descending in a corkscrewing dive. It was only ten-miles from their position and all three occupants of the King Air watched as the spiraling aircraft nosedived toward the ground. Just as the airliner's tumbling descent approached the King Air's altitude, it appeared to start separating at the tail. Two separate sections of the airliner were now falling next to each other, and then they both hit the ground.

"My God!" Paul yelled. The impact was catastrophic and two blast plumes started to rise.

From behind, John grabbed his dad's shoulder and he pointed. "Look! There's another one!" He was pointing to the left—at eleven o'clock and high.

Jim felt his heart racing and he looked out the window. Searching desperately, he'd scan one area and then move to the next. With his right hand on the dashboard, his eyes found the target and his finger pointed. "In sight!" He turned to his brother.

"Not good, Paul. Same scenario. She's coming down!"

With two men up front, and with John leaning forward between them, all three watched in horror as the passenger jet descended out of control in front of them. They stared out the window as the aircraft spiraled down just like the other one. The jet's nose would lift slightly, and then it would dip back down and roll over. As it rapidly descended out of control, the two brothers and John gasped and cringed as the helpless jet kept repeating the uncontrolled corkscrewing dive several times. Rise, dip, and roll. Rise, dip, and roll. Now breaking apart, it appeared to be headed for the eastern shores of Lake Washington.

"It could go in the lake," Paul yelled. Eyes glued to the falling airliner, he prayed. "Lord let it be in the lake!"

Approximately 15 miles to the west and in full view of the King Air's three passengers; they could see the descending airliner with its tail section flailing by a thread of torn metal. Just before impact the two sections separated completely. First, the nose section hit near the western shoreline of Mercer Island, and then a second later, the tail splashed 100 yards farther to the west and in the lake.

This time, there was a single blast plume rising from the main section's impact zone, and amazingly, the tail section was ominously visible in the water just north of the I-90 Bridge that spanned Lake Washington. There it was, a mangled tail section of an airliner, floating tail up in the sunny blue waters of the lake below. All three stared out the left side windows, mesmerized by the catastrophic events that were taking place in front of them.

"Those poor people!" John yelled from the back. He was kneeling on the seat, staring out the window.

"That was two airliners! How does that happen?" His face pale, John pulled away from the cabin window and he slid back into his sidesaddle position facing the cockpit. His mind racing, he knew the answer and it was obvious. It had to be, and he had to say something quick.

"Guys. I know what happened here. It's bad."

"What?" Paul said turning around.

"Well, my phone and laptop went dead when we lost our electrical power back there. I passed it off as a coincidence, but I don't think it is. I mean, we just saw two jets fall out of the sky—and I haven't seen any cars moving down there on the roads. I've been watching—and like I said, I thought it was a coincidence, but it's not."

Looking at his dad, he let it out. "It's an EMP. This is an electromagnetic pulse attack and it's exactly what we were warned about. This is the attack!"

Both brothers looked at each other, and then immediately, they turned and looked out the windows. Scanning the roads below, they saw no movement. No cars were moving anywhere.

"Son of a bitch! He could be right, Jim."

Still scanning, Jim could hear his little voice saying "yes."

"I just assumed we had multiple failures," he said nodding. "But it's true. This could be the attack."

His heart thumping, Jim looked at his left hand that was resting on the dashboard. "My watch is dead. We need to check everything. I think he's right."

CHAPTER 4

THE EMP EPIPHANY

So that's when it happened." Turning around, he looked at Anne. "Safe-Port was built precisely for this type of event. I'd always assumed that I'd recognize it right away. And I didn't."

Shaking his head, Jim was half-chuckling, but he wanted the record to be clear. "I was caught up in the details. I was still trying to make sense of it all, and it was my nephew that had the epiphany. He figured it out and he made the leap. He had the wherewithal to put it all together."

Turning off her digital recorder, Anne wanted to stop the interview and sort through the new facts. She needed to catch up, and she knew that Jim needed to catch his breath. He was describing an event she'd never understood, and the way that he was telling it gave her a new underlying clarity. This was an unknown story, and there was nothing about it in her file. It explained how it all began. The timing was extraordinary. She couldn't wait to hear more.

"Jim, I can see it all. Now I know how you guys got separated and I can see how this all started. The timing is what's so critical here. Everything happened for a reason, and it happened because of the unique timing. These are new facts, and none of it was in my notes. You've got to keep it coming! Just like you're doing. Tell the story your mind remembers."

Nodding, he chuckled. "It's odd. And we've talked about this. Both Ken and I think our memories are unusually vivid. We think it's strange."

Familiar with this oddity, Anne knew that it was a common thread and she wanted them to know. "FYI; and just so you're both aware. Everybody I've talked with feels the same way. From Day One forward. Total recall. It seems we can all remember the details in an unusual way."

Nearing a hundred-miles in, the trip was going well and the mission was getting accomplished. Anne was getting the details of a story she'd never heard before and she was anxious to get back to the airplane. Grabbing her notepad, she reviewed her summations thus far.

"So, like I said, I finally understand how you guys got separated." Anne leaned back and started flipping through her pages to find her notes.

"Jim, while you were flying back to Seattle, Ken was already on the ground. At the time you'd realized it was an EMP, it was Ken who was already trapped in one of those stalled cars. Am I right?"

"Yes. But he was already on foot by then. While we were in the air, he was walking on the freeway."

She flipped to another page. "Okay. Well then Ken, and we'll get to what you went through in Seattle, but by the time Jim was flying back to Paine Field, and by the time they saw the airliners falling, how long had it been since your car died on the freeway?"

"I'd estimate fifteen, maybe twenty minutes. I had plenty of indicators telling me that it was an EMP, and I'd figured it out pretty quick. It was different for Jim though. He had other worries. The signs of an EMP were overshadowed."

"Okay, but I'm still confused. So the attack occurred, and then fifteen-minutes later, maybe twenty, the airliners fell. I know this is a technical question, but why the delay? Why didn't all the airplanes crash at the same time your car died?"

Ken and Jim looked at each other, and then Ken spoke. "You need to hear the rest of the story, Anne. It was a tragedy what happened to those airliners."

With a nod from Jim, Ken gave her a short brief. "Fortunately, the King Air has cables and pulleys that operate the flight controls. Those modern airliners didn't have that and they were all fly-by-wire. With the EMP destroying all electronics, including all backup electrical systems, they had little-to-no flight control. Some were able to fly for hours while they tried to troubleshoot the problem, but a controlled descent and a safe landing turned out to be impossible. Some were able to walk away, or even swim away, but most came in catastrophically. It was an unsolvable problem, and it was pure terror for those people."

Setting her pen down, she could feel her palms getting sweaty. "I can't imagine. I just can't imagine!"

She thought about the carnage reported from the other witnesses and she wanted to know the numbers, but she'd have to wait. How many people died? How many crashes? It seemed to be unknown, and while the numbers were important, they weren't important now. She needed to get back to the epiphany.

"So—now I know. I understand the delay. And it's terrible. My God, what were you thinking when you saw this, Jim?"

"At first, I thought it was a terrorist attack. A million things went through my mind. Then John made the connection."

"Then what? John mentions an EMP, and then you notice your watch is dead. What happened next?"

Reaching for his water bottle, Jim took a long drink and he formed his response. "Dread. We weren't sure yet, but my gut started yelling and I knew John was right. We had to figure it out, and then we did."

CHAPTER 5

MOMENT OF TRUTH

Was this the attack America had been warned about? Did it happen while they were in the air? There were three theories, and only one, the EMP attack explained all symptoms in total. A simultaneous terrorist attack on the two airliners—or a mid-air collision; each would explain the two airliners falling from the sky, but only one, the EMP attack, would explain everything.

All three passengers on the crippled King Air were on a mission. Every device was checked. Luggage was opened and all electronics required an inspection. Three laptops, three phones, one watch, one camera, one small mini flashlight, and one large on-board flashlight; all were piled onto the two forward passenger seats of the King Air's cabin.

John searched for anything that worked and he failed with every attempt—except two. The tally was in. In addition to the ship's power being gone, every onboard battery-powered device—with the exception of one small calculator and an LED flashlight—was dead.

"It's not a coincidence," Paul said. "What do we do? This is bad!"

Jim's response was brief. "Standby. It's the cars that have me worried. Got to think."

The King Air was now five miles from Paine Field and it was flying at an altitude of 3,000 feet. Up until moments ago, the plan was to fly the air-plane to Paine Field, use the cell phone to receive a clearance to land, and then hand crank the landing gear down and land uneventfully. Now things had changed, and the plan needed to be revised.

The infrastructures on the ground were in serious trouble. Cars, airliners, and even small battery powered devices had been breached. If it was an EMP, then it was powerful, and if it got into the small stuff, this whole thing could be the worst case scenario. He knew it well and he knew what he needed to do. This was life and death.

The very nonstandard plan he was now considering was dicey to say the least. Like many, he'd prepared for this event, and he was an instrumental component of Idaho's SafePort defense, but he'd never contemplated he'd have to face it in the air. Unfortunately, this appeared to be the case—and worse yet, it appeared to be happening over Washington State.

The observable facts were clearly indisputable, and right now they were leading him to significant assumptions. If correct, they implied that the threat to his passengers' lives existed more so on the ground in Seattle than it did in the air. With no guarantees that his assessment was correct, he had to make a decision—and it was a big one. He had one probable offender, and the EMP theory was sound. Washington State was not a Safe state. If he landed here, nobody would get home, they'd be stranded on foot, and they'd likely die.

Jim reviewed his thoughts. If they were to continue and land at Paine Field and the infrastructure and transportation systems were truly as dead as they appeared to be, they'd be terminally stuck and on their own. It was too risky. Under any other circumstances, an electrical failure of this magnitude would compel him to land immediately. But this was different. This is life and death, Jim. He could hear his little voice. You know what to do. Just do it.

If it was nationwide, it meant a lot of people were going to start dying. All undefended states were now out of business. No food, no water, no cars, and no survival infrastructure whatsoever. If true, Jim knew the implications well. The non-SafePort states were deathtraps. Everything he'd prepared for and everything he'd learned taught him exactly what he needed to know. Escape was imperative; all means necessary must be used.

He had an opportunity to survive and he knew his decision was right. He knew the damage they'd observed suggested the event was likely catastrophic—and man-made. He knew it wasn't from a solar flare. The physics of a solar flare wouldn't take out the cars and the electronics, and the only thing that could was a high altitude nuke.

He was out of options. America was under attack. A high-altitude electromagnetic pulse had been detonated, and wherever it occurred, it made it to the West Coast. He trusted his observations and he was comfortable with his knowledge. He hoped that he was wrong, but he needed to act accordingly—and he needed to do it now.

For all three on board, the disaster forming was common knowledge. Well versed in the SafePort civil defense, each had prepared their homes and families for long-term infrastructure failure. Residing in Idaho, Jim lived in a SafePort state, and he had an official function as head of the North Idaho SafePort flight operations department, otherwise known as SafePort Civil Patrol. Even though Washington State was still undefended and had refused to sign on, its two residents on board were studiously familiar with the issues at hand. A decision had to be made—and Jim had just made it. He felt good about the new plan.

With Paine Field at their twelve o'clock position and two miles ahead, Paul and John continued to point out that there were no moving cars anywhere. As the aircraft overflew the airport, Jim maneuvered the plane into a racetrack style holding pattern that circled the runways and provided a good vantage point to fully assess the mayhem below. As Jim banked the airplane to the left to begin his southbound leg, a large Seattle Ferry boat that was awkwardly beached sideways on the shoreline came into full view.

"Wows" came from all three on board and Jim knew that it was time to get busy. He pulled on his nephew's shirt to huddle him in closer. The in-flight briefing was about to commence.

"This is how I see it guys, and this is what we're going to do." Jim cinched up his seat belt and cleared his throat.

"Based on what we're seeing down there, this is a full infrastructure failure. I hate to say it, but an EMP attack is likely responsible, and that's bad. The onboard electrical problems, the crashed airliners, and the complete shutdown of a major city." Jim pointed his finger down to the ground. "We'll never survive down there, and we all know it. It's a bad place to be, and so we're going home."

With the sound of the engines now at a slow cruise, a calm silence filled the cabin as Jim talked. "So, here's the deal. Our original plan was to come back here for an emergency landing, but she's still flying and that means I can fly us home. We've all planned for this contingency and it's time to act. Our families need us, and we're not going to screw everything up by landing on 'Starvation Island'."

His head down, Jim sighed. "My God! We need to thank God we're not stuck on the ground, because it almost happened. I kid you not, we're fortunate beyond words. I mean, we got out of there with minutes to spare. If we'd waited, those engines would've never started at the FBO."

Nodding, Paul chuckled, but it was nervous."That seems weird. Get out of here."

"Well, she's still flying, and I can keep her flying—I think. I'm worried about the electric boost pumps, but we'll keep her low. Lots to work out, but we've got to try. We're going home, and we're not getting stuck down there."

Now on the southbound leg of the holding pattern over Paine Field Airport, it was time to leave, and a left-turn would take them east. With the runway directly below, Jim departed the circling pattern with a bank to the left and he started a shallow climb. For the second time today, he established an easterly heading toward the Cascade Mountains. They'd failed to cross it in their first attempt, but now it was life and death. It was a giant wall, and for now the King Air was on the wrong side, but Jim was going to fix that.

"Get us over those mountains and we're home-free," John said, standing in the center aisle. "Fly us to Idaho, Jim. If it's still good over there, we'll drive home. If not …" John had to stop and think it out.

"That's the problem, bud. I think we'll have to consider all options." Scratching the back of his head, Jim added his thoughts.

"I'm assuming we have bigger concerns here. So how about we go with the Idaho plan, but with this contingency. First, if we observe operating vehicles on the other side of those mountains—we can then say our lives would be safer on the ground and we'll go land at the closest good runway. This would be the best case scenario, guys. And if that's how it works, then we land and we all drive home. Everybody's safe and sound. America's is still up-and-running."

With another deep breath, he looked at his brother and sighed. "But—and this is an important 'but'. If we see cars stalled on the freeways in Eastern Washington, then we're back to the worst case scenario again, and that'll change our plan. I believe this second scenario to be the most probable, and we're going to have to strategize another plan to deal with it. I've got one brewing, and I'll tell you about it now. But we'll make our decisions when we get on the other side of these hills."

Jim fine-tuned the airplane's heading so it was headed for the gap between the two peaks directly in front of them and 20 miles out. With his hands on the controls, he turned to his passengers and laid out the components of an alternate plan, should it be required.

"So," he said letting out a deep breath. "In the event we don't see any cars moving on the freeway over there, I'm flying you both to Chelan airport, and then I'm flying the aircraft back to Idaho. As long as we keep the engines running and I keep the gear down—it'll all work. And in a second here, I'll tell you how we're going to pull it off."

Jim cracked open a bottle of water, and with one tilting motion he drank half and then began his brief. "If it's worst-case, we're going to pump the gear down over the Chelan Airport and then we're going to land. The engines will stay running on the ground, and Paul, you'll open the door. Both of you will deplane. If things are indeed the way I think they are, then you'll both be walking home. I'll close the door behind you, take off, and fly home with the landing gear extended. With that big gear hanging out, I'll have to fly her slow—but I can still fly."

Another sip and he shook his head. "Still working on which airport I'd land at in Idaho, but SKYJET has shielded parts for the King Air at both the Coeur d'Alene and the Sandpoint airports. Pro's and cons with each, but I can work it out on my way back. Important thing is we get back to our families and we start managing the problem."

Finishing his water, Jim looked out his side window. "You know Paul, if this all turns out to be true, your 30-day clock begins today."

"Noted," Paul replied.

John was now standing in the center aisle behind his father and uncle. He'd heard what Jim said, and his voice was strained.

"The 30-day Get-out-of-Dodge countdown? Really? You think it's that bad? I don't think we should be jumping to any conclusions yet. I think we need to chill." His heart pumping, he knew what the 30-day clock meant and it was difficult to accept.

Paul looked back and acknowledged his rant. "You're right. We don't know what happened down there. Could be an isolated event, or it could even be a mistake or misunderstanding on our part. We just don't know." Hands open, he expressed the absence of any answers. "It is what it is, John. And because we don't know, the circumstances give us no choice. We need to prepare. We need to prepare for the worst and pray for the best."

"I know, Dad. I'm just mad! I think he's right, and that means everything is gone. If he's right, we're screwed!"

"I think he's right, too. Doesn't look good, bud."

Jim spoke up. "If it's an EMP—then it's a large-scale event. It's how they work. If we just got attacked, then our attack will cover a large area."

"Well, it's not local. Seems we would've seen the flash if it was local." Looking out the window, Paul was wondering if what he'd just said was correct. "It's hard to say. Awfully bright out there, so maybe not. But I don't think they'd waist an EMP on just Seattle. They'd blow it up."

"Yep, they would." Jim was nodding.

"So we know that it's not a solar flare, and we know that it's an EMP. It made it all the way to Seattle, and we have no choice but to assume that it was detonated out there." Jim was pointing straight ahead, and it was the same direction they were traveling. It was also due east, and led straight to the heart of America.

With clear blue skies, all three contemplated the new reality as they aimlessly looked out the windows for clues. The sunlight was bright, and with his eyes starting to hurt Jim wondered if a nuclear flash could be seen at all in the daytime. Maybe at night, he thought, and then John tapped him on the shoulder.

"Do we know for sure that it's not a solar flare? Maybe it was a big one"

"Nope. Doesn't work that way." Jim felt his knowledge kick in. "Because of that atmosphere up there," he said, pointing his finger straight up. "It's not a solar flare. The only electromagnetic frequencies that can make it down here to the surface of the Earth are the ones that affect the big stuff like our power grids and communications. Solar flares don't affect our cars and they don't affect our airplanes! This is something much worse."

Jim cleared his throat and he said what needed to be said. "We need to start preparing ourselves for something terrible. We know what this means, and I think we're in big trouble. Like Paul said, now's the time to pray."

Reaching over with his left arm, Paul placed his hand on John's knee behind him. He then turned farther to the left, and with his right arm he reached over the center console toward Jim, gathered the material of his shirt sleeve, and pulled him in closer. Paul was the official family rep when it came to talking with God, and he lowered his head, and prayed for the world. In his final request, he asked that the King Air be blessed. Fittingly, both John and Jim piled on—and they asked again.

In unison, amen's filled the cabin. The airplane was a critical component of the plan and its passengers unanimously agreed it was worthy of some divine assistance. The Cascades were now below them and all around. Some of the higher peaks were too close for comfort, but rather than climbing to a higher altitude with thinner air, Jim could see what he needed to see and he'd weave his way through.

He'd elected to fly at 10,000 feet over and through the mountain pass due to the aircraft's potential operating limitation associated with his lack of boost pumps. Without his electrically operated fuel pumps pressurizing the fuel system, there were concerns with fuel flow during certain operations.

The Operating Manual detailed specific operational flight limitations associated with the loss of certain electrical equipment. He knew that along with losing everything else, he'd very likely lost both electrically driven fuel boost pumps, which meant that the engines were obtaining fuel via gravity feed and the engine-driven fuel pumps only.

The Operating Manual recommended that all flight operations flown without boost pumps be performed at altitudes at or below 10,000 feet to avoid problems with fuel flow. Once again, and with thanks to his lucky stars, exceeding the limitations would not be required—and he could fly low. The weather was beautiful and he could see for miles and miles.

With rising terrain on his left and right, Jim flew the King Air at an altitude he didn't much care for—but it was a blessing today. If his engines quit now, there were no good options except for the winding highway directly below. Highway 2 was just cresting the summit of Stevens Pass, and there were multiple stalled vehicles in plain view. Only a few thousand feet away, groups of people were clearly visible and they were scattered along the highway. Nothing had changed, and it was clear the ramifications were becoming severe.

Suddenly from the back, John yelled. "Traffic! Ten o'clock—low. Look guys!" John pointed through the cockpit window between his dad and uncle. "That's a single engine airplane headed east. We're not the only ones. Look at that!"

"Yep, I see him," Jim said, pointing to the slower aircraft they were about to overtake.

"That's great. Surprised we haven't seen more. Just think how many airplanes are in the same boat as us? I wonder where they're headed."

The elevating emergency was becoming difficult to grasp, and Jim could hear his mind running through the basic facts. He knew there were a lot of airplanes flying when the event happened—and he knew some made it, and some didn't. He also knew there were a lot of old cars and old trucks without electronic ignitions that would survive the event, and he knew that many, including his brother Paul, were using the SafePort technique for preserving a hardened escape vehicle.

Searching for answers, he let his mind continue. How bad is this, he wondered? And how could we be so lucky? My God, he thought. Thankfully, there's a lot of people on the ground who have an extreme advantage. They have a plan and they're executing it now. They can drive away. They can round up their family members and they can escape. Some will be lucky, and some will be prepared. We've planned for this. We're ready. Paul is ready. But we didn't plan for this, did we Jim?

He thought about their situation, and he flashed on his earlier get-out-of Paine Field now feeling. This was all pure luck, and he was trying to piece it together, but he couldn't. His thoughts were swimming, and as he watched the single-engine airplane disappear behind them, he wished them well and he let his mind agree on one thing. The King Air was an advantage—and he'd use the airplane to the best of his ability. It was a wildcard, and for some crazy reason, they all had a ride home.

With the single engine Cessna no longer visible, Jim couldn't get the falling airliners out of his mind. Thank God for old technology, he thought. He looked at Paul. "A lot of airplanes crashed today. We are so lucky."

Jim needed to address what they'd seen, and he needed to address the consequences. If two were witnessed, how many more crashed? It was an uncomfortable subject, but it happened and he knew why.

"Just so you know. We're talking hundreds, here." With Paul and John leaning in, Jim laid out the details of what he knew.

"So here's the deal. If their flight control system is fly-by-wire, the manufacturer has installed multiple autonomous backup systems on board to prevent a complete electrical failure. But here's the thing. They're all electrically operated and they all use complex circuitry to accomplish the necessary task. If one system goes down, the other is there, and it all works pretty good. There's always a plan B. But if they all get damaged at the same time, like from a nuclear EMP, there's no viable backup. All systems down—and that's a complete failure. It is the one-and-only event that is not addressed in our civilian aircraft—and it's exactly what we saw."

He raised his eyebrows. "Even those backup hydraulic systems are at risk if they're using electrically actuated pumps, valves, and relays. If it was a massive attack, they probably lost everything right-away, and that's an unsolvable scenario."

"Don't they have little prop generators that can be deployed for emergency power?" Paul pointed out his right-side window. "Those little ram air turbines that catch the wind and turn?"

"Yep, they do. But it still uses circuitry technology to obtain and disburse the energy. Again, none of the safety designs contemplate EMP—except for military aircraft which harden all critical systems to withstand it. Civil aircraft are not hardened. It fried everything in here, so I have to assume it fried everything in every airliner that was both aloft and on the ground. That means everything—backup systems too."

He grabbed the control yoke and banked the aircraft left and right. "This little King Air has cables and pulleys connected to its flight controls. They don't. We can keep the sunny side up and we can fly to an airport—they couldn't." Jim was attempting to grasp what had likely happened to his fellow pilots and he had issues with what he'd seen. "It's hard to imagine. I think we saw the worst-case scenario. They shouldn't have lost it like that, but they did."

Leaning in, John was still confused. "Why did they spiral down?"

Jim noticed his palms getting sweaty as he pondered the likely struggle. "It didn't start out that way, but I suspect when they exceeded the envelope there was no way to get back and they stalled. First, they had an incident like we had, and depending on their altitude, any decompression, if they had one at all—was far worse than our little pressure dump. Truth be told, I'm still confused as to why we had a pressure dump. That outflow valve should've failed in the closed position, but it didn't, and something caused it to dump, so I don't know."

He turned to John. "Regardless of whether or not they lost pressurization, they most certainly lost flight control. I'm confident they tried everything, and if they still had thrust they tried to slow down and establish directional control for an emergency landing. The aircraft are inherently stable. Best case; they should have been able to glide to a runway, or even make a water landing, but those two didn't and something went very wrong. There's a lot of variables, and there all bad."

Defeated, he threw up his hands. "There was no way to win, and it's a horrible day. They were helpless."

Standing in the center aisle, John was between his father and uncle and he put his hands on their shoulders. "It is a horrible day, and those cars are still frozen down there. It seems you're right, Uncle Jim. I think we've been attacked. I think Washington State is over."

He sighed and looked down. "It makes me mad, Dad. They said it was a hoax. They said the President was lying. They said we were safe!"

He could feel his anger growing and he needed to calm down. "All we had to do was enact a simple plan. We could've been a Safe State, but we're not—and we're fools!"

John's anger was shared by all, but he was having a hard time remaining cool like his father and uncle. "I can guarantee that Ellen is stuck on I-5 right now, and I bet you Ken is too. I saw him in the parking lot and he told me he was headed for the Seattle airport to pick up his daughter. Can you imagine the chaos on I-5 right now? They're all screwed!"

Both Jim and Paul nodded, and they knew that his statement was true and correct. Seattle was screwed—but it didn't matter right now, and they were in the middle of an escape. They needed to make it home. They needed to pull this off, and they needed to survive. Anger was for later.

Through the hills below, Lake Chelan was becoming visible and all three looked straight ahead. The lake was fifty-miles long and it weaved its way through the valley floor of the eastern Cascades. On its eastern shoreline was the town of Chelan, and the municipal airport was another five miles farther. It was decision time, and Jim had already made it.

"There it is," he said pointing to the runway. "Here we go. It's the same over here as it was over there. Odds are, the entire nation's down, and if you ask me, I think we just got chopped off at the knees. America is down, and our priorities are at home. It's plan B. We're landing in Chelan, guys. I'll drop you off—and then I'll fly home."

Eyebrows raised, he gave a half-nod to his brother and he waited for Paul's response.

"Agreed. Take us home." Paul reached over the center console and he tapped his brother's shoulder. It seemed that fate had forced their hand and it came with a blessing. He thought about was his wife and he'd see her soon. Lisa needed him, and miraculously, he was coming home with their son. Turning to John, he couldn't believe what was happening, and then he turned around, looked out his side window and prayed.

With the ground moving quickly there was a sudden pause where nobody said anything and the cockpit went silent. The three men were thinking hard, and all three had to get a grip on their new reality. Life was changing.

"Okay guys. Ready or not, here we go. We'll be setting up for an approach and we'll be cranking down the landing gear here pretty quick. Let's make sure we're all on board with the plan and let's do a quick run through. Paul-give me a summary."

Caught off guard, he responded with confidence. "Okay. Well then here goes. Firstly, you're going to drop us off in Chelan. Unless we find this whole thing never happened, or is somehow over, John and I are going to be walking home. You're going to keep the engines running on the ground, we're hopping off, and then you're going to depart the airport and fly home with the gear down. We—John, Lisa and I—we'll start managing the emergency. Whatever it is, it'll be in accordance with the 30-day plan, to the extent we can."

Sharing his son's anger over no defense, Paul added his fears. "We'll do our part Jim, but this is Washington State. I'm afraid of what we won't be able to do. We're walking into a nightmare. This is biblical. Millions are going to die."

"I know," Jim said. "But you've got to stay alive, Paul. You've got thirty days to get to the Bluff and you need to be there."

"We will."

"With a firm nod, Jim continued. "Okay. And remember to pay strict attention to the communication procedures. In three days we can talk, but we need to be extremely careful with accessing our shielded equipment. We could have more attacks and we don't want to lose our advantage. Use the SafePort Procedures manual I gave you. Consult it and study it. It'll dictate how and when to do everything—and it'll keep you safe."

Jim knew that his brother was a unique man, and he knew that he'd have a hard time leaving others behind. He could see him struggling with it now and he knew how his mind worked. He had to say something, and he'd have to say it so he wouldn't forget.

"Paul, I need you to listen to me. I don't feel good about your situation and I'm worried this could happen quickly. If the infrastructures are fully down, then there's no surviving at your home. There'll be no other option. You can't save them all. Chelan will fall and you'll have to get your family out of there. You've got to stick with the plan."

"I know Jim," he said turning to John. "We know what we're up against. We'll follow the rules."

Nodding, he'd accept the response and he pulled the throttles back for a slight descent. Tango Lima's engines assumed a strong deep purr and the airplane began its initial approach phase. Jim was on a high extended downwind for a landing on the runway below. It was time to execute the plan— and first up was the landing gear. It would be hand cranked, and he'd do it with his right arm.

"When I fly out of here, I'll circle around and I'll take a look at the runway on Ken's property. I flew over it with Bob a few months ago and it looked good. In three days I'll let you know."

The Chelan airport was now ten miles to the north and Jim was positioning the King Air for an extended downwind entry that would circle around to the runway. With every move planned out in advance, the time to commit was approaching fast. He handed Paul the checklist to hold and then he loosened up his arm for the upcoming gear-cranking event.

"So we'll get this gear down, and then we go make a nice soft landing. Simple stuff. And we'll go step-by-step."

The hand crank for the landing gear on Tango Lima was located on the floor of the cockpit between the captain and copilot seat. It was a red cranking handle with a C-ring latch that kept it secured. The procedure for manually cranking the gear down required the pilot to first pull the landing gear circuit breaker and position the gear handle in the cockpit to the down position. Secondly, the pilot had to lift and turn the C-ring latch so that it would unlock the red lever for emergency use.

Once unlocked, the pilot would simply pump the red handle up and down until the green light illuminated on the instrument panel. Unfortunately, for Jim and his two passengers today, there was no battery power and there wouldn't be any green lights confirming anything. Whether or not the landing gear was down and locked would remain a mystery, and nobody in the King Air would know for sure until they touched the ground. Fortunately, Jim had a confidence that was contagious.

"So guys, to bring you up to speed we're not going to have any confirmation that our gear is down and locked. I'll get 'em down and I'll get 'em locked, but there's just no fancy green light to make us feel good on this one. And if they don't collapse on landing, well," he paused, eyebrows raised. "We'll know I'm right."

Smiling at Paul, he nodded. "Usually, we pump 52 times. We use full throw pumps each time, and we usually get a green light on the last pump. Today, I'm going to pump 52 full pumps and our gear will be down and locked. I'll get 'em down, but cinch up those belts and pray! Everything needs to work perfectly, so pray."

Now at a slightly higher than normal visual approach altitude, Jim gave himself a wide berth for the extra time needed to pump the gear and set up for the landing. With two-thousand feet to go before his level off altitude, Jim pulled the landing gear circuit breaker, lowered the gear handle, and then lifted the C-ring and unlocked the red handle for emergency use.

Ready to pump, he brought the power back and he started to slow the King Air. The recommended airspeed for manual gear extension was 120 knots and he had to work hard to get it there. Today, he had no flaps, and because they were electrically driven and unavailable, he had to raise the nose and reduce the power drastically. At 120 knots, he began pumping and he counted out loud so that Paul could follow.

Without flaps, the aircraft had no drag and she wanted to fly fast. Initially, Jim had to pull the power back all the way to idle so that he could obtain the 120-knot manual gear extension speed. Once he exposed the King Air's landing gear into the airstream, however, the drag on the aircraft increased dramatically and he had to compensate with added power. With Jim's constant adjustment on the throttles, the King Air's airspeed was locked at the 120-knot limitation at all times, and he was almost done.

"That's 52," he said, shaking his arm in fatigue. "They're down and locked. Let's get this done."

Jim was scanning the runway and he could see that it was clear, but he noticed something. "Check out the people gathering near the pullout on the north side. I wonder what they know. John, there's some straps in the drawer under the potty seat in back. Grab some—they could help with getting your bags home."

The King Air was now entering the approach phase and Jim performed his pre-landing checks in ritualistic style. He had a thousand things running through his mind, but he was ready and it was time to land.

"I can't think of anything else guys. Be safe and be smart. Information is your best friend. Get on it early—and stay in contact with me on the radio. If this is for real, my new duty will be to initiate the civil air patrol in Idaho. You don't have that here, so your radios are critical. All those people in Seattle and the whole west side of the mountains for that matter—that's the wild card here. Use the radio to stay away from trouble, and use it to communicate with me."

Jim looked at his brother and then back to John. "We've got a good plan, here. Let's land, and let's do this. You ready?"

"We're ready." Paul was nodding and so was John.

"We're ready, Uncle Jim. Give us a nice, soft landing. Like a feather!"

Cinching up his tie, Jim pulled his shoulder harness tight and he sat up straight and tall. This was his tell. It was a preparation maneuver, and he performed it immediately prior to engaging in the takeoff and approach phase of every flight. It was one fluid motion and it was like a switch turning on.

The King Air was now making its circling base-turn and it was heading for its final inbound course to the runway. The landing gear—with any luck—was down and locked. They'd find out soon. All pre-landing checklist items were completed and the aircraft was ready to land. With the final course approaching, Jim rolled the wings level and the runway was straight ahead.

CHAPTER 6

DROP AND GO

With three miles to go, the cockpit went silent. Amidst their prayers for a soft landing, the two passengers watched Jim maneuver the King Air with instinctive command. Paul was still learning, but Jim had done this his whole life and it showed. He watched his brother's hands traverse the controls like a musician playing an instrument. This was dicey, but Paul knew the "Drop and Go" plan had the makings of a masterpiece. It felt perfect and that meant something.

Directly below, the rugged hills looked like ripples in the ground extending out from the eastern slopes of the Cascade Range. The uneven terrain caused an immediate floating effect, and as the King Air descended the turbulent updrafts were getting worse.

Having landed at this airport many times, Jim's familiarity was coming in handy. With anticipation working in his favor, Jim's simultaneous application of rapid power reductions combined with a slight nose-down pitch successfully counteracted the floating affect. Tango Lima was right on glide path, and she was right where she needed to be.

Now on short final and rapidly approaching the runway, it was imperative the King Air maintained a stabilized descent path all the way down to the pavement. With landing flaps deployed—if he had any landing flaps to deploy—the approach would be standardized and straightforward. Today, he didn't, and that meant compromise.

An alternate method would have to be used—and thankfully Jim was good at it. He'd simply establish the King Air's landing attitude through significant reductions in power—much lower than typically desired on short final—followed by a rapid increase in thrust just at the right moment. The timely nudge of the throttles just as the aircraft neared the back side of its power curve was the key to pulling off a good landing.

The "slipping" effect established with the application of thrust and cross-control on short final placed the aircraft in a nice nose-up landing attitude with minimum float over the runway. If forced to land with no flaps while flying the King Air C90, this technique worked well and Jim was using it now.

For Paul and John, the "No Flaps" approach was something they'd never seen before and everything about it seemed odd. They'd flown with Jim many times and they'd never seen him work so hard on a landing. Temperatures on the ground with the hot August sun were somewhere in the mid-90s. The updrafts were significant and Jim had to make large control inputs with significant manipulation of thrust to manage the required stabilized approach path.

Where the inputs were aggressive, they were controlled and required. As they approached the runway, with only fifty feet to go they watched Jim make the aircraft do exactly what he wanted it to do. With their palms sweaty and their seatbelts cinched tight, the father and son passengers prayed for the gear to hold.

When the King Air touched down, the main wheels chirped and the landing gear held. Grinning hard, Jim confirmed the victory. "She's a good girl."

"Yes she is!" John yelled from the semi-crash position he'd assumed in the cabin. "Thank God!"

Throttles at idle, the aircraft was slowing down and Jim still had his two engines that were running. "Plan's working, so we're going to go with it, guys. I'm flying home." He turned to Paul and smiled. "Hard to believe."

Nodding to his brother, Paul could feel the tension mounting. Something catastrophic was occurring and it was clear that everybody was in a world of trouble. As the King Air slowed, he could see a group of people that were up ahead, and he wondered what they knew. Could there be a simple explanation? He left his hopes high, but his gut told him to be careful. It was all he could hear, and it wouldn't stop. You're going home, and you're brother is going home too. America is under attack, and it's about to get worse!

Now traveling at a normal taxi speed, the group ahead could be seen walking across the taxiway towards the transient aircraft parking. "They must think we're going to park over there," Paul said, wishing he could roll the window down and wave. "I wonder what they know."

"I wonder." His hand on the throttles, Jim pondered what Paul was about to learn. Whatever it was, he'd have to wait until later. There was no time for it now and the mission was clear. He had to go, and he had to go quickly.

Pointing straight ahead, Jim laid out the plan. "I'll turn around up here, just before where those people crossed. And then," he said, pointing behind, "I'll taxi back for takeoff and I'll drop you guys off at the other end. I'm sure they have no intention of stealing this aircraft—but let's follow the rules, and we'll make this fast. They sure look interested."

The King Air made its turn at the end of the runway and then followed the taxiway that paralleled runway 15 back to the departure end. Jim followed the taxiway to the final intersection where it then branched off and either went to the aircraft hangars or to the departure end of runway 15. He taxied the King Air just forward of the intersection and then stopped. He set the parking brake, took his hands and feet off all controls, and then he paused for a few seconds to listen. He was assessing the "at rest" health of his engines, and the sounds were strong. The hot temps and the no boost pumps was a concern, but he was happy with what he had. It wasn't perfect, but it would work.

He turned to look back at his brother and nephew who were now both in the cabin of the King Air gathering their stuff for transport. "Make sure to follow the rules, guys. If we're at war, we need to protect those radios. I love you both, and we'll talk per the SafePort schedule." Unlatching his shoulder harness, Jim confirmed that the parking brake was set—and then he turned to sit sideways in his seat. "After you deplane, don't worry about the door. I'll make sure it's closed from inside."

Paul and John opened the cabin door, and before departing they turned to look at Jim. "Go home," Paul said, pushing John towards the stairs. "We love you too. We'll talk in three days."

Exiting the aircraft, they walked their luggage over to the grass on the side of the taxiway. John had a suitcase with rollers and Paul had his overnight duffle bag. With the engines running, it was turbulent and loud—and when Paul looked back he could see that the door was closing.

"You ready for this?" he asked, putting his sunglasses on.

"Yeah, Dad. I'm ready."

Standing on the freshly mowed green grass they watched as the King Air taxied into its takeoff position. They could see Jim through the cockpit windows and they both gave him a thumbs-up, wishing him the best. With the brakes set on full, they could hear the engines advancing toward full thrust and it filled the air with the sound of power. Jim gave a quick thumbs-up back to his brother and nephew and then he popped the brakes and let the King Air roll. It quickly gained airspeed, and the aircraft raced down the runway. Jim had a ride home, and they watched as he raised the nose and headed for Idaho.

With a terrible unknown beginning to unfold, Paul and John watched as the King Air departed. Her sound echoed throughout the valley, and then it quickly faded with its departure to the east. Jim was gone, and it was now silent. This was a new world, and both could feel the weight of something heavy.

About a half mile away, and from the other side of the runway; the small group of people that had been watching the King Air land were now eagerly making their way toward the two new arrivals. Roughly a dozen, they were waving—and John waved back.

"Moment of truth, Dad. Here we go."

The two groups were on a collision course and the butterflies were stirring. Was everything as dead as it looked from the air? These people knew things that they didn't, and Paul and John had some valuable information for them too. Was it an EMP? Was America attacked? How bad is it?

At twenty feet, both groups slowed to a stop. The uncertainty was mounting, and Paul threw out the first question.

"Do you guys know what happened?"

"No," responded the older gentleman that was standing in front of the group. "We don't, but we were sure hoping you did. Nothing's working around here. There's no power, and none of the cars run."

Hoping for a simple explanation and some solid details, Paul could feel his hopes disappear. "So we're all confused," he said, extending a handshake to the older man. "I'm Paul, and this is my son, John."

"I'm Marko," he said, griping hard. "Where did you guys come from?"

John stuck out his hand. "Seattle. And it's the same over there."

Shaking his head, the older gentlemen released his grip and then turned to the others in his group. "We're all down. Seattle too."

Unsettled by the new facts, it appeared the older gentleman was confirming their fears, and Paul could feel the anxiety rising.

"Whatever caused this, it took out the cars and our phones are dead too." Marko pointed to the small parking lot that only had five or six cars. "Everything died at the same time, and I can't get anything to start. There's no juice, but that King Air was flying, so we assumed …"

Recognizing the flawed theory, Paul responded. "We were just lucky. We were in the air when it happened. We were headed here, and then it fried everything, but we still had our engines. We had stick, rudder, and thrust, and that's all. No electronics. No communication. We almost landed back in Seattle, but we didn't."

Paul looked at John. "We were lucky. My brother dropped us off here, and now he's headed for Idaho."

There was an old picnic table that was about ten feet away, and as a teenager John had used it many times to watch the airplanes take off and land after school. He knew it well, and he stood up on the bench so that everyone could hear clearly.

"It's shut down over there. It's just like here," he said nodding. "We're in big trouble. We think it's an EMP."

The crowd went silent and all movement stopped. "We saw it all, folks. Airliners crashing, beached Ferry boats, and from Seattle to here—no moving cars at all. I know we were all warned about this, and I know the whole nation could be down, but we don't know, and we need to find out fast."

His brow lowered, John had the floor and his eyes meant business. "This is life and death, and we need answers. We don't have SafePort—So we need to find out how far this goes. What happened to the rest of the country? Will we be rescued? And if not, how do we escape? How do we survive?"

From behind Marko and from the middle section of the group, a taller gal wearing a set of tan overalls and a tan shirt stepped out and addressed John. "It is an EMP," she said calmly. "It's not from a solar flare. We were attacked, and it's from a nuclear detonation—way up there."

With her arm stretched, she was pointing to the sky while looking at John. The tall woman had a small red cooler next to her, and she picked it up and walked over to the picnic table. She plopped the cooler down, and when she did, they could hear the icy water slosh inside. She opened the lid and she handed both men a bottle of cold water. "Get it while you can!"

She held out her hand and greeted them both. "Name's June. And I hate to say it, but this could be the last icy cold anything we see for a long time."

With the sun hitting her eyes, she gave them a quick once-over and continued. "I know a little bit about this stuff, and we got nailed. As far as I know, this—what we're experiencing right now—it could only happen if there was a nuclear detonation way up there."

Again she pointed straight up to the sky. "It's not only the power grids. It's all the electronics, and there's no food or running water. No food. No water. No life!"

Looking at the ground, she had a troubled smile. "This is a bad deal, everyone. Something killed the electronics in our phones and our cars—and we just lost our supply chain. It's probably nationwide and America's under attack. I think we're done!"

Looking at John, she sighed. "I think we all need to go home. We need to go home and we need to prepare for something awful."

June had long hair, and it went well below her shoulders. She was slender with a pale complexion and she wore a baseball cap with a pony tail exiting through the back. John needed to say something, but his mind was slow to respond. With the grease stains on her overalls and with the smudges on her hands, she had to be a mechanic. He'd never seen her before, and he'd remember her if he did.

"You're right, June," he said, uncapping his water bottle. "It'll be awful, but we need to survive and we need to figure this out. We still have hope."

"We do, John. But it's not here." Her head tilted, June sighed. "We need to escape and we need to get to a Safe State. This isn't America anymore and we need to leave soon."

John nodded, and she was right. Nobody would live if they stayed here, and the only hope was SafePort. He raised his bottle and took a drink.

"Did you see the airliners crashing?" she asked.

"Yep, and they were right in front of us." Again, John could hear all the movement stop and he had the group's full attention.

"That's when we knew it was an EMP. We were going to land at Paine Field, but then we saw that—and we figured it out. We weren't going to get trapped and we came here."

In a silent struggle, Paul could see the group going pale as they attempted to acknowledge the new reality that was forming. Through simple logic and commonsense the emergency was becoming verified and confirmed, and Paul could see the pain intensifying with each member. John had laid out the facts well, and he'd cut to the chase, but now they had to get moving.

"We need to move forward, folks," he said nodding to the group. From behind the picnic table, Paul walked over to his son and stood next to him.

"We need to get to our families and we need to solve this problem. Like June said, for many of us, we'll need to escape."

Sipping the last of his water, Paul set his empty bottle on the table. He'd hoped for more information by now, but the facts were becoming obvious and he knew what to say.

"I think everyone agrees. We all suspect that an EMP is responsible, and we've all surmised that America is under attack. Everything is down, we've lost our technology, and our supply chain has just been destroyed. We're on our own, and we're on foot, and the only food we have is our food at home. We've got a big problem." Rubbing the bridge of his nose, he needed to calm his thoughts and he needed impart clarity.

Taking a deep breath, he'd identify the challenge and summarize. "So what are we up against? Is everything down, and what are our options?"

Shrugging his shoulders, Paul talked it through. "We just landed here on an airplane that had two running engines, and I know the electronics, the battery, and even the starter were fatally damaged, but think about it. If these items were replaced with functioning components—we'd have a functional airplane. We have a small calculator and an LED flashlight that still works and there's got to be more. We need to go home and we need to try every-thing. Some of us have Faraday cages, and we even have old trucks and old cars that might still work. We need vehicles, and we can all work together to get our families out of here."

Listening closely, Marko spoke up. "We heard a motorcycle, or a loud car or something. It was just before you landed."

"Yeah we did," June said nodding.

"Everything was like dead quiet here, and then all of a sudden we could hear an echo off the north ridge. I think it was two Harley's and they were heading east. I know there's a lot of Faraday pods around here, so after the event they probably pulled out their motorcycles and drove 'em out of town. I think a lot of people are popping open their Faraday cages right now, but they better be careful."

"That's right." Paul looked at June and then he turned to the group. "This is a risky time and we need to be careful. Hopefully, those two motorcycles—and anybody else who had a working vehicle and tried to escape—made it to the Idaho border, but it's highly risky for the first few days. If we were to get attacked again—and it could be happening right now—any escape vehicle with preserved parts installed would be exposed to another EMP and they'd probably break down. They'd be stuck on the road and they'd be stuck in the middle of nowhere."

Standing next to Paul and John, June knew the scenario well and she knew the gravity of the situation. It was dire, and she wanted everybody to know.

"We're at 99-percent failure here, and the people that prepared are going to start leaving soon. Those that didn't are going to suffer. I agree with Paul and John. We still have hope, and if we work together—maybe we can get enough vehicles to get our families out, but it will be difficult. Maybe impossible."

Looking at John, she had tears in her eyes. "This is an apocalypse, and everyone needs to know. Millions will perish. This can't be reversed. Our leaders did this to us!"

Again, she was right and she was just as mad as he was. John nodded, and he could see Marko nodding too.

"I know what's going to happen, guys. America is over. We're going down.

Fast!" Stating her peace, June was done, and she knew that her anger was meaningless and unproductive. She was stating the facts, but the mission to survive was more important. She needed to be more positive, and while she wiped her tears she could hear her little voice telling her to buck-up.

June was capturing the full weight of what lay ahead for all Washingtonians, and the group was now fully aware. John could see the fear building and he wanted to help where he could.

"We need more information," he said, his eyes focused on June. "We need to go home and we need to set up a way to communicate so that we can all help each other. It's too soon to make drastic conclusions. We need to figure this out. We need to keep the faith and we need to focus on hope."

He turned to the group. "What's the status here? Does everybody live here and does everybody have a home they need to get to?"

Stepping forward, Marko began to introduce Paul and John to the other members of the group. They all lived in the small town of Chelan and for most everybody—home was a good five miles away.

The Chelan airport was east of town, and Lake Chelan was an oasis of green trees surrounding a long and rugged lake of blue water. Residing on the lower eastern slopes of the Cascades; to the east was the desolate landscape of Eastern Washington and to the west was the sharp rise of mountains, rich vegetation, and tall evergreens. Approximately a hundred miles away—on the other side of the mountain range was Seattle and the entire Pacific Northwest.

With a foe in common the two groups were now one. Eleven people in total were now stranded together, and they were uniting at the sleepy little airport in Lake Chelan. This group was among the few who knew the bigger picture, and because of their shared information they knew that Seattle had been affected. They knew the damage zone was at least half the state of Washington, and with that knowledge, they knew it could be the entire nation. The group was learning, and they were learning together.

On the grassy null next to the picnic table huddled a clan of eleven members. They'd been placed and stranded here separately, but now they were united with a purpose in common. Paul, John, and the rest of the group began their preparations for the long walk on the five mile road that cut through the flat dry tundra towards Lake Chelan. Marko, who was with his wife Barbara, elected to remain behind so they could ride their bicycles home once the sun started to go down. The temperature was a hot 92 degrees, and Marko didn't think they'd fare well in the heat of the afternoon.

With a travel plan that would take them through the summer desert, water would be required and June had the problem solved. The group began to walk toward the hangar where she'd been working on her father's older Cessna 310. She had a refrigerator full of water in there, and they'd need lots to make it home.

The large hangar door was half-open, and near the wingtips of the Cessna 310, the congregation assembled around the non-operating refrigerator that held the water supply. There was enough to distribute six bottles to each member and that left plenty for Marko and Barbara. Paul and John made room in their bags and the others grabbed what they could find to help cart the water along on their upcoming trek. With a good four cases distributed amongst them, June closed the hangar door and then stashed the key under the front mat for Marko to manage.

Nine members of a newly organized group began the commencement of their initial venture. As a group they left the airport grounds and started their long walk into town. Even though they were traveling through the flatlands where it was often quiet and peaceful, there was an eerie silence. Paul could hear cows mooing from what seemed like miles away. Nature was the only sound, and without society's noise to drown it out, it was odd. The silence seemed exaggerated. The group traveled close together as if there was a good reason to keep the ranks tight for safety.

For the most part, everyone was healthy and strong, but their survival had little hope and most were struggling to find answers. Survival in Washington State appeared to be impossible, and other than living off the land in a tent, Paul knew that most had no backup plan at all. With no SafePort, the President's warnings were all denied and a false trust was foolishly substituted. Guilty as charged, the walk into town was only the beginning of a constant reminder. It felt like a walk of shame and Paul could feel the guilt getting heavy.

Despair was rushing in, and the truth was brutally obvious. A great suffering was about to commence, and where only the few would survive, evil would now focus its wrath on the millions who trusted it. Paul had prepared his family, but June hadn't—nor had anyone else in the group he was walking with. He could feel the burden and it was building. It was at the forefront of his mind and his decision had already been made. It was crystal clear. He would not turn his back on others, and he would help the people who were stuck.

June's road had arrived, and now the group was down to four members. Paul watched John hand her a note as she departed the group and headed for home. He knew his son and he knew it was help that he'd offered. With his heart broken for the unprepared, Paul could see his future, and it was filled with sacrifice. His brother's 30-Day plan, most appropriately, and most unfortunately, did not take the burdens of others into consideration. Paul on the other hand, knew that he would have to. If required, he'd forfeit his lifeline to safety. He'd help the others, and he would not run.

CHAPTER 7

WORST CASE SCENARIO

Click. Anne turned the recorder off and Jim opened up his driver-side window for some fresh air. From her reclined position, Anne needed to bring her mind into the present, and she needed to organize her thoughts. Sitting up, she grabbed a small bag of salted peanuts, opened it with her teeth and started eating.

"Thank you, Jim," she said, pouring the nuts into her hand. "It's spectacular!"

Remembering her own struggle on Day One, Anne felt sympathy for Paul. "Your brother was torn, Jim. He'd made it home, he had a way out, and he had clarity on what was coming. I know we all wanted to fight for the others, but he was behind enemy lines and he was willing to stay. I know what happened and I find it impressive."

One by one, she chewed each nut and she let her eyes fixate on the side of the road as it rushed by in her passenger window. Anne was in the past, and her mind was remembering.

"For me, it was like a pressure wave. I can remember how it made me feel, and everybody around me felt the same way. We wanted to go in with the troops. We wanted to fight for the people that weren't prepared. We had hope, but they didn't, and all we wanted was for them to have it too. If we could just save them—it'd be worth our lives."

"Well, that's Paul," Jim said, nodding. "He's an attorney, but he's also a part-time preacher. I'll never forget what he told me. He knew exactly what evil was going to do, and he told me how the suffering was going to change people. He said the masses were going to turn from God—and he said there'd be a slaughter."

Glancing at Ken, he chuckled. "He was right. And just like Ken here, he had to fight an army."

Still eating her peanuts, Anne's mouth was full, but she nodded and pointed to Ken.

"That brings us to you," she said grabbing her water. "Talk about screwed. Are you ready?"

"Yep. Throw me some of those nuts. Where do you want me to start?"

Anne had her notepad on the center console and she drew a line across the page.

"We're roughly three hours into this event. Jim's trying to fly home, and you're stuck on foot in Seattle. You're walking to the airport, right?"

"Yes."

Anne tossed him a bag of peanuts and she was nervous. He should be dead, but he wasn't and she smiled. "Then start there."

CHAPTER 8

DAY 001–SEATTLE

Ken was in his tennis shoes and T-shirt. He'd shed his tie back at the car along with his briefcase and dress shoes. On his cell phone earlier, he'd tracked Sam's plane. He knew that it had landed before the event. He knew she was at the airport, but how long would she wait? *She'd realize I was trying to get to her. She'd be smart. She'll know I'm on my way. I've got to get moving.*

Westbound on I-405 and approximately five miles from the Seattle Tacoma International Airport, Ken was making good time. The car and driver that had picked him up earlier at Paine Field airport was now well behind him. He'd walked a good 10 miles already, and with the airlines crashing, he lost a good 30 minutes trying to weave through all the crowds. Following the shoulder of the highway, he was at least three hours in. He was one man with a duffle bag. With it hanging over his back, and with a low profile, Ken walked through and around the slow moving people.

He could see the airport ahead and his current estimate put him there in one hour. This was approximately five to six hours late, but he knew she was there and he knew she was alright. It was his only hope, and it was all he could think about. As long as she landed on time, then she landed before the event. He'd gone through the timeline over and over in his mind and he knew she was there. He was certain of it, and starting now, he vowed not to question it any longer. He'd stay focused and he'd strategize. You need a plan, Ken. What are you going to do?

The main exit for the SeaTac airport was just around the corner, and he could see the off-ramp lanes clogged with cars. He knew that if he crossed the highway and then hopped the fence he'd get there sooner. He could jog around the homes and he could traverse through the industrial properties that surrounded the airport. Hopping over the cement barrier, Ken walked around the stalled cars and he ran up the embankment.

Now separated from the crowds on the highway, he'd made the right move. It could get ugly quick, so staying away from the larger groups was a good tactic.

In front of him was a chain link fence and it appeared to enclose a large network of residential backyards. He threw his duffle bag over and then hopped over himself. He'd avoid other people's property at all costs, but he needed to start moving. He needed to go south and he needed to get to the other side of this hill. When able, he'd stick to the roads. If he had to—he'd cut through.

Ken continued on his shortcut toward the airport, and while walking, he worked on his plan to get his daughter out of the danger that was growing rapidly. He was upset and he knew his anger was counter-productive. He had to get perspective—and he had to get it quick. Getting caught in Seattle was ironic, and it bothered him.

He'd worked diligently for several years on helping the SafePort civil defense infrastructures come to life in Idaho. He was an Operations Manager for the Idaho zones, and now, when it really counted, he was stuck in the worst place possible. His daughter was stranded at the airport alone, and it was his schedule that put her there. I'm sorry Sam. It's my fault.

Suddenly, he could hear his little voice and it was upset.

Stop it, Ken! If you weren't here, Samantha would be stuck on her own. She could've postponed her trip, and what if she did? She'd be in Los Angeles. Get a grip!

The message was clear. If the attack had happened on any other day, Samantha would be stuck and she'd be all alone. She's here, and I'm here. Now I'm going to go find her. Twenty minutes away. Thank you, God! Thank you for everything!

Half chuckling, the sun beat down and the sweat dripped from his forehead. He could see the irony and he smiled.

Notably, over the past two years Ken had become very knowledgeable in the areas of civilian infrastructure defense and the timing couldn't be more remarkable. As the owner of a private airline, Ken had the skills and he had a good reputation, and it was his political advantage that got him his seat on the Idaho SafePort team. In the end, however, he had a knack for it and he'd done well for the state. He knew everything about SafePort, and he knew what it meant to be in Seattle without an escape plan.

When the civil defense movement first began; Ken got involved in solving the logistical challenges regarding sustenance sharing, zonal commerce, and the Civil Air Patrol. It was this part of his life that he enjoyed the most and he excelled at it.

He'd put his heart and soul into the development of a backup infrastructure system and he'd helped Idaho become one of the first ten SafePort-compliant states in the nation. With rudimentary procedures and with the shielding of standardized critical equipment, the self-sufficient system provided an emergency lifeline to everyone in the zone. It was a lifeboat and it was designed for the worst-case scenario, just like now.

Once again, he was extremely thirsty and he only had one more bottle of water from the car. They'd need a lot more, and he needed this one now—so he downed it. The airport terminal was getting close and it looked to be about a mile to the baggage claim access road. This is where he'd go.

With his mind searching for a plan, he could feel the despair slipping into his thoughts. His perspective was appropriate, and now only minutes away from his daughter, he knew why he was here and he was thankful. Nevertheless, his thoughts were all over the board. He could see the fear in everyone's eyes and he could feel the worry building. What had started out as anger and inconvenience was now turning into something else. People were waking up and he wondered how soon before they panicked. He knew it was coming, and he needed to get Sam out of here before it happened.

He was witnessing firsthand how the stunned people roaming about on the streets were beginning to realize this was not a quick-fix power outage. Hours ago, he, and perhaps thousands of others, had witnessed two jets crashing into the city. The images in Ken's mind were in full video format, and his memory had a crystal clear sound that was captured by the howling of the jet engines as they spiraled down.

Each aircraft burned a creepy and unnatural sixty-second image into his mind, and then it ended with an out-of-view explosion. Both crashes were north from his location now, and they both occurred about fifteen minutes after his car, and everyone else's car, suddenly quit.

He couldn't help but see it over and over and he recalled the distinct silence prior to witnessing the aerial event. The sounds of the city were turned off and all he could hear was the talking and occasional shouting from people nearby.

When the turbines of the spiraling jets started howling from above, everybody looked up, and with horror they stared at something they weren't prepared to observe. The crashing jets caused great concern for all who could see them, and Ken could feel the panic building behind him the whole way. The farther he traveled south, the less people were talking about it and that meant he was ahead of it for now. There were hills behind him, and the hills blocked the view. Information wasn't flowing fast—and that was good.

Unsatisfied with his progress, he needed a plan, and he needed to pick up his pace. Step by step, Ken. Walk faster.

Tonight, he'd get his daughter to a shelter, and he knew how to do it. He'd pray for the people here, and he'd pray for a way out. He'd pray that Jim made it out of Paine Field, and he'd pray that his 30-day clock was starting now. I'll handle the variables, and I'll get us to the Bluff. I can do it, he thought, but Jim needs to make it home. Wiping the sweat out of his eyes, he needed faith. We're going to make it, and Jim's already home.

Up ahead, the baggage claim terminal for the Seattle Tacoma International Airport was coming into view. He could see the large crowds congregating in the open areas, and as he got closer he could see they were flooding into the streets. With the access roadways clogged with stalled cars, taxis, and shuttle buses, he was now weaving through large groups of people and it was slowing him down. He was soaked with sweat, he was thirsty, and he was carving a path. He was almost there.

Having pierced the backside of the crowds, he was nearing the edge that was closest to the terminal and he could see a clear rout to the main baggage claim entrances. Alaska Airlines was coming up next, and it was exactly where he needed to go. He had a plan, and it needed to work. He'd enter, and then he'd immediately walk up the stairway that paralleled the escalator. He'd walk up halfway, and then he'd stand there and search for Sam. He wouldn't leave. He'd find her.

Almost there. Get around these people and keep your eyes peeled. She knows where I'll go. God let her be here.

Ken walked through the entrance and he headed for the stairway. Well over 6 feet, he had the advantage looking forward and his eyes were on a rapid scan. The crowds were thick, and as he headed up the stairway, suddenly his duffle bag was yanked backwards. His instincts kicked-in, but then he heard the voice.

"Dad!"

His heart skipped, and when he turned he saw his daughter. "My God!" he said grabbing her arm. "Sam!"

Ken pulled her to the side of the stairway and he wrapped his arms around her. Something was happening and he could feel a change. This was meant to be, and they were together, but they needed to go.

"We need to leave, Sam. Follow me."

Walking swiftly, the two weaved their way through the crowds and they headed for the exit. Once outside, he'd find a safe spot and he'd tell Sam what the plan was. The exit was directly ahead and it was filled with people, but he had a lane and he walked fast.

The loading and unloading zones were billowing with people and the crowds were in roads along with the stalled cars. Sensing the fear, Ken wanted to stay away from the larger groups and he could see an opening thirty feet away. Grabbing her hand, he pulled.

"What's happening?" she asked sternly. "Is it an EMP?"

"Yes. We've been attacked."

"I knew it!" Samantha stared at her father and her face was turning red. "That's not what they're saying in there! They're saying it's a glitch! They're telling everyone to stay here. They're lying!"

"They are, Sam, but it's good. We need the diversion."

Placing his arm around her, he pulled her behind a stalled shuttle van that was blocking the flow of people. It appeared the van was simply attempting to merge out of the passenger pickup zone when the event struck. A second vehicle had struck the shuttle van on the driver's side and it was wedged between the van and the cement barriers that lined the outer edges of the thruway.

Both Ken and his daughter huddled in the six-foot by six-foot pie slice wedge created by the fender bender and he told her what he knew. He framed the mission, he told her what he was going to do, and he kept it short.

It was ominous for both. Here they were—stuck together in the Seattle airport's loading and unloading zone. America could be in total collapse and they were stuck here, hundreds of miles from home. The people around them were confused and they were all in shock. Rumors were flying left and right, but nobody was leaving, and nobody knew what to do.

Samantha told her father about the numerous official statements being transmitted verbally by airline representatives, police, and the TSA. She told him of the many official announcements she'd heard throughout the day. Transformer explosion, cyber attack, and there was even a report saying there was a technical glitch in the upper atmosphere. The recommendations were to sit tight and wait for the systems to be restored.

Frustrated, she reached into her travel bag and pulled out a bottle of water. "You look thirsty, Dad. Drink this. I've got four more."

He was, and he reached for the bottle and then looked around. He could see others with water and the crowds were still calm, so he drank it all. "Thanks Sam. I needed that."

Ken secured his bag around his shoulder and then he had Samantha do the same. "Let's go kiddo," he said, spotting his route. He had a clear lane and it was on the grass.

"When we get over to that open road, you can use the rollers to pull your bag. Too many people here. We're going to cross over this grass and then we'll walk up that hill." He nodded to Sam. "Follow me."

Ken led his daughter through the outskirts of the crowds, over the grass field, and then up the hill that brought them to the expressway. They were on the highway and they were on a mission. They were covering ground.

In single file, and with Ken at the front, they traveled through the gaps in the endless chain of stalled vehicles. With wandering people looking for a rescue and with others like them who were on the move, the open paths between the cars and the people would expand and narrow. Most had abandoned their vehicles, but still, there were many who were sitting in their cars. They were waiting for help, and they were waiting for their phones to turn back on.

"Did you see that old couple," Sam whispered. "This is awful! What are they going to do?"

"Nothing we can do," he said grabbing her hand. "Keep focused. It's different now. We need to survive."

At a fast pace, they were traveling away from the airport via the main highway that corralled all traffic into one big eight-lane chute linking the main interstates together. Now two miles from the Baggage Claim, they hopped over the cement barricades and headed toward the residential areas east of the airport. Ken had a plan, and if it worked they'd have a shelter. Again, taking her hand they walked up the gravel embankment and they followed the chain link fence at the top of the hill. They were following the freeway and they were heading north. In one more mile, they'd hop the fence.

There was an opportunity, and although he'd told Samantha the basics he was now questioning whether the prospect had any merit. It all depended on the people and it depended on their state of mind. It's all about the timing, he thought. It's got to work, so here we go.

There was a tear in the fence and it was in the perfect spot. Ken led his daughter through and then they proceeded quickly towards the back parking lot of two motels. Stopping next to the long row of dumpsters, Ken looked behind him to see that his daughter was getting perturbed. With an obvious defect in the bag's undercarriage, she was struggling with the rollers, and they weren't rolling at all.

"We'll fix that," he said, pulling her in closer to the dumpsters.

"We need two backpacks, Dad." Samantha started working on the pull-out handle that was now stuck in the halfway position. "Not good."

"They've got empty rooms here, Sam. I'm going to get us one, and you wait here. You need to be very careful."

"I will. And use your badge. It'll work."

She'd been briefed, and she was beginning to understand his rationale. The people were confused and in shock. The retail systems were down, and the hotels were likely on standby with rooms available. He told her that if he had to, he'd use his SafePort ID and he'd require that the hotel accommodate his request. SafePort was part of the National Guard and Ken had governmental authority. It was an advantage and it needed to be used.

Waiting patiently, he'd already been gone for a good ten minutes, and Sam wanted a better view. She walked around the corner and stopped. She could see the front of the hotel and she could see the front parking lot, but she couldn't see the hotel lobby or her dad.

Out on the main road she noticed a group of police officers and others working on the removal of several stalled vehicles that were clogging the intersection. The sight made her feel better and it was good to see that something was being done to bring things back to normal. These were good people and they were working together.

While she watched the admirable efforts of the people clearing the road, she looked over to the other side of the hotel and noticed that the maid service crew was still cleaning and working as normal. It was odd, but she realized that many, including the maid service here had no concept of what was happening. They still think it's a glitch, and they still believe. Suddenly, Sam could hear her little voice yelling, and she needed to buck up. This is a travesty. They're going to suffer and die. God help them!

Samantha turned and she saw her father walking around the corner. He looked slightly unsettled, but maybe not.

"No go," he said shaking his head. "They don't have any functioning key cards to access the rooms. They said come back later."

Rolling his eyes, he continued. "So kiddo, we need to find another hotel. There's some older one's down the street and they might have metal keys."

Ken through his bag over his shoulder and he'd use his free hand to tug on Samantha's. He grabbed the handle, but then she tapped him on the back.

Sam pointed over to the maid service that was working on the outer rooms. "Those rooms have keys."

He set his bag on the ground and stared. "Yeah. Look at that. Stay here."

Grabbing his shirt, she pointed over to the dumpster and nodded. "Let me try something, Dad. Trust me. Wait until I call you over."

Before he could say anything, Samantha was gone. She walked toward the individual that was tossing garbage into the dumpster, and Ken didn't like the scenario at all. As she approached, he watched her introduce herself to the younger man and Ken could feel his adrenaline pumping. He was obviously part of the hotel's cleaning staff, and with one false move, he'd be on him.

Concerned, Ken watched, but he didn't intervene. Even from fifty feet away, it was obvious what she was up to. She was flirting, and the boy was obviously smitten with her presence. She was working something, and she looked just like her mother. He'd seen this before, but never from her. The boy handed her a metal key, and then he reached into a box and handed her a large bottle of water. Nice Job, Sam! Look at that, he thought.

Waving her father over, she'd saved the day. She shook the young man's hand, and then she patted his shoulder as her father arrived at the dumpster. "Thank you, Peter," she said smiling. "We'll be out first thing."

The two entered the room and Ken closed and locked the door. They had shelter for the night, and they'd hide from the unknowns that were building everywhere. It was Day One of a terrible new world and they were stuck in a hotel across from the Seattle International airport.

Strategic survival would now commence. Tomorrow they'd escape, but Ken only had one plan and it was a long-shot. He needed more, and he needed them quick.

CHAPTER 9

DAY 001–IDAHO

Jim's ballpark estimate said he had forty-five minutes of fuel remaining, and in the distance he could see the bend in the river as it turned north and led directly past his home. From there, it was another ten miles and he'd land in Sandpoint, Idaho. This was a non-standard flight, and over the last hour it was the amount of fuel remaining that had him concerned. His buffers were substantial—and right now he was counting on them heavily.

He had two big concerns, and it was the gear and the electric boost pumps. Dragging three tires through the air was slow and inefficient—and without his boost pumps working; there was valuable fuel in the tanks that he couldn't get to.

Under the "worst-case scenario" rule, he had to consider a sizable amount of the onboard fuel as unusable. There was a certain amount calculated by the manufacturer to be unobtainable when the engine driven fuel pumps served as the sole source in supplying fuel to the engines. Without his boost pumps assisting the fuel flow, his conservative interpretation left him with 56 gallons of jet fuel that would never make it to the engines. For good measure, he'd increased the amount to 75 gallons and he padded his estimate to reflect the gear-down flight from Chelan to here. He'd gone over it a thousand times, and he'd used sound logic. You've got enough, Jim. You'll land safely.

With only minutes to go, the final destination was approaching and he was getting antsy. The escape mission was nearly over, and soon, he'd be at home with his wife. Life would be different now, but there was hope and he was starting to feel the difference in the air. SafePort was directly ahead and he was going to make it, but there was something more. He'd seen a squadron of military aircraft traversing Eastern Washington, and it could change the equation. Management needed to know, and tomorrow morning he'd make his report.

Now crossing the border into Idaho, directly below and slightly behind was the town of Newport, Washington. The Pend Oreille River would now take him home and all he could think about was Sarah.

At the King Air's twelve o'clock position was the Albani hydroelectric dam, and it spanned the entire girth of the river. Just beyond the dam was his house, and he'd be there in minutes.

Nestled within a clearing in the woods, Jim's house was perched fifty-feet above the shoreline of the river. From this point forward, he'd continue on a direct-to course that would take him to the green metal rooftop that was just ahead.

Once there, the river would make a ninety-degree turn to the east and it would lead directly into one of the deepest lakes in the nation. Lake Pend Oreille was famous. In the 1940s; the United States Navy tested its secret submarines at the southern end of the lake, and to this day, cutting edge submersible research continues. On the lake's northwestern shoreline, where the river meets the lake, the town of Sandpoint, Idaho resides, along with its airport, ski resort, and marina.

His final destination for the day, it was only minutes away, but first, there was something more important. He had to tell Sarah he was okay.

Before turning for the airport, he'd overfly his home and he'd signal to his wife that he was safe. She's smart—and she's probably already written me off. She knows it's an EMP, and she knows I went to Seattle. I know what you're thinking, hon. But I made it.

The thought had plagued him all afternoon and his heart was starting to pound. It wasn't just Sarah he was concerned with. In about two minutes her grief would be over, but it certainly wouldn't be the case for Ken's wife, Linda. Feeling guilty, he sighed. The words slipped out and only God could hear. "Why today, Ken? Why today?"

He'd planned his descent so that his level-off would be on this side of his house and at a safe fly-by altitude. It was time to make Sarah smile. She was about five miles ahead and any second she'd hear the turbines. It was an unmistakable sound, and she'd know it was him.

Jim began his descent to roughly 500 feet above the river and he followed its centerline down the middle of the valley. With mountain ridges on both sides, the Pend Oreille River had a fairly wide girth and it had a significant amount of water that flowed through it year round. As he flew north above the river, he was approaching the Morton Slough, and he was almost to the cove below his house. He was getting close, and he hoped that Sarah could hear him by now.

To the north and just east of the river's centerline, his green metal roof was in sight. The terrain was widening and the ridges on both the eastern and western sides of the river allowed for Jim to make his maneuver. It was in this widened area of the valley where Jim initiated a tight dogleg turn to the left. He crossed the river centerline and he headed away from the house. He needed to position the King Air as close to the western ridges of the valley as possible.

With his left wingtip holding a safe distance from the trees and rocks on the western side—and at just the right moment—Jim entered a steep right banking turn and he cut across the river. With his green roof approaching fast, he leveled the wings and then rolled out on a course that was headed straight for his home. He could see his deck, and he could see that someone was standing there.

Jim knew that the sound created by the twin turbines at low altitude was flooding the valley, and for anyone nearby, it was surely an attention grabber. As he approached the house, he confirmed his sighting and it was Sarah. She was waving her arms, and Jim waved back with a roll of his wings. She couldn't see, but he was smiling from ear to ear and he'd accomplished his mission.

Sarah was at ease, and now so was Jim. He climbed to 4500 feet and then he executed a left turn to the northeast. The plan worked. Thank God, he thought. Everybody's getting home—even me.

Just ahead, and at the river's mouth where it widened and merged with Lake Pend Oreille, a two-mile bridge spanning north and south connected the two northern and southern shores of the lake and river. Appropriately, the bridge was known as the "Long Bridge" and he was overflying it now.

With the bridge behind him he began his turn toward the Sandpoint Airport. First, he'd land. Next, he'd employ his final strategy of the day. He'd maneuver the King Air into its hangar without an operating tug. He'd simply land, and then he'd taxi over to Ken's hangar—nose first.

With the engines running, he'd set the parking brake, exit the plane, and then carefully chalk the nose wheel. He'd open the hangar door, he'd turn around and come back to remove the nose wheel chalk, and then he'd get back into the cockpit. At this point, he'd simply add a nudge of power to get her rolling, kill the fuel, and then at just the right spot, he'd stop with the brakes. It went against all the rules, but it was required, and it'd be easy.

Jim's plan to land safely and then stow the aircraft in Ken's hangar worked perfectly. The big question of how far the event's damage went inland was still unknown, but he had some answers and it was a start. Everywhere between Sandpoint, Idaho, and Seattle, Washington were equally affected— and he was among the few who knew it first-hand.

Now on his way home, Jim had one of the bicycles from the hangar and he had another ten miles to go. He'd done it many times, but it was never as quiet as it was now. This was unlike anything he'd experienced before. The town of Sandpoint seemed asleep, and he wondered what Seattle was like. Was it chaos over there, and where is Ken? He peddled hard and he wanted to get home.

CHAPTER 10

MIDDLE OF NOWHERE

Looking out her passenger window, Anne couldn't stop thinking about the odds. There was something unique about Day One, and soon she'd examine the evidence in total. A tale of two Americas; she was documenting the one that had survived, and her research was revealing the presence of something extraordinary. Both men were describing the beginnings of a miracle, and now in the middle of nowhere she was confirming her personal opinion.

Outside it was desolate. With the exception of the abandoned vehicles still littering the roadside, there were no signs of human activity. These were the Rocky Mountains, and although she felt slightly nervous as they rounded the steeper cliffs, Anne felt safe and secure. Hope lived here, and she believed it to be far more than just a human emotion.

"Did I mention the extraordinary benefits we all share? The timing anomalies go far beyond SafePort. You'd be amazed with what I know about Day One."

Brows raised, she had their attention. "You gotta admit, the personal timing is extraordinary."

Setting her notepad down, she leaned forward. "How were you able to fly home? And Ken, how were you able to find your daughter? I mean, the attack had to occur exactly when it did—or it wouldn't have worked. You both talk about it in your accounts. If the timing was any different, Samantha would be stuck alone without her father, and Jim would have never departed Seattle. That's true, right?"

Both nodded, and Ken replied. "Yep, it's true. The timing was a mystery. And I know where you're at on this." Looking over to Jim, he continued. "It's either divine intervention—or it's a coincidence, and a coincidence doesn't cut it."

Leaning back, she sighed. "No. It doesn't."

The facts were becoming definitive and the timing couldn't be ignored. Where a mass coincidence might explain it, the odds were unlikely, and if not, what else could it be? Anne had seen it for herself and she wanted the people to see it too.

The answer was in the collective, and every patriot had a story, including her. It was all connected—and she could see the miracles at every turn, but she wasn't sure how to express it. She could present the details and she could expose the evidence, but maybe she should stop there. Maybe she was unqualified, and maybe the facts should speak for themselves.

"Just so you know, this whole God thing is brand-new for me. I don't know how to describe it, but just like Samantha, I had a similar experience with my dad on Day One. It was different—but similar. If the attack was on any other day, we would have been separated forever and I'd probably be dead. It was the timing, and ever since I've had faith."

Sitting up, she held out her cast. "Same thing with this. I was going to die, but I had faith, and then suddenly—I had a gun. It's strange."

With Ken nodding, she trusted them both and she wanted their opinion. "Maybe I'm going overboard here, but I see miracles everywhere and I'm not sure how to proceed. They can't be ignored, but I need to keep my opinions to myself. Maybe I should leave God out of it?"

Having gone through the same evolution, Ken had a simple answer and he wanted to help. "You're not going overboard, Anne. Same thing happen to me. Faith used to be an afterthought, and then suddenly everything changed."

Turning in his seat, he folded his knee and sat sideways. "I know what God did for me, and I can see His fingerprints everywhere, but I can't see the details you see now. We're all starving for the big picture, and until we know the whole story, we'll never understand what happened here. If you lay it all out, and if you remain objective, now you've got a powerful document. We all know it's a mystery, but we need to discover it for ourselves."

Nodding, Jim wanted in. "It is a mystery. We all have our suspicions, but we need the details to guide us. I can only imagine what you've learned, and I think Ken is right. Let us find it for ourselves."

Leaning forward, he could see her eyes in the mirror. "Did God bless America? Did God bless the patriots? Was it all a coincidence? These are the big questions and you've got an important job."

Her eyes on Jim, she sighed. "Yes. I do."

Smiling, she grabbed the recorder and took a deep breath. "Thanks for the advice, guys. You wouldn't believe what I've already discovered, and I know what's coming up. We've got a mystery to reveal, so let's continue."

Anne turned on the recorder and she put it on the center console. "Jim, Day Two. You're up."

CHAPTER 11

DAY 002–THE RECKONING

Sunday Morning 0600 PDT

Sandpoint, Idaho

With the unknowns many, Jim and his wife found that his nighttime return overshadowed everything. They were together, and last night they found peace and happiness. While others were surely haunted by the emerging terror of no food and no water, Jim and Sarah slept under the premise that together their suffering had been mitigated. Fear was secondary, and it was easily forgotten while they waited for morning.

Now awake, the burden was still here and Jim knew that it had been waiting for his recognition. Death was coming, so confront it now. You've got to get ahead of this, so figure it out. You should have an answer by now. Maybe you shouldn't have slept last night. He knew these emotions well. They were misguided and immature, and he'd learned how to deal with them.

It was the first rule of emergency management and it was the key to making good decisions. When there was more time to think, the advantage needed to be taken, and it would. This morning he'd walk his dogs—and when he got outside—he'd dig in and he'd figure it all out. It was time to get smart, it was time to think about strategy, and it was time for SafePort. It was time to wake up.

While his wife remained asleep, he could feel the tragedy rolling in. Fumbling with his socks and shoes, he sat on the footstool at the end of the bed. Still half asleep, he could feel his emotions kicking-in and he set it aside. There was no fire, and he wouldn't take the bait. It was shoes on, and then it was cobwebs out. For now, he'd turn on the autopilot and he'd get some coffee. The elephant in the room would have to wait.

Jim was a smart man and he knew how to control his weaknesses. In addition to not being fully awake, he was keenly aware of his confusion. He felt unsure as to what and how he should be thinking, and he knew it was a disaster, but he had time and he'd sharpen his bearings.

In what seemed like torrents of contrasting emotions, he knew he was compromised and he'd take precautions. He'd perform his evaluation, and he'd use the best information available. He'd refrain from any rash conclusions. He'd accept that America had been attacked, but for now he'd hold the remainder of his thoughts in limbo.

Dressed and ready, he squeezed Sarah's big toe and then he headed straight for the stairway. Halfway down, he could see that his German shepherd was still sleeping. She had a favorite pillow near the bottom of the stairs, and as he approached she opened her eyes and started to wag.

"Hey, Max," he said rounding the corner, heading for the kitchen.

Instantly she was up and she was already in front of him. She knew the routine and she knew exactly where he was going, but then Jim stopped and it confused her. He was in the middle of the kitchen and he'd forgotten. The coffee pot was electric—and just like everything else, life was changing.

Cobwebs in tow, the morning routine would have to proceed, but it was already non-standard. Maxine at his side, the priorities had to change and Jim walked from the kitchen to the mudroom without his coffee. Listening for the mudroom door, Ralphy, who was still sleeping upstairs, heard it open and he came running. Like a small horse, his gallop down the stairs shook the house. The very large, white, fluffy-haired dog ran around the corner and headed for Jim. He was happy and he was ready. It was another great day.

Grabbing the metal collars made it official, and in a final signal to Bella, who was still upstairs and sleeping with Sarah, Jim gave them a shake. It was the two-minute warning, and being the oldest dog, Bella elected to stay put. She'd slumber with Sarah. It was early Sunday morning and it was Day Two.

Sarah and Bella slept, while Jim, Maxine, and Ralph opted to go outside and check on the world.

It was the morning ritual that started the day, and everything about it was good. The combination of happy dogs and nature had a profound effect on Jim, but today—everything was different. Yesterday the world changed, and Jim's mind had awakened to what felt like a blank slate.

With loads of information and lots of assumptions stirring, up until now he'd resisted any meaningful contemplation of what had actually happened. He knew what it was, and he knew that half the country had already prepared for it, but half didn't—and that's precisely what made it unthinkable. This wasn't supposed to happen and he didn't want to contemplate it, but now he had to.

Today was the morning after, and still, it felt like a dream. In the days and weeks ahead, millions of Americans would suddenly run out of food. Death was coming, but right now, the morning was beautiful. Sandpoint, Idaho felt safe. This was a feeling that he'd never felt it before. This was a nightmare, and it wouldn't end. He needed a plan and he needed answers—and with two leashes secured—he'd find them now.

It was early morning and the sun had only been up for an hour. Except for not having any electricity and it being a little darker in the house than normal, everything looked like it did on every other day. His hand on the doorknob; Jim looked out the small window on the top of the front door. It was the deer check and the coast was clear.

"No barking, Max." Jim opened the door and they departed.

The property was 12 acres and it sat next to several hundred acres of wooded forest along the river. A little less than half of the property—or roughly five acres on the shoreline side—was partially under water during the spring and summer months. The other half of the property was located on the top of a sixty-foot benched shelf that overlooked the lower five-acre portion and the river.

It was on this upper 7 acres of the property where the home and meadowland had been carved out of the woods. On this upper shelf, the three acres of open land that rested on the edge were dedicated to the home and lawn. Behind this area was a long driveway that cut through a semi-treed meadowland that gradually became denser with cedar and pine trees as it neared the property line to the east.

In the summertime, like it was today, the meadow was filled with tall grasses and all kinds of bright colored wildflowers. The dogs had a particular affection for this area, and the summer walks were always the same. They'd smell every flower and tree within reach and they'd follow the scent until the leashes pulled them another away.

With its inherent serenity, the property was visually shielded from the outside world by a dense forest of trees. The territorial views of the river and canyon below was extensive, and with hot summers and cold winters, the land transformed with the seasons. The water level in the Pend Oreille River was manipulated by the Albani Dam—and in the summertime it was at its maximum height. Today, there was around eight feet of clear blue water, and they had their own private blue lagoon. In the wintertime, it was all ice. Each had their appeal, and for Jim, he looked forward to both.

Now firmly entrenched at dog stop number one, nearly hypnotized, Jim marveled at the Osprey that was hunting for a fish in the lagoon below. Circling above, he'd been watching its every move, and then suddenly, a familiar "schlopping" sound came from his left side. The seal created by Ralph's oversized upper lip and lower jowl had been breached, and when it happened out here, it was the human's fault.

"Doggone it! Get out of there Ralph," he yelled, pulling the leash tight. Ralph had found a new patch of deer droppings. It was the taboo treat for all three dogs, but for Ralph, it was the constant temptation he couldn't resist. Jim made a mental note of the new offender's location, and surely, Ralph did as well. The only successful strategy was to avoid the known droppings and pay attention, but with the changing environment—it was a tactical challenge. There was canine strategy afoot, and in this moment it had nothing to do with an attack on America. It was normal life with happy dogs. It was routine, and it was still here.

With Ralph forgiven, the two dogs went back to their business. Still working on the cobwebs, Jim went back to watching the Osprey. In his morning daze, it was the happiness of the dogs and nature that soothed his mind, but he couldn't get past the extreme silence.

For Jim, it had arrived upon his shutdown of the King Air's engines last night, and it still felt creepy and unnatural. Riding his bicycle from the airport to his home, he traveled through what felt like a ghost town.

The streets in Sandpoint were like giant parking lots. Stranded cars packed the streets and there was hardly anybody outside. Last night the silence was everywhere, and this morning it remained. It had a strange effect, and it felt odd. Something tragic had occurred, and the silence seemed inappropriate.

The contrast between reality and what he was observing now was confusing. Here, at his home—it felt like nothing had changed. It felt status quo. It seemed content and the silence was profound. The birds, wind, and rustling leaves were the only identifiable sounds he could discern, and they filled the air. There was no other noise. None at all—except for nature.

Before this day, and even at this early hour on a Sunday morning, the river would be alive with water skiers and boaters. Highway 2 on the other side of the river would be echoing with the sounds of civilization. The intermittent bellow of a Jake brake and the occasional roar of a Harley Davidson accelerating in the forest were common, but this morning there was no noise. Stunned by the silence, his thoughts started to roll. Is this the calm before the storm? How is this going to play out? Are we safe, and why is there no fear? My God. We're so lucky!

In rapid response, his mind argued back. That's only because you're here! What about the others? It's going to get ugly, so figure it out!

It was a strong reply, and his correction was appropriate. He felt oddly at ease, but he also felt extreme danger, and that danger needed to be understood. Just because he had a parachute, the aircraft was still going down. What if we were nuked? What about radiation? What if we were attacked again? What about the others?

These were all relevant questions, but for some reason there was a strange lack of fear. It was unusual, and he'd be cautious. As he began the morning walk, as if it were of minor importance, fear and danger was secondary and it was set aside. He'd felt it yesterday, but when he made it home last night—fear disappeared. We've got to be careful, he thought. We can't be complacent, and we can't fool ourselves just because we have the tools to survive. Hope was powerful and he could feel it in the air. It was flooding his thoughts and he was thankful, but it required due diligence. We can survive this Jim. But what about them?

Across the river and only miles to the west, in Washington State the equation was different. Over there, it was despair. Millions would start dying soon, and it was a preventable consequence that shouldn't have happened. My God! They have no options! This can't be fixed!

In the middle of nature, Jim was struggling. The reality was unimaginable, but it was real. All they'd have to eat was their food on hand. There's no running water and they can't go to the store. It's over. It's either escape or die, and they don't have much time. Shoot—what about Ken?

His heart sinking, he caught it quickly. There were too many unknowns, but he'd figure them out and he'd go step-by-step. Vowing to save both Paul and Ken, his confidence was unshakable and he knew he'd prevail. I'll get 'em out, but first things first.

The morning splendor was astounding—but there was a storm brewing and he knew that it was unstoppable. He knew that it could destroy the nation, and he knew that beginning today, it was likely that all unprepared states across the country were entering their final days of existence. Starvation and death was coming, and it couldn't be reversed. Starting today, the nation would pay.

Dogs happy, Jim found his anger and it was rising. We blew it! We blew it big time, and doggone it, those poor people. Son of a bitch! How stupid! We should've stepped in!

The undeniable facts were clear. SafePort defended America, but it only defended America for the people that were prepared. It was the new reality, and it came with guilt and sorrow. The hopeful would live—and the others wouldn't. There was no escape, and the penalty was harsh. It was inescapable, and the verdict identified exactly who was responsible.

His thoughts flowed and he knew they were raw. Climate change was a national emergency, but the people's duty to defend life and liberty was an archaic philosophy that was inherently wrong. Our nation was divided and our morals were in decline, but then SafePort came along and it made the patriots strong. Another year, he thought. If we'd had one more year the deceivers would've failed. The United States would be strong. We'd all have hope, and we'd all deserve it, but now—there's no more time. It is what it is, Jim. Figure it out. Survive. Do your job.

Still waiting for Max to finish her business, he felt a calm sense of direction capture his attention. While the dogs did their thing, he'd let his thoughts take over. Standing on the edge of the bank, he directed his gaze out on the river and Ralph shuffled up next to him.

Watching the Osprey hunt over the lagoon, he'd found one that was in a hover. A master of flight, he'd swoop in and then slow to a hover while assessing his potential target. He'd hover for several seconds, and if it wasn't a "go," he'd continue around for another swoop and hover in the next adjoining spot. When they attacked, they'd hit the water hard, and when they caught a fish they'd fly out of the water and head for land. It was a sight to behold, and while he watched he found his mind wandering.

If indeed the worst case scenario, the people in the non-SafePort states were going to eat their food and drink their water with absolutely no hope for continued survival. For most, the only hope would be a delusional hope. Many would wait for rescue. When their food and water dried up, many would begin to die. Many would steal and kill to live another day.

He quickly reflected that before SafePort, everyone was complacent. Back then, our government wanted us weak, we all survived by a thread, and there was no civil defense plan at all. It was wrong then, and it's wrong now. How could the states be so foolish? Again, Jim was mad.

Overhead, a second Osprey entered the hunt, and with its entrance Jim now had both targets in sight. As he watched, he found his thoughts reflecting on the country. He recalled how the federal government, prior to the civil defense movement, only protected its own continuity. Special countermeasures were implemented so that it could survive modern-day threats, however, there were no such contingencies for the American people.

Threats were concealed, and the republic became weak and helpless. It was a hoax. The liberal establishment, the deep state, and the mainstream news media were all at the forefront of our national sabotage. Guns were for them, and the people didn't have to worry anymore. The people were safe, and the President was lying.

Before SafePort came along, the people were weak—but now they had a civil defense and they had a shield from modern-day weapons like EMP. If all states would've joined—America would've been protected. This wouldn't be happening. The President wasn't lying!

Looking up, he sighed. It is what it is! Lost in his thoughts, the Osprey was nowhere to be found. And as far as he knew, it could have caught a fish and he'd missed everything.

"Come on Max! Get a move on," he yelled. Jim tugged on her leash and told her what a good girl she was. It worked every time, and it was working now. She wagged her tail and with ears raised, she got down to business. Free to move on, with a tug on the leash they proceeded toward the path that would bring them through the forest. Once on the narrow trail, it would circle them around to the east and then make a sharp right turn inward toward the center of the open meadow.

Jim staggered the leashes and formed a single file formation as they entered the trail. It was a natural game path made by all the critters wandering through, and it was filled with frequent "stop and go" smells for the dogs at every bend. This part of the journey was theirs to lead, and it was up to them to set the pace.

Jim lagged behind and he pulled up the rear. He was fully awake now. Similar to the flood of emotions he felt earlier while putting on his shoes, he felt a new rush of concern and it was rising. This time he was ready to deal, and his mind was sharp. He dove in, and what he found surprised him.

The big picture was devastating. He was beginning to realize the full gravity of SafePort's effect on the country. Using logic and reason, what he'd seen yesterday gave him the full authority to postulate rational theories about the nation, and his observations were more than just clues. Through simple deductions, he'd awakened to a new reality. The contiguous U.S was likely attacked with a high altitude EMP, or in military terms, a catastrophic weapon known as HEMP. Some U.S cities may have been nuked, but Seattle wasn't. It was the worst-case scenario, and the suffering would be unimaginable.

Following his two dogs through the path in the woods, Jim could feel his mind boiling it down, and he said it out loud. "War! We win or we die. It's inescapable."

With few details, Jim's morning analysis required critical assumptions be made, and he knew that his observations pointed to a horror story. He'd seen Pacific Northwest and he'd seen the devastation. The critical infrastructures were down, and it was the same here—so it had to be nationwide. A fatal blow meant no food, no water, no communication, and no cars. Only those citizens with backup infrastructures would have any chance at surviving anything beyond days and weeks, and if America was to survive, only the SafePort states could make it happen. These were big assumptions, but he was making headway.

There was a new hero in America, and it was called the SafePort Act. The term was an acronym, and it described an infrastructure for preserving life, liberty, and freedom in a treacherous world. The Survival Area Freedom Enforcement Project Operational Reach Territory Act provided federal dollars so the states and their citizens could effectively defend themselves from an inevitable danger. SafePort provided for a backup supply chain, law and order, civil defense, and emergency services.

Within each SafePort boundary, the entrenched populace residing within each zone worked together with experts on the planning and development of a backup off-grid emergency infrastructure. Each zone was unique to the survival needs of the local inhabitants, and each capitalized on the survival assets existing within each specific territory. In a nutshell, each zone was a pre-positioned emergency network, and its primary function was to produce and disperse critical lifesaving goods and services throughout its territory.

With the zones' practical use of Faraday cage shielding, these backup emergency infrastructures were protected from most all threats—including the granddaddy of them all—the HEMP weapon. Precisely because of its high confidence integrity against the electromagnetic pulse, SafePort was the preferred, go-to defensive countermeasure for all threats against the civilian populations of America. It was the prudent solution to protecting freedom, and with the SafePort Act, America's new President made it so.

The ultimate goal was to supplement the national infrastructures with both a local and regional backup infrastructure system for all cities and all states throughout the country. Should the national grids or national supply chains fail for extended periods, the protected backup systems would not fail and the basic survival requirements of the country would be met. At the time of enactment, the President announced that our national railway system was to be the first official SafePort zone of the country.

The heavy lift capabilities from the time of our grandparents became the dedicated emergency supply chain provider in time of war or national disaster. The railway system provided a hub and spoke system that facilitated the interconnection of local SafePort zones and regional SafePort territories. With the effective supply-chain capabilities of the railways, survival needs of the highly populated cities could be met and it was precisely this capability that opened the floodgates for SafePort development everywhere. One after the other, state after state joined in.

Each SafePort zone was different, but the critical off-grid electrical components needed for long-term survival was standard. Portable generators, ham radio networks, basic transportation, water pumps, fuel pumps, tools, refrigeration, automatic controllers, essential equipment, etc. were all preserved in various EMP-proof Faraday cage enclosures throughout all zones.

Silently, Jim started to cheer. The water companies and co-ops were going to save millions of lives. He'd reviewed SafePort's water protection systems in the manual a few months ago, and it was both brilliantly simple—and effective.

Each SafePort water supplier was required to have an onsite Faraday cage enclosure with one complete backup of all electrical pumping and controlling equipment used in its water delivery system. Additionally, for each operation, the company or co-op was required to have at least one self-contained power generating unit of sufficient size shielded in an enclosure and stored onsite. Like many, Jim had a well, but he was cheering for the others who didn't. It was huge, and it solved a big problem. The people would get their water back. Millions could now use their homes as shelter instead of moving closer to a lake or river.

With tension on both leashes, it seemed the dogs were in a hurry and the trio moved quickly through the path in the woods. Around the next corner they'd be in the meadow, and it was clear the dogs wanted to get there pronto. Pulling Jim along, they knew the procedure—and once there—it was leashes off. The open meadow was freedom, and it was always the same. At the big cedar tree they'd be let loose, and while they frolicked, Jim would stand in the shade and watch. It was happiness, and it was guaranteed.

"Good girl, Max." She'd found a stick and she was proud of it. Prancing up to the cedar tree, she taunted Ralph with her new toy, but when they got there Ralph found another stick and it was better. It was a common scenario, and the game was on. Jim unlatched the leashes and the dogs were free.

Standing next to the tree where he'd usually sip his coffee, this morning was different and so he walked out into the meadow to think. The sun felt good. Arms spread, he stretched, and he was ready to embark on his new life. There was a plan—and everybody in Idaho had prepared for this contingency. I've got a job to do, his thoughts yelled. I've got to keep my family alive, and I've got to get the SafePort flight department up and running.

There were rules and procedures and the system needed to be activated. He was ready, and he knew the plan would work. Breathing deep, he was organizing his thoughts, but then he could feel his mind saying stop. What about this? So now you know.

Again, his heart sunk. It was the timing, and the more he thought about it, the more it became clear. "My God!"

It was an unbelievable circumstance, but now it could be confirmed. The rational explanation wasn't cutting it, and where his arrival in Sandpoint last night was lucky—luck couldn't explain the rest. It was the big picture, and now Jim and everybody else could finally see.

How did SafePort save us in time? He knew the answer, but the answer described a miracle, and it was a miracle that would now save millions of lives. History revealed the true story, and on Day Two, Jim could see the proof of how an evil force almost destroyed America. If it weren't for the two congressmen, and if it weren't for our new President, we'd all be dead.

Today, it could all be traced back, and it all started on one special day. Nearly two-years ago, two U.S congressmen addressed the American people and it sent shockwaves throughout the nation. They described a special weapon, and it was a weapon that most of us had never heard of. They explained that it could destroy American instantly, and they explained that our radicalized enemies now had the power to kill us at any given moment. Suddenly, our new President broke the silence, and he told us it was time.

The new threat had been concealed for decades, and it was concealed to keep the people weak. In defiance of the elite, our new President exposed everything and he told us how to prepare. He said mutually assured destruction was no-longer a valid restraint, and he said that our enemies would inevitably launch the weapon, and they'd launch it because their God was telling them to.

Jim could remember every word. It spread across the nation like a tidal wave and the patriots did the rest. America needed a war shield, and SafePort was borne. It was the establishment versus the patriots, and the new President talked about a new freedom.

With his pen, the SafePort Act was signed and the states starting opting in. It was the SAFE STATE movement, and it was transforming the nation, but it was already divided and the liberal states doubled-down. They said no. They said the people needed to give up their guns and they said the Safe States needed to be prosecuted. They said we were racist and radical. They said we were evil.

His memories flashing by like a movie on fast-forward, Jim recalled it all. While some states were SafePort, others were not, but some were coming around. He sighed, and then Max came over and dropped her stick on the ground.

Her eyes alert, she wanted to play and so he picked up the stick and threw it. "Another year," he said watching her run. "They would've come around!"

Maybe not, he thought. Maybe never. And it doesn't matter anymore. The attack happened—and it happened now. It is what it is.

"C'mon dogs," he said, shaking the leashes. Time was short, and the morning walk would have to end. Sum it up, he thought. Get a move on. Stick to the facts. He fastened the leashes, and he'd finish on the move.

This was all concealed. We were sabotaged. SafePort came along, and SafePort changed everything. We had just enough time. We defended ourselves, and then we got attacked. It's all happening—and it's all happening now. We must survive. We've got guns, shelter, food, and we'll defend our freedom. His thoughts were clear and he could feel his heart pump. We're at war. I've got a job to do.

There were a myriad of potential struggles ahead. He'd need more time to work things through, but he'd found some answers on the morning walk. Life and death, hope and despair, each were finding balance and his mind was clear. He had a foundation and the chaos was getting organized. He had a plan.

On the driveway and at a steady pace, the morning walk was only a few yards from being over. Up the steps and onto the porch, Jim opened the front door. "Shush," he said, walking the dogs quietly into the mudroom.

The mudroom was designed as a front "pre-entrance" room where one could remove any unwanted bulky coats, muddy shoes, boots, snow shoes, or dogs, before entering the home through its secondary entrance. Maxine and Ralph were sufficiently tuckered, and while Jim stashed the leashes they went straight for the entrance door. When it opened, it was the path to their inside world and it was pure habit that dictated the next few steps.

Knowing them well, once opened they'd both run upstairs as fast as they could—and they'd go find Sarah and Bella. This was the routine, and he was counting on it to be the same as it had always been before. With his thumb on the lever, he grabbed the door handle and pushed it down to disengage the bolt from the door jam. As usual, the sound had an effect and both dogs were frozen with anticipation.

Jim bent down and whispered. "Where's Sarah? Go find her!" And with a slight delay to let the effect reach its fullest, he pulled open the door and the dogs raced down the hallway at full speed. There we go, he thought closing the door behind them. "Good dogs," he said quietly, and he headed back outside.

Standing on the front porch, he felt energized. The sun was calming, and there were orange colored light-beams that were piercing through the cedar trees and lighting up the house. The porch was getting warm, and to his left was the deck chair where he'd usually have his second cup of coffee. Not today, he thought—and then he walked over and sat down.

The barrage of uncertainty was slowing and he'd assessed the big picture. His observations gave him an edge, but by tomorrow the SafePort states would be official, and the information would flow. The clock was running and it was time to manage the emergency.

The rules were simple. Asses the event for three days, and do not open or compromise the shielding enclosures. On Day Three—perform integrity checks on all equipment and monitor the HAM radio system for commencement communiqué. SafePort was on auto-pilot, and the cure was on its way.

CHAPTER 12

THE CURE

Deep into the unknowns; he'd found peace and he had solid footing, but his situational awareness was only superficial. America was prepared, but a portion of it was intentionally sabotaged and it made it difficult to decipher the true predicament.

The suffering was preventable, and the departure from reason was both calculated and premeditated. It was clear. They took advantage of the people and they undermined the system. They kept them weak. They had open borders, and they gave sanctuary to illegal immigrants and said it was moral. Justice was lost, and it never came back, so was it even America?

Jim's grasp on the future was minimal. He knew the horrors were coming, but he was still confused and he wasn't ready to make any assumptions. Half the nation was going down; but these were the states that were willing to destroy America for a sinister goal. Their plan was working, and they wanted to vote the patriots out. They did terrible things and they did them with no remorse, but now they've failed—so how should we feel?

Confused, his assessment was vile, and he focused on the innocent. These people were betrayed and now they're helpless. Jim couldn't stop thinking about all his friends that were now trapped and they didn't have an escape plan like Ken and Paul. He didn't know how to feel, and it was odd. There seemed to be a wall, and what resided on the other side was inconceivable.

He grieved for the innocent, but he wanted the deceivers to fry. It's good versus evil, God. What do we do?

Besieged with an apparent response, his little voice yelled and he got out of his chair with vigor. It was hope, and he could feel it rushing in. The patriots would live—and America was still alive. We've got a purpose, and we must survive. For now, nothing else matters.

Inspired, Jim leaned against the deck rail and sorted his thoughts. It was simple. Half the states were SafePort compliant and half were not. The equation was set and it couldn't be reversed. We're at war and all bets were off. It was time to go to work, and tomorrow, he'd accept his command. Destiny would explain the rest, and accountability was for later.

We can help, he thought. We're still alive and we're strong. We can save lives and maybe we can save Washington State. Shaking his head, he looked down. "Maybe. I just don't know."

From out on the deck, he could hear that it was still quiet inside and that meant Sarah was still asleep. For the moment he was free and he'd use it to his advantage. He needed to review the plan. He needed the manuals, and he needed some coffee.

Through the front door and down the stairs, Jim headed for his basement office. With no lights and with the windows still in the shade, he was struggling to see. This is no good, he thought. Time for a new office. Time for lanterns and candles. Got to get used to this.

Rummaging in the dark, his thoughts were on the initial SafePort procedures. As time progressed, it would all come together. We need our supply chain. If we all do our part, the plan will work. We'll be fine. I need to get busy.

As the Director of Flight Ops, his role served a unique function, and he was ready to take it on. It was an appointed position, and he'd refrained from making any official request, but his connection with Ken likely sealed the deal.

Appointed last year, he'd helped Ken build the primary surveillance infrastructure for SafePort, and it was certified for on-demand operations six months ago. As the Flight Director, he had a team and he had all the preserved equipment necessary for indefinite operations. There were five SafePort zones within the North Idaho Territory and Jim was responsible for all flight operations within each zone. With unique authority, he reported directly to both the Territory Commander and the governor, and his flight department performed the necessary function of a modern-day civil air patrol.

Looking for a pen, he had two large binders in his arms, and there was a clipboard full of notes held tightly under his armpit. Searching for his favorite, his fingers sorted blindly through the assortment stored in a large beer mug on the top of his desk. It was his red pen and they all looked the same.

Jim pulled out a handful and walked over to the window. "Damn!" It didn't matter, and he walked upstairs, quietly. He had a thousand things on his mind, and all he needed was fifteen more minutes. He headed for the front door, opened it slowly and then shut it behind him. Sarah was still asleep. Not much time Jim. Hurry it up.

Back outside and with his reference material spread across the patio table, this would be his desk for the day. He could see, the sun was bright, and there was a lot to read.

Jim believed the SafePort manual system was the key ingredient to selling the countermeasure to the patriots. It was an easy three-step process, and it turned a complex countermeasure system into a simple plan. It was easy to follow, and with its standardized methods and procedures, it was easy to comply with. Its framework was unique in that it enabled the survival experts to provide expanded details, and it drove the market. The civil defense industry became profitable, and the demand was inherent. Best of all, everyone was on the same page, and it was all because SafePort had a well organized General Operating Manual (GOM).

The SafePort GOM's were standardized countermeasure manuals, however, and each zone had an operating manual that was specific to that area. The procedures spelled out precisely how each operation of the system would be performed, and additionally, the duties and responsibilities for each participant were specifically identified. This included the general populace, the sector managers within each zone, the zone commander, state managers, directors, and the territory commanders. The structure was comprehensive—but it was simple and it was built to succeed.

Implemented solely as an emergency backup infrastructure, when required due to national emergency, the elected state governors assumed full command over their respective SafePort infrastructures, to include the civil defense forces and the state guard. In the event of a national emergency resulting in supply chain failure, it was the state governor who would declare the official commencement of any SafePort operations.

This official commencement—per SafePort's Emergency Radio Network—would be declared at some time no sooner than the third day following a catastrophic "Infrastructure Down" event. Additionally, in concurrence with the commencement guidelines, an official meeting in all zones was pre-scheduled so that all managers and directors would meet on this third day. Tomorrow was Day 3, and Jim would be attending. It'll be historical, he thought. Tomorrow we start the machine! We get organized and we survive.

He had two manuals on the table. The Bonner County SafePort GOM, and most importantly, the North Idaho SafePort Territory Flight Operations Manual—called the NIST FOM. Only Jim, his duly assigned flight operations personnel, the territory directors and commanders, and the governor had access to the NIST FOM. From around the country, a national team of experts had developed the SafePort flight-mission parameters, policies, and procedures, and Ken was on the approval team. In the end, they'd produced a good document and Jim believed the drafting of the standardized manual was an impressive achievement. He knew it well, and starting today the NIST FOM was the new playbook he'd live by.

Once up and running, the daily operation of the county zone was designed to operate as a function of the community. It was during the initial days and weeks that a lot happened. Many critical actions were recommended or required and each had to be performed in accordance with specified calendar days that accrued from Day One of the emergency event. As of now, he was no longer the Chief Pilot for U.S. SKYJET. The company was gone forever, and all duties were now SafePort duties. Barring some miracle—this was his new life and it started today.

He could feel the pressure ramping up, but he needed to slow it down and he needed to get ready for Sarah. She'll want the fast-track. He needed to bypass the emotions he'd already dealt with—and if he did—she'll see the hope quicker and it'll be better. He knew what to say and he'd explain it all when she woke up. The manuals could wait. Go to the pump house, Jim. Make sure she's got water pressure. She'll want coffee too. Get ready.

He'd resisted long enough. His jolt of reality approaching the coffee machine earlier was a heart stopper. As of this morning, his automatic brew of freshly ground coffee was a thing of the past, but there was a simple solution. The old campfire-seared percolating coffee pot was in the garage somewhere and he'd find it. It was his first dilemma and he'd solve it now. No more waiting, he thought. He'd find the percolator and he'd fire it up. Coffee on first, then it's off to the pump house.

It was still early and the sun had only been up for two hours. The sky was bright blue and it was already warm. He'd sorted through the shelves in the garage and he'd found the percolator. Things were about to get a whole lot better, and as he headed around the deck towards the back door, he stopped at the gas barbeque and pulled off the vinyl cover. Strategically positioned so that its operator could overlook the river while tending to the food, the view in front of him caught his attention, and he couldn't stop looking at it.

It was the Washington border, and it was just on the other side of the mountains across the river. Looking to the west, he wondered. Just on the other side of those hills, Spokane is waking up to the end. No food, no water, and their cars won't start. That's a quarter million people and they're all trapped. They're screwed!

Jim sighed, and his thoughts continued. Plenty of food. No damn plan. Even if we sent in the food, they have no process. They can't receive it and they can't distribute it. It's a done deal. We can't fix this. It'll get bad!

Reality was sinking in and he was being ambushed at the barbecue. We're the closest targets! What if they all rush in? We've got food and water here. We've got hope, but if they take it, we've got nothing! We all go down. America goes down!

The scenarios were horrific, and he was starting to see something he wasn't prepared to see. These thoughts had to stop. He wasn't ready. Contemplating them now produced nothing but disturbing revelations, and Jim wanted no part in assessing it any further. Not now, he thought. Later, and with a nervous chuckle he flipped on his crisis switch, turned off his thoughts, and headed inside. Okay—coffee and water.

The camping grade coffee pot he'd proudly gathered was quickly becoming inferior. Quietly rummaging through the kitchen cabinet, he'd discovered the French Press coffee maker and it was a game changer. He was searching through an area rarely explored, and like a kid emptying his toy box on the floor—Jim had what he wanted. He gathered all the coffee in stock and he had three and a half bags. Coffee was now a luxury.

Got to get used to it, he thought. It's a different world. Then he heard his little voice, and it was the voice that liked to question his perceptions. "What if it's not as bad as you think, Jim? What if the rest of the nation is unaffected? What if the power comes back on?"

This was his counter-balance, and its sole purpose was to question his thoughts and actions. Where unverified assumptions were often dangerous, it had its place, and Jim smiled at the question. He grabbed the tea kettle for his hot water, the French Press, and a small ration of the precious coffee. Yes, he thought. The power could come back on, and maybe I'm missing something here. His gut said no, but he'd allow the question.

Back at his patio office, it was time for some hot water. With his manuals waiting for inspection, he moved the tea kettle onto the barbecue and filled it with four bottles of water. With his hand on the gas knob and with a lighter ready, he hesitated. There was a particular memory that was starting to bother him, and there was something he'd thought he'd seen in the manual.

"I know exactly where to find it," he said to himself. "Let's clear this up."

The countermeasure manual had an essential chapter that was specifically dedicated to post-event emergency assessment. Provided as a tool to help users identify and decipher the national emergency; it used a flow chart that converted user observations into meaningful information. Jim thought the flow chart was brilliant, and for the general populace it was perfect. When the communications were down, the people could still figure out what they're up against, and they could make educated survival decisions.

He'd read the chapter many times, and it's precisely why he knew the event was not from a solar flare. It was definitely an EMP, and his observations confirmed it, but there was something about magnitude—and he needed to check. Still quiet inside, Sarah was still sleeping and it surprised him. Good for her, he thought. Let her sleep. I need to figure this out.

With a flip of the tab titled "Event Analysis" he flung open the manual. The GOM published accurate data that was up-to-date and based on scientific principles and facts. It removed the chaotic effect of misinformation, and it provided the user with critical information and unique tools for properly assessing the emergency at hand.

Jim, as did all SafePort residents who studied the manual in depth, acquired a comprehensive understanding of the EMP weapon and its effects on various electronics. It was the new nation killer and knowing its potential effect on American citizens was critical to one's personal defense. SafePort was for the patriots who wanted to survive, and that meant the patriots had their flow charts out. They know it's not a solar flare. They know we've been attacked—and they know it's an EMP.

Per the GOM, an Electromagnetic Pulse had three distinct pulse signals. The three signals consisted of the E1 pulse, the E2, and the E3. Each pulse frequency had its own signature, and their ability to reach the ground was dependent upon the location of the source, relative to the Earth's atmosphere.

Unlike solar flares, gamma rays emitted by a nuclear detonation at high altitudes, but below the upper atmosphere, emitted all three pulse signals toward the surface of the earth. Solar flares, however, caused an electromagnetic pulse that had to first penetrate the Earth's atmosphere to reach the ground, and the only frequency that could do that with any force was the E3. Whereas the solar event's E1 signal was absorbed and nullified by the atmosphere, alternatively, the HEMP weapon capitalized on the Earth's atmosphere and used it to magnify the effects of all three frequencies.

With a HEMP detonation; E1, E2, and E3 frequencies are hurled directly towards the ground, but the E1 and E3 frequencies are the primary killers. The E1 is small, rabid, and fast. Occurring within nanoseconds from detonation; the E1 frequency is unique in that it can penetrate and destroy the critical circuits within our small electronics. Regardless of whether they're plugged in or turned off, the E1 was a technology stripper, and it was precisely why Jim knew that it wasn't a solar flare. If it destroyed our cars and our autonomous electronics, it was a high-altitude electromagnetic pulse (HEMP).

Where the E1 pulse was perfect for the small stuff, the E3 went straight for the large. Antennas, power lines, and distribution infrastructures were no match for the E3, and where the solar flare was a grid-killer because of it; today it was the result of a nuclear weapon detonated at a high altitude.

HEMP was a double-whammy. The E1 and E3 worked together in

wiping out technology instantly, whereas the solar flare could only remove our power grids and communications. Both events were existential, but the worst case scenario happened yesterday.

Rubbing his forehead, everything he read was in support of his current understanding. The E1 pulse was clearly observable, and the damage told the story.

Jim turned the page, and on the top there was a graph titled Observable Effects. It was here where the damage observed by the user was used to identify the suspected source—whether HEMP or solar. This was what he needed to check and he was starting to remember. It seemed the observable condition was unusually severe, and it required that he refer to a separate classification that was listed at the bottom of the page.

Reading through the notes, they failed to mention anything about airliners, but it did reference the cars. Apparently, the observable failure of all modern-day vehicles was considered an extreme damage environment. On the scale of Pulse Magnitude versus Damage, the countermeasure manual referenced this extreme environment as one having additional survival requirements and challenges.

Most notably, it assigned a term for the unique magnitude. It was strange, and he'd expected something more clinical than a *Super EMP*. Nodding, he chuckled. "It was super."

He skimmed through the rest of the notes, and they were all bad. As he read on, it appeared his observations played an important role in determining survivability. The Super EMP was an elevated calamity, and the analysis matrix appeared to be alluding to advanced hardening and shielding requirements for survivability.

His heart sinking fast, the manual directed the user to review potential considerations that may affect the functional operation of SafePort zones if a Super EMP was detected. Reading the words, Jim was getting scared. Do we have advanced shielding? Is our equipment safe?

Scanning for a caveat to relieve his concerns, he found none. Yesterday's attack was a military grade weapon and it was powerful. The manual suggested the possibility that some Super EMP weapons—if used—could exceed the shielding effectiveness of certain preservation enclosures. These Super EMP weapons were noted by the experts to have magnitudes that were classified, but it also stated in big bold print that it was a known and existing technology. With an asterisk, it stated, "Considered to be in the arsenal of most nuclear nations."

FaraSafe Inc. was an official contributor to SafePort and they were a common supplier of preservation shielding enclosures throughout the nation. Their official statement in this area was that they incorporated a shielding effectiveness capable of protecting equipment from weaponized EMP technology.

The very common and lightweight FaraBox was FaraSafe's lowest rated shielding effectiveness enclosure, and it was suggested that due to its unique double Faraday cage within a Faraday cage design, its shielding effectiveness was still sufficient to withstand—or reduce to a nominal level—the effects of a modernized HEMP weapon.

Where Day Three was the official day for SafePort integrity checks, the manual suggested all users perform an immediate inspection to confirm enclosure reliability if a Super EMP was detected. Specifically, it recommended that the FaraBox safety check and all non-rigid Faraday cage enclosures should be among the first integrity checks performed. This last suggestion got his heart pumping. He knew they got hit hard, but what if the preservation enclosures didn't work? We'd be toast. We'd be just like them. His stomach was churning, and he stood up.

In addition to the quarter-inch steel Faraday cage he had buried in the meadow, Jim had several FaraBoxes in the garage, and they were nothing more than special metal bags that were sandwiched between cardboard. He was headed there now and he'd do a quick test. He rounded the corner and ran into the garage. Palms sweaty, he should've done this earlier—and he felt sick.

When he got there, he opened up one of the FaraBoxes and performed his test. After a few fumbling moments, he was reassured. "Thank God!" he said sighing hard. He was scared, but he was recovering.

Jim had checked several of his hand radios and the equipment worked fine. The FaraBoxes had held strong and his sour stomach went away. Hope was back, and a simple metal box would now save his family. That was way too close, he thought, sighing again. Way too close, and he walked out of the garage.

The Faraday Cage enclosure was the essential component of every Safe-Port zone, and if they failed to protect the equipment inside there was no way to rebuild the supply chain, keep the community alive, or survive as a nation. Used by the military to defend critical technology on the battlefield, it was a simple device that served as a portable shield for all equipment that wasn't internally hardened. Nothing more than a metal enclosure, it was discovered in 1836 by an English scientist named Michael Faraday. He'd found there was a canceling effect of electrical fields within the interior of enclosures made out of conductive materials, and it became an essential tool in the electronics industry.

Discovered long ago; the canceling effect was a fundamental principle, and now it was saving the nation. There wasn't much to it, but when defending from HEMP, enclosures reliability was essential. Millions were using the FaraSafe enclosures, and Jim knew that he wasn't the only the one with sweaty palms.

With his equipment safe, he felt hope return and it was time to embrace the moment. He'd deal with the manuals later—and he was anxious to talk with Sarah. He'd been on a rollercoaster all morning, and he wanted to calm down. It was time to smell the roses, and it was time to go to the pump house.

Jim's property had well water, and thanks to SafePort, today he'd be able to pump the water by hand. Last year he'd installed a manual hand pump so he could get emergency water from the well when the power went out. The hand pump was a SafePort requirement, and it was mandatory backup for all wells in the zone.

Jim's system was also connected to his pressure tank, and it allowed him to pump the water pressure so that it was available at the faucet on demand. With the new technology in leverage physics, it wasn't that hard to pump up the pressure tank, and after a shower or two, you'd simply go back to the pump house and pump it up again. It was saving the day, and Jim knew that everyone living off a well in his zone had water flowing.

Within days, the community systems and water companies would be back online—and that meant everyone else would have their water too. Millions were about to be saved—and it was an amazing accomplishment. The water was protected, and it would flow, except for over there. In Washington

State; they'd have to leave their homes, and soon they'd become refugees with no shelter.

It was horrible, and Jim didn't want to think about anymore. His arm was tired and he looked at the pressure gauge to confirm that it was good. This'll work, he thought, and he stowed the pump handle and walked away. It was time for Sarah, and he could see her in the window as he walked towards the house.

Headed for the back door, Jim was on the deck and he was turning the final corner. He had ten more steps, but before he got there, Sarah opened the door and stuck her head out. She was sleepy.

"Mornin', hon. Thanks for pumping the water."

"Morning'," he said, arriving at the door. "I know it's only cold, but I'll fix that later."

He could see the upper corner of her mouth start to quiver. "Yeah, I know. Not good, Jim. But we'll deal with it." Stepping out on the deck, she walked into his arms. "Give me a few minutes. I'll get dressed and we'll talk. We're going to be okay, right?"

"We'll survive," he said nodding. "There's a lot of bad, but there's a lot of good, and its all here. Go get dressed. I'll give you the run down."

He watched Sarah close the door he could see the worry on her face as she turned and walked away. She was waking up to the same unknowns that he'd already faced, and he wanted to simplify the process. This was a new life and it was scary. It wasn't a dream. It was real. Millions would die—and America was at war. It was all bad, but she needed to focus on the hope. The quicker she got there, the better.

He knew what to do, and with Sarah upstairs he walked into the house and headed for the kitchen. He grabbed his supplies, and with his arms full he walked back outside to start breakfast. He had the good stuff and he laid it all out on the patio table. It was Sunday and it was time to eat. It was time to embrace life.

The tea kettle had a slow boil and he poured it into the French Press. With the burner still on, he put the cast iron pan on the barbecue and filled it with bacon. It was strange, and he wondered how many other people were doing the same thing. It made him smile, and it felt like a celebration. We defended ourselves. We live!

Jim opened up the door and yelled the good news. "Coffee's on! And its bacon and eggs, hon."

"Excellent, Jim. I'm hungry." Leaning over the balcony, she looked down. "Almost done. Happy Sunday!"

"Happy Sunday."

Sarah had special power and it blew him away. Where most would only see fear and uncertainty—she'd seize the faith, and she'd find the good. She was scared, but her heart was always happy and it was a unique strength. It was powerful, and Jim admired the trait.

She was ready for anything, and from here on out they'd deal with the problem together. His, "Hi honey, I'm home," grand entrance last night went from pitch black fumbling in the mudroom, through a three dog obstacle course, and then directly upstairs and into bed. He told her the short story, but all she could hear was that he was home. She wanted everyone on the bed, and she wanted her family to fall asleep together. Everything else was put on hold until morning.

The fry pan was starting to sizzle, and the coffee tasted spectacular. Eggs, bacon, toast, coffee, and juice—it was a tall order, but it was worth every bit of effort. This was hope, and it meant food, water, and shelter. Jim thought it was historical, and a full course breakfast was perfect.

With the patio table set, food was on its way. Sarah brought out the dogs, and with the gates closed the deck became a first-class kennel in the middle of nature. Jim pulled out a chair at the makeshift table. "Have a seat," he said holding a platter of bacon. "Eggs and toast are almost done."

"Smells fantastic, Jim. Just like camping."

On the deck in Idaho, it was Sunday morning and it was Day Two. Together they witnessed the new world and they talked about everything. Jim told her what he'd seen on his flight yesterday, and he walked his wife through his morning analysis. Together they found hope, and they found purpose. They were a team, and the team had a job to do.

On the edge of her seat, Jim was telling her about the plan for getting his brother Paul and Ken out of Washington State. She'd heard some of it before, but now it was real and her heart was racing.

Suddenly, Ralph barked from under the table. It was a deep single bark, and he got up and shuffled over to the deck rail. Both Jim and Sarah could hear something coming down the driveway—and it was getting louder. Maxine got up, but she only walked a few steps and then she lied back down.

It was George, and he was on his bicycle. The dogs loved George, but especially Ralph, and his tail was wagging. Jim stood up and he walked over to the deck rail.

"Morning, George! You beat me to it. Was headed your way after breakfast."

"That was you in the King Air, right?"

Jim nodded. "Figured you'd hear it."

Leaning his bike against the rail, George opened the deck gate and he was greeted by Ralph. "Morning boy!" Bending down, he scratched his chest with both hands.

"Yeah, I heard it. And then I ran out and watched you fly over. What the hell?"

Shaking his hand, Jim chuckled. "Have a seat. Lot's to talk about."

George was their closest neighbor on the river and he was a good friend. They'd known each other for years, and over the last two they'd worked closely together on improving the SafePort infrastructure.

George was a sector manager, and starting tomorrow he'd be in charge of Bonner County's Fish and Game. He was retired Army, but when he got to Idaho he took a job with the state running its Fish and Wildlife Preservation Project. His experience was vast, and he was the perfect man for the job. He knew where the food was, and he knew how to get it. Most importantly, he knew how to organize, and he was an expert at directing boots on the ground.

While George sat down, Sarah got out of her chair and started to clean up the mess from the breakfast shenanigans. Jim still had eggs on his plate, and with his fork in hand he slid over the coffee thermos and pointed towards the cups stacked at the end of the table.

"You know something," George said, grabbing a cup. "How far does this go? Is it local?"

"From Seattle to here, George. All the way. And probably to the east coast. Worst case scenario."

Jim told him everything. He told him what he saw and he told him about the C130's and the Army helicopters he'd seen to the northwest of Spokane.

"I don't know what it means, but they weren't crippled like I was. They were flying tight. Low and tight. I saw two formations, and they were both heading north."

Sitting in his chair, George leaned back and took a sip of his coffee. He was thinking, and he was shaking his head. "Hard to say."

He took another sip and leaned forward. "If Seattle's down, then we've got to assume it's coast to coast. I'm guessing you were about three hours in—so I don't think those helicopters departed from an unaffected area. They're beefed-up, and they probably survived the attack. I'm thinking it's a good sign."

Jim was nodding, and he was letting George soak it in. He could see his eyes getting angry.

"So where's the King Air now?"

"She's in the Sandpoint hangar. She's safe, but she needs her mechanic. She needs fresh parts. First priority."

Standing up, George had more facts than he'd expected and Jim's observations made it clear. His mind racing, he sighed. "I'm sorry to hear about Ken. It's a damn shame."

Leaning over, he set his coffee cup down and looked at Jim. His face red, he put his fists on the table. "We knew this was coming. And so did they!"

Pointing due west, across the river and towards Washington State, George shook his finger and nodded. "They knew everything about this threat. They had all the intelligence—and they knew the people wouldn't survive. This will get ugly! We're on the front lines. We're in trouble!"

CHAPTER 13

THE BETRAYAL

Sitting up, Anne was smiling.

"That's the part I wanted, Jim. The fear and the anger. The battle for hope. How should we feel? Your story nailed it."

Stretching in his seat, Jim leaned back so that he could see her in the mirror. "It was that anger that got me. I tried to turn it off, but I never could. It was the betrayal. I still can't shake it."

He looked to Ken. "I know we're supposed to forgive, but they were traitors. They were murderers. They caused this, and I can't let it go."

"I don't think we have to, Jim. Not yet, anyway." Looking at the map, he was shaking his head. "We're still at war, and this isn't over yet. Justice first, forgiveness later. We'll get there."

Turning around, Ken nodded to Anne. "Somebody needs to do a story on them. We need facts. We need to find out who survived—and we need to track them down. What about those governors? Where are the senators? Where did they go, and can they be prosecuted?"

Anne shrugged. "In the works, but only the military has access. Still too dangerous, and the journalists can't get in. I know there's a pool heading into California with the Army this month, and I just heard New York is on the verge of becoming controlled territory. I know it's slow, but the facts are coming."

"Good. We need closure."

"I agree. But I'm with Jim on the forgiveness thing. I know they didn't want people to die, but they led the people over a cliff—and they said it wasn't there so that they could get more power. They were deceivers, and they tried to trick us all. How are we supposed to forgive?"

The cab fell silent, and then Jim turned to Anne. "It's the betrayal."

"Yep ... It's the betrayal." Leaning forward, she wanted to pursue the topic.

"It's the hardest thing. And in hindsight we can see it all. There was an evil force and it was targeting us. It used our own government, and then it used an EMP. It wanted to kill the real America, but it had to kill us—or it had to vote us away so that it could succeed. It used temptation, greed, and vanity, and our offenders took the deal. They almost got us, but then something happened, and they failed. And now we're here."

Anne sighed. "I know the betrayal is difficult, but I think there's something else, and I think it's critical. We know they wanted to destroy us—and we've got the proof. But what if we had proof of something else? I think we do. And maybe it can help us on the forgiveness thing."

Intrigued, Ken was now sitting sideways and his foot was on the center console. "What do you mean?"

"Think about the timing. On Day 1. Now back it up a year, and think about the timing of those congressmen and our President who revealed everything. Think about the countermeasure that was intentionally concealed, and remember how everything changed once the people found out. The establishment crumbled and the patriots united. The media lost the con and the patriots were given the tools to defend America. We had one year, and we had one chance, and we did it. Then we got attacked."

Tapping her cast against Jim's arm, she smiled. "What are the odds of that? And why did it happen? What I'm saying here is that we have two parts to the equation. Where evil's plan is now provable, so is God's. And in hindsight, we can see it all. And I think it's critical to our recovery. What if—"

Ken held up his hand. "Was that an RPM drop?"

"Yes." Staring at his gauges, Jim was preparing for a full failure. "Split second. I saw it drop. All the way to zero—then back to normal. Son of a bitch!"

"I heard that," Anne said, motionless.

Scanning for signs of danger, Ken looked out the window, and then his eyes went back to the gauges.

"What are you looking for?" Heart racing, Anne slid over to her side window and looked outside.

"We're still gun-shy, aren't we?" Ken was smiling. "It's not an EMP, Anne."

"No its not," Jim said, firmly. "It still gets my heart pumping, though. She's fine. Bad connection, or maybe it's a loose fitting."

"Thank God." Anne had a crackle in her voice and her fear was fleeting. The mountain roads were bordered by steep hills on both sides, and she could only see directly above. Her first thought was that they had just dodged another pulse, but now she was smiling too.

"Get Rob on the horn." Eyes still glued on gauges, Jim wanted the expert opinion. "It was a bumpy ride back there and I know we hit some good potholes. Maybe a wiring harness is loose? Maybe we should pull over? He'll know."

"Roger." Ken grabbed the radio.

"Leader One. You up Rob?"

"Loud and clear. How's the ride, boss."

"Good, but we've got an issue. We had a split-second loss of power. Three minutes ago. RPM went to zero—then back to normal. It's solid now, but do we let it go?"

"For now, yes. We'll get the experts on it later. Probably a loose wiring harness. I can pop the hatch at Overland and we'll take a quick look. We're about two-hours out, but if it keeps happening—find a good spot and we'll pull over. We've got tools and we've got full spares on board, so we're covered. Just keep me informed."

"Roger. She seems fine now. We'll see ya there. Thanks Rob."

Ken put the radio down and looked at Jim. "Avoid the potholes."

Laughing, Anne grabbed her notepad and leaned back. "Nothing like a good boost of adrenaline. Wide awake back here. What are we, halfway through?"

Jim looked at his watch. "Just about. We'll lose a half-hour or so at Overland, but we're on time."

"That's awesome, guys! We're moving right along." Her head down, writing in her notepad, Anne picked up the recorder with her bad arm. She set her pen down and tapped Jim's shoulder.

"Now it's his turn. You get a break."

Putting his sun glasses on, Jim smiled. "You're up, bud. I'll watch for the potholes, you talk for a couple hours. Anne, throw me some nuts."

Tossing him a bag, she laughed.

"And now for the great escape." She drew a line on her notepad and looked at Ken.

"So, before we begin, I want you to know where I'm on this story. I heard the live report when they first ran it on the SafePort networks, but I only heard the brief facts that could be told on the radio. It was a spectacular report, but I know there's much more to the story."

Anne started the recorder and set it down. "So now you're sitting in front of me. I have a file on this, and between what the file says and what I've heard from my Dad, I've learned a little bit more, but not much. There's no information on how you pulled it off. There's no mention of this 30-day clock, and today, I've heard both of you talk about it. It's these details that tell the story, and I want to hear your thoughts. It's Day Two and you've left the hotel—I want to hear it all."

Nodding, Ken took a deep breath and he let it out slowly. "I can do that. But it's not pretty. I was a wreck, Anne. I had to find hope, and I needed faith, and it took me a while. In the end, I think it was a test, but it felt like a lesson. I struggled, but I learned."

Scratching the back of his head, he smiled. "Just like you, I found my faith, and then I met evil."

CHAPTER 14

THE BRIDGE

O n the day after the attack, America was in shock. For those entrenched in the SafePort states, hope had arrived and they'd be spared. For all others, the countdown to terror and panic had begun. Within a very short time measured in hours and not days, the unprepared would erupt. For Ken and Samantha, trapped in the city of Seattle, this lull before the storm was a tactical advantage. If they could escape now, they'd get out before the panic. The longer Seattle remained stunned, the better.

It was getting lighter now and Ken could see the narrow cement sidewalk they'd been blindly walking on for the last mile. Headed east-bound, they'd been feeling their way through Seattle's I-90 tunnel, but now they could see. The end was near, and Ken could see the lake.

Thirty minutes ago, it was dangerously dark as they entered, but it was a good decision and they were almost out. They were headed for the floating bridge which would take them across the lake and arrive at the eastern shores of Lake Washington. They were headed away from downtown, and if it weren't for the fortuitous timing of their sliding merge out onto the I-90 freeway, their access to the bridge would've taken them a lot longer. If it wasn't for the armed escort, the tunnel wouldn't have been an option.

Thankfully, the opportunity presented itself at the bottom of a steep grassy hill where three police officers were leading a large group of people headed for the bridge. Ken and Samantha had their ticket through the dark tunnel, but at the top of a steep hill, they had to get down.

Officer Raddicheck, who had his right arm in a makeshift sling, watched as they both slid down the grassy hill to the edge of the pavement. With a graceful left-foot-forward surfing stance, Samantha made it all the way—but then she tripped and fell down at the bottom. Ken was still on his way down when he saw Samantha fall, and thankfully, he saw her rescue.

Officer Raddicheck, who resembled a 300-pound linebacker, helped Samantha up and over the guardrail and onto the highway's pavement. He was already on the move when Ken got to his daughter, but if they ever caught-up; he'd be thanking him for his help.

It was a big morale boost to see officers in full uniform and serving. They hadn't seen any all day, and Samantha had postulated that many must have opted to remove their uniforms in an effort to blend in while making their walk home. These three officers, who were 100 feet or so ahead of them and leading a long line of appreciative followers through the tunnel, were Seattle's finest. They were serving proudly, and they represented law and order in a city that was falling apart. The selflessness was impressive, and Ken considered them heroes.

Thanks to three loaded guns, going through the tunnel, as opposed to around the tunnel, was deemed the better option. They'd been walking for hours now and the bottled water Samantha procured from the hotel staff earlier was now gone. Every step forward cost valuable energy and they needed to be mindful. Ken could see the three officers ahead and they were now exiting the tunnel. He and Samantha were almost there, and he was relieved to be through it.

"I'm glad we took the shortcut Sam. We saved a good hour."

Now out in the open, it was back to the dilemma he'd been working on all day. He was frustrated with his lack of viable options—and he was not performing. It felt like a mental block, and he didn't like it.

Aside from the thick shadows cast by the metal bridge trusses extending out from the tunnels and onto the bridge deck, the sunlight was bright and warm. Samantha slowed her pace and fumbled for her sunglasses she'd stashed in a zipped pocket on the outside of her makeshift carry-on bag. She'd turned it into a backpack, and with a few attempts, she'd unzipped the pouch and on went her glasses.

Tapping her father's shoulder, she stopped so that he would stop too. "It's getting bad here, Dad," she said, lowering her glasses. "I'm thinking your estimate was too conservative."

"Yep. I think so." He put his arm around her and they continued walking.

You need a strategy, Ken. He could hear his thoughts elevating and he knew that Samantha's comment was accurate. The vibes were different, and it did feel as if the lull, if it could be called that, was now coming to a close. That point in time, just prior to panic, when the mind assesses threat and withholds its determination—had passed. Panic, dread, and terror was arriving. It was beginning to grow. He could feel it.

He suspected this quicker than anticipated transition from shock and dismay to rapid comprehension of the life-threatening danger was due in large part to the fairly recent increase in HEMP knowledge. Most people could understand what a catastrophic grid failure looked like, and they were quickly realizing that this was it.

Over the last eight or nine hours on their journey east they'd seen many desperate people doing many desperate things. Now it seemed to be everywhere. He saw it on everyone's faces—and in everyone's eyes. Word of an EMP attack was spreading fast, and it seemed that everyone they'd passed was talking about it.

The sudden arrival of panic and revolt plagued Ken's tactical planning. The timing of this transition was critically important to their escape, and with it now expiring, the urgency of getting his daughter out of the city and away from large groups of desperate people was escalating. He was good under pressure, but not today.

Ken had his mind in the zone, and it was filled with free-flowing thoughts. He had a big net to capture the good ones, and he was ready for rapid sorting and then practical application. He excelled at problem solving and he could manage chaos well. But today he was having a problem. He couldn't come up with anything, and at present, there was only plan A and it was a long shot.

Failing to come up with any alternatives, he was left with only one option. As of now, he and his daughter were at the mercy of fate, and without his friend Otto—who lived on the other side of Lake Washington—there wouldn't be a plan at all. Otto's home was on the shoreline of Mercer Island, and it was about a half mile south of the I-90 Bridge they were on now.

He'd been resisting the reality of his situation all day. Never before had the challenges been so overwhelming. It seemed that everything was out of his control and he was unable to inflict any advantageous influence on the environment around him. After hours of seemingly useless contemplation, he could see that the sun was now low in the horizon and it was well into the late afternoon. Like a diver low on air, Ken was out of ideas and he starting to feel frantic. He was defeated and it offended him. He found himself failing at the most important moment of his life. He had nothing in his bag of tricks beyond Otto.

Like a hurricane in slow-motion, dread had been flowing into the city all day, and Ken felt it pass through him now like a tidal wave. In a way he'd never experienced before, he felt utter defeat. He was losing the battle and he was helpless to help his daughter. They were trapped hundreds of miles from home and they were deep in the middle of a major city that was about to explode with suffering.

Chaos had won. He'd failed. All he had was one idea. He had one hope—and that wasn't going to cut it. His analysis was deficient and his lack of a viable plan other than asking a friend for help was unacceptable. He would not rest, and he objected to fate controlling their destiny. There were other solutions. It was his duty—and he'd find them.

Samantha watched the flow of foot traffic ahead begin to slow and widen. There were people pointing at something and she pulled on Ken's shirt to slow him down and get his eyes forward. The people traveling in front of them were at the top of a slightly elevated portion of the bridge deck, and it was obvious they were seeing something across the lake. The next twenty-feet placed Ken and Samantha at the same spot.

Cresting the top of the slight incline, the entire view of the lake and its eastern shoreline opened up. On the other side of the bridge at what appeared to be the shoreline just north of the bridge was a plume of billowing smoke. With the afternoon winds the smoke was headed east and into the mountains. It was a thick dirty brown color and it was converging from two separate areas that were relatively close to one another.

"I suspect it's one of those downed airliners I saw yesterday, Sam. Location makes sense." He moved slightly to the left and stood off to the side in the center lane for a better view. "Hard to say though," he said, stretching to see. "Guess it could be anything. We'll find out soon."

He weaved his daughter through the abandoned and disabled vehicles on the center lanes of the bridge and merged the two of them back to the right and into the flow of the people traffic headed eastbound. They continued forward, and they were both lost in their own thoughts of worry and fret.

Somewhere around the mid-point of the floating bridge, as Ken was fully entrenched in his strategic planning, Samantha, who had been keeping pace with her father and was directly behind him, broke the silence. "Dad, there might be injuries up ahead. It looks significant."

She cleared her throat and then continued. "If there are, then maybe we can help?" She said it with a slight question in her tone. Samantha continued walking forward while she waited for her father's response.

Ken's pace forward did not slow. Ten steps went by. Twenty steps. Thirty. He heard every word she'd said. He had no good response, but he knew he needed to respond now.

He searched for an answer that was sufficient. Should he tell her they might have to break into Otto's house if nobody was there? Should he tell her they might have to set up camp in the woods and live off the land tonight?

Scrambling for answers, he struggled over the lack of alternatives—and he knew what it meant. He had no solutions, no answers, and no clear plan. He had nothing and he felt panic enter his thoughts. *What's wrong with me? This isn't right.* Deadly threats were prevailing, and unlike every other battle he'd faced in life before, this time he had nothing. No magic. No strategy. There was only Otto. "Lord, help me!"

Ken slowed and then he stopped abruptly. He took in a full deep breath and then he let it out slowly. A light bulb had gone on, and it'd happened fast. It was like waking up from a nightmare, and he was feeling the rush of a new reality that made everything better. Suddenly, he'd realized how irrational he'd been. Another light bulb went on and Samantha saw it. He had an answer, or maybe it was an idea, but he had something and she could see it forming.

"I should have known, Sam."

Staring at him, she was intrigued. She'd seen it before and she'd seen it many times. She'd become accustomed to her dad's mental acrobatics, and this was his tell. It was his look of victory, and she knew he'd had an epiphany and he'd figured something out. All day she'd been watching him struggle in his own thoughts, and now he was at ease. It meant something, and he was about to deliver. She knew it would be good and she was ready.

Ken talked with his daughter and he found words he'd never contemplated before. As he and Sam discussed the situation, they found their missing strategy. As they talked, his mind performed a full review. Thinking clearly now, he could see his foolishness, and he could see the folly of his limited perspective. It was his small mindedness that had kept him from seeing it, but now he did.

From his mind's eye, he could see himself on the bridge—50 feet behind—and searching frantically for a plan. He could see the desperation on his face. Like a commander leading his troops through a mine field with no map, he could see himself lost and terrified to make any uninformed steps. With this he found his clarity and it was smacking him in the face.

Things changed for Ken on the I-90 Bridge in Seattle, and the change brought him peace. His new epiphany on the mission was simple. Both the plan and their fate were unknowable, and that was exactly how it was supposed to be.

He laid it out and he brought her up to speed. He explained how the purpose to get back home was a purpose with hope, and hope was all they needed. It was okay they didn't have a solid plan. It was okay they didn't know what to do. They weren't helpless, and all they had to do was believe.

The epiphany hit again, and Samantha added the flair. "Well duh! We're so stupid, aren't we? Dad, I set it all aside, and I don't know what I was thinking. It's weird. I felt oppressed, and I felt lost. Now I don't. Thank you!"

"I know, Sam. It is weird. But from this point forward, we go step by step. We trust in God. Nothing else matters."

Walking side by side, he lowered his voice and leaned in. "Our purpose between here, this bridge in Seattle, and our home in Idaho is unknown. We're at the mercy of everything. And fittingly, we don't know what that is. That's life, Sam. That's how it's supposed to be. Faith is a beautiful thing, and I'd forgotten all about it."

"Faith drives the ship, Dad."

"That's right! We use what we've been given and we work smart. Every moment counts and we give it our all. That's all we can do, and that's all that's required. It's not the end of the world, Sam, but as you can see—it is here.

We can't out-think this, so we let faith do it for us. We hand over the reins and we accept everything it brings."

Walking faster now, he pointed to the smoke ahead. "You're a nurse. If there's anybody that needs your help up here, He'll let us know. He's given us Otto, and for now, we'll rest our hopes there.

"Step by step. I like it, Dad."

Samantha was at ease. Her father wasn't a religious man—but today he was. It astounded her, and the tears were starting to run. She'd released her fears and her father reminded her of the bigger picture. The dread was gone—and its spell had been broken. Everything was different.

Inspired, she took the lead. She grabbed her dad's hand and pulled. "I feel better. The butterflies are gone. Off to Otto's."

At peace, they forged ahead. The sun was hot and their clothes were drenched with sweat. They were running on empty.

"I'm sooo thirsty." Samantha tipped the empty water bottle and she got a teaspoon.

"It'll be dark in a couple hours. If we cut the corner up here and walk on the shoreline we should be at Otto's in less than an hour."

Ken stopped and pointed to a small waterfront home on Mercer Island just south of the bridge. "See that house with the brown shingled boathouse over there? That's Otto's. Let's pick up the pace and get off this bridge."

It had been a hard day. The three-mile crossing, now finally behind them and seemingly much more than just a bridge—felt like the longest three miles of the day. The billowing smoke suspected by Ken to be the impact zone of a downed airliner, was indeed the impact zone of a downed airliner.

On the eastern side of the bridge and approximately one mile to the north stood the ripped and mangled tail section of an airliner rising up vertically out of the water. It was a hundred feet off the shoreline and it was surreal.

These catastrophic images, combined with the unprecedented, never-before-heard dead silence of a city in the daytime, burned an ominous warning in the minds of all who bore witness. It was a devastating scene and it was a reminder of how much the world had changed since yesterday. Something terrible was coming, and Ken knew that it was about to begin.

They were worn out. Shelter, food, and water were now critical to survival.

They had hope, but they had nothing of what they urgently needed. Faith was a heavy load to bear, but it was enough and it was mounting with every step forward. It seemed to be the one and only ingredient their lives required, and without it survival was futile. Fear and despair were everywhere, but for Ken and Samantha, something had changed. The world was different.

Now on the shoreline, it would take them to Otto's house. The sand was hot, but near the water it was moist and cool. Samantha couldn't resist taking off her shoes and socks for a little foot therapy on the cool sand. Ken watched his daughter and contemplated the relief. It looked good and so he followed suit, and they both walked toward Otto's carrying their shoes.

As thirst quenching and lifesaving as the lake water looked, there'd be no drinking it yet. Ken had already had the displeasure of drinking bad water before and the debilitating effects were profound. It was too soon to add risk, and they were almost there. He could see the boathouse clearly now. Hope was alive.

Approaching the enclosure, he noticed the sunlight was beaming through. Although there were sides built onto the boathouse—they only protruded down to a few feet above the waterline. From Ken's ground level view he could see under the sides and into the boathouse. There was no boat.

Ken had known Otto for almost twenty years. His life revolved around his boat, and he and his wife Lynne spent more time on the water than on land. They were both retired, and they were enjoying the sunset years they had worked hard to obtain. For them it was on a boat, and Ken admired that. He'd been on it several times and he found it to be an impressive vessel. At almost seventy feet long, she was well suited for worldwide travel—and today—she wasn't here.

They must be gone, he thought. Good for them, but don't lose hope. Almost there, Ken. Keep moving. Guiding Samantha up and onto the landscaped portion of Otto's neighbor's backyard, he kept the empty boathouse to himself. They put their shoes back on and they headed for Otto's walkway thirty steps ahead.

He helped Samantha step up on the walkway and then he stepped up himself. Now, slightly more elevated, they could clearly see Otto's backyard patio straight ahead. At twenty feet in, he noticed something, and then he could smell it. There was a fire in the fire pit, and more specifically, there was a fire cooking food. Someone was here, but was it Otto? Using his hand to shade his eyes, Ken squinted in an effort to see through the large windows that looked into the interior of the home.

The sun was nearing sunset and the windows had an orange glare that made it difficult to see anything on the other side. Samantha, directly behind her father and slightly to the left, obviously did, and she grabbed her dad's shirtsleeve and stopped. She pointed to the sliding window near the back patio—and then suddenly, it started to open very slowly. Using his left arm, Ken moved Samantha behind him and then he called out.

"Otto! Is that you?"

"Who is that?"

"It's Ken."

The older gentleman exited the house and he stood there grinning. "Kenny!"

"Otto! Thank God!" Ken pulled Samantha's hand and they started walking closer.

Again, the slider door opened and out came Lynne.

She ran to Ken and wrapped her arms around him. "Son of a bitch Kenny! How'd you get here? What the Hell's going on? Are you okay? Who's this?" She looked into Samantha's eyes.

"This is my daughter, guys. Otto and Lynne, this is Samantha."

Introduction's were made and the hugs ensued. Here they were. They'd made it all the way and they were safe. Sam was overjoyed and she was glad to finally meet Lynne. She'd been told much and she'd been a fan for years. Lynne was a firecracker, and she liked her.

"Where's your boat, Otto? I thought for sure you were gone."

"She's in dry dock. New paint, can you believe that?"

While Samantha and Lynne got acquainted, Otto called out to the two other individuals inside his home and told them it was okay to come outside.

Out came an older couple. Both of them had big smiles on their faces and each was carrying a large gun. The man had a rifle and the woman had a shotgun, and it was obvious they were very comfortable with their weapons. Retired something, he thought. Maybe law enforcement? Ken didn't know, but he suspected. He guessed they were a married couple and somewhere in their mid 70s. They appeared to be a happy crew.

The two senior citizens, who surely had a bead on both Ken and his daughter as they advanced down the walkway, were in-fact Otto's longtime neighbors, Tom and Betty. These two, as he'd heard before, were indeed very genuine and happy folks. They had interesting personalities, and Ken was uniquely impressed. In the face of tragedy, it seemed a great deal of joy was beginning to commence. Six souls were converging, and they all had the same very big problem. On the backyard patio at Otto's home; Ken, Samantha, Otto, Lynne, Tom, and Betty were all together. Starting now, they were a team.

Weak and thirsty, they needed food and water. The distinct odor of cooking food noticed by Ken as they approached the house was correct. Lynne had a large cast iron Dutch oven that was stashed on the coals in the fire pit and it was full of beef stew. Her motherly skills kicked in and Ken and Sam were well taken care of. The beef stew, French bread, and fresh water did wonders. Ken's body was tired, but like a fast-acting drug, the full course meal gave him energy, and he needed energy so he could plan.

Their plates empty, he'd been working the problem and he had the basics down. There were some challenges, but it was an escape plan that would get them all to safety, and maybe even Idaho if Jim made it home. The bluff was a good hundred miles away, and he knew that Otto had four bikes, so they needed two more. It's doable, he thought. We'll find a way, and then he downed his water and stood up from the kitchen table.

"Kenny?" Lynne was pointing to the wine rack on the dining room wall. He declined, but she had a thumb up from Samantha, and she uncorked a bottle of wine and poured two tall glasses.

"Here you go sweetie," she said, sliding the glass to Samantha. "It's been a rough day, hasn't it? Let's take these outside."

With no time to spare, it was time to collaborate. Waiting outside near the fire pit were Otto and Tom. Anxious to get the discussion started, they'd insisted that Ken and his daughter first submit to Lynne's care so they could revive their bodies. With the sun setting it was getting dark quick, and Betty proceeded to light several kerosene lanterns that were positioned around the fire pit. Ken, Samantha, and Lynne walked out of the house and they all grabbed a seat around the fire.

The patio's fire pit was round, approximately four feet in diameter. There was a cement bench that encircled the pit, and it served well as a high seat or a short beverage table for the patio chairs. Tonight, it was a round table and it had a fire in the middle. All six huddled as if it were a makeshift conference room, and then Ken stood up so that he could lay it all out.

"I need to get right into this, so let me start with the basics. You guys saved us today, and I'm pretty sure that I can return the favor. It's going to be rough and we've got some challenges, but I've got a plan and I'm going to talk it through." With his intro delivered, he sat down and started to continue, but he was interrupted.

"We've been holding our tongues while you guys ate, but we've got some information." Tom looked over to Otto.

Otto followed. "I'm not sure, but I don't think you know what we know."

Heart racing, he looked at Otto and replied. "What do you know?"

Tom reached into the knapsack that was sitting on the cement bench between him and Otto and pulled out a small handheld HAM radio. "We've got these, and they work. We've been listening all day." He proudly held out the portable radio in his left hand. Having them was a distinct advantage—and for Ken it changed everything.

Otto continued. "The Amateur Radio Emergency Service networks are up and running. Information's coming in from all over, and it's bad." Otto grabbed his notepad from the knapsack and then stood up. His foot braced on the fire pit's cement bench, he held out his notepad to capture the light.

"So, this is what we've heard." Otto lowered his readers to the optimum position.

"Several reports … Scratch that—all reports have declared the same emergency we're experiencing here. Severe electronic damage; and it's being reported by multiple observers nationwide."

He lifted his glasses. "We've been listening to reports from all over. It's catastrophic, Ken. Just like here. Total failure. ARES is also reporting that all equipment preserved in Faraday cages appear to be unharmed—and thanks to Tom, it's precisely why we've got a working radio here—but there's more we have to worry about. And I'm talking about nukes."

Holding his notes under the light, he pulled his glasses down. "So we need to be careful here, and I've heard conflicting reports. It's possible that New York City, Paris, and London have all been nuked, and given our situation here it wouldn't surprise me if it's all true. We're obviously at war, and we can confirm America is down, so it's bad." He paused, and then he dropped his notepad on the bench and sat down.

"It's the end, Ken. The Safe States will survive, but not us. We were warned, but we failed. Time's up."

Defeated, he threw out his hands. "It's over. There's no second chance. The suffering is coming, and it can't be stopped."

Head spinning, Ken worked on the logistics while he responded. "We're going to escape, Otto. And that radio changes everything. You know that, don't you?"

Tom stood up and he was smiling. "What if we had more than just a radio?"

CHAPTER 15

BIG SURPRISE

think we can help here," Otto said, stretching out his legs on the fire pit bench. "I think we have a better plan."

He opened his can of beer and looked over to Tom. "We, Tom and I that is, we've prepared for this. We've made some big decisions and we've followed through. Just like you, Ken. And now you're here, and we all need to leave, and you came to the right place."

Otto sat up and leaned in. "I submit to you all, this was meant to be. It's a privilege and we're going to get you home. You've got a job to, and now so do we." Otto was determined, and when he looked at Tom they both nodded. Clearly, they had something up their sleeves.

"Wait till you see," Tom said, smiling. "We've got a vehicle and I can get it to run. It's big enough for everybody." He chuckled. "Retirement is gone. Plan's change and it's a new world. Now, it's what we have in our pockets. It's what we carry on our backs—and even better—it's what we've got in the garage."

Standing up, he caught Betty's eyes. "Life's over in Seattle. There's no saving it now. Time to leave. We're ready." Tom had a slow and deliberate tone. "It's clear. We go now, and our ticket is in the garage."

His arm around his wife Lynne, Otto addressed the group. "We've had all day to mull this over. The worst case scenario happened yesterday. We know what's going to happen here, and I don't want to see it, and I don't want Lynne to see it either. It's not America anymore, and the people trapped here, well, they're going to die and it'll be horrible. We tried, but it's over."

Breathing deep, he sighed. "We're going to leave this place forever Ken. Mission number one—we get to a Safe State. We go where there's still hope and where America still exists." Another deep breath and he looked at Lynne. "We'll miss our life here, but we've got no choice and we've got to leave now."

Ken was blown away, and he didn't know what to say so he folded his arms and smiled. He looked at Sam and then he looked at Otto. "So we're leaving, and we're all going to Idaho in a car that you've got preserved in the garage. That's pretty amazing, Otto. You just saved our lives."

Reaching for Sam's wine glass, he took a big sip. "So, let's go with your plan. It's far better, and we'll use mine as a backup. In twenty eight days I have an emergency airlift planned that uses one of our King Airs. If for some reason your vehicle fails, then we go with plan B. All we've got to do is get to a private airstrip on the other side of the Cascades, and the King Air will do the rest. That was my big plan, but yours is beautiful. Way to go, guys. I'm impressed!"

Standing up, he walked over to the cooler and grabbed a bottle of water. "Idaho's a seven-hour drive at normal highway speed. With the stranded cars—and believe me, there's a lot of 'em—we could be looking at double that or more. So, a few tactical issues, but doable. We'll need to leave soon."

Nodding, Tom chimed in. "I'm thinking tomorrow night, right after sundown. The people will hear us, but they won't see us like they would in the daylight. Our security will be difficult, but we'll have better odds at night."

Guzzling the rest of his water, Ken agreed. "Good point, Tom. What's the vehicle status?"

"Betty and I will work on it tonight. It'll be running by morning, and we can load up all the boxes tomorrow."

In the end it didn't matter, but Ken was getting curious as to what kind of vehicle they had. "So, what exactly do you guys have in the garage? How big is this car?"

Lighting up his cigar, Otto took a puff and smiled. "Well, it's a highly modified 1992 Dodge motor home. It's a small RV, and Tom and I bought it last year just so we'd have an escape vehicle. We've got tons of spare parts, and there all in the Faraday cage. We've gone through the drill a couple times, and in about four-hours—the parts will be in."

Ken was impressed with every word he was hearing. The world was changing, and from the bridge forward, life had become exhilarating and new. Every thought and every action seemed to have a purpose, and it was much greater than he'd ever known before. This was the real plan A, and it was organized and designed without his knowledge. He was in awe, and it felt good, but suddenly, an ominous sound got his attention.

In stark contrast to the eerie silence of a dying city, the sound of automatic gunfire rang out with multiple two-second bursts. The first rattle was from heavy firepower, and it had come from somewhere north of Otto's.

It filled the air with a mechanical echo unlike any other sound, and it represented anger. Then, after a thirty second pause following the first rally of gunfire, a second series of rattling bursts came from the west, somewhere near the downtown area of Seattle. It was clear that aggression was being announced, and Ken could feel the insanity that he knew was here. It was a primitive "I hear your gun, so hear my gun too" communication of power, and it marked the beginning of something horrible.

The terrible sound announced to all that desperation was here. Good and Evil would now go to war, and Ken knew precisely what evil men were about to do.

The hearts of Americans would now choose their sides. He'd studied it and he knew the horror that was about to happen. The sound of gunfire was a signal to all that soon there would be no middle ground, no grey areas, no deception, and no disguise. It was good or evil, and for the starving there'd be no in-between. The sell was on, and free-will would establish two teams. For food, many would give their souls—and many would not.

"I'd say that gunfire is our cue. Let's go to the garage." Ken wanted to see the goods. "Tomorrow night will be here soon. Plus, I gotta see this! Definitely impressed!"

"We did it for the women," Tom said with a straight face and a wink for Betty standing next to him. "We'd just as soon go down with the ship and shoot it out but seems the wives see it differently." Joking around, Tom let the question slip. "How's Linda? Does she have a radio?"

Realizing his question had no tact, he looked at Betty and she threw up her arms.

"No, but she will tomorrow." Ken said it with a slight chuckle. "She only knows that I flew into Seattle yesterday and that so did Sam. Tomorrow's Day Three, and thanks to you guys—I can call her then."

He tried to stop it, but he could feel his heart flutter at the thought of his wife. Tomorrow was Day Three—and it was the predetermined time when the SafePort radios would be taken out from their protected enclosures. Tomorrow, official communications would begin, and he knew Linda would wait until this third day before accessing the radios. Tomorrow he'd transmit a series of messages, both official to SafePort Operations—and personal to his wife. He was only hours away, and in the morning he'd use Tom's radio to call.

Samantha had finished her wine and it was obvious she was getting sleepy. It was time to finish the meeting and Ken was tired too. He stood up, and while Otto put out his cigar they started to hear something. From off in the distance the faint sound of a float plane taking off could be heard. The noise was getting louder and it seemed to be headed in their direction. All three men started walking toward the boathouse hoping to see the airplane. Scanning the moonlit sky, it was headed their way—and for all, it was a beautiful sound.

Noticing Samantha hadn't followed them, Ken looked back to the fire pit and saw her still sitting on her chair. It looked like she was crying. Before he could get one foot forward, he saw Betty pull up a five gallon bucket that was lying on its side behind Samantha. He watched her plop it down next to her, sit down, and then place her hand on Sam's shoulder. With a squeeze and a hug, she had the situation under control. Thanks Betty, he thought. The kids are getting the shaft. Sam needs her mom.

With the sound of the engine now overhead, he looked back up in the sky and he could see the floatplane reflect off the moon. No lights, no strobe; just a ghost plane leaving a dead city. Nice job, guys. Way to go!

The distraction of the plane was profound, its sound now well to the east and fading fast. As it climbed up and away from Seattle and east toward the Cascade Mountains, Ken walked over to where Tom was standing near the boat house, still looking into the sky. "Well there you go," he said, smiling. "Somebody's getting out in style." Tom raised his coffee cup in a silent salute.

Ken thought about the courageous occupants who'd just escaped, and he wondered which SafePort state they were headed for. With millions left behind with no food and water, despair was everywhere, and yet still and among some, there was a sense of honor. He could feel the admiration building and he was certain the floatplane's departure was cheered by many. He thought about Jim. He'd made it out too. He had to, and he'd confirm it tomorrow.

He wondered how many others were on the verge of executing an escape plan. There were a lot of smart patriots out here and he suspected many were commencing their departure plans now. That's how I'd do it, he thought. Just like the King Air, but if we lived here on this lake, shoot I'd have a floatplane instead. I'd shield her parts in a FaraBox or two and that's all it'd take. Heck, some of these older piston would start just fine with a hand prop. Tons of ways to get out of here—if you planned.

"Are you ready," Tom said. "How about some show-and-tell?"

Thirty feet away, Otto was standing on the walkway and he had a lantern. "Let's go to the garage, guys."

Back at the fire pit, Otto packed up their notes and Ken watched Tom put the radio into a FaraBag that was inside his backpack. A secondary HEMP attack was a plausible war strategy and its purpose would be to kill any exposed backup systems. Ken was glad to see that the radio was still being protected. He wondered if Linda had a radio sitting on the nightstand right now. She'd know I'd be following SafePort procedures, and she'd wait until morning. But what if she didn't? What if it was on, and what if he could call her right now? He felt the knot tightening in his stomach, and then he let it go. It's all about faith, and she's got it.

Tom grabbed the other lantern for the trek to the garage, and then from out of his pocket he flicked a momentary flashlight beam on Ken's chest to let him know he had one. "I'm an impatient man. Couldn't wait for the "three-day" rule. I had to check status."

Again, he flicked it on and off and then nodded. "Everything works. FaraBoxes did their job."

While Otto dampened the fire, Samantha walked over and gave her father a hug. They were going home, and she squeezed him tight. "The girls and I will get some beds ready for us to sleep on tonight. Betty said she's going to stay up with Tom tonight in the garage, and get this, she's going to work security while he installs the new parts on the RV."

Ken wasn't surprised, and he'd been wondering about her background all night. With a slow nod, he looked down to his daughter. "Good."

"Yeah, Dad. She's a cool chick. And she knows her stuff. I don't think you heard, but both Tom and Betty are retired U.S. Marshals. I think we're in good hands." She covered her mouth to hide a full blown yawn.

"I think so too. Go get some sleep Sam. Tomorrow's a big day."

"You too. You need strength for tomorrow." Another yawn, she shuffled toward the sliding glass door and waited for the group to enter the house.

Otto, Tom, and Ken followed behind the three girls in front leading the single file line into the dark house. Lynne stood at the front and she held her lantern high so she could illuminate the obstacles they'd all have to dodge. Otto was at the rear, and he carried the remaining lantern so he could light the pathway leading to the garage.

Once inside, the three men continued forward through the hallways with Otto and his lantern leading the way. The women remained near the kitchen and they huddled at the dining room table to plan the attack for tomorrow. Betty loaded up the percolator and she lit the gas stove so that her and Tom would have enough coffee for the night shift.

Assessing the equipment corralled in the garage, Ken was extremely impressed. The vehicle was pristine, and it only had thirty-thousand original miles. With the exception of the galley, all original interior equipment was removed and replaced with basic sleeping cots and storage. Compared to newer vehicles with computers and computer chips, the electronics were limited and the engine's ignition parts were simple and few.

Tom was the mechanic and he knew the engine like the back of his hand. Both he and Otto had a dozen or so FaraBoxes between them, and they were full of shielded parts, tools, and equipment. There were even two homemade Faraday cage enclosures that had a small generator in each. Otto had a rigid FaraTube mounted on the top of the RV and it was filled with spare parts galore.

The revamped RV would carry a lot, but it was clear that it wouldn't carry everything. Critical decisions were approaching, and so they'd sleep on it. Tomorrow they'd decide what went—and what stayed.

Raring to get started, Tom already had his overalls on and he was opening up the Faraday cage with fresh ignition parts. At a still young and very strong seventy-five, he was now an adamant nap taker and he'd just awakened from three hours on the hammock in the boathouse before Ken's arrival earlier. He was still fresh and Betty would join him for moral support and guard duty.

Both Ken and Otto left Tom to do his thing, and with the flick of a lighter, they stumbled through the doorways and hallways on their way to the kitchen. The morning would come soon and tomorrow's sundown departure was less than a day away.

As the night wore on, random sounds of technology echoed in the silent air. Roaming motorcycles could be heard in the distance, and as Ken lay in his bed he heard several vehicles crossing the bridge, headed east. Sporadic gunfire continued, and the locations were different each time. Exhausted and trying to sleep, he wondered how many of the bullets were aimed at humans on the other end. At what point, he wondered, would evil make its play?

Among many things, he was an analyst. He'd worked civilian vulnerability models backward and forward, and he knew better than most that a societal breakdown brought evil into the equation fast. With evil came mayhem, and great atrocities would soon follow. It would happen. The food and water would be gone in days. Insanity is coming. We need to leave. You've got to stop thinking. Go to sleep.

CHAPTER 16

OVERLAND

Both the United States military and SafePort civil defense had transportation checkpoints established throughout the nation. Using the hub and spoke system for overlapping defense, a secure roadway was established for all controlled territory, and most checkpoints were built along the roads and highways that bordered the failed-states.

Effective ground surveillance had to be maintained at all times, and national defense relied heavily on the combined efforts of both the military and SafePort. Heavily armed with well equipped troops, each checkpoint was served by the U.S Army, civil defense forces, and the civil air patrol. Where high confidence defense was required, and where large territories needed to be controlled, each checkpoint incorporated a series of outposts along its circumference, and drones were becoming the primary surveillance tool.

Alternatively, the failed states were still under the control of rebel forces. Through exploiting major seaports on both the east and west coasts; the use of covert supply chain shipments were still in use and they were operating under the guise of humanitarian aid. Replenished with weapons and supplies, the rebel forces had become aligned with unknown parties, but thanks to the U.S Navy, the majority of their supply ships were now under a military blockade.

Today, their troop numbers were on a steady decline and the equation was changing. Slowly, but surely; survival colonies were expanding. Patriots were clearing the path and the rebel forces were disbanding. Territory was being regained, and atrocities were being documented. Interstate commerce was expanding, the power grids and the communications infrastructures were returning—and America was getting strong.

For the tractor trailer and its two security vehicles heading south towards Salt Lake City, safe travel was a condition to be wary of. Today, the convoy had extra protection—and in the middle of nowhere it felt good. They were government transport. They had an elevated clearance and they had military escorts, both on the ground and in the air. If needed, they had special equipment and they could take care of themselves. Defending America was the name of the game, and around here—the U.S. Army checkpoint that made it all possible was straight ahead. On the crest of a rugged mountain range, Overland was an American muscle. It had brute force and it was impressive.

Putting down her notepad, Anne turned off the recorder. "So we'll stop it here," she said, sitting up and scooting towards the center console. "It's fantastic, Ken. We'll pick it up on the other side."

"Sounds good." His eyes on the roadblock a half-mile ahead, Ken was organizing their paperwork.

"I think you'll like this place, Anne." Jim took his foot off the gas and the truck slowed. "It's pretty cool. This is the American Giant."

"It's a lot bigger than I thought." Her eyes scanning the area, there was a shallow basin on the backside of a steep mountain and it was filled with military troops and facilities. "Wow! There's the airfield."

Just ahead, the two soldiers manning the forward security line stepped out in front and directed the fleet of three towards the left-hand lane that led through the gates and into the compound.

Once inside, they followed the left-lane to the main dispatch facility and when they got there Jim had a flagger pointing to the fuel truck. Around the cement barriers, and then a sharp right turn and he'd be lined up for the orange cones. "Here we go."

"Remember she's long. I've got your six on this side." Ken used his index finger as a supplementary instrument and he pointed it where Jim needed to go.

At the signal to stop, Jim's heavy foot brought the fully loaded tractor trailer to a rapid standstill. "Oops, sorry about that," he said, setting the brake. "I'm too far. Look back there, Ken. That's tight." Both were leaning forward and both were studying the right-hand mirror.

"Yeah, it's tight. See if you can get 'em to move those barrel cones and it'll give me another two feet."

"Roger. I got it from here. Go check us in and call Linda."

While Jim turned off the key and shut the engine down, Ken opened his door, grabbed the handrail and stood out on the top stair. Directly below, Rob was smiling.

"Afternoon, boss." Sun in his eyes, he flashed his toolbox. "How about I take a look?"

Ken hopped down the two steps onto the ground. "Just be careful. If it looks funky, leave it alone. We can fix it later."

"Looking for the loose connection and that's all." Walking around to the two front fenders, Rob opened the latches on each side and then raised the hood exposing the engine compartment. "Only happened once, right?"

"Only once. And it's been good since." Putting his sun glasses on, Ken patted him on the shoulder. "I'll see you in a few."

Thirty minutes later, all fuel tanks were filled to the top and the security checks were complete. Both Ken and Anne were still inside the building and Rob continued his search for an obvious offender. The unique semitruck was a brand-new and heavily modified version built for post-war transport. It was getting a lot of attention, and Rob noticed several who couldn't resist sticking their head into where it didn't belong.

"You know, when Stan gets back from lunch, he'd probably help ya." The armed guard who was on a shift change walked over to where Rob was standing and stuck his head into the engine compartment. "I've heard about these rigs. What's the problem?"

"Well, there's really no problem. Just checking on a few things." Rob grunted as he reached out with his foot to find the engine step on the left side. Leaning back, he pushed himself up and then he jumped down to the ground. He'd found nothing and he was ready to close it up. Too many tire kickers on what was supposed to be a classified vehicle. He was unsure of his protocol—and he didn't feel uncomfortable.

"Stan said you got some big guns on board. Is that a turret?"

Rob closed the hood and smiled. "Secured compartmentalized information. I'm not allowed to say."

"Well, it's fully hardened. And I love the tires. Hell of a machine, dude!"

"It is at that," he said nodding. Cleaning his hands on a rag, Rob smiled again. "You'll be seeing a lot of these pretty soon. They give a whole new meaning to secured freight."

Inside the main facility, Ken had completed his check-in procedure and he'd called his wife. Exiting the radio room, he saw Anne looking through the dispatch window at the airfield and hangars that filled the valley below.

"Quite an operation, isn't it?"

"It's amazing, Ken. I had no idea there were this many people up here."

Packed with troops and equipment, the airfield was bustling. "They're getting ready for another advance. Lot's happening right now. America's coming back."

Comforted by what she was seeing, Anne felt proud to be a patriot. It was freedom they were fighting for, and she knew something that Ken didn't know, so she'd tell him now. First she'd ask him about his special equipment.

"So what's with all the aviation stuff in the back of the truck?"

Unsure if she was cleared to know, he was caught off-guard, but then she turned and smiled.

"It's okay. My dad told me about the air cargo project and I think it's great. Just curious about the timing. Maybe we should talk about a Press Release. What if I could arrange some national news coverage?"

Anne reached into her pocket and handed him a business card. "When the time is right. We should talk."

Slightly confused, he held out the card and read it. FNN—24 Hour Satellite News. Anne Wilkes; Salt Lake City.

"Is this national broadcasting? Live news?"

"Yep. We're getting our news back, Ken. We're on a two-month countdown. You're right. America's coming back."

Where the story of the patriots had only just begun, Anne was on a mission to bring the victories of America to the people. She knew that both Ken and Jim were among the leads on a new air cargo revitalization project and she wanted the story.

The modern-day world of overnight delivery, air freight, and even passenger service was on its way back to the Homeland, and Ken filled her in on the basics.

Inside the semi's trailer were the essential communications components of a retrofit air traffic control center, and on the west coast it would start with Salt Lake City. It was only the beginning of an infrastructure rebuild that would soon be expanding throughout the nation, and as of two-weeks ago, both Ken and Jim were working for the U.S government. Anne had her story, and Ken would let her know when it was time. It was an American victory, and she was happy. It was a beautiful day.

Now back at the semi, Ken would be the driver for the final leg into SLC. "Are we secure?" he asked Rob, stepping up the stair and grabbing the handrail.

"All good." Wiping off the grease stains he'd put on the hood, he looked up. "Found nothing. Everything's tight. She's secure"

"Thanks, bud. Let's roll."

With the scheduled driver swap, Ken was in the "hot seat" and Jim would be a passenger for the rest of the trip. Anne was in the galley at the back of the cab heating up some water for afternoon coffee.

"If you open the bottom drawer, you'll see some Kona blend in that sealed bag there. That's it! That's the good stuff!"

"Thanks, Jim. Awesome!"

"Ready?" Ken was adjusting his mirrors and seat to find the perfect fit.

"We're ready," Jim replied. "I got you another two-feet on right side. Watch those brakes. They're touchy."

Ken released the parking brake and slowly maneuvered the truck and trailer through the narrow lane of orange cones and barrels that would lead them back onto the highway. Passing through the final gate, the convoy of three was on the move.

At the top of the last mountain they'd have to cross, from here it was all downhill. Steep grades and sharp turns were ahead, and with the flatlands fifty miles away—they were just coming into view. With two blinks on his brake lights, Ken signaled for Rob to take the lead.

"It'll get a lot easier when we get down there," Jim said, pointing. "Watch out for the Gs on these turns. They caught me off guard. Be careful."

"Yep, I see that. Okay, we're going slow."

"Here's your coffee, guys."

"Thanks Anne." Ken grabbed his cup and took a sip. "So I know we're getting ready for the big escape, but what about this." He took another sip.

"Day Three is when SafePort engaged—and that's when Jim went to the commencement meeting in Sandpoint. You'll want to hear about this, Anne. You'll want to hear about Sarah." Glancing over to Jim, he nodded.

"This is when the crazies came out—and we should tell it in order. It was a chain reaction, and it all started on that morning. When we left at sundown, the insanity was well under way—and then it got worse. So you tell her about Idaho first, and then I'll tell her about Seattle."

Anne held up the recorder. "Sounds good. I have nothing in my file about the SafePort meeting or Sarah, so fill me in. Jim, you're up. Ken, you're next."

Holding his coffee cup, Jim loosened his seatbelt and sat sideways. "Okay. You'll like this part. It's got heroes."

CHAPTER 17

COMMENCEMENT DAY

Sandpoint, Idaho

He'd been up and working for a good hour. It was Day Three and the sun had just started to rise. From his bed and straight to the garage, the early morning radio brief was a disturbing revelation, but now that it was over, the slate was clean. Reality had been clarified and it was real. Finally in the meadow and at his Faraday cage, Jim was happy. This was the "big" moment—and today it all began.

The morning had great potential and he was eager to seize every drop. FaraBoxes, FaraBags, and Faraday cage enclosures of all kinds were spread across the country. They were about to save millions. Day Three was here and the patriots had a green light to implement their backup.

Rays of sunlight were streaming through the tops of the trees and reflecting off the access door he was currently engaged in breaching. The quarter inch steel door was getting warm from the sun—and so was he. He had four bolts to go and without his cordless drill, it was turning out to be quite a process. This was the first time he'd accessed the door by hand, and without his little helper it was taking a long time. It was glaringly obvious that with thirty-six bolts in total, the access door to his Faraday cage in the meadow was not designed for at-whim opening.

Other than loading and unloading, the door's primary function was to maintain proper continuity throughout its entire circumference when closed. The most common weak link in all Faraday cage enclosures was the point of entry. Whether it was an access door or ventilation system for removing unwanted interior moisture, if a breach in the electrical continuity of the enclosure walls exceeded more than the approximate diameter of a large nail, the shielding effectiveness went to minimal. To ensure proper continuity, Jim used a copper compression seal placed around the entire circumference of the access door and thirty-six bolts to compress it tightly. A modified 8000-gallon steel tank, he'd built it strong.

When the cages hit the market, he embraced the challenge of building his own, but it was the 8000-gallon steel tank for sale down the road that cinched the deal. He liked projects, and he elected to build his own instead of buying one that was ready to go.

He hired a welder who'd made a business out of Faraday cage manufacturing and he had him customize the tank and install a five-foot by five-foot access door with slide hinges positioned at the end of the cylinder shaped tank. Jim buried it in the meadow and then built a stone wall façade at the front end of the exposed tank. With George's tractor—he'd carved out a twenty-foot ramp that sloped down to meet the access panel and then he planted grass to keep ramp from eroding. It worked well, and he'd just trimmed the grass last week.

With the last bolt removed, he opened up the door and he pulled it out on its hinges and then swung it to the right. The tank was full of equipment, but what he was after was loaded at the very front, and it was loaded that way by design.

"There she is," he said, smiling.

With the sun now rising above the tree line to the east, the beautiful machine he'd been dreaming of all night stood proudly. Glimmering in the orange sunrise, he grasped the handlebars of what would soon be his two-wheeled transportation to the SafePort meeting in Sandpoint. With a few heavy pulls, he had both wheels on the centerline of the metal ramp, and with a good tug he had it out and it was standing on its own.

He had two options. He could wait for Sarah's help and together they could push and pull the motorcycle up the twenty-foot grass ramp, or he could simply fill it with gas and drive it up himself. The sun was shining and there was plenty of room to work. I'll grab the gas, and I'll start her up.

The motorbike was an official standard-issue SafePort motorcycle. It was a 500cc enduro model that was well suited for both paved and off-road conditions. To optimize readiness, for the purposes of preservation storage all SafePort managers were issued appropriate transportation vehicles. In Idaho, that included the motorcycle backup in addition to the community preserved four-wheel drive vehicles. For standardization, all motorcycles were identical. They fit in the Faraday cages easily and they served the function of immediate transportation. Provided it wasn't wintertime, they were a strategic advantage.

He'd been against two wheels from the start, and there was a community backup plan that used dedicated vehicles to get the system up and running during the snow, but now it didn't matter. It was still summer and the motorcycles were here. It was perfect.

Everything was working as planned. As he filled the fuel tank with gas, he couldn't believe what he was about to do, and he couldn't believe what he'd heard. The reports made him angry and he could feel his stomach churning.

Within minutes from waking and with a push of a button, while he sat on his stool in the garage the ham radio came alive. He'd listened to reports from all over the country, and even parts of Canada and Mexico were experiencing the same levels of exposure.

Everyone was reporting the same thing—total grid failure, electronic failure, and a complete shutdown of the transportation infrastructure. He'd listened to confusing reports that seemingly attempted to define inaccuracies of previous reports suggesting that a nuclear detonation had occurred on the ground in New York City, Paris, and London. Apparently, they were all wrong, but at the same time, these updated reports were suggesting that a nuclear detonation did occur in Israel. It was blatantly obvious; on the morning of Day Three, chaos ruled.

Among the reports, they were all unconfirmed, but in Jim's mind the reports about Israel pointed a suspicious finger at the likely offender of the American EMP. The news appeared to be flooding the airways, and if correct, it put Iran at the top of Jim's list. Regardless of it being unconfirmed, the reports made his instincts take notice. It felt personal.

The insight gained on the morning of the third day was significant. Battered by his emotions, he sat on his stool and he listened while his heart pounded. He wanted to be free of rage, but the anger had merit. Right or wrong—he didn't know. Somebody wanted us dead, but he was confused, so he'd let the anger lead. He couldn't stop it and he prayed hard that the U.S. military would find their target and destroy it forever.

At thirty minutes in, he'd gotten the gist of it. The primary frequencies were all transmitting the same thing. He'd heard the official SafePort communications and he'd heard the other, but in hindsight, and with high emotions, he wasn't sure who was who. To his surprise, he found no reports being issued from any federal government agency. It was disappointing, and what came in loud and clear was the fact that the worst case scenario had just occurred.

Whether or not a nuclear detonation happened somewhere on the ground in America was in Jim's opinion, the least of everyone's worries. Sad if true, but it was nothing more than salt on a wound. The deathblow to America came from above, and starting now, the country was shut down completely. The fuse had been lit and it couldn't be extinguished.

There was no going back. Based on the reports he'd heard this morning, every town and every city in America had been affected. All citizens without a SafePort zone were now helpless and frozen in place. Without food and water, and with no electricity and no transportation—they were on their own and they wouldn't survive without help. Unfortunately, help was impossible and the consequences were unstoppable. All in all, it was unthinkable.

His knowledge gained in the garage was an official confirmation of everything he'd suspected to be true. It was no surprise, but the truth brought a heavy weight, and that weight would have to be carried.

He knew how to do it, and the gift of SafePort was his go-to refuge. It was an undisputable fact. America had been given a second chance, and with it he could feel the anger and vengeance spawned in the garage fleeting. With hope driving his soul, he freed himself from the chaos of the alternative. He'd save the vengeance for later. SafePort would work. Today was a victory.

By the end of his third cup of coffee, Jim had the SafePort motorcycle parked in front of the garage and it was ready to go. With his To-Do list stacking up, he quickly organized the remaining items within his Faraday cage according to priority. Tomorrow he'd start work on re-installing fresh components for his off-grid power producers. Jim was fortunate to have both hydro-electric and wind power systems on his property. Both systems had protected backup electronic controllers that were fresh from the factory—and they were both still in their shipping boxes just inside the enclosure.

Next to those, Jim had a brand-new electronic brain box for his unprotected 20 kilowatt standby generator that was mounted on a cement pad behind his garage. The generator's backup digital controller was ready to snap in, and like much of the rest of the equipment in the Faraday cage, most was paid for in full by SafePort and its federal funding.

The generator provided more than enough power to run the entire home and in the past it had kept the hot tub hot throughout many two and three-day power outages. It was the first piece of unprotected equipment he'd checked for damage, and sure enough, the digital controller installed on his outside generator was toast just like everything else.

While attending the SafePort meeting this afternoon, Sarah's task for the day was to get the propane freezer up and running. With the hand dolly, he'd pulled the unit out, tugged it over to the garage, and set it near the electric chest freezer that was filled with food and ice. The SafePort manual recommended that half the freezer be stored with ice, and so far it had worked well. The frozen meat was still frozen—for now.

He'd heard generators running in the valley from all directions yesterday afternoon, and now in hindsight, he wished he'd broken the three-day rule himself. If nothing else, at least getting the propane freezer fired up would have been a smart move. There was a good month's worth of frozen food at stake, and if the backup freezer took too long to cool down, the opportunity for a safe transfer was shot. Having that extra day to play with would've been nice. Three days was cutting it too close, and he didn't want to eat nuts or berries, or worse, deplete SafePort reserves meant for other people's emergencies. Live and learn, he thought. No do-over's, idiot!

The third morning was setting a trend and the American way of life was being revised. Chaos was circling, and a countermeasure was in play. Good men were in a battle against evil, and the intelligence of patriots was proving to be superior.

Embracing the challenge, Jim played his part in ripping victory from evil's hands. He'd been wide awake and raring to go since he hopped out of bed early this morning. The morning's pace had been on quick time and the high priorities were getting accomplished. His Faraday cage enclosures had all been accessed, and all was protected. His download of official communication was complete, he'd left a transmittal message for Linda, and he'd talked with Paul at 0800. All morning tasks and preparations had been done. Everything was set and he was ready for the next step.

It was 11:30 a.m. and his departure was approaching. The meeting was only hours away, and in the eastern states, they'd already commenced. America was rising and Jim could feel it. It was time to load up. He had to go to George's house. Steve would be there, and then all three would caravan to the meeting downtown.

He filled the motorcycle's side bags with water and supplies, and then he fired up the engine and let it warm up while he said goodbye. Holding his helmet, Sarah was on the front porch, and he ran over to give her a hug.

"It's time. Do what you can while I'm gone. I love you."

"I love you too."

"I put the operating instructions on top of the new freezer. It's just like we did in practice."

"I know, Jim. I got it." Fumbling with his helmet straps, she looked up and sighed. "Just get it done—and then get home. I don't like us being separated right now." She handed over the helmet and gave him a kiss. "Be careful!"

He threw on his helmet and headed for his ride. "Back before dark," he said slinging over his leg and hopping on. It had been awhile, but he added gas and it felt good. It felt surreal, and he couldn't believe what he was doing.

The driveway that led to George's home on the river was a mile farther down the road than Jim's. So far, he'd only made it halfway and he'd been stopped twice. The patriotic neighbors waving him down and wishing him luck at the meeting were great, but at this rate, if he were to stop at every wave over, he'd never make it to the meeting.

Just wave back and keep riding, he thought kicking in the gas to see what she had. The bike had solid power and it was a firm but forgiving ride on the dirt road. It was a good machine and Jim was having fun. It'd been a good ten years since he'd ridden on two wheels, and with the bend in the road, he quickly realized he wasn't being careful. "Whoa," he mumbled, and then he slowed down.

George's driveway, like his, was winding as it cut a path through the trees. He was just rounding the last bend when he saw the home, George, and Steve coming into full view. He was happy with what he saw, and he too was ready to fuel up and eat some food. It was lunch and the barbeque was on. With the meeting scheduled at 2 p.m., there was still plenty of time to kill. Six hot dogs went on the grill, and the three managers with brand new lives sat down for lunch.

Jim had met Steve briefly once before. He'd heard a lot about his qualifications and he was glad to hear that Steve was designated as the water manager for this zone. There was no doubt he played an important role.

Water was the key to life and water distribution was the highest SafePort priority in every zone across the country. Aside from private wells, Bonner County had over thirty community water systems throughout its zone and most of them were located in the western sector. Each community system was required to have fully shielded replacement pumps, controllers, and generators, as well as a full year's worth of propane stored on site and dedicated to SafePort's emergency operations.

Steve's job was to manage the systems, but initially his job was to get them all up and running, and his mission started today.

Jim knew how lucky he was to have his own well, and even better, a river on his own property. Most people didn't have easy water access like he did. In fact, most people lived in a home that prohibited sustainable living—and without any technology to pump the water where it needed to go; they'd be forced to move elsewhere. In modern society, and especially here in the U.S., most depended on the water coming to their home. If it suddenly didn't, sustainability was nil.

Steve knew the water game well and that was good for the zone. On the second hotdog, he even told Jim that by tomorrow or the next, he "guesstimated" that most people would have their water back and it would be flowing at the faucets. Water pressure in the people's homes was a primary function of SafePort. Without water in the homes, residents would be forced into refugee camps and SafePort would fail. Steve's job was to make sure that didn't happen, and his two-day estimate was amazing. Jim, having under-estimated a thing or two himself, concluded that even if you doubled Steve's guesstimate on the repair time, it was still remarkable.

After two hotdogs each, they fired up their engines and all three departed George's house. Once again, the silence had been broken. In a land where there were few, the three motorcycles were getting a lot of attention. As they headed for the county road, neighbors who they'd never seen before were running out to throw a wave. Now passing his own driveway, Jim knew Sarah could hear it all. Get that freezer working, hon. Get her cool.

The downtown high school was the designated destination and there were a little over four hundred individuals with the SafePort classification of "provider" that were expected to attend.

Standardized designations of the populace residing within SafePort zones used a simple and straightforward process. You were either designated as a consumer, or as a provider. The populace in total carried the class of consumer and those directly responsible for providing sustenance or products beneficial to SafePort operations held the additional classification of provider. All providers in the Bonner County SafePort Zone would be attending this first meeting, and the machine that would save millions was about to launch.

It was a twenty-mile trek, and as they rode through the streets they passed many along the way who went to great effort in showing their support. They'd made it across the river on the Long Bridge and the two miles spanning its entire length were lined with citizens waving flags and patriotic thumbs up. The SafePort missions were many, and raising national spirit was one of them. The spirit displayed along the Long Bridge in Sandpoint, Idaho was extraordinary. Jim was impressed, and so was everyone. America was more than just alive, she had pride and she was ready to fight.

The high school parking lot looked a lot like a biker's convention as they entered and maneuvered to find an open parking spot. The generators outside were humming and it seemed there was a full house. First thing on the To-Do list was registration. SafePort procedures were specifically designed to establish a sound organizational structure that functioned effectively without the need for technology.

The registration process at SafePort meetings was a key function in linking providers with SafePort operations and management departments. By registering, providers would accept and claim previously assigned responsibilities with their presence, and the lack thereof played a key function in identifying critical responsibilities or communications that had gaps in coverage.

As Jim approached the registration desk, he could see that he knew one of the gals behind the counter. He'd met her at the last SafePort prep meeting a few months ago, and she'd assisted Dean Simmonds, who was now the zone commander. When her eyes caught Jim's, she waved him over.

"Jim, I have something for you." She fumbled through the stack of paper that was on a clipboard and she pulled out a one page document. "Here it is… It's a transmission communiqué and I'll need you to perform a read and copy. You can go over to that table and copy it down, and then when you're done, just give it back to me and I'll have you put your initials down in this binder right here."

"Okay, you got it," he said headed for the table.

George saw him reading the communiqué and walked over. "Is that from Ken?"

Jim was nodding. "Yep. It's from Ken. I'll read it to you, 'Have Samantha and four others including Otto. Planning road trip departing tonight. Expected arrival tomorrow night. Linda has been advised.'" They both looked at each other and then George smiled.

Jim copied the message down and then got back in the registration line so he could initial his receipt. "Well, I know who Otto is. And if I were to guess, I'd say they've teamed up. I know where he lives and it's real close to where that airliner went down."

Reliving the crash scene in his head, Jim summed it up. "So, Ken found his daughter and they made it to Otto's house. Tonight, they're driving to Idaho. That's pretty amazing, George. Hopefully, there's a lot of people escaping Seattle right now."

Jim returned the communiqué and signed the Read and Initial file completing the process. He submitted his official report designated for the zone commander, and then he signed his name in the registration binder signifying his presence at the meeting. By doing this, he was accepting his duties and his service to America started now.

It was 2 p.m., and the meeting was officially commencing with Dean

Simmonds at the podium. He'd known Dean for a little over a year now and he was impressed with his demonstrated leadership skills. He was a good commander, and the Bonner County SafePort Zone was ready for business because of it.

There was a large half circle of 4 x 8-foot tables that were designated for each department of the emergency system and they lined the perimeter of the high school's gymnasium. He'd found his Flight Operations table ahead, and he could already see that the inbox was stacking up. He'd sit down for a minute, but he needed to find his mechanic. Jerry should be here waiting for him, but he wasn't, and Jim was getting worried.

Well that's stupid, he thought. I should've checked the registration binder to see if he's here. Then, and just as he'd stood up and prepared to make his way back to the registration desk to check on Jerry, the lights in the gymnasium suddenly went out. Immediately, the generators outside began to rev at a higher idle speed signifying they'd lost the electrical load of the lights inside. The entire room was on edge to say the least.

At first, everyone gasped when the lights failed, but the generators running outside made it all better. Now that society was turning itself back on, sudden silence was feared by all. For Americans, silence came from an EMP. Another attack was entirely possible and nobody knew what to expect.

Dean was preparing to display the distribution charts on the overhead projector when the lights went out, and now he and everyone else were in the middle of some nervous chuckling. "Well," he said laughing. "Good thing there's a lot of windows in here, and at least we can still see. We'll put the charts on hold. Boy, it's good to hear those generators isn't it? Never thought I'd love that sound."

He grabbed one of his sheets from the projector and used it as a flag to get the attention of the crowd. In an elevated voice Dean addressed the entire room.

"While they work on the lights I want to talk about the big picture here. There's a lot of information coming in right now and we don't know much, but we do know that our country was hit hard with an EMP three days ago. We've all heard the reports and it's clear that it knocked out everything. The biggest problem we're facing right now folks—and I know this sounds trivial, but I gotta say it because it only takes one mistake—is our emotions. We've got to be wary. We've got a good system here, and it will save us all, but we've got to be extremely cautious."

Looking out over the entire crowd, he needed to talk about the new priorities and he needed to address the obvious sorrow.

"Over the last year I've dedicated my life to SafePort, and I'll tell you, it's impressive. We've worked hard on this and I know it'll work well. But I also know we're all dreadfully concerned for our fellow brothers and sisters who are living out there in these non-SafePort states. These are our friends and our family members, and shoot, folks, they're fellow Americans. It's one hell of a story for the history books, and I contend—and we must all contend— in the end it'll be America that prevails. We have a duty to preserve it. We have to defend it, but it'll be tough and we have to make hard decisions."

Nodding, he continued. "We did the right thing. We built our SafePort and we built it fast, but the others didn't, and now we have to deal with it. I know it's sad. But it's true. We can save our states and we can save America, but anything else is questionable. Maybe we can help Washington, but that's a big "maybe" and we need to be careful on that one folks. What I'm getting at here is that every one of us wants to rush in and save the day, and frankly, what we have here is the birth of a new mission—and it's a mission we'd never contemplated. We all want to help the undefended states, and if we can, we will. It's all part of the program now, but we have to go step by step. We have new priorities to follow, so let's talk about 'em. Let's go through the basics."

Walking over to his now useless overhead projector, Dean put his hand on it and smiled. "I had a really cool chart that would've made this easier, but it doesn't matter. I know they're scrambling with the fuses out there, but we don't have to wait. It's straightforward. It's one, two, three, and it's precisely in that order."

Dean held up his index finger for a number one count. "First, we start the machine—and that's what we're doing today. We start it up and we work out the bugs. Secondly, we crank it up! We maximize our production and we get strong. Then folks; number three," he stuck out his third finger and he held his hand up high. "That's when we can help… and that's when we'll save the others. Step by step folks. We gotta get strong first. We can't let our emotions over task the system. It's only with our strength that we can help.

If we're strong, America has a chance, but if we're not—we all go down. Sad but true, and we can't forget it."

With a new circuit breaker installed, the lighting crew had Dean's lights back on and suddenly his overhead projector came back to life. "Fantastic guys. Thank you!"

"Before I get to these flow charts, a few things more. Timing ... Timing is an important component for us here in the Inland Northwest. Even though its eighty degrees outside, everyone who's lived here for a while knows that in as little as a month or so, snow could start falling. That means any coordinated sustenance deliveries into the interior of Washington State will likely have to wait until spring. With the exception of food and water that we can bring up to the state line, that means we're looking at six months to prepare for mission number three. Most importantly, it also means we have a month or so to get things running smoothly around here, or it's going to be a cold and hungry winter for everybody."

Flipping through the pages in his notepad, Dean was sorting through the important stuff and he was checking things off.

"Propane. It's our new lifeblood, and it's imperative that the distribution networks keep it flowing. Get on the list to get your tanks topped off now because those trucks aren't built for the unplowed roads that are coming soon. Also, snowy roads. This is a big one folks. We have a few operating snowplow trucks for the zone but we need more people with snowplows on their pickups to help keep the distribution lines open. If you know of any individuals with snowplows on operating vehicles, get them down here and get 'em registered as a provider. We need more providers. The more the better."

Going down his list, he was pacing back and forth as he went through each item. "Okay ... Another big one. Transportation. I'm told that our car dealerships—we have eleven of on board—have all announced this morning that they expect to have the shielded replacement parts installed by the end of this week for all designated vehicles. If you're on the vehicle list—or you require it and you're not—get the ball rolling now. It's a new system and we're going to have problems, so let's dive in and let's find them now. The SafePort GOM and its procedures are now the official law of the land. So use 'em and let's work to improve. If there's a better way, submit your process through the manual's revision and amendment process. Day by day, step by step. Let's work out the bugs and let's make it purr."

Listening closely, Jim felt a tug on his shirt. It was Jerry and he'd been ten feet away the whole time. When the lights went out, Jim had sat down to listen to Dean's address, and Jerry had been filling out paperwork for emergency medical services at the table behind him. Jerry was diabetic, and he needed insulin on a regular basis to survive. George's wife would have to do this too, and before he left the meeting he'd have to get Darlene signed up for emergency insulin.

SafePorts across the country had a standardized Medical Services Department. The primary function was to provide for autonomous medication production and distribution within each zone. These medication-producing facilities were standalone, independent of one another, and self-sufficient. With full-time generators and solar power, they were able to produce and store basic medications such as insulin, antibiotics, and other surgical medications such as anesthesia and dental medications. The pharmaceutical production service was one of the most important services that SafePort provided to its citizens, and the facilities across the country were now poised to save millions.

With Jerry's presence at the meeting confirmed, the day had just gotten a whole lot better. There was a lot to talk about, and when he was done with his medical forms he'd fill him in. Jerry was the former director of quality assurance for U.S. SKYJET and he officially retired from the company last year. He was the second victim of Sandpoint, Idaho behind Jim, and he'd moved here from Scottsdale, Arizona where he'd run the company maintenance base for the last eight years. He'd been deemed the "golden child" by Ken and he was a master at managing the complexities of an airline maintenance program. As the company expanded, he was instrumental in keeping the fleet safe, and Ken was forever grateful.

Although officially retired, Jerry had been retained as Tango Lima's personal mechanic. He had both Ken and Jim's absolute trust, and Jim was thankful he'd agreed to serve as the director of maintenance for SafePort.

In less than five minutes, he had Jerry up-to-date with the in-flight failure, his flight home, and the associated predicament of Ken being trapped in Seattle. Up till moments ago, and per the latest published SKYJET flight schedule, Jerry had assumed the King Air was still at the Coeur D'Alene airport.

Impressed with Jim's Day One adventure, Jerry made a comment and it was accurate. "Tango Lima is an angel my friend. She saved you guys again."

He pointed his pencil at Jim and then he tapped the air. "I know the boss didn't fare so well, but it sounds like you and his airplane did. If this drive out of Seattle mission fails, I'll have her ready. She's one hell of a lucky girl, so if you need her for Ken, she'll be ready. I'll grab the wife and we'll start on it tonight. We'll stay at the hangar till it's done."

Scratching the back of his head, Jerry scanned the crowd. "Have you seen Mike yet? We need his airplanes too. Lots to coordinate."

Mike was an aviation design and certification engineer who was a recent transplant from California. Jerry had known him for years and he now worked for the newly certified aircraft manufacturing company that had just recently based their manufacturing plant at the Sandpoint Airport.

The company was building a new single engine airplane which incorporated a highly reliable turbine engine with a non-pressurized cabin and fixed gear. It was a workhorse and Jim was impressed with the aircraft. It even had an option for floats. He'd been planning on presenting the idea to his brother, and if it weren't for the EMP interruption on their last flight, he'd have probably brought it up then.

"Well let's find Mike, but first …" Jim held up a small handheld radio and dangled it in front like a carrot. "These have distinct frequencies and they're just for us. I've got a box full of 'em. Let's go over to the table and I want you to grab a few."

At two hours in, his duties were completed. Jerry had found Mike and the maintenance department had a plan. SafePort Flight Ops was ready for business. He'd met with all his teammates and to his amazement; there were no gaps in coverage. Emergency procedures were implemented and the mission was clear. Scheduled surveillance flights would begin next week and the SafePort border would be under full control twenty-four seven. Bonner County would survive, and so would he and Sarah. Everything was working perfectly—and he couldn't wait to get home.

★ ★ ★

Now alone, the silence was a constant reminder and it was getting to her. She knew that America was on the verge of life and death, and she was ready to fight for survival, but with Jim gone she could feel her courage waning. He'd briefed her on the official reports, and when he was here she felt brave, but what if SafePort didn't work? What if they had to fight off marauders and what if they had to run into the mountains just to escape a dying world?

This was the real thing and millions didn't prepare. They had no hope, and when they realized it, what would they do? What if SafePort fails and what if its resources become a target? What if there was an enemy invasion, and where's our military? She felt nervous, and it bothered her. She needed to be more positive.

"I don't like this, Max!" Setting up her work area in the garage, Sarah was scared.

She pulled over a chair from the work bench behind her and sat down. She was thirsty. Now on day three of its final thaw, instructions in hand, she sat in front of the old chest freezer and planned her attack with a fresh bottle of water.

Before he'd left, Jim positioned the new propane freezer next to the main gas line, and all she had to do now was connect the lines and then start it up. It was a simple procedure, but as she read the instructions it listed critical steps that needed to be followed. The chair felt good. Another minute and some more water and she'd be ready. It was hot outside and she could feel her energy draining.

With Ralph and Bella inside, Maxine had the honors. Because she was a good girl and she minded, she was on the outside team with Sarah. Having brought her own bone, Max claimed her spot on the cement floor of the detached double-car garage that sat sideways next to the home. Inside it was a mess, and with all the chaos, Jim had boxes, tools, and Faraday cages scattered everywhere.

Feeling better, the two-minute break gave her an emotional boost and she was ready to tackle the freezer. She stood up, she gave Max the rest of her water, and then she opened up the garage door for some more sunlight. Where's the lemonade, she thought. Wish I had some tunes. She looked at Maxine and pointed her finger. "Tomorrow, we're playing music!"

The four-step procedure for starting up the freezer was confirmed. It was simple, and she was ready for step one. The gas line was unobstructed and she had plenty of length. She'd done this with Jim and she knew how to connect the fitting. Kneeling down she made sure the gas valve was off. I hope there's no pressure on this, she thought. She wasn't sure if it made any difference, but she was fatigued and she stood up to think twice. Looking into the meadow, she stretched her back and reviewed what she was about to do. It's just a fitting. There's no pressure, and if there is, it's okay. It's simple. Just do it. Then she saw a deer.

Lying on the floor next to her, Maxine was content with her bone. Happy as can be, she hadn't seen the deer yet—and Sarah didn't want her to. Now out by the well house and near the edge of the meadow, the deer was grazing on the taller grass and it appeared to be alone. If Max caught sight of it, she'd bark, and then Sarah would have to yell. It was an easy solution and the diversion commenced, but this time, the deer moved first and started running. It was too late.

Maxine stood up and she let it rip. Sarah yelled. "No Max!"

Ears perked and still barking, she marched out of the garage and into the driveway. She stopped moving forward and watched. With the deer running across the meadow, Sarah issued her commands from behind. "Stay, Max. Stay!"

Maxine looked back, and with a small wag she let her know that she wasn't going anywhere. It had been two years since the deer event and she'd learned well. She'd run after one before and she didn't come home for two days. That was then, and this is now. She was a good girl, and she'd learned her lesson.

Standing in the driveway, they both followed the sound of the running deer. Together, they watched for a glimpse through the trees and they could hear the sticks crackling on the other side of the meadow as it ran deeper into the woods. It seemed extra loud with all the silence, but then it faded and the sound was gone. For Maxine it was over. She strolled back into the garage and picked up her bone. For Sarah, it was back to the freezer. "Good dog, Max! Let's get this done. You're such a good girl."

No more distractions, she thought. Wiping the sweat off her forehead, she grabbed the gas line from the new freezer and then knelt in front of the fitting she'd been struggling with. The main gas line from the propane tank outside was piped into the garage, and it had a connecter stubbed out of the wall at about two feet high. Gas line in hand, the connection was about to occur. "Okey dokey, so it goes like—"

She was hoping there wouldn't be any pressure, but as she inserted the fitting Max barked, and instantly, Sarah jerked back, heart pounding. Frustrated, she dropped the gas line and stood up. "Maxine! Stop!" It was her aggressive bark and at any second, Sarah knew she'd run. "Stay, Max! Stay!"

Maxine held her ground. This was the bark that meant business, but in the end it was always a nuisance and a false alarm. She was famous for it at night. On the leash and out of the blue, sometimes she'd bark into the darkness like she was scared. It was an aggressive alert and Sarah hated it. It always made her jump and there was no time for it now. She grabbed her collar and Max went silent. She was just standing there. Looking.

"What the heck Max. What is it?" Holding her collar tight, Sarah looked for the culprit. She could see the hair on Maxine's back rising, and she was staring straight at the well house. "I don't see anything. There's nothing there. You stay!" Suddenly, something moved and Sarah froze. "What is that?"

Bet it's a bunny, she thought. Maybe a turkey? Then, on the other side of the well house she saw a shadow move and it was large. Now she thought it was a deer. It's not a bunny. "What is that?"

Max started growling and then she saw it. It was a man and he was peering around the edge of the well house. Someone was looking straight at her! Suddenly, he moved from the edge and out into the open grass, and her heart stopped. Maxine went off and her bark was like a scream. She'd never heard it before and she grabbed her collar tight and yelled. "Who's there? Who is that?"

Suddenly, she could see who it was. He was standing in full view. God, what do I do? It's the crazy neighbor! He's dangerous. Why isn't he answering? Again, she yelled. "What are you doing here?"

"It's okay!" he responded sharply. "I just need transportation. It's an emergency. Thought I'd ask."

"We don't have any transportation!" Sarah was scared and she was struggling to keep Max under control. He shouldn't be here. Again she yelled. "Everything is fried!" Standing on the other side of the lawn, he looked agitated and Sarah was shaking. "But if you need help, I'll try and send you some later. Is everything okay?"

"Ha! I know you're lying! I just saw your sorry-ass husband on a motorcycle." Standing in the open grass, the man shook his head and then oddly, he smiled. "I need to go somewhere and I need to go now! I'm taking what you have! Get inside!" Sarah noticed the holstered gun at his side. "If you let that dog loose, I'll kill it!"

From inside the house, trying to get out, Ralph was going ballistic. He'd gone to the upstairs loft where he could see through the window that looked down on the driveway and the front lawn. His front paws were hitting the window hard and Sarah was scared he'd break through. Holding Max, she needed to diffuse the nightmare that was happening fast.

"You stop! You need to go!" Her mind was racing.

She had a gun, but it was ten steps away. She'd just seen it. In fact, she'd just moved it to the backside of the table and it had a full clip sitting next to it. She looked behind her and the path wasn't clear. Stuff was in the way, and she'd have to go over and around. Looking back to the man, he'd moved closer. "Stop now!"

Again, Max barked and she wanted Sarah to let her go. "We have bicycles!" she yelled. "You stop! I'll set a bike out at the gate and you can have it! It's all yours. But you have to go now!"

"I need pain killers. Get inside." He started walking toward her and he was two hundred feet away. Walking faster, he pulled out his gun.

Pulling on Max and walking backward, she tried to push her way through the boxes. Plowing through the obstacles toward the rear corner of the garage, she headed for the gun, but she tripped. Desperate to hold on, falling backward, she lost her grip and Max ran toward the man.

On the ground, from the corner of her eye she could see the man running toward Max and she sprung up on her feet. Her heart sunk. Inside, Ralph was pounding against the window with his feet and she knew that it would break any second. She was losing everything.

At lightning speed, she bashed through the clutter keeping her from the pistol and clip. The very next second, she had it in her hand and the clip went in. Then she heard the shot.

Running out of the garage, she was crying for her dog, but Maxine was still circling. He'd missed, but he was going to shoot her again and Sarah yelled. "I'll shoot you! Drop the gun!"

Her finger on the trigger, she pointed it straight at him, but she was still a hundred feet away. He aimed at Max. "No! Don't! Don't do it!"

He looked at Sarah and smiled. With Maxine at his feet, his gun was at point blank range and she could hear her little voice start to yell. Get closer Sarah. Shoot him now. As she ran, he pointed the barrel at Maxine's head and pulled the trigger.

It didn't fire. He looked surprised and then he pulled again. Still it didn't fire and Sarah was ten feet away. She had to do it. Shoot him, Sarah! Kill him now!

She was paralyzed, and Maxine got hold of his leg, but he kicked her away. Yelling, he charged Max, but she dodged his kick and circled around. Max was scared. She started to circle, and then again, she lunged, but he got her! He kicked her hard and she screamed. She was down! Trying to move, she cried in pain as the man approached to kick her again. Taking aim, Sarah yelled. "I'll kill you!"

He laughed and then stumbled back and raised his gun at Sarah. "Don't think so, honey," and then he winked. Sarah pulled the trigger. She pulled it again and again, and then he dropped. She needed him dead, and she walked over to his head and fired two more.

It was over and she ran to Maxine. She dropped to the ground and hugged her. "You're such a good girl! Are you okay?"

Maxine got up and wagged, and Ralph stopped barking. She needed help, and she needed it now. Jim! Come home!

His duties completed, George made his way over to Jim's table and sat down next to his friend. Feeling anxious, there was something on his mind. "So, I was listening to our Sheriff talk about the drug addicts around here, and I thought about our neighbor. Did you hear him last night?"

Jim was shaking his head. "No. I didn't hear anything."

"He was yelling. And I know we've heard it before, but it sounded worse. I've been meaning to talk with you all afternoon."

His stomach churning, Jim leaned back and dropped his pen.

"Thought it'd be a good idea if we asked Johansen to send out some deputies. Maybe a little pop-over visit to check on things."

Nodding to George, he was disappointed with himself and he should've remembered. "Forgot all about him. I think a pop-over visit would be smart. What was he yelling about?"

"Couldn't tell, but he was angry. He was bashing on things and screaming."

"Great." Shaking his head, Jim sighed. "That's a problem."

The new rules had begun, and there was no room for troublemakers. The unstable were a huge threat, and his neighbor was clearly one of them. He should have remembered, and he could feel his worry elevating.

In all of his thoughts over the last couple days, he'd completely forgotten about the danger that lived in the woods. His cabin was only a half-mile away. He was usually gone, but when he was there, he'd seem to always make his presence known. Jim didn't hear anything last night and he was kicking himself for missing it.

Two years ago, he'd gotten into a verbal argument with this guy—and it was clear he was mentally unbalanced. Arrested several times, he was a risk and he was unpredictable, and Jim and Sarah were left with only one option. If they wanted to maintain their peace and tranquility, they'd have to ignore him and they'd have to pretend he wasn't there.

Leaning back in his chair, Jim had a new priority and he folded his arms. This needs to be dealt with, he thought. We need to make sure this guy's okay. We need to be proactive!

Today, SafePort was a Godsend, but it was no bed of roses. SafePort was a wartime act, and in America it was wartime. It was bad all over—and soon, bad people were going to start doing bad things. Little did he know, the chain reaction had already begun and the mentally ill were imploding. Insanity was here, and it was everywhere, and when he got home he'd find that his wife was alive and that his neighbor was dead. Soon, he'd find his body lying in his driveway.

Suddenly, the speaker got his attention. He heard the word" refugee" and he wanted to listen.

"It's a conundrum, folks. And we'd all do it. If I were trapped on the other side with my family—I'd grab them now and I'd make a run for a SafePort.

I'd follow the rules, and I wouldn't hurt anybody, but we need to remember, many will."

The speaker was shaking his head. "It'll happen here, and I'm sure it's happening right now. We have to be on guard and we have to protect our resources. It's up to the armed citizens now—and that's us. Watch your stuff and help people when you can, but don't let anyone steal anything. Theft is a high crime now and it can be punishable by death."

Again, he shook his head. "This is serious business. If you have to, protect your family with deadly force."

Listening closely, Jim was glad to hear the speaker talking about reality.

"They'll be headed our way, folks. Their homes are useless, and they'll be on foot. American refugees looking for food and water. It'll be horrible, but we have to defend SafePort."

There was that word again. Refugees. American refugees. I wonder how many?

"So I know the zone commander spoke of our mission to help the people on the other side, but until that happens—the best we can possibly do now is to corral the transient people along our western borders. We can bring food and water to the state-line and it can be managed appropriately. What we can't do yet, even though we'd like to, is let them in. It would overwhelm our system, and that's just the way it is. God bless the ones who had an escape plan and who can slip in now. I'm cheering for them all, but it's the masses on foot we must stop. I know it's terrible, but if they get in—the system will fall, and we all go down."

It was a sad reality, but it had to be heard. The speaker was addressing the brutal truth and he was narrowing in on the brutal mission. Jim knew it well, and today, so did everybody else. The speaker's words made it official, and it was historic.

"For now, the primary function of this newly activated SafePort Civil Defense, along with the Idaho Guard is the protection and enforcement of our SafePort borders with undefended states. Idaho's got two of 'em. For us it's Washington State. Our base in Boise is handling Oregon and everything south of the Columbia River. Canada is SafePort compliant, so we don't have to worry about them. But, with Montana and Utah being SafePort states; our western border is smack-dab on the front lines."

The speaker pointed. "Right out there, folks! The stage is set and they'll be here soon. For us, it'll start with Spokane, and when they get here it'll be a bottle-neck on the two main highways coming in. We're all working on the solutions now, but we've got to be ready and we've got to follow procedure."

The speaker went on and he talked about procedures for reporting suspicious activity, and how to engage law enforcement and civil defense forces when needed. If encroachments of the border became an elevated issue; he explained how the State Guard would take command of all defense forces and direct their operations. He also explained how the U.S military had final authority, and how that authority would be exercised if it were to emerge. All in all, it was a good lesson of a new, but temporary system.

Jim had worked with Captain Sullivan in establishing unifying procedures for SafePort Flight Operations, Guard operations, and civil defense. The mission of border patrol was the primary function and it was time to put the plan in motion. According to the schedule he'd found in the Flight Operations inbox this afternoon, he had an appointment with the captain this Friday. Captain Sullivan was formally with the Idaho National Guard, but as of today he and his organization were now the sole property of the governor of Idaho.

George signaled to Jim that he was done and ready to go. Half the participants had already left the building, and when they shut the lights off and shut the generators down outside, the sound of mass motorcycles departing the town of Sandpoint filled the air. Steve had already departed an hour ago with several crews of technicians in tow to begin the night shift. With continued round-the-clock retrofits of each community's water system; the people would get their water back soon.

The first day of a new America had begun, and with the commencement meeting over hope was overflowing. In the face of a decapitating HEMP attack on the nation, it was an impressive sight to see. The American Giant was indeed powerful, and today it was historical. The patriots were defending freedom, and freedom was winning.

With one exception, the ride home was much like the ride into town with patriotic citizens waving flags and cheering. The exception occurring immediately before the Long Bridge came from a rather large group of disgruntled anarchists who were yelling at the SafePort attendees and objecting to everything. As Jim passed the angry group on his motorcycle he attempted to read some of their signs, but he could only make out two.

"NO SLAVE TO SAFEPORT!"

"FOOD IS A RIGHT!"

He smiled at the group and rode on by. What a difference a plan makes! No free lunch! Earn your keep! He tried to come up with some more, but all he could think about was Sarah. He had lots to tell.

CHAPTER 18

ESCAPE

Sunset: Day 3
Seattle, Washington

Samantha was helping Betty and Lynne pack and they'd been at it all afternoon. The agreed upon allotment was five medium sized boxes each. The escape pod, as Otto and Tom were calling it now, was a shared venture and there was only enough space for each family to move an equally allotted amount of belongings.

She'd just returned from next door where she'd been helping Betty with her five boxes and now she was with Lynne. The ten-box limit was a mutual agreement, and it was based entirely on the recent loading scenarios Tom and Otto had performed after breakfast. There was much that hadn't been considered, and prioritizing belongings was one of them.

They were leaving everything behind except for what they could carry. Just like everyone else in the post-EMP America, their money in the bank was gone and what they had in their wallets meant nothing. Each family would depart with their entire net worth, and whatever made the cut would be loaded in the RV. What they were leaving behind, they were leaving to be pillaged. In no time at all, their home would be ensnared in an inhospitable land and they were fully aware of what the future held. Their former life was over and tonight they'd leave it behind.

Samantha was the most fortunate team member of them all when it came to emotional ties. She'd left her apartment in Carson, California with her bags packed for only a few weeks, but today when it counted, they were stuffed with most everything that was important to her. Samantha was young and she was living the life of a student. She was exploring the world's opportunities on her own, and with no significant others in her life, it seemed her emotional strings were reserved for the future.

For this she was lucky, and all she'd leave behind was her temporary position at the SOCAL Research Center for Cancer in LA. While she studied, and while she worked at climbing the ladder of experience, her life in California was only a steppingstone. At 24, she'd done well at keeping her attachments at arm's length.

She let the tears flow with both Betty and Lynne, and she was there as they packed their memories and valuables into five boxes each and then said goodbye to all the rest. It was an emotional time and she felt sad for them both. It seemed the process had an enlightening effect. She could see what was important—and what was not. Although lacking in the keepsakes, she found solace in that her life was an open book.

There were a host of unknowns and there were exciting chapters ahead. There was a purpose coming and she was beginning to hear its call. Freedom and liberty were still alive and in the Safe states they were being defended. That's where America was, and the nation needed her patriots to step up. Sam wanted to fight for the country and as of this morning, striving to be a part of it was now driving her every move. Her fire was igniting, and step by step she'd pursue it in full.

It was 9 pm, and on Day Three the sun had just dropped below the horizon. It was getting dark. "Operation Drive out of Seattle" was about to begin and the participants were ready. Tom had the motor home's exhaust pipe plugged into a duct in the garage that ran the fumes outside. The engine was running and the garage door was closed while they loaded up the final items.

All required systems on the motor home were checked and re-checked. Once the garage door was opened, the escape pod would be ready for launch. Tom's mechanical advantage was coming in handy, and he had the engine running smooth and strong. The RV was ready, and he'd packed every spare part imaginable in his "fix-it-in-the-field" go-bag. Operational confidence was high and Tom's preplanning measures were well appreciated.

All equipment and cargo had been loaded. With the departure looming and chaos outside rising, safety was the primary concern. It was their initial departure through the residential streets of the immediate neighborhood that had the greatest exposure. The slower speeds on their way to the interstate highway added an extra level of undesirable vulnerability. Close proximity to the dense populations at slow speed was an issue, and Ken was starting to see the value of one modification in particular. Apparently, Tom and Otto had made it for just this occasion.

Directly in the center of the vehicle and ten feet back from the driver was a heavy-duty pull-down rigid ladder with a man-size hatch on the ceiling that slid open. The ladder had a support structure for standing on, and if needed, it provided a stable platform for overhead weapon support if required. It was decided that during this vulnerable stage from the house to the highway, the ladder would be pulled down and the hatch slid open for quick access to the roof. It was also unanimously decided that Tom and Betty would mind this rear defense with their weapons at the ready.

It was time to leave, the sun had set, and duty called. Nobody was brave or stoic—and their departure was based entirely on fear. Six souls in Seattle were making their escape—and not a minute too soon. Makeshift funerals had already begun with two of their close neighbors having failed pacemakers. Both had been buried in their respective backyards today, and Tom and Betty and Otto and Lynne were among those paying their respects. Nothing was the same and the insanity was starting. They had to get out.

Only hours ago, while Otto was securing the boathouse, he watched a pickup drive out to the midpoint of the I-90 Bridge and then stop for about sixty seconds. The truck then turned around and raced back toward the east. While he stood watching, he was contemplating the truck's purpose—and then the bridge exploded. He dropped to his knees and took cover, but he quickly realized that it was a smaller explosion that probably didn't do much damage.

The city was frantic and the people were losing composure. Like fish out of water, they were flopping and scrambling. The calm before the storm was over. The desperate were beginning to take action. The bad would take from the good. The weak and vulnerable would be defiled. Delay could mean death and the escape had to be now.

With the ducting connected to the exhaust pipe removed, Otto hopped in the driver's seat and signaled to Tom for him to roll up the garage door. It opened up quickly and Otto drove out slowly with only inches to spare on each side. With the RV clear of the door, he stopped. Tom closed the garage door and then ran around to the passenger side and hopped in. There wasn't a soul in sight—and Otto drove the RV out onto the street, turned left, and accelerated.

"Pretty sure I forgot to lock your garage door," Tom said, clicking his seatbelt.

"Good," Otto snickered. "Now they won't have to break in."

Leaning forward to catch one last view in his driver's side mirror, he turned the corner and they were off.

Tom needed to switch seats and he traded spots with Ken. The plan was in motion and he and Betty took their positions while Lynne and Samantha sat at the RV's modified bench and table behind Ken in the front passenger seat. It was approximately 10 p.m. and it was dark. They had all running lights turned off and they were doing their best to remain invisible. The moon was bright enough to see without the headlights, but it was also, unfortunately, bright enough for them to be seen.

"It's Randy!" Otto yelled. "Sorry buddy. I can't stop," he said, waiving to his neighbor as he drove by. They passed the visibly stunned man who was waving to Otto. With desperation and shock, he started to run toward the departing RV with his arms flailing. Through his rearview mirror, Otto watched his neighbor slow to a stop looking exhausted and defeated. He'd turned his back on a friend and it made him sick. He turned to his passengers and then made an announcement. "This is it everyone! We get one shot. And we won't stop for anything!"

Cinching his seatbelt tight, Otto took command of his captain's seat like a bull rider preparing for a bumpy ride. He was focused and Ken appreciated the confidence and determination. It reminded him of Jim.

With no headlights it was difficult to see the road ahead. They had to proceed slowly as they navigated through the residential streets that were still littered with abandoned cars. Ken and Otto's eyes were peeled for obstacles and threats. Their forward scan could only focus a couple hundred feet, and all points beyond faded into blackness. It was creepy, and it was uncomfortable.

Ken was unfamiliar with the back roads Otto had chosen, but it was clear he was navigating the RV to the interstate highway in the most safe and effective manner. There was nobody around and the trees were blocking the view from any residential houses. This was a good way to go and it was better than what Ken had imagined.

"Good job, Otto." His eyes adjusting, Ken was scanning the area and he was trying to get his bearings. "Now where's the highway?"

At the top of a hill and coming down, Tom came up from behind and pointed straight ahead and into the blackness. "The on-ramp for I-90 is at the bottom of this hill. About a mile ahead."

He tried to make out any visual references resembling an on-ramp, but he couldn't. It was too dark and it was too far ahead—so he kept looking.

Now traveling at its fastest speed of the night, the RV was approaching 30 mph while coming down the hill. So far, the congestion caused by stranded vehicles had been fairly easy to circumnavigate, but as they proceeded down the hill, the congestion started to increase.

There was a main intersection with a three lane road running north and south at the bottom. It looked tight, but they'd have to cross it in order to get onto the on-ramp for I-90. If needed, they'd have to bash their way through, and Ken was starting to appreciate the bumper modification. As a last resort—the RV had a rigid steel bumper on the front that could easily facilitate the ramming and moving of any obstacles in its path.

Otto slowed the RV as the stalled traffic from the stoplight ahead filled the road. Ken spotted a light flickering and then he lost it the darkness. The hill had an obvious bend in the road, and as the turn started to straighten out, the intersection below and a small crowd of people came into full view.

"Those are fires," Tom said, standing in the center aisle.

Now focused on the intersection, Ken pointed. "That's a crowd of people down there. That's exactly what we don't want."

Otto maneuvered the RV through the gauntlet of cars and trucks that were stacking up as they approached the main intersection. There appeared to be a path on the right side that allowed for unfettered travel across the main road and onto the interstate's on-ramp. Now in the center of the three-lane road, they were still going down the hill, but the intersection was approaching quickly. With inches to spare, Otto slipped the RV in front of a stalled cement truck and assumed the right side of the road.

Again, he cinched up his seatbelt and his hands gripped the steering wheel like a vise at the ten and two o'clock positions. Watching Otto prepare, Ken had a sudden vision of the RV's captain ramming his way through the crowd of people and cars ahead like a tank commander busting through a barricade. He quickly wondered what fate had in store at the intersection below.

With his game-face on, Otto turned to Ken and then, with a glance back to Tom, he began his briefing on the plan. His tone was calm and relaxed. "So we're going through this intersection on the right hand side. We're going through slow and steady. Tom, you man the hatch. Be ready if things get tight. We don't know anything about these folks up here, so let's just pray they let us pass on by. Verify doors locked and the hatch open gentlemen. Thirty seconds and we're through."

Steering toward the right-hand side of the road and traveling along the shoulder, the path seemed clear ahead and the on-ramp was getting close. Ken's concern of having an overzealous captain at the controls was quickly replaced with confidence. Controlled force was an asset. Otto had it.

Veering to the right and then onto the shoulder, the RV dodged the stalled vehicles in the turning lane, and from his right side Ken caught a glimpse of two shadowy figures. Darting out from a car that was parked in the grassy area beyond the shoulder; they had purpose. When his eyes caught up to the moving targets, he could see they had guns. He yelled out the position for Tom in the back. "Right side—two o'clock—two targets, armed."

Tom was ready. "Back off! I'll kill you now!" he yelled from the open hatch.

Just then, two additional men from behind a car fifty feet ahead stood up and started to walk away fast. From atop the RV, Tom's upper body was holding an AK47 and he had it trained on both men as the RV rolled through the intersection. The groups of people that were gathered on both sides watched intently as the RV rolled through, slow and steady. Now accelerating on the on-ramp, the four menacing men were still walking away as Tom kept his aim.

Weaving around the traffic, the RV merged onto the highway and they were now headed eastbound on I-90. Next stop was Idaho, and from the passenger compartment, Betty, Samantha, and Lynne cheered. "Good job! Way to go!"

The stalled cars were everywhere, but Otto was finding a path. Oddly enough, it appeared that most moved over to the right once their engines lost power, and so far, the fast lane was somewhat clear. They had a 40-mph cruise, and once they headed up the mountain pass, it should get even faster.

"Lord—let it be smooth," Otto said, relaxing his grip on the steering wheel. "Good job everyone. We're out of here!"

With Seattle behind them, soon the RV would be passing through the city of Issaquah. This was the last major town of the Seattle metropolis and it was at the base of the western slopes of the Cascades Mountain range. Beyond Issaquah, it was straight up the mountain and through Snoqualmie Pass to get over to the eastern side of the state. Once on the other side, the forest and the mountains would be behind them, and the terrain would become flat and desolate.

On the other side, it'd be smooth sailing, and they'd be out of the trap they were in now. Death was here, but if they got to the other side they'd escape the suffering that was coming for everyone.

Releasing the tension in his seatbelt, Otto readjusted his seat so it had a slight incline. He pulled out a pack of unopened cigarettes from his pocket and smiled.

"If anyone has a reasonable objection—I won't light up," he said holding up the pack for all to see.

"Light it up, Otto. We can deal with it," Lynne yelled from behind.

"Thanks honey. I owe you one." He looked at Ken.

"Smoke it up, Otto."

He lit the cigarette, inhaled, and opened his window. "Maybe some coffee too?" He turned to Lynne and smiled.

"You got it."

He wasn't much of a smoker, but he used to be. He'd found a full carton on the top shelf of his bedroom closet this morning and he brought them because they were a commodity. With the exception of a cigar once or twice a week, he'd quit smoking five years ago. He had no plans to start it up again—but right now and with no regrets, he would enjoy his pack of cigarettes.

With Issaquah in the rearview mirror, they were now officially headed up the mountain pass. The population densities from here on out would decrease with every mile. The RV was able to maintain an acceptable cruising speed as the stranded vehicles were becoming more and more spread out. Much like a giant slalom course and without the need for a blinker, Otto weaved the RV up the long hill on the interstate and was doing so at a good clip, with an average speed of 50 to 60 miles per hour. If they could keep it up, they'd arrive at Ken's home in Idaho sooner than they thought.

His cigarette now comfortably nestled between his left two fingers, Otto reclined his seat back one more notch and then folded down his right side arm rest. There was a new feeling in the RV and it was starting to grow. Success was beginning to resonate and freedom felt close.

Ken's passenger seat had a swivel option and he elected to swing it to the left so that he could recline and cross his right leg over his left. In this position, his right leg and knee rested comfortably on the large center console, and he was looking for the sweet spot. He'd noticed Otto was looking at him, and after a few more adjustments on his seat, he looked back. "How's it going bud?" he asked, cracking open the bottle of water that was stashed in his cup holder.

"Well, I've got some questions." He took a long drag and then he blew the smoke out the window. "Been thinking a lot. Trying to hash it out."

Weaving around another car, he raised his brow and looked at Ken.

"I know what's going to happen here. I know that Seattle and every town and city west of the SafePort state lines are going to crumble within days. Within weeks, there'll be a massive die-off. We all know what we're leaving behind here and it's sick!" Another drag and he shook his head.

"These people are going to suffer. I mean, what happens when you put a million people on an island with no food. This has never happened before and we just lost half the nation. Their homes are useless and they have no food or water. They have no cars, and they can't communicate. They're all trapped, and it'll be bad. Real bad."

Snuffing out his cigarette in an empty water bottle, he needed to frame his question. "Like us in this RV. Sure there's a lot of patriots getting out, but everybody else is left behind, and they're all trapped behind these mountains. No Safe States to the south. Just more starving people. In a month it'll be wintertime, and pretty soon ... You know what's going to happen, Ken." Otto was shaking his head. "It's unthinkable."

"Here's your coffee, guys." Lynne handed Otto his cup and then tossed some cookies on the center console. "Eat those. There's two each. And there's plenty of coffee, so drink up."

While Ken went for the cookies, Otto smiled and then winked. "Thanks Lynney."

Coffee in hand, he returned to his inquiry. "So what does it all mean? And are we fooling ourselves? I mean, it's not like another country can ride in on a white horse and save the day. We're at war, and wars are all about controlling the territory. Look at what's happening here. It's the writing on the walls, and it looks bad."

Setting his cup down, Otto grabbed a cookie and looked at his friend. "It's all about America now, so I've got to ask. Will SafePort work? What do we have here? Is the infrastructure sufficient? Are we fighting, or are we abandoning ship?"

Otto's question perked everyone's ears—and without the road noise you could hear a pin drop. Behind the center console, Ken noticed that the pillows and sleeping bags had been arranged into a comfortable seating area, and everyone was waiting for his response.

At its core, it was a simple question, but he felt unqualified to answer it. He'd been struggling with it all day and he kept running into the unknowns. It required a calculated prediction, and even though he'd studied the risk assessments over and over, this scenario was unique and there were too many variables. Scrambling to provide a worthy answer, he needed the right words and he took a deep breath.

"So you've asked the most important question, and because I know quite a bit about our civil defense forces, I should be able to give you an answer." Turning to the group, he had to be candid about his confusion.

"But it's too soon, guys. I've been thinking about this all day, and I just don't know. We're at war. We have no idea what's going on out there, and Otto, you're right—we've already lost half our nation. Can we save the rest?

Can we save America? Too soon to say, and the circumstances are way too confusing. There's no good answer yet."

He picked up a cookie and took a bite. "I've been going round and round on this, and I keep coming back to the essential differences between us and them. Look at what we have here. Think about it what it means."

He took another bite and set it down. "We're in an RV, and like many others—we took steps to protect ourselves. It was an inevitable event, and we defended ourselves, but the others didn't. We've got millions who will survive—and that means we've got an army who will fight. Remember how those congressmen and our President exposed the big secret. Remember how SafePort swept through America. Remember how we united against the establishment that wanted us weak, disarmed, and divided, and remember why we're here. We have food, water, and guns, and we have the will to defend freedom. They don't, and that's got to mean something."

Knowing his answer was vague, he sighed. "Something profound is occurring, and we're all part of it. That's all I know. It's my gut feeling, and I believe mighty forces have been helping us the whole way."

"I'll second that," Tom yelled from the back.

"Me too," Otto said, smiling. "Good answer Kenny. Sorry to put you on the spot."

Moving into the fast lane, Otto hit the gas and the RV shifted into overdrive and climbed up the hill. Reaching for his cigarettes on the dash, he flicked his lighter in the darkness and then he flicked it again and took a drag.

"So I've got another question. Big picture stuff."

"Fire away, Otto."

"Rebuilding the grids, readiness teams, replacement parts … that kind of stuff. Where are we at? We've heard different stories, and a few months ago we read a SafePort report on the teams being denied access in Washington State. Was it just Washington? And does it have an effect on the national grid repair?"

"It wasn't just Washington. All the non-SafePort states refused access. And it's more than just the readiness teams, but we found a workaround."

Ken smiled. "I'm glad you read the report. It only scratched the surface, though, so here's the summary. Washington and all non-SafePort states refused to allow the readiness teams to stockpile and preserve any backup parts for the electrical grids within their borders. We had the same denial for the railroad teams. Even though the federal government assigned the national railways as a federal SafePort Zone, because they wouldn't allow access—all pre-staged operations have been temporarily positioned within the borders of the SafePort states. It'll cause problems, but the backup parts are still preserved and the dedicated teams are still ready when required."

Standing in the center aisle, Tom sighed. "It's good we have a work-around, but the denial is telling."

"I agree. We kept hoping they'd come around, but they never did, at least not in time."

"They were a sham. They were traitors." Tom looked at Otto and he was mad.

"They'd never acknowledge SafePort as a legitimate defense. They spent all their time convincing the new voters that it was dangerous. I know a lot of people that thought eventually we'd become a Safe State, but if that happened—they'd never be able to take away our guns. SafePort was a contradiction, and it exposed their deception—so they despised it. It's all very clear."

Nodding, Ken concurred, and there was nothing else to say. He grabbed his coffee cup and held it up to Tom and Otto. "Very clear."

A profound change in the road was taking place and everyone began to notice they weren't climbing anymore. Currently they were traversing the summit and they'd been traveling on relatively flat road for the last few miles. In another few, they'd reach the descent point, and the downhill portion would commence. Safety was getting closer.

They'd been traveling for a few hours now and it was well past midnight. The moon had risen to its highest point in the sky and the visibility was fantastic. At 40 mph—Otto didn't have to use his headlights at all. He'd use them occasionally when traveling behind a mountain or in a shadow, but for the most part—the lights-out tactic was working.

With a full thermos for the coffee drinkers, Lynne placed her hand on Otto's shoulder while she waited for him to sip the last bit of cold beverage at the bottom. He was well known for not wasting anything, and Lynne could prove it with the paper bag full of half smoked cigars she'd just found stuffed in the side of one of their personal boxes. She knew him well, and it was obvious.

They'd been married for fifty-three years and they'd both lived a hard life. Otto started out as a logger with his dad, and together they had grown a successful timber business with mills established throughout the Pacific Northwest. He and Lynne married at eighteen and they had a son and daughter who died tragically in a horrible car accident more than twenty years ago. Five years ago, Lynne was diagnosed with colon cancer and she began a long treatment that eventually sent the cancer into remission. It was obvious to all observers; Otto and Lynne had a few extra connections in the relationship department.

"Here you go, darlin. How about a half cup."

She filled Otto's cup halfway and then grabbed Ken's from his cup holder on the center console. "Get it while it's hot," she said with the thermos held out. As Ken hesitated, she tilted the thermos and started to fill. "I'm pouring it anyway. You guys need to stay awake."

"Yeah Dad," Samantha said from the back. "Drink up."

"Look!" Otto yelled. "That's a car behind us." All eyes turned and Ken focused on the passenger mirror.

"Yep, we got company," Tom said, staring out the rear window. "He's going fast Otto. Let him pass. He's coming up quick."

"I'll give him a wide birth and he can take the lead. Not a bad idea to caravan our way through this. We're in the middle of nowhere and it's good to know we're not alone."

They were indeed deep in the middle of nowhere and they'd just started their way down from the summit of Snoqualmie Pass. Everyone onboard felt a sense of unity with the fellow escapees that were traveling behind them. The vehicle had its lights on—and to help illuminate the road ahead and provide for a safe pass—Otto turned his lights on too.

The interstate was now descending down a fairly steep grade with a constant switchback from left to right as it cut through the steep ridges of the mountains. Otto wanted to find a good length of road that would allow the vehicle to pass on a straightaway. With the moonlight reflecting off the mountains and his high beams on, he could see the ridges in front of them start to widen out. Having traveled across this pass many times, he knew that in a few more miles the highway would start to open up, and this was where he'd slow down and give the car plenty of room to pass.

Coming out of a left turn and into a sharp right turn, Ken's attention was grabbed by a flash that appeared to bounce off the rock-faced ridge ahead and to the left. "Did you see that?" he asked while leaning forward.

Otto's head was blocking his view of the ridge through the driver's side window, so Ken leaned forward on the dashboard. He saw it again before Otto could respond. "There it is again. That's a flasher!"

"Yes it is," Otto replied as he tried to look over his left shoulder and drive at the same time. "Holy cow, that's a cop flasher! It's got blue in it—doesn't it?"

The RV was maneuvering through tight left and right switchbacks, and with every turn back to the northeast they would see the ridge reflecting the flashing light. There also seemed to be a slight mist in the upper elevation of the ridges and it too reflected the flashing light into the sky above. Now heading northeast, Otto slowed and both he and Ken leaned forward to get a bearing on its location.

"It's got to be up and around that next turn," Tom yelled from behind. "I've lost sight of the car behind us." He'd been keeping a close eye on the trailing vehicle and he'd expected it to be on the RV's tail by now. "Guess they slowed down too."

Confused, Otto turned to Ken. "Could there be authorities up here?"

"Don't know," Ken replied with the same bewilderment. "Those lights came from multiple sources. You could see them overlapping in the mist. Guess we'll find out in a minute. Remember what's at stake here, everyone. We've got to play this right. Like Otto said earlier, we only have one shot. Make sure that hatch is open Tom, and be ready for anything—but don't raise that gun unless we need to."

Ken was working a thousand scenarios in his head, and the scenario unfolding was increasingly uncomfortable. It was another unexpected event he'd not considered. The flashers were confusing, and confusion was bad. Why would authorities be up here? If it was military, then it's simple. We're on their side and we're just surviving. If it were anything else, he was drawing blanks and he'd have to wait and see. As of today, his official SafePort authority would supersede all state and local police, and his credentials should get them through anything, even an official checkpoint, if there was such a thing.

The idea of an official checkpoint on the top of Snoqualmie Pass made little sense. Ken's mind was working fast, and he knew that if there was a checkpoint up here, it meant the government was alive and well and they were likely enforcing marshal law. After all, he thought, we are at war—maybe that's what's going on here.

If for any reason their travel east was denied, the mission to escape would fail. Failure wasn't an option and under the fog of national collapse, he knew that most anything could be happening. His mind raced and he worked the problem the best he could. It was happening fast, and as they proceeded to enter the turn that would lead them to the source of the flashing lights, he could feel all command being stripped from their control. They were committed, and the situation would have to be faced. He asked for God's help and then reached into his jacket and unsnapped the strap that held his 9MM pistol.

"Slow down a bit Otto, I think they have the road blocked."

Coming out of the turn they could see at least two vehicles ahead with flashers in the middle of the road. Behind the vehicles it appeared two or three people were moving around with flashlights. Otto slowed the RV and from out of nowhere a large truck or SUV with its high beams flashing on and off came up directly behind them and assumed an aggressive position. Tom slid the upper hatch open and pumped a live shell into his shotgun while Betty readied the assault rifles for quick access.

Struggling to decipher what was happening, and once again his gut instinct was on overload. There simply wasn't enough information, and just like the I-90 Bridge, strategy was futile. All he could do was be ready.

Otto began slowing the RV with the intention of stopping a good hundred yards in front of the vehicles ahead. "They've got it blocked alright."

He slowed to a stop as the forward edge of the RV's high beams cast a dim light on the vehicles that were blocking the road. "Doesn't seem right," he said as they both leaned forward to make out what was ahead.

Ken unbuckled his seatbelt and then put both hands on the dashboard and leaned forward even more. Just then, the entire forward compartment of the RV lit up with a spotlight that was being cast from ahead. As he struggled to see through the glare on the front windshield, the truck's high beams that were flashing on and off repeatedly from the rear now had the addition of a handheld spotlight that was sticking out from the passenger side.

Boxed in—they were now ensnared. Is it a gate or a trap? An overwhelming pressure hit Ken and he could feel a dose of adrenaline starting to pump.

He turned around toward Samantha to see where she was at, and as he did so, the spotlight from behind illuminated the rear interior of the RV. Betty jumped up and closed the blinds on the rear windows to shield the offending intrusion.

"This is bad," Betty yelled. She immediately started pulling down every window blind in the back of the RV. "They're not going to like this, and we've got big problems. This isn't official. No way. It's not standard. I'm not buying it, Tom!" She'd gotten their privacy back but in no way did she mince her words. She'd stated her case and it was convincing.

"Standby. Guns down—but be ready." Ken motioned to Samantha and he needed her on the floor. He needed more information and he needed it quick. Spinning forward, he scanned for more visual clues, but it was too dark and it was too bright with the spotlights. At the current pace, any answers were too slow and they were losing control. Failure wasn't an option, and if he had to—he'd change the game.

In the nick of time, what happened next was the first official act they'd seen, and it took the edge off of what was beginning to look like an assured ambush. From out of the darkness and from behind the spotlight in front of them, one individual began an approach. He was carrying a flashlight in his right hand. He was of a large stature and he had his left hand held up high signifying the "halt" command. He proceeded toward the RV, and it was difficult to see if he was wearing a uniform.

"Doesn't feel right," Otto said, alarmed.

"I agree. And by the time we confirm it, it'll be too late. So, here's the plan. You need to be spring loaded to ram that vehicle behind us. If it turns out that we need to bust through this, you've got to do it. And Otto, if you gotta cut and run, you need to ram that vehicle and then you gotta go—even if I stay behind."

"What do you mean?"

"We're at an unacceptable disadvantage here, so in thirty seconds when he's fifty feet away, I'm out the door to force a change. We need confirmation this is official—or we need a distraction to give you a head start. This'll give you one or the other. It's our only option. Just promise you'll go without me Otto. No time to think, just promise!"

"Okay. I promise and I'm ready. But just hold it for a second, would ya?"

Otto's tank commander confidence was at full and he reached down and cinched his seatbelt as tight as it would go.

As the approaching figure began to enter into the light beams coming from the spotlights, a weapon could be seen and it was slung across his torso. As the man continued to approach, the uniform provided no clues. It was nondescript, and yet it was reminiscent of military battle attire. Over the next three steps—his body armor became fully illuminated.

Tom yelled from behind. "Not good, Otto! Where's the flag? This is wrong!" Just then the approaching individual lowered his left hand and then he started to wave his arms back and forth. He was less than a hundred feet away and he was walking fast.

Ken's time had arrived. This was a crossroad. He couldn't let it pass. If his sacrifice saved the rest, he was ready and he was at peace. The unknown man now had his arms down and his right hand appeared to be resting on his rifle.

Otto's driver's side window was slightly down. "Identify yourself and do it now!" he yelled through the four-inch opening. "Stop now! Halt! Identify yourself!"

With no reaction from the approaching man, Ken turned to his daughter. "Samantha, you get on the floor and you stay there!" He looked over and caught Otto's eyes. He gave a nod and then he reached for his passenger door handle, and he pulled it.

As the door swung open and before he moved an inch, gunshots rang out. Otto yelled in pain.

Ken slammed the door shut and snapped his attention back to Otto. He felt the RV start to move slightly as if Otto's foot had come off the brake pedal. Something horrible was happening. Within microseconds he realized Otto had been shot in the head and was writhing in pain. The front windshield had been breached by several bullets and they were under full attack. Evil was here and it wanted them dead.

Ken needed Otto out of the driver's seat immediately and he reached down for Otto's seatbelt latch on his right side. Before getting to it, Otto swung back with force from his position against the driver's side window. In his last moments of consciousness he groaned in pain, and then he slammed on the brakes.

In the sudden stop, Ken fell forward against the front dashboard and windshield. As he regained his balance and righted himself, Otto's body went limp and he slumped over the steering wheel. While reaching again for the seatbelt release, Ken was able to unclick it, but at the same time, unconscious Otto had regained his movement—and while he moaned in pain again, his foot hit the accelerator and he floored it.

The RV lurched forward and Ken fell backward into Tom who was securely holding on and blocking the path. As he fell rearward, he was able to grab Otto and pull his foot off the accelerator.

From behind, Tom pulled his friend out of the driver's seat and Ken went for the brakes. Headed for the edge, it was too fast. Tom leaped for the steering wheel, but he was too late. The right front tire fell off the edge and the RV veered. They were going to roll over, and it was starting now.

The drop-off from the road onto the dirt was severe and it sloped down into a shallow ravine at the bottom. The RV began to tilt aggressively to the right as it slowed down. Just before coming to a stop, the lateral center of gravity was exceeded and the RV rolled over. It was now upside down and it was on its back in the dirt. Ken wasn't buckled in, and as the RV flipped over he hit the back of his head on the metal edge of the built-in cabinets.

It was dead silent. He found himself dazed and lying in pain on the roof of the RV. His head felt like it was going to explode and all he could do was hold it with both hands. He was wedged in the forward corner and as he looked up he could see the front passenger seat hanging there directly above him. The creepy silence was back and all he could hear was the dust settling outside. Lynne cried out and then his vision went blurry and all he could see were stars. He was struggling to maintain consciousness and he quickly yelled out. "Is everybody okay?"

He reached into his unsecured holster to pull out his gun and it was there. Samantha responded, "I'm okay Dad. I think I got hit in the leg, but I'm okay." He could only see her body and she was face down in the middle of the RV's roof. He caught Tom's eye, and just before he spoke, Tom signaled to stop and listen.

They nodded and with their fingers they pointed to the outside sounds that were approaching. Tom and Betty were right next to each other and Lynne had crawled over to where Otto was lying in the front corner of the roof. Whoever did this was now approaching to finish the job. Tom and

Betty were having none of it. Working in unison, they separated their fire-power to both sides in the rear corners of the upside-down RV. Ken was fading fast and he feared he'd be of no help in the upcoming fight for life.

They were losing everything. All the advantages were gone and in moments from now they'd likely be shot and left for dead in the ravine. Should have known better, he thought to himself. My God, it's the end of the world out here. How stupid to think we could just roll on through with an RV full of supplies. He held out his gun and he prayed for help. They needed it desperately and they needed it now. Someone was approaching.

Footsteps were on the other side and they were turning the corner at the rear of the RV. Tom paced the moving target and he stood with his shotgun barrel an inch away and pointing outside. He was ready to pull.

Suddenly, the sound of footsteps stopped cold and from off in the distance the sound of another vehicle could be heard. It was getting louder, and it was getting louder fast. Then the door bashed open and Tom and Betty unloaded.

Ken could see an armed man rush the door with his rifle barrel rising toward Samantha. Time was up. He was going to pass out, but from the side he aimed center-mass and pulled the trigger. The gunshots echoed. Everything went black.

CHAPTER 19

STILL ALIVE

Scratching the back of his head, Ken started to chuckle. "I thought we were home free. I should have known better, but we learned."

Stunned, she set the recorder down and scooted towards the center console. "So this is how it all began?" Tapping his arm with her cast, she leaned in closer. "That's incredible. I can't believe you made it. You were trapped out there for four months."

Still recovering from his wounds, he wanted to make sure that their mistakes were noted in the record. "Yeah well, in the end we made it, but we made critical errors and it nearly killed us. Just like Sarah, we were lucky. We had a second chance."

Pointing to Jim, he provided the supporting evidence. "She should have dropped that guy sooner, but in the end she was given a second chance. She finely saw evil for what it was, and when she saw it, she took it out. For those of us who survived our first post-event encounter, we learned a valuable lesson."

Writing down Ken's words in her notebook, Anne looked up. "We all presumed too much, didn't we? We thought they'd be amenable to our pre-planned survival. We thought the undefended would still have honor."

"Bingo," he replied. "We knew that most would have guilt and remorse regarding their own decisions, but because we were fellow Americans—we assumed they'd honor ours. We were wrong. A great many chose murder, rape, and slaughter. We didn't know it would happen so fast, and we misjudged their resolve."

"They've killed millions," Jim said with a scowl. "They still call themselves Americans, but they never were. They have no morals and they don't believe in the golden rule. When the grids went down, the veil was removed. We had to learn fast, and we did."

Transcribing the emotions coming from her two subjects, Anne knew their perceptions were first-hand and highly relevant. The battle for America was between good and evil, and it was simple, but there were grey areas, and she had to ask.

Tapping her pen on the notepad, she was searching for the right words. "It's just sad."

Ann looked down at her notes and she could feel the heartbreak that all patriots had to bear. It was at the core of everything, and it was betrayal.

"I think they hated God, and they hated us. Their armies are still out there today, and they're fighting under the impression that it's the patriots who are evil. It's a messed-up equation, and its way beyond my scope, but I've got a question. It's for both of you."

Drawing a line across the page, she wrote REFUGEES in big bold letters. "So this is when the wicked came out of the shadows. It was backed into a corner, and it exploded in a way that none of us ever imagined. Both of you had an extraordinary vantage point, and Ken, I can't even imagine what you lived through … But I want to back up for a second. Before we proceed, I want to categorize the people on the battlefield."

With her notepad resting sideways on the center console, she watched Jim read her title and then nod. She circled it and then set her pen down. "So we've got three groups. We've got the patriots and the marauders, and we've got the refugees. Who are the refugees? And where do they fit in?"

Both hands on the wheel, Ken looked over his shoulder. "They're heroes."

A single nod and he looked at Jim. "What do you think?"

"I think they're unique. Highly unique."

Curious, she wrote down the word and circled it. "Unique?"

"Yes. Extremely." Jim turned and sat sideways.

"For the most part; these were the patriots that either failed to defend themselves in time, or did—and it was all taken away by the marauders. These are the people who rejected evil while they watched their families suffer and die. They waited for their countrymen and they prayed to be saved. Some were wicked, and the wicked did terrible things, but most were good, and the good were heroes. I respect them greatly."

"What about the killers?" Anne needed to drill down. "I mean—on the border states. A lot of them got in disguised as refugees, and I know my attackers were on the Watch List."

Not surprised, both men sighed and Ken responded.

"Were they confirmed?"

"Yep. And I just found out. My dad told me yesterday."

Confronted with his former responsibilities, Jim had been concerned with the new military transition regarding refugee management. He knew about the gaps in protocol and he struggled with an appropriate response. "We need a better system and we need our internet back. They shouldn't have got in."

"I know. But in the end they didn't. There were six of them, and because they were all wanted they had to hide-out in Montana. Now they're dead."

Anne leaned forward. "And if I didn't do it, somebody else would have. They were executed on the spot. Appropriately."

Smiling, she wanted Jim to know that she was grateful. "It was your Watch List. I don't know what the evidence was, but my dad said they were confirmed targets from Spokane—and they've been on the wanted list for several months. Your system worked Jim! And your evidence makes me feel better. They deserved every single bullet."

"That's good, Anne. And I'm sorry it was you, but way to go!" Rubbing his forehead, Jim was impressed.

"We watched them for months," he said leaning in closer. "We documented everything. We had high resolution cameras. We had spies in the refugee camps, we had spies in the cities, and we had airplanes in the air. It started out slow, but after a while we figured out their tactics and we started to win."

Tilting his head, he sighed. "You need to hear the rest of the story. The military's running the show now, but when we did it, we watched evil at its very worst. We documented everything, and we saw the unthinkable."

"You're right. I need to hear the rest of the story and you were both there. Ken, you were trapped in Washington State, and Jim, you were in the air. Where do we begin? I need it all."

Watching their eyes meet, Anne could see they were on the same page. Jim held out his arms as if it were the obvious choice.

"Rescue! Day 122! The President's address. The big day!"

CHAPTER 20

DAY 122

Sandpoint, Idaho
0800: Pacific Standard Time

H is heart beating fast, Jim walked out of the radio room and proceeded down the hallway. The mission was on and he was anxious to get it done. Reaching the doorway to his office, he entered and yelled down to Rob, who was just around the corner.

"We're on bud. Wheels up at 0900."

Before he could sit down, running from the Dispatch desk he saw Rob standing in front his office and he had a clipboard hanging from his crutches.

"I'm on it," he said spinning towards Jim. "How many passengers? Do we know yet?"

"You're getting good on those."

Jim was impressed with his clipboard hanger and he had to say something. "You need a coffee cup holder. Put it on the other crutch and it'll balance it out."

Rob looked down and laughed. "Yeah, that's good. Never thought about that." He vaulted into his office, grabbed his clipboard and readied his pen.

"We've got two passengers on the return leg."

Opening his folder, Jim sorted through his paperwork. "Water and meds only. Here's the checklist and I want you to double-check every med. Go get the maintenance sheet back from Jerry on those two passenger seats. Let's go with ten bags on the water."

"Got it, Jim. He's installing the seats now."

Rob, who was standing on his good foot and dead center in front of Jim's desk, was getting proficient at maneuvering quickly. His three legged skills were impressive, and although he had a broken foot, he was far from handicapped.

With little room to maneuver, he hung up his clipboard and positioned his crutches like an athlete getting into his stance. A solid plant on one, he turned on a dime and then swung his body through the narrow exit and into the hallway. From there, it'd be a two-hundred-foot skip to the hangar. It was a straight shot all the way down. But before he could launch, Jim had a revision.

"Let's go with fourteen bags. But tell Jerry that I want two water bags each strapped to those passenger seats. So that's four bags on the chairs, the rest in cargo."

Nodding, Rob wanted to confirm that he was done, but Jim beat him to it.

"That's it. We'll talk in a minute."

Racing down the hallway, Rob was the new office helper and SafePort had assigned him to the Flight Ops department per Jim's request. Last month, Rob had broken his foot while cutting firewood for the SafePort winter stores. Roberto Garcia was twenty-four years old. He held the class of consumer within the Bonner County SafePort system—and he was hoping to serve in the civil defense.

At eighteen, all residents had the legal right to opt out of the SafePort Sustenance Delivery System, or SSDS, and survive on their own. Opting out removed the nonparticipant, or if acting as the legal designated family representative, removed the family from receiving SafePort benefits which included, among other things, food, water, and medical services. Many residents living in Bonner County had homes that were in remote areas, and because of their geographical location it made it difficult or impossible for them to participate as a user in the SSDS program.

These residents were among the many that had appropriately opted out, and they'd done so in exchange for meeting their own self-sufficiency requirements. This sector of the populace, including the many survivalists who'd made arrangements to survive on their own, performed the honorable function of contributing to the community systems without taxing any reserves.

Most residents, however, were like Rob, and they chose to participate in SafePort's SSDS program out of necessity. The systems were working, and at four months in—those who'd participated were healthy and strong. Everybody worked as a team, and everybody owed their lives to it.

Roberto had caught Jim's attention during last month's SafePort meeting. He'd been hobbling around on his crutches all day and he was lining up various duties to perform from various departments. He was offering his labor out to everyone he could find and he was managing his own schedule. He was freelancing. He was working when he didn't have to, and Jim asked him why? His response was the clincher.

He argued that he could still work and that he could still pull his own weight. He said he had to make up for his injury and that he would. He said it was his duty.

As an injured consumer and per the SafePort regulations, Rob's physical status removed him from the work requirement until healed and he was told not to report. It was black and white, and for many it was a sound policy, but in this circumstance he didn't agree and he took it upon himself to remedy the situation. He said he needed to work, and Jim had an idea.

Territory-wide, the SafePort flight departments needed more personnel. With the expanding mission, skilled labor was a hot commodity and additional help was needed everywhere. Jim had been working diligently at expanding the North Idaho Civil Air Patrol, and to increase its capabilities he needed more pilots in several zones. Unfortunately, the local pilot pool was minimal, and he'd been forced to employ other tactics.

Rob was his first candidate. Once trained, he'd be the first of many "non-pilot" flight crewmembers to assist in the new endeavor. Six aircraft in total had been assigned to the North Idaho Territory and Jim had to allocate them appropriately. For now, he'd assigned four aircraft to the Kootenai County SafePort Zone, which was the adjoining zone to the south. Population densities were much higher in this zone and he needed the expanded coverage. The refugee camp on I-90 was smack dab on the Kootenai county border with Washington State, and because of its growing size he needed to maximize his aircraft, maximize his crews, and delegate effectively.

Over the last two months he'd given Jerry's counterpart, Mike, the operational control responsibilities for all four aircraft in Kootenai County, and they were all based at the Coeur d'Alene airport. The assets to meet the current mission were getting dialed in, and for now the primary function in North Idaho was protecting the borders and the refugees. The job was getting done, but it was all about to change and Jim had a new structure that would accommodate the expansion.

With the dispatch systems working well and with both the Sandpoint and the Coeur d'Alene departments ready for increased surveillance, Jim had a new crew arrangement and it was nearly complete. The weak link was unacceptable and his "on call" readiness needed to be improved. He needed more flight crews, and if the pilots lived elsewhere he needed to substitute safety for new recruits.

To meet the expanding needs there were few options. Until they got more airplanes—and more two-man crews—his current tactic was the only tactic he could choose. He needed to adapt, and he did, and Rob was his first candidate.

For surveillance purposes, flight missions were best served with at least two qualified occupants on board. One would serve as the Pilot in Command, and barring any emergencies the other would handle the cameras and perform all ground observations. When able, Jim would dispatch each flight mission with two qualified pilots, but the atrocities were expanding and it was getting tough to do. The policy optimized safety, but when multiple incidents were occurring in Washington State, there simply weren't enough staff pilots and the department was rendered over-tasked.

The dedicated aircraft in SafePort's fleet were all certified to be flown with a single pilot. Up until now, the second crewmember had always been a fully rated pilot, there for backup, but primarily assigned to the non-flying duties such as ground surveillance and the management of cargo. During the initial startup, the two-pilot crews were an advantage that maximized both the flight mission potential and the survivability of both crewmembers. In the event of an emergency landing, two were better than one in the uncontrolled territory.

Now everybody was getting used to it, but back then it was a lot scarier.

In the beginning, routine departures had the flight crews fully armed. Each pilot carried enough food and ammo to survive for a month. Dispatching all flights with a second pilot gave the mission an edge, and the crews knew that if needed, one might be able to save the other in a pinch. Now, safety was a luxury, and Jim had to adjust.

At three weeks in, his new plan was in full-swing, and he'd officially trained Rob to be a non-flying crewmember. The new structure would have an immediate effect on his dispatch capabilities, and with another four candidates only a week behind Rob, his crew-base was about to expand significantly.

It was Rob's spirited attitude that got him the job, and Jim wanted to make it official. Rob was the first of five that were undergoing the new training program, and each would undergo a final check ride with Jim to be certified and signed-off. Rob was up first, and Jim knew that he was ready.

Only minutes away, and presently unbeknownst to the spirited trainee, it was Roberto who'd be assisting Jim, and today they'd perform an overdue rescue. With a hundred and twenty-two days on the calendar, Ken and Samantha were finally coming home. Jim needed an assistant—and he felt confident Roberto was the right man for the job. He still hadn't seen the refugee camps and he hadn't flown across the border, but today he would, and then Jim would sign him off.

Where the full weight of the catastrophic attack was just beginning, Jim knew the insanity was at full-tilt and he needed his civil air patrol to be ready for what was coming. At four months in, death was administering its most powerful blow. Starvation was hitting the country hard, and in a cruel twist of fate, it was the non-SafePort states that had the highest population densities of all.

Somehow, Ken had found a way to beat the odds and his actions had likely saved many lives. Most had already succumbed, but there were many that were still flailing in their attempt to outsmart death. Millions were dropping dead in the streets—and the death toll was far higher than on any month before. At four months in; a mass decay of the unburied was spreading across the nation. It was a horrific reality—and it was inexcusable.

Over the next few months the accumulation of rotting bodies would likely fester into the remaining populace, and with certainty, it would surely lead to many more dying of disease and infection. Month four was bad, and the part of America that refused to defend itself was dying a horrible death.

The SafePort territories had their losses too. Anyone dependent on modern technology or special medicine to stay alive was either gone already or on death's door. Life was precious and it was fragile. Only the well defended, the lucky, and the determined were surviving the ordeal, but oddly enough, if you were a marauder in Washington State—the equation was different. The marauders were thriving and they were building an army.

The reality was confusing, and like all patriots, Jim struggled with the betrayal. Ken had outsmarted them, but the fate of his brother was still up in the air. Jim worried that Paul and the entire Chelan group was clinging to life somewhere, or maybe they'd already let it go. He didn't think so, but he didn't know and it was a continuous struggle.

With his flight planning completed, he had a half hour to kill and he needed to get his mind clear. He'd be seeing Ken today, and when he did there'd be a lot to go over. So much had happened. The last few months had been a blur and he could only imagine what it was like to be on the ground. It was getting worse. The evil forces were killing people for food, and they were doing it on a grand scale. Something needed to be done, and Jim wanted to do more than just document it.

With matching rationale, both Ken and Paul had relinquished their personal escape and both opted out of the airlift plan using the King Air. From the midst of circumstances known only to them, they were both leading large groups of fellow survivors and the members-only airlift was no longer an appropriate solution. It was admirable, and they were both answering the call to save others.

The private airlift was meant for the few and not the many. For similar reasons, they adapted their tactics so that all had a chance at escape. After today, he didn't have to worry about Ken anymore. Paul's group, however, were still missing. It had been over three weeks since he lost all communications with his brother. The outlook was grim.

Paul's group had made their initial departure out of the town of Chelan two months ago on Day 70. With help from June, the airport mechanic they'd met on Day 1, the group's convoy of misfit vehicles included three yellow school buses, a semitrailer full of operable equipment, plus two pickup trucks and two RVs. It was both amazing and impressive, and it was a caravan that many had helped build.

It seemed that Paul's part-time preaching at his local church had an effect. He'd been preaching preparedness for a year now and it seemed his SafePort sermons had inspired fruit. Apparently, June the mechanic had a field day with the preserved engine parts. They were shielded by several church members, and Paul said she was a Godsend. June and her helpers were able to salvage six large transport vehicles, and like Noah's Ark, the Chelan team built a life raft that was big enough for all. It was impressive, but they'd been forced to leave before they were ready—and now they were lost.

Upon their initial departure from Chelan—and in what should have only been a one-day travel event—the convoy broke down on the side of the road after having only traveled a couple hours. Jim spoke with Paul on the radio several times from a small town just east of Coulee City on Highway 2 where they were stranded and making repairs. Highway 2 was the preferred east/west highway in northern Washington, and from Chelan it took them east, just like I-90 did for Ken and his group coming from the more southern location of Seattle. It was a simple day trip, but it turned into a blunder.

After a month-long breakdown and from a tiny town off of Highway 2, in his conversation with Paul three weeks ago, he was told they'd solved their problem and that they were going for it. They'd made repairs, they had a break in the weather, and in less than twelve hours they'd be at the refugee camp. That was the last he'd heard from Paul.

Maybe today's the day, he thought as he looked out of the windows in his office. Maybe today I'll spot 'em. Before his brother left Chelan, he confirmed Paul's compliance with his recommendation to paint a big red X on the roof of his RV and on the roof of the three yellow buses. He'd been assured that it was done, and after the weather broke he scoured the countryside. For the last two weeks he'd been looking for red Xs and he'd had no luck at all.

Winter was here and so was the snow. Everything on the ground was white—including the roofs of all vehicles. If the roof was clean, however, he'd see the red Xs and they'd stick out like sore thumb. If they'd just clean off the snow, he thought. Show me the signal and I'll find you Paul.

He was forced to assume that his brother's group had left their holdup position on Highway 2 under the false assumption that the bad weather was breaking. Northern Idaho had been socked in for the last month and a half, and with the exception of a few days with brief clearing, it was only recently that he'd been able to fly any meaningful surveillance flights at all. When Paul departed the small town three weeks ago, Jim had no clue what the weather was doing two-hundred miles away.

For the most part, the weather had been low overcast and it'd been dumping snow every other day in Sandpoint , Idaho. It kept Jim grounded, which meant he had zero information on the marauders, and he had zero information on the status of the snow on the highway. These were critical components, and Jim knew the airplanes were essential. He wanted them to wait until the weather fully cleared—but for some reason, they thought it was doable.

His worst fear remained. They got stranded and they froze to death. It was happening everywhere—and he'd seen it over and over. For all he knew the snows could have come and covered all of their tracks. Hence, no red Xs, and no Paul.

As the only team member who'd made it to the safety of Idaho, Jim performed the function of a third base coach and he watched the battlefield for openings. With a dedicated airplane and a set of radios he rallied the advancement of both groups toward the safety of home plate—and today it would be Ken making the next score. They were all underdogs, and they were all within the opponent's grasp, but if Paul could make it—they'd win the game.

Over the last month, the future of America was getting difficult to determine. Failed states were imploding, survivors were being slaughtered, and both Ken and Paul were forced to make critical decisions in an effort to survive. These were battlefield decisions and they were made on the fly.

In both cases they were directly attributable to either life or death. The outcome of Paul's decision was unknown. Two weeks ago, Ken's decision saved hundreds. It was a new world in Washington State and the wicked were taking control. For those still trapped, in many cases, escaping east toward Idaho was no longer the best option. Ken was forced to decide—and so was Paul.

With the assault on Snoqualmie Pass now a well known news brief, Ken and the others had become overnight heroes in Idaho. Jim had only heard bits and pieces over the radio regarding his friend's brush with death on the night of Day 3, but he knew that Ken and the small group he'd left Seattle with were more than lucky to be alive.

It seems their near-death experience sparked a new path. What had started out as a small group traveling east in a little RV, and thanks to the arrival of two new heroes, over the next few months the group of fellow escapees rapidly evolved into a large hundred-plus member clan. On the night of the escape, on Day 3, the two Kittitas County police officers that had followed Otto's motor home and rushed to its rescue were now champions.

In the nick of time, they'd rolled up on the roll-over assault and their actions were miraculous. In Idaho, these two officers were famous, and their selfless, brave, and noble act had accomplished much more than just saving the lives of six people. It was here where the greater mission was born, and so far, the mission was getting accomplished.

Ken's rundown of the deputies' actions astounded him. They came from out of nowhere. They fought evil. They saved Ken's group from assassination, and they'd been instrumental in the formation and success of a large survival group. These were the guys that Jim wanted to meet. Apparently, the mountain pass attackers were ruthless. They'd killed a smattering of others before setting their sights on Otto's RV, and if the two cops weren't there they would've kept on doing it.

As the story goes, the two officers had been waiting for the killers to make another move—and in Jim's assessment, their timing was miraculous. Had they rolled up on the scene one second later, everyone would have been dead. It was then, on the night of Day 3— on the top of Snoqualmie Pass—where destiny intervened. It was here where the components of a grand plan were added to the mix, and it was here when the first ingredients came together. It'd been four months and now the group was a walking army. They were winners, and they were heroes. They were still alive.

Following the attack on the pass, the two deputies had taken all six into their homes and they helped everybody recover from their varying wounds. Over the last several months, the fellowship expanded. They worked together and with Ken they united the local patriots that were losing the battle on their own. It was all fate, and if you were with them—you were living.

Both deputies lived on farmland just east of Ellensburg, Washington, and by chance, each of their family's two properties joined at the corner. The opportune arrangement of land and property lines worked well for the group's base camp, and within the first few weeks after the attack, the surrounding hillside and valley had banded together. The whole area had become strong and it was a protected territory where the marauders couldn't get through.

In a place where families knew families and neighbors knew neighbors, the good people sought out the good. From near and far, word of mouth was spreading and some risked everything to be a part of the small army.

Injuries had to heal, and while the patriots expanded their local forces the new plan appeared to benefit from the delay. Where both Ken and Otto suffered severe concussions, Otto got shot in the head and he lived to tell about it. Samantha was shot in the leg, but she recovered quickly and she was up and walking.

It was Day 122, and at four months in, much had occurred. There were distinct reasons for everything, and to keep up with the changing world, Paul and Ken's best laid plans were changed repeatedly. Both groups were being squeezed from all sides by the marauders desperate for food. Gangs of the hopeless and frantic were growing bigger by the day, and large portions of the populace were now throwing in the towel on their humanity.

They were killing to stay alive and both Paul and Ken's groups had become known commodities. Their Chelan and Ellensburg locations were no longer defendable, and both groups had to depart quickly before the larger gangs stormed in.

No choice, he thought. Jim had assessed it over and over and it always the same. They had to run. Time was up.

Managing the variables was no easy task, and Ken and Paul had been on the hot seat for months. Which plan were they on now? Seven ... Maybe it's eight? I wonder? He still had some time to kill, and looking out his office window he thought about the first.

In Plan A, Ken was going to drive across eastern Washington with his daughter and four fellow survivors. They'd enter Idaho where Ken was a resident, and after that he'd politically adopt his four friends and then they'd all live on his property as part of the SafePort team. It was a great plan, and it should have worked, but it didn't.

Sure has changed, he thought scratching his head. You almost made it Ken, but you didn't lose. You're coming home. I'll see you soon.

Following the incident on the mountain pass, Ken and his cohorts dedicated their lives to a greater purpose. As the group of six nursed their wounds and regrouped, their fellowship with others spread and the people of good spirit banded together.

The group became larger and larger and simply crossing into the land of SafePort for political asylum with Ken was no longer a valid option. He couldn't adopt a hundred plus members—and until the supply chains were ready—SafePort couldn't allow it. As the days went on, together they survived and together they assessed the region around them.

Jim's connection with Ken was instrumental. The advantage was in the airplane, and Ken squeezed it for every drop. Waiting for good weather; Ken's group bunkered down and waited for the airplane to raise their odds. It was the only way to win, but while waiting to move eastward toward the safety of the refugee camps, the region near the border crumbled quickly and then so did their hopes. With real-time information coming from Jim, escape plans were in turmoil and quick decisions were required.

Gangs across the nation were killing their countrymen at alarming rates. If they didn't go, they'd be killed. If they stayed another day, they might lose it all. Good options were far and few and the lives of many depended on good decisions.

At about thirty-days in; the refugee camps started. By Day 60, hordes of people from the eastern Washington region had made the desolate crossing. Upon arrival, they then piled themselves into the two SafePort refugee camps on North Idaho's border. They came in droves, and even in the winter snow there were thousands who were on foot. People were flocking to the camps. Some went to the I-90 camp and some went north to Highway 2. The hopes for food and water were being answered, and the camps were saving lives.

At two months in, the camps were still safe, they were separated from the marauders, and they were preventing starvation. For most, other than the prepared, if they wanted any chance of surviving through the winter, getting to the camps was an appropriate measure to be taken. Although many died trying, on Day 60 people were still helping people, and in the camps it it was

Americans helping Americans. Refugees were surviving. Law and order was being managed, and once there, survival odds would increase. For most, it was the only solution, but as time went on, things changed.

By Day 70, Paul's group had run out of time. They were forced to make a move—or die. If they stayed any longer they'd be overtaken and they'd be killed. With no alternative, from Chelan they deployed their caravan east toward the safety of the Highway 2 refugee camp. With the gangs moving in, they'd departed in haste. Noah's Ark had gotten off to a bad start, and then it broke down. As far as history knew, the outcome was still unknown.

Ken's group was also ready to deploy on Day 70, but the new information was halting their advance. Instead, they held back and weighed their options. The attack on America was killing its people fast. Even though the EMP was measured in milliseconds, the ensuing consequences were ramping up. By Day 70, things were becoming different. In Washington State—the horror was growing at an alarming rate and there was an army hunting patriots.

With Jim's frontline view of both the refugee camps and the marauders lying in wait, the information he was getting back to Ken was the game changer. There was an evolution occurring, and it was putting evil at the top—fat and happy. Marauders owned the land and they were decimating the groups headed for the border. The camps were getting out of control and the marauders were getting in under the disguise of good. Suddenly, cannibalism to survive was becoming an accepted technique. A decision was required, and unanimously, Ken's group pulled out the wild card.

He was in good company. His group had intelligent minds working together, and like him, strategy was their specialty. They'd seen the writing on the wall since Day 60 and they now believed the refugee camps to be equally as dangerous as staying put. Their decision to hold back, in hindsight, was the correct one. The refugees were out of control. By Day 70, I-90's camp had effectively merged with the city of Spokane, and today, there was well over a hundred thousand people looking for clean water and food.

On Day 70—the same day that Paul's group had narrowly escaped Chelan with their lives—Ken's group chose the alternate plan. Based on the deteriorating conditions between them and the SafePort borders to the east, they would not proceed to the refugee camp on I-90.

Plan B was simple and appropriate. They had well over a hundred members. With each member contributing food stores to the group, in total they had at least another four months' worth of food on hand. They could survive together on the stores they had, and with a defendable location secured, they could keep their stores from getting taken. Ken's Bluff was fifty miles to the north. From there, they could fend off an army if they had to.

One month later, on Day 105, they finally made it. With Jim's help from the air and with a fully armed battalion of determined patriots leading the way, they traversed the fifty miles that cut through the easternmost slopes of the Cascade Mountain range and they made it to Ken's Bluff.

It was the third attempt and it was no picnic. They were lucky. It was only with Jim's aerial surveillance that they avoided the traps and outmaneuvered the enemy. On their first attempt and while crossing the flatlands just east of the Columbia River Gorge, Jim spotted two separate groups of marauders that were strategically positioned on both sides of the surrounding hills. They were both preparing to engage, and with no other option the advance to Ken's Bluff was halted. Unable to proceed or remain, not once, but twice, the group was forced to retreat back to their temporary base camp near the Columbia River.

With Jim's overhead surveillance the key to a successful advance, now it was the weather that controlled the schedule for the next attempt. With several days of low clouds and with time on their side, Ken's group sent out scouts to investigate the two separate locations of marauders that were keeping them trapped. What they'd found was tragic. When the weather cleared, Jim's surveillance confirmed the locations of the atrocities.

Separated by the valley and I-90, it appeared each gang controlled the high point positions of about twenty miles north and twenty miles south of the interstate gauntlet. Coming from the south, that left forty miles of highways and roads rigged for assault against Ken's group. Jim's pictures revealed close to fifty vehicles for each clan, and while most were being used as mobile barricades to ensnare the passerby, all were suspected to be operational. Near every trap, there were shallow pits with dead bodies visible from the air. It was a killing field. What they'd discovered was a horror and it was insanity. It affected all, and "Pay Back" became part of the plan.

As it turned out, Ken's group had talent. Many of its members had battle skills, and attempt number two was nothing more than a practical test.

They needed to see how the enemy groups would advance when tempted, and attempt number two was a ploy. With pre-positioned scouts and Jim in the air, everything needed for an upcoming ambush was gained. It was a beautiful plan and when the weather broke again, the logistics paid off. On Day 105, with blue skies and with Jim high above, the trap was set. The mission had two goals and each was met. The marauders were all dead and Ken's group made their final advance.

It had been a long, hard road. From the beginning, many had died. On this mission alone, they'd lost five, but they were winning. They were on the top of Ken's Bluff, they had all their vehicles, guns, and supplies, and they could defend their position. They were safe, and with a nudge to the odds, evil had lost.

Today, surviving in the wastelands of eastern Washington required help, and there were many other groups like Ken's that were still alive and hanging on. SafePort Flight Ops was tracking several groups near the border, and just recently, Jim had established radio communications and visual contact with several others operating near Ken's group in the central part of the state. Still gazing out the window, he wished his brother's was among them.

"Let it be today, Lord. Just hold on, Paul." The danger was severe, and evil was flourishing everywhere. Without his eye in the sky, Paul had an extreme disadvantage. You need my help—and you need it now. Killers everywhere! Call me, Paul! Thinking hard, he hoped his brother could hear.

The marauders were vile. Their ranks had increased tenfold over the last three months and their primary targets were groups of traveling survivors. With the mass exodus of people headed for the refugee camps on Idaho's border, the open terrain over the last month had become a bloodbath. The preferred method was the roadblock, and with it the marauders were spreading carnage throughout the state. Jim watched it all and he was among the few who knew the big picture. Many had gone insane, and in Washington State there was a deathtrap around every corner.

Typically, the nefarious roadblocks were all staged in small valleys. With a low side and a high side, each one he'd observed had the attackers sheltering in wait on the hillsides above. From high overhead he could see how they strategically placed vehicles and then used them as barricades to trap and corral their prey. The common tactic being used by the marauders was that they'd allow the vehicle or caravan to enter into the trap fully, and then once in, they'd barricade the exits and cinch up the trap. They'd begin their assault from the high ground and the advantage was all theirs.

With thousands looking for free food and supplies to steal, the moving vehicle trap had become the preferred tactic. Like fish nets, they were popping up all over, and from the air Jim could spot them right away. Staged on blind curves; unless you had someone in the air guiding you around, the caravans were easy targets. Once in the trap—they were caught.

Over the last two months, Jim had seen many who had suffered the consequences. Either killed on the spot or left on their own with only a shirt on their back, countless had been robbed of their survival supplies. Both were equally heinous and both constituted murder. For the wicked with no remorse, it was the sin of choice, and where many were initially allowing their victims to walk away with their lives, things were changing.

Jim had seen more and more traps that were engaging in pure evil. With easy food getting harder to find, stealing and killing for supplies wasn't cutting it anymore. There was a shortage of meat, and evil needed to grow bigger and stronger. There needed to be a solution, and to keep the gangs from turning on themselves, they enacted a substitute that would feed everyone. It was vile change in tactics, and the marauders were now treating humans like manna from heaven.

Without his advantage from above on the roadblocks that sought to wreak havoc on Ken's group, things would have gotten deadly on the fifty-mile mission to the Bluff. With Tango Lima, however, the game was changed and the advantage saved the group. Today, and fittingly, that same airplane would land, drop off supplies, and take Ken and his daughter back home to safety.

On Day 1, Jim had only circled Ken's Bluff once before he turned and made his way home. Today, he'd land. He'd drop off the supplies and then he'd load up Ken and his daughter and he'd fly them to Idaho. Yesterday, Ken plowed the runway. This morning on the radio Jim got the all clear. On Day 122 and on Tango Lima, Ken and his daughter were coming home. After four months of hell, it was an amazing feat and it was an astounding accomplishment. He'd done well and he'd saved lives. It was time for a break.

Jim logged his flight plan in the SafePort dispatch binder and he was ready to perform the mission. With a few more minutes before departure, he sat in his chair and slid it over to the windows. He couldn't help but picture Paul, Lisa, and John curled up in the back of a school bus somewhere, freezing and starving and stuck in the snow. He admonished his thoughts, but they kept coming. Knowing them to be unacceptable, he countered. The day would bring good news, he argued. Today, everything could change. Ken was coming home and Paul could call on the radio at any moment. Anything could happen.

He stood up and walked around to the front of his desk. Shake it off, Jim. He stood there, and he reviewed the good. It was a big day. Ken was coming home, and tonight, the President was making his third national radio address. It would be the most important since the attack, and tonight, everyone hoped he'd unite the country with a clear direction and some good news.

So far, this hadn't happened, and it was starting to appear as though both the military and the government may have lost its continuity. Information was either unknown or it wasn't being provided appropriately. Tonight, it was expected to flow. Death rates were skyrocketing and the patriots were being decimated. We need the military—and we need to go in!

He better have a plan, he thought, adding it to his list of hopes which was getting longer and longer every day. The ghastly horrors were just beginning, and the country needed its federal government to step up and lead. The President needed to rally the people, and Jim expected he would.

The day had great potential, and with this, the negative thoughts of his brother's demise were fleeting. Jim grabbed his coat from the rack in the corner. He walked over to the window and he returned his gaze on the blue sky. With Ken coming home and the President's speech, how could he not feel good? This was a special day and life was remarkable.

On top of everything else, the day's itinerary had George and Darlene coming over for dinner tonight. The weekly event was a highlight. With dinner at six—and the President's address at eight, what could be better? Good company and fantastic food were a certainty, and with any luck, good information for the country would finally come.

Jim put his hands on the windowsill. With a sigh, he leaned forward and lowered his head. "Lord, my brother needs help. Help his family and help his group. Let the red Xs be found." His mind was at a loss, but he threw in what he could. "Get us home safe and how about some good news on the country. We're on the edge down here." Looking down, he shook his head. It wasn't pretty, but he hoped he'd covered the bases. "Help us all, and help me do what I'm supposed to do. I'm off to get Ken—amen."

Jim was a manager of very large and complex things. Variables, unknowns, and gaps in the big picture were a nuisance, but specifically, there was a lack of relevant information they should have known by now that annoyed him. SafePort was impressive and everyone was eating, but as he zipped up his winter coat, he couldn't help but shake his head. *We have no idea what's going on, and what about the enemy? This feels like limbo.*

With four months of Hell, the country was confused and still writhing in shock. The health of the nation and its military was unknown—and the people wanted answers. The big picture was obscured, and based on the tragic reports coming from everywhere; there was no telling what the true state of the nation really was. Tonight's speech was an extremely important event. If he left now, he'd fly his route, pick up Ken and his daughter, and be home with an hour or two to spare. It felt like a good day, and if Rob passed the test—he'd sign his paperwork and he'd have a new crewmember.

Grabbing his flight bag, he walked out of his office and headed for the dispatch board. Rob was seated on a stool, and he watched Jim grab the marker and smile. He wrote Rob's name in the crew block column on the large white board. Turning around, he gave the order.

"You're up. And if you pass, I'll sign you off."

Rob leaped off the stool and landed on his good leg. "I'll see you out there," he said, grinning. Hopping on his good foot, he headed out the tarmac door, but before it closed, he stuck his crutch out to stop it. He poked his head back inside, and with an awkward confidence, he lowered his brow and nodded. "Thanks for the opportunity, Jim! I'll work hard."

Sitting in the crew room next to the tarmac door, Jerry couldn't resist. With Rob outside, he stood up and poked his head around the corner. "Did he just say, thanks for the opportunity?"

"Yep, sure did." Jim walked over and handed him the flight release form.

He signed it and then smiled. "Good pick on that guy. I like the way he thinks, and he's smart." Handing the form back to Jim, he stood there and waited for his eyes to come off the paperwork. "By the way, I closed Alpha Two this morning. Don't use it. I'm stashing my snow there."

"Got it," he said, moving his eyes back on Jerry. "No Alpha Two. And we're out of here. See ya soon."

Jerry opened the door and he patted Jim's shoulder. "Go get the boss. Find Paul."

CHAPTER 21

REFUGEES, PATRIOTS, *AND* MARAUDERS

Dispatched at 0900, they departed on time and the weather was thirty-two degrees and sunny. With Jim at the controls and with Rob learning the ropes, Tango Lima flew her standard surveillance route to the south and they were at 3,000 feet above the ground. Currently over the Pend Oreille River near the western border of Idaho, they had a good view and they were following the state line that separated Kootenai County's SafePort border with Washington State. Twenty miles ahead, they'd turn right. They'd cross the border at I-90, and they'd fly over the main refugee camp where tens of thousands were trying to survive in the cold.

The large interstate highway entered into the state of Idaho through the city of Post Falls. The state's western border was on lockdown, and with the help of the railway system from adjoining territories to the east, Idaho's Safe-Port was funneling as much food and water as they could into the refugee camps in Washington State. With the civil defense forces manning the border, the Civil Air Patrol watched from above, and the system worked. Safe-Port was able to hold the lines. Corridors of food, water, and supplies were making it into the camps, and where the lawlessness was getting worse, Safe-Port was saving lives—at least for now.

It was here on the state line where the flatland's of eastern Washington ended, and eastward, the mountains of Idaho began. Fifteen miles to the east was a large lake, full of fresh, clear water. Known as Lake Coeur d'Alene, the terrain was visibly stunning and both the lake and its city were nestled at the base of the Bitterroot Mountains. If one were to continue east, Interstate 90 followed the lake's shoreline and then it went up-and-over the mountain pass into Montana.

West of the refugee camp, and throughout central Washington; it was desolate. For nearly two-hundred miles to the west the land was barren and dry. Without irrigation, it was void of any meaningful nourishment, but eastward into the SafePort states—into Idaho, Montana, and beyond—the land was fertile and hardy.

Just ahead, there was a barricade that separated the two—and Rob was about to see what it looked like. He'd been wondering for months, and he couldn't picture it in his mind, but today he'd see it all and he was getting anxious.

Over the last thirty days, the full weight of the HEMP attack was beginning to surface and SafePort's Civil Air Patrol mission was expanding. With the rapid influx of survivors on foot, the refugee camp populations were exploding and overhead security was increasingly required. The risks were becoming severe, and aerial surveillance was the only way to mitigate the danger to Idaho.

Where the two camp perimeters had been formed by the refugees themselves, they were now part of controlled territory, and if Jim's plan worked—he'd have enough crewmembers for the upcoming mission. SafePort had a strategy, and the civil defense forces were preparing to advance into the refugee camp territory. Starting next month, law and order would be regained, and to pull it off, the expanded readiness of his flight department was mandatory.

Thankfully, his first applicant was sitting next to him, and if he passed the final check, he'd sign him off as an official crewmember. There was nothing standard about the test, and to be approved as a crewman it required a unique set of emotional skills. It was all about his mental fitness, and today he'd assess Rob in the field. He'd test his reason, his focus, and his emotional stability in a time of war. There were bad things ahead, and the first test was almost here. It was a heart-stopper, and where Jim expected courage, he also expected shock and anger.

The current size and scope of the refugee crisis was now on a need-to-know basis, and Rob was about to learn the brutal truth. There was no correct way to respond, but a balanced understanding and a stable attitude was an essential requirement.

Approaching ground-zero, today he'd see the crime scene first-hand, and it was in a place where the survival of man had been swindled and stolen. From the safety of the King Air, he'd see the suffering up-close, and he'd observe the indescribable.

From the air, both camps resembled a wide funnel which then compacted into two tight corridors along the two major highways entering into Idaho's panhandle. Camps were being established on both I-90 and Highway 2—and with both camps growing at alarming rates, SafePort's ability to distribute food and water to the masses was becoming less effective and increasingly difficult.

Where law and order used to be controlled by the refugees themselves, it was now becoming impossible, and with the new arrivals there appeared to be internal battles getting out of control. Marauders were infiltrating the camps, and where Jim had been tracking several approaching groups, he knew that several had gotten in.

I-90's camp was the big one, and as they flew south along the state border it would soon come into view. Behind them, and almost fifty miles to the north, Highway 2 was the other major freeway into Idaho—and today they'd make a big circle and they'd overfly the northern camp on their way home. The refugee camp on Highway 2 was significantly smaller, but it too was growing rapidly.

Highway 2 was the biggest threat to Bonner County's survival zone. As a crow flies, its location was only twenty miles to the west of Jim's home on the river. Everyone in town knew it wouldn't take much for a single camp to unite and then overrun the entire zone. A breach in the border was a major concern, and it was the primary mission of both the ground forces and aerial surveillance to ensure that it never happened. It was estimated the camp on Highway 2 had a current population of forty-thousand, and roughly half had arrived over the last two weeks. I-90's estimates were off the charts, and with its merge into Spokane the numbers were unknown.

Today's flight was special, and for both occupants it was profound. Upon completion of the southern route, they'd then turn west and they'd perform the rescue mission that everybody had been waiting for. They'd land at Ken's Bluff, and then on departure they'd have two extra passengers. Ken and Samantha were coming home. Secondly, and of equal importance, their return leg would intersect with Highway 2 at the last known location of Paul's group. The flight home would commence with four sets of eyes, and with the advantage, Jim was feeling the potential. Heroes were coming home. Others might be found. Just like Rob, he was getting anxious too.

With clear blue sky and with Tango Lima and all her systems running strong, it was a good day and the border was looking status-quo. It was time to get busy, and it was time for Rob. Jim had several goals—and the first was to assess standardized procedures. The right-seat crewmember had special duties and today's observations needed to be documented properly. It was Rob's new job, and with his clipboard and binoculars he was executing the task in accordance with his training.

Jim was giving him a snap-shot and it would be Rob's base-line observation from this point forward. From Sandpoint south, he identified all the known survival groups and homesteaders that were setting up shop outside the range of any SafePort assistance, and he showed Rob all the components that required a constant measurement of normal activity. Anomalies were the concern, and as a surveillance crewmember he had to be able to recognize all changes.

Now elevated, and for good reason; a primary function was to alert the defense forces of any large incursions, and to document the locations of large groups amassing at critical points along the northern border. Rapid Response Teams were on call and ready for any large-scale breach, but as of yet, it hadn't happened.

Over the last two weeks, and following two weeks of bad weather with no flights at all, Jim had observed a dramatic influx of people establishing homesteads along the riverbanks near the border. It didn't surprise him, and he'd been wondering when they'd show, but the one's that got his attention were just outside the humanitarian aid boundaries of the Highway 2 refugee camp. They were on the Idaho side of the river, and it was an odd place to be, but if you were a survivalist who didn't want to be a refugee—it was perfect.

Within Idaho, many citizens were setting up homestead camps along the shores of lakes and rivers, and they were doing it for good reason. It was the logical result of North Idaho residents leaving their snowed-in homes to survive the winter. If you lived outside the plow zone, sustenance acquisition was becoming difficult, and for some it was nearly impossible.

For many, harvesting easy water and sharing emergency food to keep their families alive during the winter was becoming the best choice. Over the next several weeks, he expected more to make the leap, but he suspected the people he'd observed near the border were likely doing it for other reasons. His best guess—they were clever Washingtonians. They'd simply crossed the river and they set up camp outside of the SafePort system. They weren't asking for help. They weren't refugees. They were Americans surviving off the land, and it was a good thing.

So far, these isolated intrusions were only being documented and the general rule was to leave them alone. Jim believed the SafePort regulations did nothing to preclude any citizen from self-survival, and if the good people slipped in, and if they set up their camp so they could survive on their own, well good for them and way to go. There were hundreds of miles along the Rocky Mountains that could be accessed within Idaho and Montana, and he hoped and suspected there were many thousands there now. Living off the land and feeding your own family was the American way.

On every over-flight, he'd cheered for the homesteaders on the river, and today he even rocked his wings in a "way to go" salute. If he were in their shoes, he'd be somewhere on a river and he'd be far away from large groups. Even with the sustenance being delivered into the camps, with the chaos and lawlessness, there was likely more food and a better chance at survival away from the starving people. Provided you had the skills to pull it off, the wilderness was where it was at, and it seemed to be the one and only choice that came with any dignity.

Happy with Rob's performance, he'd documented everything appropriately and it was time to head west. With I-90 approaching, Jim made the right turn, and at 10,000 feet they were headed for Washington State. Fifteen miles ahead; the hills and the forest met the eastern edge of the valley, and in a matter of seconds, the perimeter of I-90's refugee camp would be clearly visible.

With anxiety filling the cockpit, the picture forming ahead was

indescribable. It took about thirty-seconds for the visual to fully material-
ize in Rob's mind, and when it did, Jim watched it happen. He'd been there
himself and he felt bad for the first-timers. As he flew closer, he waited for
what he knew was coming. There was distress, and he could feel it mounting.

"My God!" Rob cleared his throat and his heart started to pound. "I
didn't …"

He stopped talking and raised his binoculars. He scanned the camp and
it wasn't what he expected. "This is huge! What the hell?"

Back on his binoculars, he started to focus in on the people.

"They're skin and bones. There's thousands." Scanning the interior of
camp, he stopped and put his binoculars down.

"I had no idea. That's a death camp, Jim."

He could feel a lump in his throat and he swallowed. "They're all dying.
And they're freezing. How do they survive?"

"Most don't." Jim pointed to one of the mass grave sites and he told Rob
to look closer. "That's just one. They're all over."

Rob had it in focus and Jim could see his anger.

"I know I'm supposed to be composed, but I'm not." Leaning back, he
sighed. "I'm pissed! And I apologize."

"It's normal. It's what I expected."

He needed Rob to soak it in and he pointed to the smoke that was billowing into one large cloud near the center of the camp. Now at 5000 feet,
Jim's flight path was traversing the southern edge of the camp's populations.
There were hundreds of cooking and warming fires from all directions and
they peppered the landscape below.

The plumes of smoke from each fire rose to about a thousand feet and
then they merged at the center of the camp into one dark billowing layer.
Visibility within a ten-nautical-mile radius of center was nil. The smell of
fire and smoke began to infiltrate the cabin of the aircraft. There was a bad
taste in the air, and their eyes started to sting. The odors of burning rubber
and other unknowns were heavy and Jim banked the aircraft upwind. He
was ready to pull the oxygen masks if they didn't get clean air soon.

The camp's radius had grown a good mile since his last flight two days
ago. Every time he was here it was a difficult sight to endure, but in the
King Air they were only getting the sanitized version from overhead, and

like spectators, they were only getting the view from the outside looking in. Other than the SafePort scouts and the survivors themselves, few on the outside had a grasp of the true horrors existing on the ground.

He tapped Rob's shoulder and pointed forward. "Up here by the mall is where the food and water stops. We've got ten distribution sites throughout the camp, and this is the closest one to Spokane."

"What about Spokane? Does any food get into the city?"

Back on his binoculars, Rob could see thousands of muddy tents and they were all packed into the mall parking lots.

"Not anymore. The city's off limits. They have enough trucks to manage the delivery, and we send in tons of food, but it's all run by the refugees. There seems to be a line—and its right up here. Nobody will cross it anymore."

With a glance to his right, he could see the reality flooding in fast, and he knew it was like a fire hose. He needed Rob to see the bigger picture and he needed him to process it quickly.

"Because they didn't want SafePort, they didn't want a backup system to distribute food and water. What you're seeing below is the penalty for that— and it's extreme. We have trainloads of food, but if we sent it all in, it'd just sit on the tracks. Eventually, the marauders would raid it, and none of it would ever get to the people. Without a protected and prearranged system, emergency food distribution is impossible—and they knew it. Because they wanted the people weak, this is the consequence."

His eyes scanning the ground, Rob thought about the betrayal, and he wanted pay back. He wanted vengeance, but he didn't want Jim to see his anger. He was at a loss for words, but he had to say something.

"I can't believe what I'm seeing. It's unbelievable."

"Yep, it's bad. But we're trying and it's the best we can do. Until we get our supply chain through Spokane and into the rest of the state, the food ends here."

Jim pointed down. "That's why the crowds are here."

He chuckled, but it was in a defeated tone. "Food and water. The last dining room is straight down there. Everything to the west is strictly self-survival."

His head tilted, he turned. "This is where it gets bad. And it's a lot worse than you've heard."

Only twenty-miles to the west of Idaho's border; Spokane, Washington was a big city for being in the middle of nowhere. With its population of a quarter-million, there were a lot of dead people and there were a lot of people on the edge. The city had become a haven for gangs, and likewise it had become the final barrier between hope and despair. For the survivors headed east with their families, Spokane was becoming a trap few could escape.

It was a bad setup, but it came with the deal. All people traveling out of Washington State and headed east on I-90 had to first successfully divert and go around—or navigate through the city of Spokane to get to the border's refugee camp on the other side. It was precisely why Ken's group had aborted the plan and opted for the Bluff, and it was the right choice.

"I heard it's like the Old West down there." Back on his binoculars, Rob was looking for any activity near the edge of the city.

Banking to the right, Jim established a large circling pattern over the mall, and then he corrected his crewmember. "Nope. You heard wrong. Try the Old West with the marauders who want to kill you for food. It gets worse, but we'll leave it there."

Looking out the window, Roberto could feel his gut telling him to listen and learn. He'd been avoiding the subject for weeks, but today was different.

"So, it's true? They're eating the people down there? That's how the marauders are thriving?"

Jim was expecting the question, but he could only give the short answer for now.

"Yes. And I'll brief you on it later. When it's official, you'll have full access. You'll be part of the team that collects the evidence."

The line needed to be crossed and he was measuring his new applicant carefully. He needed to push, and he believed Rob had what it took, but he'd do it slowly and he'd let his crewmember decide for himself. He'd give him one more clue, and then he'd move on.

"All I can say is that the atrocities are rampant, and it's not like the Donner party down there. They're killing for food. They're demanding allegiance and they're taking full control of the state. You wouldn't believe what our cameras are documenting."

Tango Lima had special cameras mounted on its belly, and from inside the crew was able to control its functions from a touch screen mounted on the center instrument panel. It took Jim a few days to catch-on, and now it was Rob's turn. He cleared all functions and turned the cameras off.

"Jerry told me you had this down, so let's do a test. How about a forward pan, 160 degrees, down thirty. And give me a two-mile ground track on the rear camera."

Rob punched it in like a pro, and he was passing the test nicely. Jim checked his clock and it was time to depart for the Bluff. Still circling, he added some power and started a climb.

Rolling through due west, the King Air was now at 10,000 feet and over the western edge of the city. Still climbing, Jim leveled the wings and established a northwesterly heading toward Ken's Bluff. It was a hundred-plus miles away—and he set the autopilot so that it would level off at 15,000 feet. It was time to discuss the battlefield.

Rob's understanding was required. He was angry, and it was appropriate, but was it balanced? Did he understand what was going on, and could he perform the mission? He'd give him a few minutes, and if his crewmember didn't open the conversation, he would.

Still struggling, Rob was trying to conceal his emotions. Somebody needed to pay. It was the politicians and the marauders, and it was all he could think about. But why did they do it? And how did the marauders become so evil?

This is a crime, he thought. We were all betrayed! His mind was searching, and he was mad.

In defeat, he looked to his boss for help.

"It doesn't make any sense, Jim. This was an inevitable attack, and if we'd all prepared, we'd all be safe. They took that away."

While Jim nodded, Rob took a deep breath and sat up straight. "Last week I heard Jerry say we've known about this for decades. He said that because the groups controlling the mainstream messaging didn't like the storyline, it never got out until the President started talking about Safe-Port. He said SafePort was the establishment's worst fear, and he said it was all about our guns. He said they were trying to steal America—and they needed us weak."

Raising his brow, and before Jim could respond, he continued. "I think he's right, but it still doesn't make any sense. I mean, we all knew this was coming. And how could those people still believe in those politicians? They distorted the truth, and everybody with a brain knew they were lying. It was so obvious, and I don't understand how they pulled it off. Is this what they wanted? I don't get it."

Now facing forward and with his eyes distant, he was in the muck and he could feel himself sinking. He'd asked the hard questions, but his mind kept coming up with more. Nothing made sense. Watching the evolution, Jim was about to respond, but Rob wasn't done yet.

"The system works ... so why didn't they do it? Makes no sense. It seems wrong. Criminally wrong! Washington, Oregon, California; all of them, Jim. And what about the East Coast? They should've all been SafePorts!"

Rob cleared his throat and did his best to shrug off the gloom that was setting in. With earnest tone, he turned.

"It's the hoax that gets me." Looking down, he fumbled with his cast.

"Millions believed, and I was one."

Turning to Jim, he shook his head. "It was my mom. She believed, and so did I, but then we didn't. It was psychotic, and it was obvious, so we walked away."

Still fumbling, he raised his head and sighed. "I thought everybody would see, but I was wrong. Jerry says they're building armies and they're calling us the enemy. He says it's just like before—but I still don't get it. It doesn't make any sense. Why wouldn't they feel betrayed? And why would they hate us? There's no logic here."

At 225 knots, the approach into Ken's Bluff was another fifteen minutes down the road and the subject had to be addressed. Jim had the short answer, and Rob was asking the right questions. He'd heard Jerry's two-cents, but he needed the full story and he'd get it. The evidence was substantial, and he'd start with the basics.

"There's a good answer for that, but it has nothing to do with logic. It's all part of a bigger plan—and there's a major glitch we need to understand." With no course guidance, he was navigating over the ground and he could see that he was drifting.

"For starters, this isn't what our deceivers had in mind. They fulfilled an important role by seducing half of our populace, but the attack on

America—and what we see outside our windows—this is the result of something far more powerful than our elitist establishment. In hindsight, we can see the framework and it explains everything."

Fighting a cross-wind, he was following a lone road and he was headed for a snowy hilltop that was now visible on the horizon. Twenty-miles south of Ken's Bluff there was a known caravan camp and he wanted to overfly it and show Rob. He had ten minutes, and he'd talk fast.

"So you might be too young, but I don't think so. Look at what we've witnessed over the last decade."

Turning to his crewmember, he laid it out. "Suddenly, the abnormal became normal, and all the lessons we were taught as children were reversed. We saw our elitist government using the temptation of entitlements, and the lure of open borders to change our culture into something new. We knew that it was a power grab—and we knew they were trying to vote us out, but we were stunned. They called us racist and immoral, but still, they expected our trust. We were the targets, we were the victims, and we didn't know what to do."

His attention spread, Jim prepared for the approach while he continued. "Remember what it was like when everything changed?"

He held out his fingers and started counting. "We learned that our enemies could wipe us out with a single weapon. We had congressmen warning us that the countermeasure was being concealed and we had a new President that told us everything about SafePort. Suddenly, we were united. We had a President on our side, and he led the patriots in defending the country. Our strength allowed us to vote out the establishment and demand justice. Freedom was winning, and then we uncovered their crimes. Remember what happened then?"

Rob was nodding. "Yeah! They called us liars. They doubled-down."

"Exactly. And it's that state of mind we've got to remember here. They have no remorse. They'll do anything for more power—and they'll do anything not to get caught. These are the common criminals who found power in American politics and they concocted a sinister plot. Evil is evil and we've got to remember they have no sorrow."

Sighing, Jim had a chuckle in his exhale. "Think about it. Using all the basic sins; evil consumed half of America. It convinced its followers to shut down free speech, and it told them they needed safe-spaces. They stopped communicating with anyone who disagreed, and then suddenly, our nation became split between the SafePort states and the states who believed in something strange and un-American."

With the caravan camp getting close, Jim started a slow descent and kept talking.

"All the while, and this is the key element we've got to remember. When America was being attacked from within, and when America was being weakened by its conspirators, evil was empowering our enemies with a radical religion, radical agendas, and a secret weapon. It was a grand plan—and this is it—but it required us to be weak, and it was supposed to take out the patriots. We were the only target evil had to destroy and we were the only living force standing in its way. The sheep were incidental, but we the reasonable had to be taken out, and we're still here."

With his eyebrows raised, Rob turned. "So we're the glitch. We live, America wins."

"Yep. And I know this doesn't answer your question, but hold on. When we woke up, we defended ourselves and we changed everything. When we defied evil, they doubled-down. They refused to defend, and they refused to be wrong. Remember what we were finding out just before we got attacked. They were all criminals, and just like the bank robber they only wanted the cash. They weren't concerned about jail—and they weren't concerned about HEMP. All they wanted was to secure their power—and they were willing to do terrible things to acquire it. They had to win—and as long as they did—there'd be profits with no consequence. They'd steal the money and they'd shoot their way out. Whatever it took."

Looking out the window, he pointed to the ground. "First thing you need to know. The bad people are winning down there. They're winning because an extraordinary amount of people are exercising evil without any consequence. They have no remorse, they're killing patriots, and they're getting away with it. It's a catastrophic formula, and it's a product of the hoax, but we need to be careful with our assessment. It's not the liberals versus conservatives and it has nothing to do with political viewpoints."

He turned. "That's how they pulled it off, Rob. They took the two political views our republic is built upon, and then they tried to convince us that it was simply a natural dispute between the two. It was a bait-and-switch, and that's how the abnormal became normal. Under the guise of good, the radicals hopped on, and with a disguise they became the new Democratic Party. Our deceivers said it was a natural evolution, but we the reasonable knew otherwise."

Jim wanted to be honest, and he smiled. "Just like you. I believed them too, but then I saw the deception and I ran. So when I say 'we the reasonable' … I mean we who seek the truth."

He was deep in the weeds, but he needed to be clear. "Just remember—the marauders have no remorse. These are the people who were exploited by the ruling class and now they're a cult. Both the elitists and the radicals wanted more power, and so they used nefarious tactics to achieve it. They used our presumptive trust. They convinced the uninformed and impressionable that they were ordinary liberals who were fighting for justice. The Republicans, the conservatives, and all their opponents were evil people, and it's okay to hate them because the Democratic Party says it's righteous and proper."

"That's what they did, Jim! Psychological warfare. Betrayal."

"Yep, and our history proves it. After the patriots united under SafePort the elitist went crazy. They had to make their followers hate us even more—and so they did. They said the Safe States were evil, and so were the people who lived there. They went after Christians and Jews, they said the American patriots were Nazi's, and they sided with the Muslims. It was a coup. Some could see through it, but some couldn't."

Leveling off, he added power and finished his statement. "They hated us back then, and now they've lost their food and water." Scanning his instruments, he thought about the new reports coming in from Seattle. "It's different now. It's far more than hatred."

For Rob, the mechanics were becoming clear and he could feel his instincts learning. "They need to be dealt with," he said, staring out his side window. "How many? Do we have numbers?"

"Not yet. But we're on it and I'll brief you later." Jim liked what he was hearing and he was ready to certify Rob and make it official. "As far as the plan goes, we'll talk about it, but there's a take-away, and I've got a final question."

With the caravan camp approaching, he had two minutes and he could do it in one. He turned to Rob and gave him the spiel.

"Just remember the basics. The marauders are forming armies—and they're decimating the good people who are trying to survive. We don't know who they are, but they're thriving at an alarming rate and they've assumed the same core hatred for patriots that we observed before. The refugees are different. And because evil lurks everywhere, you'll see terrible things happening down there, but for the most part they're heroes. They've accepted their fate and they've survived without killing or stealing. Its good against evil, Rob. It's a big mess, and we've got to figure it out."

He grabbed the approach checklist and set it on his lap. "For now, our purpose is limited. We expose they're crimes. We look for they're weaknesses, and we assist the forces of good. We learn the battlefield. We wait to do more."

Looking forward, he reduced the power and began a shallow turn. "If you want I'll sign you off and you can join the club. Your call."

"Was that the question?"

"Yep. You're good to go."

"Then I'm in."

"Good." Jim's attention was on the ground and he pointed to an old pickup on the side of the road.

"Get your binoculars' out on that truck down there. This used to be a survival camp."

Rob focused in on the truck and Jim zoomed in with the cameras. There was nobody in the area and the camp looked vacated.

"Looks abandoned." Rob could see their make-shift shelters next to the stream between two hills, but he couldn't see any people. "How many were here?"

"We've got it at thirty-three souls. They had eight vehicles here two-weeks ago." Jim was reading the surveillance logs and he knew the camp had been in contact with SafePort Flight Ops for almost a month now.

"I don't see any fowl play here." He made a note and then closed the logbook. "Let's hope they've moved to another location. We've got a two-day lag on these surveillance logs, and the communication logs take even longer. You'll need to research this when we get back."

Banking the aircraft hard right, Jim headed for Ken's Bluff and he could see it in the distance. With the rolling hills behind them, the smooth terrain below resembled a sea of thin white snow and the Bluff looked like a flat rock sticking up in the middle of nowhere. Like a ship spotting the shoreline, Rob pointed straight ahead.

"Is that it?"

"Yep. That's it."

He raised his binoculars and took a closer look. "Wow. Sure looks small."

"Plowed and prepped last night, so we're good to go." Jim cinched up his shoulder harness and then scooted his seat up a notch.

"You should strap yourself in tight for this one."

Jim looked over to his copilot and smiled. "Sorry bud. Couldn't help it. The approach is pretty cool and I can guarantee the views are unlike anything you've seen before."

He watched Rob tighten up his shoulder harness. "Actually, it's a very stable approach. Hardly any wind out here so the landing should be nice and calm."

With a read of his copilot's body language he could tell that he was getting nervous. "No worries worries, Rob. The landing's going to be fine. We've got five thousand feet of runway and that's twice what she needs. I know it looks small, but just wait until we get on short final. It'll look way worse."

Jim smiled again, and then so did Rob. "Good. You're ready. And I promise it'll be safe. You'll see."

"I'm ready. No fear." He had his binoculars back up and he could see the runway. "And it does look pretty cool."

"Well there you go. Embrace it."

Jim handed him the approach and landing checklist. He wanted Roberto focused on a duty, and better yet, he wanted him to learn. There was no better time than the present, and with his help, Tango Lima descended and then maneuvered for a five-mile straight-in approach to the runway at Ken's Bluff. She was here to save the day. She had loads of water, medical supplies, and two passenger seats to whisk Ken and his daughter back home.

It was a good day and it was about to get better. It felt historical.

CHAPTER 22

RESCUE

Ken's Bluff, Eastern Washington
1100 AM: Pacific Standard Time

With five hundred feet to go, the final approach to the runway was smooth. Rob's death grip on the dashboard was loosening, and it seemed that now in the final seconds of the flight, he was actually enjoying the view.

Both unique, and visually stunning, Ken's Bluff was the unofficial name for a small outcrop of rock that formed a small mountain in the middle of nowhere. Positioned near Quincy, Washington, the rock protrusion had a flat top and steep cliffs all the way down. It rose up sharply from the desolate valley floor, and like an oasis in the middle of the desert, its position was approximately twelve miles from the vegetation-rich tree line on the eastern slopes of the Cascade Mountain Range. Its highest point above the surrounding valley floor approached three hundred feet—and its diameter was a good two miles.

In the wintertime months, the natural formation created the appearance of a snowcapped island that was in the middle of a frozen white sea. It was one of a kind, and it was Ken's father who had the foresight to capitalize on its advantages. The flat terrain on top extended from edge to edge, and the private runway made it into a very special location.

Built to maximize length, the paved runway could handle the weight and performance requirements of most midsized aircraft. For the King Air it had more than enough strength and length, and it was right in front of them. Approaching fast, the runway threshold was a hundred feet ahead. The sharp edge of the cliff was just now passing below. Descending at 120 knots, the ground was moving in rapidly.

With final confirmation of the wheels down and locked, Jim had his landing flaps deployed and he finessed the airplane so that it would float down. With a foot to go, he could feel his wheels skimming the snow, and then suddenly they were on the runway.

"Nice and soft," he said, smiling. His throttles at idle, he didn't need reverse and the King Air was slowing down. "Told you it was pretty cool."

"It is, Jim." Taking it all in, Rob could see the buildings sitting on top of the small hill that overlooked the runway. "This is a big setup. Is it all Ken's?"

Approaching his preferred taxi speed, Jim gave him the quick rundown.

"It used to be his dad's and then Ken got it. We've put a lot of work into this place and it's fully stocked. It's a lifeboat, and it's hard to believe."

The timing was significant, and for Jim it felt like a dream. "These people are set," he said stowing the checklist. "Check out those two buildings above the barn."

"They both have wood stoves, propane heat, full kitchens, bathrooms, and even showers. They're industrial, but they can shelter a lot of people and each one has a shielded generator."

Jim pointed to the barn that was that was at the end of the tarmac. "You see those two red shielding containers over there? Those are the backup parts and they're both stuffed. Well pumps, generator parts, solar power, you name it and it's in there."

Jim could see the barn door open and he knew that it was Ken walking out. He had an orange cone and he was waving it in the air.

"Is that him?" Rob asked.

"Yep. That's him." Jim turned on his landing light, and then he turned it off. "He's got a beard."

The King Air's engines were smooth, and as he taxied towards the barn they purred in the cold crisp air. The snow was light and fluffy and the flakes in the prop wash whooshed off the ground and then swirled into the air. Behind the King Air was a screen of billowing snow, but standing in front was a man that Jim knew well, and he was smiling.

Slow and steady, he taxied up to the orange cone triangle that Ken had placed in front of the barn. With his nose-wheel at the forward cone, he cut the fuel and set the brakes. They were here, and the silence came rushing in.

At first there was a wind down of the engine noise, but then it faded and it became ultra-quiet. The anticipation was nearing its peak—and Jim could feel his senses operating at maximum. He performed the shutdown checklist, and he could hear Ken chalk the nose wheel. He heard the snow crunching under his feet, and then he heard the familiar sound of three loving taps on her left-side wingtip. Suddenly, the sound waves from the rotating door latch filled the air and the two worlds were about to meet. Everything seemed extra loud, and it felt like victory.

From the outside, Tango Lima's door fell into the waiting arms of her one true owner. Like holding a lady's hand, gracefully, and with a bend in his knees, Ken lowered it down. Jim still had his headset on and he was finalizing his checklist items when he realized he had a smile that couldn't be removed. He peeled it off and turned around.

In the middle of the passenger cabin, their eyes met. Ken hadn't shaved in months and his beard concealed much of his face and expression. The wrinkled up corner of his eyes and bunched up forehead was a dead give-away. He was grinning from ear to ear, and so was Jim.

"How was the approach?" Ken asked, deflecting his emotion. After four months of war, he and his daughter had almost died. Jim and the airplane were the blessings of a lifetime, and right now he didn't want his emotions to get in the way of anything.

"It was good," he said with a nod to his copilot. "And it's good to see you. About time, huh?"

Standing in the center aisle, Ken walked between the water bags and headed for the two passenger seats at the front of the cabin. With his head down, he put his forearms on top of the seat-backs and looked up.

"It's good to see you, Jim. And you should know—the folks around here are pretty happy to see this King Air land. I don't know if you can hear them, but they're all cheering inside that building over there."

Ken's smile was at full. "Gentlemen, it's a good day at the Bluff," he said walking back to the cabin door. He popped his head outside and waved to the group that was looking down from above.

Ken reentered the cabin. As he did, he walked toward the cockpit staring dead center on the new guy. "Hey Rob. It's a pleasure," he said, hand extended. "Those are your's?" Ken was pointing to the crutches.

"Yes sir. They're mine. Stupid logging accident, but it's getting better."

"Good. And I'm glad you're here. There's a convoy of wheelbarrows coming down to help with the water, so hop on out and stretch your legs. We'll send the doc down to pick up the med's—and Jim, you come with me. We won't be long."

Rob stayed with the airplane, and Jim went with Ken. Standing on the tarmac, he could see Ken leading the way up the gravel path and then they both disappeared around the corner.

How amazing, he thought. The King Air was like a priceless diamond, and he could feel the spotlight shining down. He was here, and he was a part of it, and for now, she was under his watch. He'd protect her with his life and he was thankful for this new duty. Today, the privilege to serve had a new meaning, and for Rob everything had changed.

Walking up the path that led to the mobile home where Ken's father used to live, the two men passed the chain of people that were coming down with wheelbarrows to help Rob unload the water. Both Ken and Jim had been here together several times while flying in supplies, and Jim's first experience was when Ken's dad was still alive. He recognized the overabundance of passing wheelbarrows and he'd used them many times himself. They were the preferred method for hauling supplies from the tarmac to the living quarters, and although the tractor worked too, the wheelbarrows didn't use any gas. Apparently, Ken had adopted his dad's procedures.

Now at the top of the small hill next to the runway, around the next corner they'd continue towards the two steel buildings located in front of and slightly below the mobile home. The mobile home's vantage point was stunning. It was positioned at the highest elevation of the bluff and it overlooked the entire valley on all sides. As they turned the corner, Jim noticed that the right side building's roll up door was wide open.

Both inside and outside, a large portion of the group appeared to be milling about. As they walked on by, Jim looked inside—and right off the bat he saw Samantha. She was in the corner standing over a garbage can. She was peeling potatoes, and then she saw Jim and ran.

With a running limp, she arrived, arms stretched.

"Look at you, Sam. You're okay."

"I'm okay," she said hugging him like a bear. She'd known him since she was a little girl, and Jim was like an uncle.

"Wait till you see my gunshot wound. Clean through. In and out, dude!"

She walked over to grab her makeshift cane that was leaning against the outside of the building, and with a slight side-step limp she laughed at her own awkwardness. She took several steps forward toward Jim and her father—and then she stopped at about five feet out. With her hand cupped over her brow to shield the sun, she tilted her head and smiled at her dad.

"Did you tell him?"

"Nope. I haven't told him yet." He turned to Jim.

"She's staying here. There's a lot to do. Doc needs her help and so do the people. So, I guess I'm glad. I'm proud she's staying."

Ken was looking straight at Samantha, and with one firm nod he'd given her his full respect. Over the last few days he'd been uncertain about her decision, but today he'd come around.

"It's a good decision Sam. I'm with you."

She smiled and shuffled up next to her father. "Thanks Dad. It is a good decision. Plus, I'm the only one who knows where everything is. I've been crawling around this mountain since I was five years old. I'll be fine."

She kissed her dad on the cheek and then, with a pat on Jim's shoulder, she limped back inside to resume peeling her potatoes.

With a matter-of-fact braveness, she walked off and both men stared at her like she was riding into the sunset.

"You know about Pete don't you?" Ken said it, and it broke the gaze. He turned to Jim.

"That's the other reason she's staying put."

Jim looked confused, so he lowered his sunglasses and released the clue. "Pete's one of the deputies that saved us on the pass."

"Ah …" Jim looked down, and then he laughed. "Yeah, that explains it."

Tapping his shoulder, he took pity on his friend. "Linda won't like this, will she?"

"Nope. She'll be mad. And I should have told her, but I just decided this morning. Should be interesting."

With a soft laugh, he motioned to the path and Jim started walking. From behind, Ken kept talking.

"It's a strange world, Jim. The surprises keep coming, but I think I'm getting better with the big ones. I gotta say, this time I'm actually okay with it. Pete's a good guy. And if it weren't for that—this wouldn't be happening."

"Where is Pete?" Jim asked, turning his head. "I'd like to meet him before we go."

"Hunting party."

Now at the bottom of the steps to the mobile home, Jim walked up, and Ken followed.

"Both he and Bickford left this morning for elk. Bick's the other deputy from pass, and Tom's with them too. He's another guy you'll want to meet. We've been watching some small herds come in and out of the valley over the last two weeks. Hard to believe, but there's still meat out there."

At the top of the porch, Ken opened the front door and they both walked inside. At first look, Jim could see that the forward part of the building was serving as the lookout. Spotting scopes lined the windows on all three sides and they had a radio station set up in the middle of this forward room.

While Jim stood and admired the view, Ken threw his coat on the chair and headed for the hallway that extended forty feet back and ran dead center down the middle of the home.

"Back here is the hospital. You need to see this."

Jim followed, and he was impressed.

"Jack Walters is our doc, and we all call him Doc."

Headed toward the back of the building, and at its southern end, Ken was pointing to a room on the left-hand side, and as Jim walked by, he caught the eyes of the doctor. Wearing a surgical mask, he raised his brow and held up his finger in a signal to give him a second.

Inside, he could see there were multiple patients lying on makeshift cots behind the doctor, and three of them raised their heads and waved. Jim waved back and then Ken tapped his shoulder.

"He's anxious to get those meds. We've lost fifteen so far," and then he pointed to the closed door behind him.

"SafePort or no SafePort, the two in here are out of time because they're out of meds they'll never get. The room behind you has three more the doc thinks he can save with what you brought today. We've got twelve more on insulin. Another week—hey would've been out if it weren't for you."

He smiled and scratched his beard. "So that airplane out there. This place here. It works pretty good, doesn't it?"

"Yes. It does."

Nodding, Ken walked to the end of the hallway and stopped in front of the large walk-in closet with two double doors.

"You know," he said opening the doors. "It's the hope that drives us all. Without it we lose."

Walking in the closet, he turned to Jim. "SafePort is our hope. Every time we saw you in the air—you brought it out here. It's powerful Jim, and it's the magic ingredient here."

Scanning the shelves, he continued. "Today, with you and our girl out there—these folks just got a big boost of it, and it means they have a future to look forward to. It's life changing."

He pulled out his packed duffle bag from the top shelf, and while he held it, he looked at his friend.

"Still blows my mind. You got out of Seattle just in time, and now you're here."

Jim rolled his eyes. "I know. Pretty amazing, huh?"

Ken let his duffle bag drop to the floor. "How's Sarah?"

"She's good. We heard Linda told you about her little incident."

"Damn, Jim. She told me about last week." His head tilted, he'd wished Jim had mentioned it sooner, but he understood why.

"I'm just glad she did what she did." Nodding, Ken raised his brow. "They caught us all off guard, didn't they? Day Three—they went insane."

Bending down, he took a knee and he fumbled with the shoulder strap that was now tangled in a series of failed field repairs using duct tape and twine. Looking up, he wanted to get down to business—and it was time to break the ice.

"Shall we talk freely?" He smiled, and then pointed to the radio. "We've had to keep our mouths shut this whole time. Everything we said was being listened to, but we're not on it now, so let's talk strategy."

"I've been holding my tongue, Ken. Where do we begin?"

Back on his shoulder strap, he fumbled while he talked. "Well, let's start with them. They're only getting away with the carnage because they're not being watched. You changed that for us, and it's why we've got a winning hand. Without aerial support, the Bluff would have never worked. We'd be bunkered down in a ditch, or we'd be dead like all the rest."

Frustrated with the tangle, he stood up and threw his duffle bag on the table. "I know things are getting crazy on the border, and I know you're struggling with getting more airplanes in the air, but I've been working on a simplified plan."

His fingers back on the tangle, he looked up. "I assume you're preparing for phase two?"

"Yes. But we're behind the curve."

While Ken struggled with his bag, he'd put it in context. "It's all about organization, and these first few months have been chaotic to say the least. It's the nature of the beast, but it's getting better. We've got an offensive planned for next month, and its coming together."

He'd give him the short story, and he'd summarize the details, but just as he spoke, the bedroom door opened and it was Doctor Walters.

"You're Jim—and you've got a present for me," he said extending his hand. "I'm Jack, and it's good to meet you."

"A pleasure to meet you, Jack." Jim shook his hand, and then he pulled out an inventory list from his coat pocket. "As requested, it's all in the cooler on the airplane. If you go down there, Rob will show you where it is."

"You brought the full order?"

"Sure did. It's all there."

Doctor Walters threw on his jacket and headed for the door. As he grabbed the doorknob, he stopped and turned around. "So Rob is at the airplane now?"

"He's the tall lad with a cast on his foot. Let him know who you are and he'll show you where the cooler is."

Moving his eyes onto Ken, the doctor raised his brow. "This changes everything!"

He turned around and opened the door. As it often did, the wind had picked up, and he struggled to keep the buffeting door open while he stepped outside. With the wind working against him and his right hand pushing the door closed, he caught Jim's eyes inside.

"Thanks, Jim," he yelled. "We're cooking with fire now!" The door closed and he was off.

"Doc's happy," Ken said smiling. "I told you this was a good day on the Bluff."

Jim sat down on the chair next to the table and he put his hands in his jacket pockets. "He's right, though. It changes everything."

By no means was he a tactician and he had no military experience, but Jim knew the Bluff was something special. It was an outpost. It was well defended. It was a sanctuary, and it was managed by the survivors themselves.

"So I mentioned an offensive. It's only to regain control over the refugee camps, and we're still struggling on how to regain control out here. But it's interesting, Ken."

He could feel the potential growing, but it was only a seed and he was still thinking. "This is a small refugee camp out here, and it's the same model we're dealing with over there. I have no doubt we can regain control of the camps on the border, and if we can manage the border, why can't we manage camps out here?"

"Bingo, Jim! That's what I've been thinking too. But then I got another idea."

Head cocked, he smiled. "I've been thinking about this for weeks. From the minute we got here, it suddenly clicked. I've got an idea, but I think it's better if I show you. Let's talk in the air. And then we'll go find Paul."

Ignoring the tangled strap, Ken slung his duffle bag over his shoulder and grabbed his gun. "Let's go."

Looking at each other, they knew they were knee-deep into something highly unusual. Without a word, they headed outside and they walked single-file on the gravel walkway. As they approached the two main outbuildings, they could see the legs of the group's members that were congregated inside. The large roll up door was partially closed, and at four feet up, there were a lot of legs milling about.

Once spotted, the doors came up and the entire group was there to wish Ken good luck. As they approached, Jim stepped back and he watched Ken say his good-byes. With a short speech, he told them that the Bluff was their home for now and that he'd be back very soon. His duty to the group was now best served from the shorelines of SafePort, and he told them the patriots were united in saving America. He gave Samantha a hug, and then passed his baton onto her shoulders. Otto, Lynne, and Betty came over to say their goodbyes and it appeared to Jim the group had become a large family.

While waiting for his two bosses to have their meeting in the mobile home, it seemed Roberto had been talking it up with the group that was corralled in front of the two buildings. He'd told them of the stories and news from his side of the SafePort line, and it appeared he had some charismatic skills.

As Jim signaled for him to accompany them to the aircraft, it was clear he'd gained the hearts of several members. With a genuine "so long" and "see you soon", it almost seemed like he'd known them from the beginning.

Now on their own, all three headed for the King Air. They walked down the hill, and about halfway down, Ken stopped and dropped his bag.

"So, it's quite the view, isn't it?" He turned and then pointed up the hill at the mobile home. "From up there, you can see all this to the north—plus everything else to the south."

Rob was impressed with the location "It feels like we're on top of an island."

"It does," Ken said, nodding. He grabbed his bag, and continued down the hill. "Let's do some circles on our way out, I want to show you a few things."

"Roger." Walking down the hill, Jim was getting curious. It was good to have Ken back, and he missed his style.

Watching his footing as they proceeded down the incline, for a split-second he looked up, and suddenly he could see the large gash that was still healing on the back of Ken's head. He hadn't noticed it before, but from behind he could see it clearly.

"Hell of a scar, Ken."

"I've never seen it before, but I can feel it." Ken started rubbing his head, and then he turned around. "Never did the two mirror thing. I hope Linda likes it."

Jim laughed and so did Rob. Leading the way to the bottom of the trail, Ken stepped off the path and then all three were on the pavement. Thirty yards later, they were at the airplane.

Thanks to a chain gang of helpers and wheelbarrows, Tango Lima's payload of extra water had been fully unloaded and she was ready for departure.

It was time to take the boss home, and with everybody inside—Jim closed the cabin door. Ken hopped in the right seat and Roberto hopped in the back. Starting now—the rescue would commence.

Buckled in his captain seat, he performed his checklist items quickly, and then he fired up both engines, one after the other. With the turbines running, the airplane came alive and then Jim fired up all of her systems.

"Jerry did a good job, didn't he?" Ken was admiring the new surveillance instrumentation mounted on the center panel.

"If it needed replacing, he replaced it. We've got these camera systems on six of our aircraft so far." Jim pushed the button and he activated the touch screen. "It's pretty cool."

He released the brake and the King Air began to roll.

Slow and steady, Jim taxied to the far end of the five-thousand-foot runway, and when ready for takeoff he set the brakes, took a deep breath, and sighed. "It changes everything, Ken. If we can land here on demand, this isn't a rescue mission anymore."

Looking at his friend, he couldn't help but smile at the new advantage. "So we're just giving you a ride home—and that's all. This is SafePort now."

"Yep," he said, nodding. "Just catching a ride home."

Still smiling and with his foot on the brakes, Jim eased her throttles forward and set full takeoff power. With all gauges in the green, he let the King Air roll, and with a tornado of billowing snow the airplane roared down the runway. Within seconds, the magic airspeed was obtained and Jim raised her nose. Seconds later, she leaped off the runway and the valley echoed.

Per Ken's instructions, Jim climbed to an altitude of 500 feet above the ground and then he entered a circling pattern flying clockwise around the Bluff. Pointing out various strategic advantages, Ken provided Rob with a guided tour.

The small mountain had steep cliffs on all sides and it had a corkscrew road carved out of its edge that went all the way around and from the bottom up to the top. From above, its defensive attributes were impressive, and it had a good ten miles of flat terrain where nobody could get close without being seen. Beyond that, and to the north, south, and east, there were a few rolling hills, but ten miles due west, the rugged slopes of the Cascade Mountains rose up dramatically.

Circling through south, the westerly heading toward the mountains was approaching rapidly, and Jim handed over the controls so that Ken could maneuver the aircraft where he wanted. There was an area of rising terrain with trees and large boulders, and it was the closest area that couldn't be seen from the Bluff. As he approached the area of interest, he flew the aircraft so that his target would remain visible to all occupants above the right-side wingtip.

"Right down there," Ken said banking hard right and pointing below. "That tree-line on the sloping ridge is the only blind spot we have out here. If a menacing group were to organize there, they'd be able to see us and we wouldn't even know. It's the only hole in our defense, but we're working on it."

Ken nudged the wingtip down a little farther and pointed. "Next week, we'll have a lookout post, and we're putting it right there. Just in front of that tree-line."

Approaching an easterly heading, he rolled the wings level and turned to his friend. "These are strong people, Jim. They're some of the strongest I've ever known. The one's that made it here—and the thousands of others who are still out there. They're all being hunted down and they all want to fight. They're hardened soldiers, and we've got an army."

His opening statements were over and he'd described the main components. There was another ingredient, and it was time to put it all together. "Here, Jim. You fly. I'll talk."

Intrigued, he was beginning to sense the significance of Ken's battlefield experience. He'd been out here for months and he knew what he was talking about. "Roger," he said, taking the controls. "My airplane. But you've got to spit it out. I feel like I'm missing something here."

Smiling, Ken reached down and slid his chair slide to its most rearward position.

"Okay. Let's start with the basics." Turning sideways, he motioned to Rob to join the discussion.

"Precisely because of the King Air and the Bluff, these folks have been provided with the essential ingredients necessary to survive and fight. We've created a miniature SafePort here, and through our Civil Air Patrol—we're connected to the outside. I know it's a unique situation, and I know it came to us on the fly, but now that we've got it—it's not all that unique. The ingredients are everywhere, and it's a recipe that can be duplicated."

Nodding, he raised his brow. "It can be multiplied. And if done properly—we could defend the territory between here and the border. We could build a supply chain. We could use the armies that are already out here to defend it. We could locate all the refugees that are trapped out here, and we could provide safe passage and run convoys of trucks and trains. We can do it all the way to Seattle, Jim. And we can begin here. Simplified tactics. That's all we need."

Looking back, he pointed with his thumb. "Rob here, he mentioned the Bluff was like an island. What if instead, we thought of it like a ship?"

Scratching his beard, he elaborated. "So, if it was a ship, why couldn't it be several? And of course, we're talking aircraft carriers here."

Ken knew the immense power of his idea and he spelled it out. "It's all about the airplanes, and it's precisely how we win. Not only could we insert survival assets, but we could insert military assets and we could establish surveillance countermeasures around each outpost. In a nutshell, Jim, we could establish our outposts at fifty-mile increments, and we could build a supply chain into Washington State. SafePort gave us the Civil Air Patrol, and this is how we use it."

His head tilted, he smiled. "We need to toss out our airline mentality, Jim. There's an extreme advantage that comes with added risk—and we need to start embracing it. We're not flying the general public, and we're not flying heavy bombers or fighter jets. These are small airplanes, and there a dime a dozen. They can land almost anywhere. We could easily modify I-90, Highway 2, or any road for that matter as an outpost runway, and if we fly 'em like crop dusters we can accomplish the task. I know we've got some hurdles, but it's doable."

Eager to discuss the new concept, Jim pulled back on the throttles and he started a slow descent. "So we create a hub and spoke system linked directly to SafePort, and we set up the outposts in strategic locations along the highways."

Chuckling, the more he thought about it, the more he liked it. "You're right, Ken. We could make it safe. We could base the smaller airplanes along the highway outposts, and we could use the Bluff for larger transport. We can pick our spots, and we can overlap our surveillance. It'd work, but we need a lot more airplanes—and a lot more crew."

"Yep," he said back on his beard. "Those are the hurdles, but they're all solvable."

Ken was nodding and he had a simple solution. "We know the older piston airplanes can all be started with a hand-prop, and if the maintenance department can't fix the ignition systems, then we start 'em up with a hand-prop as part of our normal procedures. We don't need any electronics or navigation. All we need is a handheld radio, a propeller that spins, and a capable pilot that can take-off and land."

His eyebrows raised, the crew arrangement was simple, and it required simplified thinking. "And if we can't find enough pilots, you're a flight instructor, and so am I. In fact, all of our pilots could teach others to fly."

"That's true," he said, nodding. Again he chuckled, and Jim was amazed at the plan being discussed.

"We could do it. Its fair weather flying, Ken. On the older pistons I could have Rob checked out on takeoffs and landings in two-weeks. If we throw out the old standards, give us a hundred applicants and I can give you fifty pilots that can perform the job."

Ken was nodding. "I concur."

"Me too." Standing in the center aisle, Rob leaned forward and he stuck his head in the cockpit. "I could do it, Jim."

"Yes, you could." He gave him a nod and then looked at Ken.

"Keep this to yourself, Rob. And get that cast off."

The Highway 2 intercept was just ahead and Jim was approaching his predetermined starting point for today's search. Still descending, he had a thousand thoughts running through his mind, and using the highways as a runway system was something he'd never thought of. It was a unique circumstance and it was a game changer. They weren't highways anymore. They were long stretches of pavement. With a little man power, the snow and abandoned cars could be easily removed.

Ken's idea had great merit, and the more he thought about it, the more he believed it was the solution to everything. Without a military, the supply chain into Washington State would have to be secured by SafePort's civil defense, and if they didn't do it quickly, the marauders would take over the territory and they'd kill all the patriots who were still trapped. Next month, the refugee camps would be secured, and the next logical move would be to extend the supply chains westward. It was perfect timing, and it was a brilliant idea. His mind was racing, and for Paul, he needed to calm it down.

Approaching his search altitude, Jim raised the nose and added power. "So I'm intrigued and I'll be up all night thinking about this. When you're up to speed, let's set a meeting. I've got a full briefing binder in your truck and it'll fill you in."

"How's tomorrow at 2pm? I've already asked the commander, and he said he'd be there. I'll drive up in the morning and we can talk at your office."

"Works good, Ken. Let's have Jerry there too."

"Excellent!" He knew the plan would work, and Ken could feel the power of an idea that was important. He could see it growing in Jim's mind, and tomorrow it would meet the world. It was becoming real. It was off his chest, and he felt better.

"Now let's find your brother," he said, sliding his seat forward. He grabbed his binoculars and then turned to Rob. "Find his brother and you're a hero."

"I'll try, sir."

With the mission clear, Jim established the King Air over Paul's last known position. Flying at 3,000 feet above the ground, the search was on, and Jim was hoping for something strange. If it was unusual, or if it was out of the ordinary, he'd see it.

"We'll run across several known camps out here, and we'll check them off as we go. We're looking for red X's, but if you see any signs of people on the move or gathered together—point 'em out."

Jim set the cameras, marked his location, and started the clock. All search flights were logged, and the flight tracks determined which areas still needed to be flown. He'd planned his route out last night and he'd used the most recent data. Although some was repetitive, some was new, and with a little good luck, maybe he'd find the sweet spot. Rob was right. It felt like a good day, and his hopes were elevated.

If nothing else—he'd make sure his new crewmember learned the search area, and there was no better way than to give him the reigns. Starting now, Rob would lead the search by announcing what's ahead. He'd manage the search log and all observations. At all documented camps—he'd build his baseline and he'd manage any new findings.

In no time at all, Rob had it down and his attention to detail was impressive. At a slow cruise, they'd already covered the majority of the search zone, and other than a few isolated cars moving down the road, there was nothing new. It was a big area, and there was life down there, but no red X's and no Paul. Another forty miles and they'd be over the Idaho border. Maybe his group got lost? Maybe they went farther north? Maybe they were five-miles ahead?

There was still hope, and Jim was flying a new profile that examined previously unviewed territory. So far, the known camps were all status quo, and he had to assume Paul's group was operating under the same dynamics. There was a new strategy in town and it was becoming obvious that everybody was using it. They were all sheltering near the highway, they were all stopped near a water source, and they were all hiding.

Per the logbook, many had established radio contact within the last two weeks—and Jim knew their most recent communications reaffirmed the common thread of all patriots trapped in Washington State. With the bad weather, most had been held up for nearly a month, but over the last couple of weeks it had gotten much better. The snow wasn't that deep anymore, and it could only mean one thing. They weren't moving because of fear. A change had occurred, and it was the same change that compelled Ken's group to go to the Bluff. People were hiding and they were sheltering in-place. They were scared. The marauders had roaming armies, fleets of vehicles, and superior firepower. Nobody wanted to get spotted, and so they were bunkered down.

Now approaching another known camp, at five-miles out Jim couldn't see any smoke yet—and it was odd. He was slightly north and he took his new vantage point into consideration, but the wind was calm, so he should be seeing it. At three-miles out, he started a descent and altered course for a direct intercept. At two-miles out, there was still no smoke and he brought it to Rob's attention.

"Camp 42 has no smoke."

Coming into view, it was clear they'd let the fire burn out and it was starting to look like nobody was around. The vehicles were still there, but what about the people? Every time and without fail, the sound of the approaching

King Air at low altitude had a morale boosting effect on the stranded people. Most would come out of their shelters and wave to him when he flew by. The camp was directly below, and it wasn't happening this time.

"I was just here," Jim said, cinching up his seatbelt. He set his heading bug and prepared for a course reversal.

"That was two days ago. And why are all the vehicles still there? I counted seven. What's the logbook say?"

"Six." Rob had it in front of him and he was nodding. "So there's an extra?"

"I guess so." Jim looked at Ken. "Let's find out."

Now a good three miles beyond the camp, Jim banked the airplane into a shallow left turn. Seconds later, he followed with a slight descent and then a hard right turn—all the way around. With its wings level, the King Air had reversed course and it was heading back. Jim wanted a closer look.

"No movement," Ken said, steadying his binoculars on the campsite.

"If they were still there—they'd be out in that field, Ken." Descending rapidly, Jim was getting concerned.

"It's just flatland and snow down there." Rob had his binoculars braced against the side window and he was scanning fast. "I see some tracks, but it's just a bunch of ragged circles. Maybe snow machines or ATVs?"

"Keep looking. And look for any tracks coming from that tree-line to the south. I think that black truck is new."

Jim wanted to go lower, but for now he'd hold his altitude at three-hundred feet above the ground. The terrain was flat, and there were no obstacles other than the power lines along the highway and a few areas of dense trees. For a better angle, his ground track approaching the target paralleled the opposite side of the freeway from their first over-flight. This time, and unlike the first, they'd get a clear shot into the center of the camp. The search mission was on-hold, and Jim set the cameras to one-half mile.

"There!" Roberto yelled, standing in the center aisle. He was pointing straight ahead. "I see three ... No—I see four. I've got four people under that black truck down there. They're hiding, Jim!"

"A little to the right," Ken said, pointing. "I want to see what they're doing."

"Roger."

With a quick roll to the right and then wings level, Jim nudged the King

Air in tight. The truck was at the one o'clock position and it was approaching fast. Jim dipped the nose, and with a hundred feet to go, they were low and slow. A little left rudder to keep her flying straight, he lowered the right wing-tip, and then suddenly the bloody scene behind the truck became visible.

In full view, there was a large pit in the snow and it was filled with muti-lated body parts. At first sight, Jim added full power and climbed.

"My God!" he said, banking hard left.

In a steep turn back to the east, he kept the throttles at full and he low-ered the nose for maximum airspeed.

"Limbs and torsos, Rob. Mark it down!"

With the centrifugal force increasing, Rob used his good foot to pivot to other the side of the airplane, and in one fluid motion he had his binoculars back on the crime scene. "Those are humans! What are they doing?"

Looking back, Ken watched as he tried to steady himself against the side window during the turn. He could see Rob's expression and it was painful to watch. The truth hurt, and he was seeing it now.

"That's the Devil, Rob. He's in their minds. Those were the marauders."

As Jim leveled the wings, Rob stood up in the center aisle and he braced himself behind the cockpit. He'd seen it all, and he was trying to calm him-self. "Was that the entire camp? Did you see that little girl? What the Hell!"

Looking up, Ken responded. "Yes, I saw her."

"I did too," Jim said with his heart pounding.

On the edge of the pit, there was a young girl lying face down in the snow. Behind the black truck there was a large stack of human carcasses with no legs and no arms, and there was blood everywhere. It was obvious what they were doing to the little girl. She was being processed like an ani-mal, and they were half way through. She had blond hair, and as they flew on by, Ken saw her leg and it was partially attached. It was unbearable, and he had to look away.

He felt bad for Roberto. He was trying to be strong, but as he looked up he could see that his eyes were troubled and confused. It was a nightmare, and it was terrifying, and he needed help.

"Nobody should see this, Rob. It shouldn't exist." Turning around, Ken nodded. "It's an abomination, but it's real. This is who they are. This is what evil does when it gets desperate."

He nodded again. "You're here for a reason, Rob. You need to know. Listen up."

Ken watched his eyes getting wider and he summed it up.

"They blame us, and they hate us. They murdered those people because they wouldn't capitulate. They believe they're morally entitled to take what they want, and they believe they should survive at all costs. They still call themselves the "Resistance", and they believe the American patriots must be exterminated."

He'd seen the hard evidence and he wanted Rob to know it too. "It's their call to arms. They've been spreading their messages and propaganda on signs and billboards everywhere. They're feeding their armies with human flesh and they're tempting others to join—or die. That was an ice chest down there, and I've seen them up close and personal. First, they raid the camp, and if the camp won't join, they murder everybody and then they cut 'em all up. Those were butchers down there, and they were packing the meat in the snow."

His eyes sad, he looked at Rob and pointed down. "That's our enemy, son. Where they used to hide under the guise of good, and where they used to parade as noble warriors for the elitist left—now they're souls are exposed. They believe we're evil and they say our enemies are justified. They've been fundamentally transformed, and now we've got to stop them."

Sorting through the facts, Rob had seen the brutal truth for himself and there were four faces burned into his memory. His adrenaline was pumping, and he wanted revenge, but he was clear-minded and he felt strong. Oddly, he was standing on his bad leg, but there was no pain.

"It's insanity," he said, shifting his full weight. "There's something wrong with their minds."

Calmly, and with his nerves steady, he looked at Ken. "I like your plan. I'm ready."

His courage building, Rob sat down in the passenger seat behind the cockpit and he could feel his world changing. He put on his seatbelt, and he opened the log.

"Marking it down, Jim."

"Roger. I've got us on camera 2. Start time is at 33 minutes, 11 seconds."

Leveling off, Jim reduced the power setting and then he engaged the autopilot. At a slow cruise, they were back where they'd left off, but he needed some more time and he flew the King Air in a big circle. There was an elephant in the room, and he needed to tell his crewmembers.

"So, Rob. I haven't briefed you on this yet, and Ken, you'll read about this your file tonight."

His brow raised, he turned. "It's Seattle. We've got some new reports, and if they're accurate, our problems just got a whole lot bigger."

Jim had their attention, and he sighed. "We just got 'em a couple days ago, and I haven't seen the supporting evidence yet, but I'm told it's coming. If correct, we're talking about a slaughterhouse network. Like a cattle farm. And if they're doing it in Seattle, they're doing it everywhere."

Where the reports detailed an organized network, Jim knew what it meant. "It's profound, gentlemen. They've solved their food problem." He couldn't believe it was real, but it was, and he shook his head.

"So this is what they're doing. In Seattle—it's much warmer over there, and they can't freeze their meat. They don't have ice chests, and so they're capturing large groups of people and they're keeping 'em alive until they're needed. They've solved for X, and it's going to happen out here. The numbers were staggering, Ken. And if it's spreading …"

Jim shook his head. "I'm just afraid we're running out of time. We need to get busy."

"Agreed."

Scratching his beard, he knew Jim was right. He wondered how many people had already been killed, and he wondered how many people had joined the marauders. We need our military back. We need to get busy.

He took a deep breath and turned to his friend. "We've got a plan, Jim. We need to have faith. We need patience."

Ken raised his brow. "We've got another thirty miles left on the search. Let's find Paul. Let's keep the faith and let's do our job. It's how we win."

While Jim responded with a single nod, Rob held up his thumb. The search area was directly below and they were back on course. They needed to focus on the mission, and if they could find Paul—everything would be better. As they scanned the area, each found their minds clouded by the pit, and each did their best to recover.

Jim had his eyes on the ground—and he had the cameras on, but he couldn't get his mind off the little girl. Stop thinking about it. You need to turn it off. He glanced over to Ken and then back to Rob, and he knew he wasn't the only one.

It was a unique burden, and for Jim it was taking its toll. All he wanted was retaliation, but instead he had to watch, and he had to let the wicked get away with murder over and over. He wanted guns, and he wanted bombs, and he wanted the consequences to start raining. The marauders had to be stopped, but for now, he had to turn it off, and he needed to stop thinking about it. He needed patience and strength, and it felt like an impossible task, but he had to do it, so he did.

In the battle of good against evil—Jim found his strength from above. This was the patriot's inalienable advantage, and it was precisely what evil didn't have or want. Step by step, we'll make it through. He knew it was true, and he felt better.

They performed low-approaches, s-turns, and circles, and throughout the entire search Jim did his best to find Paul, and so did his crewmembers. As a team they scoured the area, but they found no clues, and the ground was void of any new groups that hadn't already been spotted. The Highway 2 refugee camp was directly ahead, and if Paul was this close—he would've established communications by now. The crowds were coming into view and it was time to call it off. Paul was still lost and the mission was over.

With the Sun setting behind them, the King Air had done its job and the three men were coming home. With the border just ahead, the refugee camp was directly below, and with both Ken and Rob on their binoculars, they said it didn't look real.

It had a unique feature where Highway 20 and Highway 2 converged to form a "Y" just before the Idaho border. In the town of Newport Washington, the river separated the two states and the refugee camp encircled the whole town. From the air, it looked like a gigantic swath of humans swarming a city and making it into a cocoon. The snow was deeper up here, and there were strange features where long igloos expanded outward from the buildings of the town. It was odd, and it didn't look real.

Now crossing the river into Idaho, the sunlight was getting dimmer and the air was smooth. Jim entered a shallow turn and his new heading would take them directly to Sandpoint.

He didn't find Paul, but Ken was coming home and he was bringing a new battle plan that could solve everything. He had a new crewmember and he could see that Rob was becoming a soldier. In a world gone bad, it was a good day to be alive, but it was also terrible and horrific, and it was difficult to balance.

How strange, he thought. If felt like a dream, and there were portions of reality that didn't make sense anymore. He had a unique window, and depending on where he traveled—he could see good and evil and he could see the boundary beneath him changing. He'd seen the horrors over and over, and then he'd come home. There were two worlds, and he flew an airplane that wandered in-between. It was surreal, and he worried about the future. He knew it could get much worse and he needed to work on his strength. He took a deep breath, and then he felt his stomach grumbling. He was hungry.

Tonight he'd be eating hamburgers with his neighbor and he couldn't wait. Even better the President's Address was only a few hours away. As he looked out the window, he was getting excited. It was good to be going home.

Running on empty, Jim reached into his flight bag and he pulled out three power bars. He'd lost ten pounds over the last four months, and it looked like Ken had lost twenty. He tossed him a bar, and then he threw one to Rob.

"Wow," Jim said pointing straight ahead. "That's a full moon."

"It'll be a bright one tonight," Rob said from behind.

While eating his power bar, Ken thought it was exceptional, but there was something strange going on and he could feel it in his bones. Something was different. He felt hypersensitive and it was weird. He turned to see if Rob was noticing it too, but he was focused on his paperwork.

Resting his forehead against his side-window, Ken peered down and he could see the trees, the homes, and the farms rushing by. He could see fishing boats in the river and he could see roads with moving cars.

It was just how he'd pictured it and he was fully aware of his unique circumstance, but he'd failed to prepare for this. Lifting his eyes, he scanned the horizon and he knew exactly what he was feeling. This was true freedom. It was indescribable. He could feel it in his soul, and then he heard Jim.

"You ready?"

"Yes."

CHAPTER 23

THE PRESIDENT'S ADDRESS

Jim's cabin; Sandpoint, Idaho

A little after six o'clock, he'd finally made it to his gate and he was still on schedule. With it closed tight, he secured the latch and then he walked back to his truck. His adrenaline was still pumping. He needed to talk with George. He needed to hear the President. He needed to prepare for tomorrow's meeting with Ken. He got in and closed the door. Slow it down, Jim. Breathe.

His mind racing, he knew what to do. The bloody pit was real, but the marauders were on the other side of the mountains and they'd have to wait. His memory of the little girl wouldn't stop, but his sorrow had to stay here. These were the new rules, and they were getting harder to follow, but they helped and he put his truck in gear.

Anxious to get to the other side, he turned on his high beams and headed for the snow covered forest. His driveway looked like a tunnel of ice and as he entered he watched the moonlight fade away instantly. It was dark in here, and it was dangerously cold, but he had a good road and he'd plowed every inch of it. Thanks to George's tractor, he could do it in less than an hour and he was keeping up with the storms. With packed snow under his tires and with eight-foot snow banks on each side, he followed the path he'd been carving all winter and he thanked God for the snowplow. It was an impressive tool, and it was essential to his personal survival, but he'd found another advantage and it was pretty cool.

Last week, and following the latest snow, he'd discovered it all by accident and it started with a simple goal. He wanted a new parking spot for the SafePort meetings and he wanted it closer to the house. He had a large front yard, and if he plowed it perpendicular to the driveway he could fit five or six vehicles and he'd still have room for the turn-around. As long as he pushed the snow far enough, it wouldn't affect the carport or the garage and it was all doable. He wanted a parking lot, and he got one—but he got a wall too.

It was an early Sunday morning and he'd spent an hour moving snow, but he'd pushed a big pile of it in front of the home and it had to go. With his plow lowered he was about to push it away, but then he realized something and he stopped cold. He couldn't see his house—and if he built the snow bank a little higher he'd have a wall. He could hide his home from the driveway. He could conceal it from any trespassers in the woods and he could take the tactical advantage. It was a rudimentary defense, but it was a cruel world, and he wanted to be ready.

With the snow chirping under his tires, Jim thought about Sarah and he knew the risks were growing. Surrounded by darkness, just beyond his headlights it was pitch-black and he was fully aware that his local woods were becoming dangerous. Across the border the wicked had full control, but in Idaho they didn't. They were on the run and they were hiding in the shadows. Murderers were killing people in their homes and they were using the forest to scuttle their plunder. Less than a mile away, one of his neighbors had just been attacked, and he'd survived, but he lost his wife and son. Scanning the darkness, Jim rolled up his window and he looked at his gun. He wanted justice. He wanted to fight. He wanted the war to be over.

Just ahead he could see the moonlight breaking through and he took a deep breath and thought about dinner. He could see his meadow coming into view, and then suddenly it got bright and he could see the stars. He was home. Directly in front of him he could see a wall of snow and it cut straight across his driveway. Look at that, he thought. It was a work of art and he liked the new addition.

At ten-feet high, he merged with the snow bank on his right-hand side and then followed it to the very end. He had plenty of room, but to get inside he'd have to crank it hard, and he did. Now behind the wall, he could see that George was already here. Perfect, he thought. Now it's a party. Pulling up behind him, he was eager to talk with his friend.

Turning off his truck, Jim gazed at the barrier one more time and he could hear his ears ringing in the silence. The wall was bright, and it was almost shimmering. After the next storm he'd make it better. Maybe taller, he thought. We'll see. He pulled out the key and sighed. What if we have to leave?

Offended by the question, Jim opened the driver's door and hopped out of his truck. The marauders were off-limits and he needed to shake it off. Over the last month it was getting harder and harder to stop thinking about it, and he could feel his instincts telling him to be careful. It was an internal struggle, and he wasn't sure what it meant, but he needed to shake it off.

With his flight bag slung over his shoulder, he locked his truck and started walking towards the front porch. He thought he could hear laughing, but on every footstep he could hear the snow squeaking beneath his feet and he wasn't sure what he was hearing. It was loud, and he almost stopped, but when walked up the steps the squeaking went away. He put his key in the front door, and then he heard Darleen.

Jim walked into the mudroom and then he heard it again. It sounded good and he could hear laughing in the living room. He set his flight bag down, took off his coat, and then he sat down on the bench and commenced his boot removal. He could smell food, and he could hear George talking in the kitchen. He heard Sarah's voice, and then suddenly, she opened the door and she was walking fast.

"Thank God," she said grabbing his shirt. "Mission accomplished?"

Jim was nodding, but then he stopped. "Sort of ..."

"Ken's home—but it's a long story." Eyebrows raised, he hugged her and he used his free hand to fend off Ralph and Maxine. "I'll tell you later."

"What about Paul?"

Bending down, he shook his head. "Nothing. But we'll find him."

Grabbing Sarah's belt, he went to his knees and held on. Tales wagging, Ralph and Maxine let him have it.

"Wait until you see what Darleen brought."

Braced against her leg, he looked up. "Really?"

Doing his best to steady himself, the two dogs were like bumper cars and Ralph had no concept of size. Maxine could handle it, but Bella knew better and as Jim stood up he could see her waiting for him in the corner.

Well past the juvenile years, she knew the group hug with Maxine and Ralph required too much energy and she didn't want to get hurt. Bella was wise, and with her tail wagging, she looked into Jim's eyes. He held her head and then he gave her a hug. Love was here, and he turned to Sarah.

"Good to be home, honey. What's that smell?"

Sarah smiled and then she grabbed his hand. "I don't know. Let's go see."

Together with the dogs, they walked inside and Jim closed the mudroom door behind them. Instantly, he could feel the temperature rise and he could see that the woodstove was on high. At five-steps in he could hear the sound of meat cooking in the kitchen. They were almost there, and on every step the smell got stronger, but then suddenly, George came around the corner.

"Welcome back," he said extending his hand. "How's Ken?"

"Home-base, George. I'll fill you in."

With a secret handshake that said "let's talk later", George knew the backstory and he had a dinner schedule to keep on track.

"Good! I got the burgers on. You're going to love these." Headed for the kitchen, he was on cooking detail and he was the chef in charge. "Old school, Jim. We've got ten minutes

They both followed him into the kitchen and as they turned the corner they saw Darlene standing next to the center island. She had something in her hands and he couldn't believe what he was seeing. It was odd, and he couldn't take his eyes off of it.

A pre-war pastry, Jim could feel his memories surfacing and he was speechless as she raised it to his nose. It was a peach pie—and it was still warm.

"Isn't it just delightful?"

Her southern accent thick, Darleen let the vapors swirl and then she set it down on the countertop. "It's for good luck. And it's because I can. It's because our President did the right thing."

Staring at the pie, she'd been thinking about him all afternoon and she was astounded with the synchronistic details of what he'd done. "He's a hero, Jim. We need to pray for him."

Darleen had a way with words and she had a grit that Jim liked. This was her wind-up, and so he nodded.

"Think about it, Jim. When we were most vulnerable, God sent us a leader that couldn't be bought. When the others said he was lying, he told us the truth and he helped us defend our families. He saved America, and this proves it. We're alive and we're united. We can survive. We can eat pie … And we're going to."

Bending down, he gave her a hug and said, "Bingo, Darleen." It was true, and he fully concurred. "You're spot on. It's good to see you."

It was seven o'clock and the greetings were complete. Huddled in the kitchen, the group of four crafted a game-plan, synchronized their watches, and then dispersed. The race was on, and while Jim ran upstairs to get out of his work clothes, Sarah, Darleen, and George worked as a team to get dinner ready.

Upstairs it was hot and Jim cracked-open the bathroom window to get some cool air. He washed his face and brushed his teeth. Dinner with friends was about to begin and he could feel his afternoon dread fading away. He thought about how happy Linda was when she saw Ken at the hangar. He thought about Paul, but he'd leave it there. He was hungry, and he thought about dinner.

Survival cooking was the new norm and everybody was getting used to it, but if you worked hard the expanded menu was becoming feasible. Darlene's dessert was a guaranteed home run and George's burgers looked mouthwatering and exquisite. The hamburger was a special blend, and per George's bartering buddy at the Food Distribution Center in Sandpoint, it allegedly came from the more desirable part of the cow. Recruited by the governor of Idaho, George was no longer serving as the sector manager for the Fish and Game Department, but his old position came with perks—and the perks tasted good.

Hamburger meat was standard issue, and it was becoming the preferred meal for many. Known for its high protein and high calories, it was healthy red meat, and it was filled with fat to keep the populace strong. Standard weekly allotment was two pounds of meat per person, and the choices were many. Chicken, beef, pork, and fish were all available, as were other various game animals from time to time.

As an independent survival zone, Bonner County had hit the jackpot of sustenance in the form of plentiful food and water for everyone. Gourmet food was on hold, but the good old meat and potatoes were making it to the plates of everyone in the zone. It was the key to success—and at four months in—the populace was healthy.

Wearing his winter slippers and favorite sweatshirt, Jim ran down the stairs and he headed for the dinner table. Everybody was there and the food looked incredible. The buns for the hamburgers were made by Sarah and she made little potatoes that were charred in pan with onions and bacon fat. There was no salad, but there was frozen corn, and with the salt, pepper, and ketchup, everything tasted spectacular.

Whether standard issue, or whether a special perk from George; for the four neighbors in North Idaho, the weekly events inspired fellowship. They talked about everything, and tonight they talked about Ken and Linda, Samantha, Bella, and the President. Life was new, and it was a scary world, but as a group they walked forward in the confusion. They were friends, and they'd figure it out together.

There was a team spirit, and as Jim sat at the table he thanked God for the arrangement. He couldn't wait to tell George about Ken's plan, and he couldn't wait to hear his response. The more he thought about it, the more he liked it, and he knew George would too, but it seemed oddly fortuitous. George had the governor's ear. Tonight he'd hear the plan, and he'd hear it on the same day that Jim heard it from Ken. It was the timing, and it was almost too perfect.

With his plate empty, Jim wondered what it meant, and he wondered if it meant anything. Maybe Ken's plan had already been contemplated? Maybe the military was ready to deploy? He didn't know and he'd have to wait. He'd talk with George after the President.

Jim pointed at the clock on the wall and they had twenty minutes. "Good timing, everyone," he said standing up. "Shall we get ready?"

He turned to Sarah and Darleen. "I'll wash the dishes. You guys serve pie?"

"Deal," Darleen said, cracking a smile. She looked at Sarah and they both laughed.

"We like your plan, honey. But it's still game-night." Pointing her finger at Jim, she shook it. "After the President—no more news."

Like a good husband, he nodded and then glanced over to George. "Yes dear."

Standing up, George patted him on the shoulder. "I'll help you wash."

Inside the cabin it was toasty warm, but outside it was approaching single digits. With the wood stove blazing, Sarah had to crack open the windows just to keep the house temperature below 80 degrees. The winter storms were here, but tonight it was crystal clear and the valley was frozen solid. In the moonlight it seemed eerie, but the brightness added something special to the mood. There was a question in the air, and everybody could feel it.

With fifteen minutes to go; the clock was ticking and there was an elevated sense of excitement. At 8 p.m. the President might unveil the enemy, and if he did, everybody wanted to hear. It was time for clarity and the unknowns were getting old. The President had information, and the people needed to know.

More than half-way through, and with the dishes flying from one hand to the other, George and Jim were making a good team. With the girls elsewhere—George wanted to talk shop.

"So, how's Ken?" he said waiting for another plate.

"Happy." Jim stopped and turned. "I think it hit him when he saw his wife at the hangar."

"What about the Bluff? Was it safe?"

"Yes. Very. But we need to talk."

Back to the scrubbing, he nodded. "I had an illuminating day," he said passing him a fork. "After the President, I'll tell you what I mean."

George wiped it dry and then he set it on the stack. "Roger. Two cigars. We'll go to the deck."

While the two men finished their chores, Sarah walked out onto the front porch and grabbed the four bottles of root beer she'd stuck in the snow before dinner. Icy cold, she brought them inside, and she did it while George wasn't looking. It was a surprise, and with the bottles in hand, she walked over to the large coffee table in front of the couch. She set the bottles down, and when she did, George walked in.

Focused on the radio station next to the chair, he was closing in, and at ten-feet away he saw the beverages.

"Is that root beer?" He was staring at the bottles and he looked at Sarah as she walked by.

"I found 'em last week. They're icy-cold. Enjoy!" Walking out of the room, she knew it was his favorite. A trade for wine, it was worth every penny.

His butterflies stirring, Jim walked into the living room and he headed for the couch. With only minutes to go, both Sarah and Darleen were scrambling in the kitchen, George had the radio on, and there was a sense of tension in the air. He sat down and shook his head.

"This better be good," Jim said, sliding over a bottle. "We need our military, and we need it now."

Grabbing the beverage, George leaned back in his chair and reached into his front pocket.

"We'll see, Jim. I know we're getting close."

Still reaching, George was searching for a multi-tool in his pocket, and Ralph, who was sprawled out in front of him, watched him pull it out. For some reason the tool got his attention and he was curious. Jowls at full droop, Ralph lifted his head off the floor and he watched with his ears perked. He saw the bottle cap fly off and it made him wag. He got up, and he walked over to George.

"Good boy," he said scratching his head. George set the bottle on the table and pointed to the clock.

"Where's the pie?"

Jim laughed, but then Sarah walked into the room and Darline was behind her. Darlene had four slices of pie and Sarah had four cold mugs. Everything was set, but Sarah wanted it right.

"You sit next to Darleen, George. I'll sit in the chair. Jim; you stay." Sarah was getting organized, but she was anxious and Jim could tell.

"Ralphy, you sit down. Give him some room. We know you love George."

With three on the couch, Sarah was on the chair, and all four started pouring. The big event was about to begin and with forks in hand they all had a bite of peach pie. They were a team, and they'd hear their destiny together. Three bites later, the radio came alive and George turned up the volume.

"… *To the great people of America. Patriots! Hear my call! This is an emergency communiqué, and I call on my countrymen! My brothers and sisters. Listen to me now, for the time has come. You must learn the truth, and it is the truth that will reveal our enemy. I come as your Commander in Chief. I am the President of our United States. I am here to lead us into battle.*

"*To all who are listening, and to all who will spread my message, I come with an urgent call for rescue. The enemy is upon us. Foreign troops are landing on our shores. The time is now, so prepare your souls. Listen carefully.*

"*It is with great sadness I must report that our homeland is under attack. If we do not act, and if we do not act now, our great nation will be lost forever. If we fail, the enemy of our loving God will consume us all—and the world will suffer. Great patriots of America, I ask you to lend me your ears and to open your hearts. I have critical news. Take heed. Listen now!*

"*Yesterday, reports of two breaches along our western shoreline were officially confirmed. It is with resolute declaration—and I must confirm this to you now, and I must confirm to the world—this has indeed occurred.*

"*At this very hour, two of our undefended cities, both Seattle and San Francisco have been infiltrated and commandeered. We see it from the air and we see it from the ground, and all reports confirm that an invasion force is building its infrastructure. Foreign troops have landed, and they've brought their war machines with them. It is now, America. And it must be known by the world. We are the great nation that opposes evil. We are the giant that serves freedom. We are the giant that defends God.*

"*Let it be known to all; fleets of unmarked ships are staging off key points along our eastern and western shorelines. Where two of our U.S cities have already been conquered, we expect more to follow—and woe to them who march over our fallen, trespass on our land, and disguise their immoral will. Our forces are mighty, and while we observe a great number of vessels from unknown origins obscuring their identity, we watch as they plan their plunder, plot their betrayal, and gnash their teeth. Under the flag of humanitarian aid, they advance under the guise of good, and they lie to hide their true purpose.*

"*Great patriots, let it be known. We have confirmed these ships to be carrying hidden armies. We've seen their secret payloads and we've seen their camouflaged troops. Beware good people. They shroud themselves and they plot against our souls. With the sword of the devil and from behind a rock; it is the enemies of America who ride these ships, and it is the enemies of freedom who conspire to help them.*

"It is tonight, America. And oh Lord, let it be heard. It is we who are being called. The strain of the world has brought us to this day—and it is our freedom that has allowed us to prepare an army. As God has blessed this nation, it is we who must fight for our inalienable rights, and it is we who must fight for the world. Let it be known—it is a good day, for we are alive and strong!

"Great patriots. We are here, and so is God. Let the world hear! We know who the enemy is! We know how to win! We've broken the devil's chain, and we have the power of true freedom!

"Listen to me closely. I'll tell you what I know."

At three bites in; the peach pie sat on the table. In Northern Idaho, the group of four was in shock and they were glued to the President's every word. This was their destiny, and they were learning it now. History was being made. America was rising.

CHAPTER 24

INVASION

The President's address was over and it was almost 9:00 p.m. Groaning, George reached over and turned down the volume on the radio. They were stunned, and with the exception of the crackling fire, there was an uncomfortable silence.

Suddenly, Sarah jumped out of her chair. "Who is it, then? Who's on our shores? Is it Russia or is it China?"

Watching from the couch, George, Darlene, and Jim sat speechless. Nobody had a definitive answer and everybody was confused. Reaching over to Sarah's belt, Jim wrapped his finger around it and he pulled her in closer.

"Too soon, hon. But we're about to find out." Cringing before he'd finished, he could see her eyes getting bigger and he didn't know what to say.

"He's right," George said jumping in. "But it's not China or Russia."

His assessment forming, George could hear the silence return and he had the floor. Breathing deep, he'd take the lead.

"So, if the Russians are on our southern border—they're probably in Canada too. If our airspace is being violated by China, then it's dangerously unprotected, and we know that our defenses are stretched thin. These are all simple deductions, and they're not only based on what the President just said, but they match our observable world. The attack lasted one day. America and Israel were the two targets. The world is in freefall, and the superpowers are being cautious."

Leaning forward, he shook his head. "It's peculiar, isn't it? No retaliation and no escalation. Mutually assured destruction is still in-play, and if we were attacked by China or Russia we would've instantly retaliated with a nuclear response. I think the President chose his words very carefully. He gave us the details we didn't have, and frankly, I think he solved the anomaly."

Measuring the clues, George could feel his instincts kicking in.

"So, now we know. Whoever attacked us—they did it anonymously— and they used confusion to buy time. This was a Hail Mary. If our enemy had any sustainable firepower they would've used it by now. It's been four months. The President said they used a high-altitude weather balloon to deliver the first weapon. Did you hear that? That's critical."

Looking down, he took a breath. "Superpowers don't use weather balloons. It's not Russia. It's not China. And there were at least two weapons."

While Sarah sat down on the couch, George could hear the silence return and he used it to organize his thoughts. The wondering was over and he could finally see the horizon. He could identify the enemy, and he could confirm its weakness. The facts were telling, but he had to talk it through.

"It's absurd. We've got a hidden army—and they're using humanitarian aid to sneak into our undefended ports. That's strange, Jim. Terrorists would do that, and it's a weakness."

Pushing his half-eaten pie off to the side, the new information was no surprise, but it was extremely odd, and it was familiar. "I think it's pretty clear. Both Russia and China have been identified and our enemy remains veiled. Our President made that distinction and he was loud and clear. Those secret ships landing on our west coast are here to kill us, but China and Russia have been distinctly visible, and they're waiting to see what happens."

With the trickery getting old, the masquerading tactics were both confirming and easily deduced. "Our enemy hides," he said raising his brow. "And they're not logical."

There was a golden nugget in the facts and George could see it clearly. His heart rate accelerating, he addressed the group.

"There's a distinct weakness here, and I'm telling you—it's time to spell it out. It's all confirmable and it's all traceable. This is the chain reaction we all knew was coming and it's exactly why we built SafePort. It began with 'Death to America' in the Middle East, and then it came here disguised as the good people versus the 'Deplorable'. It's the same enemy we've defeated before, and it's the same enemy we're about to defeat now. We know who it is, and our history proves it."

Clearing his throat, he had all the evidence he needed and the President's address was the final component. He could validate the truth, and with everyone's attention, he scooted to the edge of the couch.

"Just think about it for a second. We can confirm our instincts. Now we know." George needed the right words, but he only had a few.

"We can follow the facts. For the enemy to win; America had to be destroyed or it had to be transformed, and we've seen our enemy execute both attempts. Initially, the first attack used our all means necessary to undermine the American people and the American way. The second attack exploited our weakness with an EMP. We know the two conspirators, and we watched the relationship grow. We saw it all—and it was worldwide. The global establishment used the Muslim religion to change our western culture. Radical Islam used our global establishment to help conceal their true goals. Suddenly, we noticed the change in our values and we saw the conflict, but if we questioned it—we were attacked by both groups."

It was much easier than he thought, and he used history to reveal the big picture. "Remember what we've seen. We've experienced the attempts, and now we're knee-deep in the consequences. They were supposed to defeat us, but they didn't. While the patriots got stronger, suddenly their co-conspirators—who incidentally counted on our elitist officials to keep us weak—were in a pinch. The opportunity was fading fast, and because the patriots had a defense, America was becoming resilient to EMP. To prevail, they had to attack us quickly, and they did."

Half-chuckling, George shook his head. "Remember what the President said. He said they had help. He said they had a special advantage. I think it's a big clue, and we can only wonder, but I know this. We saw a special hate. We saw a political party incite civil unrest. We saw them sacrificing the people just so they could win. Before the attack, remember what was happening. Big players were under investigation. People were heading for jail, but now they're not, and it makes me wonder."

Nodding to his friend, Jim was in full agreement and he knew George was right. There were many forces attempting to defile the world, but these were the two that exploited each other for the same benefit, and these were the two that needed us gone to win.

"It's all true, George." Nodding again, he raised his brow. "It's unstoppable. Whoever they are, they need to kill us now or they'll lose. This is their last chance. It's another Hail Mary, but we're ready."

"Yes. We are." Putting his hand on his wife's knee, George leaned forward. "And that's precisely why we win. We're fighting an irrational enemy that had to fool us into losing. They had to incite hate, deceive the people, and trick our presumptive trust. We know the hoax well. It happened here, it happened in other nations, and it's the same lie that's corrupting the Muslim faith all over the world. It is unstoppable, and you're right, Jim. We're ready."

George took a deep breath and sighed. "Point being; we saw the ruse. We built SafePort because we couldn't trust the world, and it saved us. We didn't get fooled, and we're not getting fooled now."

Leaning back, he could hear his little voice and it was reciting the new evidence. "If they can take us out with a weather balloon—then our sabotage is confirmed and so is the enemy. The Devil said lie, and they did, but we didn't fall for it."

George took a deep breath and he stood up in his exhale. Starting now, he had a new job to do and he was ready. With his mind on the battlefield, he could feel the betrayal for what it was. It was predictable, it was weak, and it was a sign that the enemy had no bricks to support its foundation.

"It doesn't matter who attacked us," he said, standing in front of the coffee table. "And it doesn't matter who's on our shores. Our enemy is a deceiver, and that's all we need to know. Maybe it's Iran? Maybe it's not? Maybe it's a madman?"

George looked down at the group and he shook his head. "Whoever it is, if they come here they'll lose. We built a countermeasure to defend our freedom, and we've got an army that will defeat them all."

Bending down, he picked up his half-eaten pie from the coffee table and he started to load his fork. "It's amazing, Jim. Two-months ago we started this whole merge process. When I talked with the governor, he said he wanted his civil defense ready in 60 days."

Now at room temperature, the pie had an intense flavor and George could feel his heart rate calming. "Now that's some good timing," he said with his mouth full.

"And I know we don't have fighter jets and tanks, but we're a heavily armed force, and we have big guns, Jim. We have communications, troop transport, and overhead surveillance. While they're hiding and sneaking around, we can find them and we can kill them on the spot. Not bad."

Again, he chuckled while heading for another bite. "We're ready. How amazing!"

Nodding to his friend, Jim stood up and he walked over to the large windows at the west end of the cabin. George had been officially reassigned by SafePort to help merge Idaho's Guard and civil defense forces into one infrastructure, and Jim had seen his resume. He had the skills Idaho needed and he was well respected. George could see the battle in his mind and he had a unique talent for getting others to see the big picture. Today was no different and he'd done it again. The timing was amazing, but he still hadn't heard about Ken.

Over the last several months, George and several other retired military specialists were now serving at the sole request of the governor, and they were all seasoned commanders proficient at mobilizing troops. George was becoming a key figure in helping Jim merge the Civil Air Patrol functions with the ground force strategy being planned for the refugee camps. He was a tactical advisor, and George had clout with the decision makers. He needed to know about Ken's plan. He needed to know everything, and he needed to know it now.

Standing behind the woodstove and next to the large windows, Jim had to spill the beans, and as he reached for the pull handle to open the blinds he could feel the risk growing. Over the last month, the marauders actions had been kept on the down-low, and even though George had access to the sensitive information, he hadn't talked with him about it for several weeks.

Their sole mission was to secure the refugee camps, and they were preparing for Phase Two. They were almost ready, but the marauders were Phase Three—and he'd avoided the subject with George. He'd kept his mind on the mission and he'd remained focused. He'd assumed his friend had done the same, but he didn't know for sure, and Jim wondered how much he knew.

The world was changing fast and he could feel the weight getting heavier. It was all adding up, and now the refugees, the marauders, and the invaders all had to be dealt with simultaneously. Ken's plan, he thought. We need to revise our priorities. We need to get to Seattle.

With the pull rod in his hand, he was ready to open the blinds, but again he thought about the unique timing, and he just stood there. It was a familiar advantage, and for Jim it felt like outside help. Thank God, he thought, and he could remember Day One. He breathed deep, but then he sighed, and he heard his mind lay on the guilt.

The marauders strength, numbers, and tactics had all been concealed. He was complicit. He'd been ill-advised by his own judgment. Assuming it was the right thing to do, he'd kept his mouth shut regarding the marauders atrocities and he'd only discussed the elevated threat with other approved SafePort personnel. It was the new policy, but he'd used for his own selfish reasons and he'd used it to cope. Sarah didn't know, and he didn't want her to know unless she absolutely had to. It was the same excuse for everyone— and he used it often.

The people were on edge, and they needed to rebuild America. Death was everywhere, but in the Safe States there was hope, and hope needed to be protected. These were the vile and wicked things, and for right now, the people needed to focus on getting better. SafePort would take the burden, and Jim could hear his voice reminding him how he'd simply turn it off when he got home.

It was selfish and it was wrong and he could see the consequences forming. While he worked hard to keep evil from being seen, evil wanted to be concealed—and it was. The slaughter of our fellow patriots and the marauders military strength should be the talk of the town, but there were no official details issued from SafePort and nothing could be confirmed. Jim could see the trap, and it was hitting him hard. He'd been hiding the truth, and it needed to stop now.

The two-story windows spanned the entire west end of the main floor and they overlooked the river valley to the west. Having one main vertical blind in the center and two smaller blinds at each end, all three were closed, and the moonlight was beaming along their edges. Standing still, and with the pull rod getting sweaty in his hand, Jim turned to George, and he shook his head.

"You're right," he said, nodding. "It doesn't matter who they are, and we are ready. But I do have some new details—and it changes things."

With his words unleashed, slow and steady he began to pull open the blinds. With one down, and two to go, he could feel his thoughts rushing in. Now at the halfway point, he stopped and turned around.

"You know some of this George, but not all, and you need to."

With the blinds fully open, the river valley and distant mountains sparkled in the moonlight. It was a full moon, but it seemed brighter than usual and Jim was amazed at the nighttime visibility. He could see the entire valley, and as he began his briefing he stared out the window. With Sarah listening, he held nothing back and he revealed terrible things.

He began with the marauders extermination motives and he explained how they were recruiting an army to rebuild their new America. He described the atrocities in detail and he revealed the new reports coming in from Seattle. He told the group about the Bluff, and then he told George everything he knew about Ken's plan.

It was both an epiphany and it was validating, and after Jim let it all out, Sarah said it confirmed everything George had just stated about the enemy. She said they'd gone mad and that the patriots were prepared and ready, and that there was no other way to perceive it. Everybody knew it was true, and with these facts the group found clarity.

Suddenly, Sarah said the word again.

"Timing!" She looked to George for his reaction, and then her eyes went back to Jim. "This all happened today. The plan ..." Again, she looked at George.

"Is it a good one?"

Nodding, he leaned back in the couch and smiled. "Maybe."

George was unpacking everything he'd just heard, and Jim was right. He hadn't seen the Seattle report, and he'd been focused on Phase Two. The marauders were a significant force and they were more than a distraction. Most of all, he was impressed with Ken's plan, and it appeared to solve everything.

"It's like a ladder, Jim. We've assessed the railway system for this same strategy, but they've already destroyed key portions of the track and we know they'll destroy more. We need the roads and the highways to move our troops. We need to own the territory, and we need to own it fast. This plan has merit."

Standing up, George walked towards the window. He'd avoided the view, but it had a pull and he'd felt it all night. It was like daytime, and with the snow and the moonlight, he could almost see everything. He could see the ridges on the other side of the valley and he could even see the trees. It was spectacular, and then he thought about the marauders. It was a betrayal of the worst-kind, and it was unthinkable. They were infected. Redemption was impossible. They needed to be removed.

Taking it all in, George turned from the view and he looked at his wife and two friends sitting on the couch. He needed to accelerate the conversation and he needed to get Jim up-to-speed so he could go home and crunch the numbers. Idaho was on the front lines and the governor would need a working plan by tomorrow. He wanted his maps, his laptop, and a full pot of coffee. The clock was ticking and he needed to go home, but first he had to tell Jim what he didn't know.

Walking over to the couch, he let it fly. "I've got some info, Jim. We had to keep this quiet, but not anymore."

Standing next to his wife, he raised his brow and sighed. "This is our back-story—so here goes."

With Jim, Sarah, and Darleen sitting on the couch, the fire crackled and the moonlight beamed as George told the group his trade secrets. They weren't classified and they weren't definitive, but they were all relevant and they were a product of his private communications with other retired commanders.

He had the scoop, and although much of it was still vague, Jim learned many things. He'd learned that the formation of C130's and military helicopters he'd seen on Day One came from the now abandoned Fairchild Air Force Base located in Spokane, Washington. He learned that most of our military aircraft and weaponry that were located in undefended states were scuttled to other locations throughout the nation. George talked about the tight seal on all information regarding military readiness, and he explained how the military infrastructure in the Homeland was still in place, but unfortunately, lacked its qualified personnel.

Most notably, George explained the extreme importance of our civil defense forces to hold the line while America waited for its military to revive itself. He said that if it were a month from now—they'd likely be here. But right now, he said they were non-functional and that we needed to wait while the new recruits received specialized training.

George laid out the hidden truths, and he revealed our strengths and weaknesses. He said the patriots would have to fight a dirty battle, and he said the civil defense forces were well-equipped—care of the U.S military. He said the patriots had a unique power, and with the airplanes overhead, he said we could cut through Washington State like it was nothing. He said we can outfight anybody, and he told Jim that he needed to get busy with airplanes and pilots.

All in all, it was good information—and for both men—they were square. It had been a long day, and the night was just beginning. It was time to dig deep and the SAFE STATE mission had just been elevated. The "Draft" had been enacted, and starting now, thousands would be following the SafePort reporting procedures for civil defense. The next seventy-two hours would be a blur, and for Jim and George it was all about managing the plan and making things work.

"So then, I'll get on the radio tonight and I'll set up a strategy meeting for tomorrow morning." George looked at his watch and he took a deep breath. "I'll hash this out when I get home, but in the morning I'll need you and Ken to help me with the surveillance challenges."

Jim was nodding. "The 'Draft', George. I can pull pilots from anywhere—airplanes too."

Standing next to his wife, he tilted his head. "You can only make the request—but I can demand it tomorrow." Looking down, he nodded to Darleen. "Maybe thats why we're all here. The timing. The circumstance. It feels valuable."

Turning to Jim, Darleen had a "look" and it spoke volumes.

Valuable ... It was a good word, and he breathed it in. "We'll have a plan by morning, George. First thing."

With a battle to win, they had the tools they needed and George could feel his wish-list growing. Together, they carved out their tasks and the next critical steps were straight-forward. It was time to go to work, and by tomorrow, George would have a working plan that he could submit to the governor.

With his confidence high, Jim walked over to the wood stove and he threw another log into the fire. The cabin was hot, but the coals needed some company, and after he added the log he opened the window a smidge for climate control. The cold air felt good, and as he breathed it in—it was the view that got his attention.

With the snow reflecting in the moonlight, it was an eerie site to behold. Both the cabin and the valley were brighter than on any other night before. Again, he was in awe. The powdery snow made the mountains look smooth and the visibility went on for miles. The air was crisp and still, and as he looked westward towards Washington State he could see the distant ridge marking the border. It was fuzzy, but he could see it and his eyes were trying to zero-in. My God, he thought. His eyes focusing, he felt something odd and then suddenly he knew what it was. He'd never felt it from here. It was fleeting, but he didn't like it and he turned around.

Knowing something was wrong; the dogs were feeling it too. Ears down, Maxine walked over to where Jim was standing near the window. Both Ralph and Bella went straight for Sarah on the couch. The silence was back, and Jim and Sarah locked eyes.

"Jim?" she asked with the dogs at her side.

"Yeah, hon."

"I'm sorry you had to keep all that stuff bottled up."

"I'm sorry I did."

Sarah knew why he did it and he'd get a full pardon. Like Jim, she hated the wickedness, and she'd avoided it too, but suddenly, she thought about the marauders motives and her face went pale.

"You saw them up-close, didn't you?"

"Yep." Jim gave her a nod and he could see the bloody pit in full view. "I saw them today. I've watched from the beginning."

Sarah sighed, and she'd seen the same murderous vile. She had to speak her mind, and with her adrenaline pumping she had to do it now.

"You need to hunt them down, Jim. They're infected and they won't stop. This needs to end."

Darleen was sitting next to her, and when George said "yep" from behind, Sarah turned. "You tell my husband what you need, and he'll give it to you. Screw accountability. We can't put 'em all in jail! It's us or them."

Putting her arm around Sarah, Darleen agreed. "That's right, darlin," she said with her southern drawl thick. "We've been so thirsty for accountability, and we've tried so hard, but this game is over. We have to defend."

George looked at his wife and then over to Jim. Both men nodded, and the girls wanted a response, so George answered.

"They'll be executed. Quick and dirty. Marauders, invaders … There's no other way."

It was a hybrid war, and it was the traitors and invaders versus the patriots. For Sarah, it was the inevitable and she knew what it meant. It was extraordinary. It was an indescribable feeling, and before she could stop herself she blurted-out the words.

"Karma! It's here!"

With Bella at her feet, she reached down to pet her worried dog.

"We've had faith, Jim. We took responsibility and we've done all the right things. I know this is terrible, and I know it's going to get worse, but something good is happening too. I know it!"

Ralph, who'd been waiting patiently under the coffee table, had taken notice of Bella's hands-on attention and he sat up to claim his turn. Eyes sad, he placed his front paw on her lap and he asked for her hand. Grabbing it, Sarah held his paw and she turned to Jim.

"This is it!" she said, smiling. "It's a turning point. I can feel it." Looking at Ralph, she took a deep breath and it felt good.

Jim smiled at his wife and then he bent down to pet Maxine. She still had her ears down and it was unusual. Petting her head, he told her she was a good girl, but then he looked up and he was confused. Sarah was motionless, and he saw George and Darleen stopping mid-stride in the middle of the room.

Jim stood up, and when he did he felt a vibration on his feet. He looked at Sarah, and then suddenly, her eyes lit up and the sound came in hard.

Instantly, he knew what it was and he and George ran towards the windows. It was bright enough to see everything, but they saw nothing.

"Helicopters," he said, running for the deck door. "Big ones, George!"

The back door flew open and they both stumbled outside. With the sound guiding them, they plowed through the snow and they headed for the edge of the deck. The noise was coming from over the river and it was getting louder. Bracing their legs up-against the snow bank that covered the deck rail, side by side, they stared to the south. The air was vibrating hard, and at any second, multiple helicopters would appear.

Suddenly, George dropped to his knees and yelled.

"Get down now," he said, pulling on Jim's shirt.

"What's happening?" Sarah yelled from the door. "What do we do?"

"Get back from the windows," George yelled. "We're playing it safe."

Nodding to George, Sarah shut the back door and he could see Darleen pulling her into the kitchen.

"They're military, Jim. We've got to be cautious."

"You're right!" Groaning, he squeezed in tight next to his friend. "But it can't be the enemy. Too soon."

The noise vibrated, and the thunderous sound was now approaching slow. Puzzled, George knew that it was over the river and he knew that it was just behind the tree line.

"Should've been here by now," George said struggling to get a glimpse.

"I think they've stopped." Jim was listening for a pitch change and the sound was steady.

"Yep, I think so. And I'm guessing two gunships. Maybe three, but it's hard to say." Kneeling behind the snow pile, George was confident he knew exactly where the helicopters were hovering. "They're over the Morton Slough now. Low-level. Stopped. Just above the water."

Turning around, Jim looked through the windows to find Sarah and all he could see were Ralph and Maxine. He pointed down, but they weren't buying it, and then he saw Sarah holding up his binoculars and waiving. Panning right, he looked at the spotting scope. It was on a tripod and it was just inside the door.

He tapped George on the shoulder and then he rushed into the house. It was nighttime, but it wasn't dark and Jim could see everything. He grabbed the scope and the binoculars and then he was back in thirty-seconds.

"Try the scope," he said kneeling in the snow. "You're in a better spot. You might be able to pierce through the trees."

George tried, but it was too thick. He moved from spot to spot and he even stood up to find a better angle, but the snow covered trees made it impossible.

"In two minutes, I'm going to run over to your fire pit, Jim." The noise was loud and George had to yell. "I can see from over there. We need to know who this is. It's got to be ours!"

Suddenly, Jim heard the sound multiply. There was a new oscillation and his eyes went straight to a new target. "Look! Coming over the ridge!" Jim pointed across the valley and it was bright enough to see. "No lights. Who is that?"

George had the scope dialed in and there was a new gunship descending into the valley. "It's not ours, Jim! No markings. Get down!"

George swiveled his body toward the house and then sat up on his knees to yell through the window. Thanks to the hot fire inside—and just in front of him—the window had been left ajar. It was noisy, but his yell would be heard.

"Take cover now!" he said cupping his hands. "Hide and don't move!"

The sound waves of big turbines and rotor blades shook the ground hard. George felt it reverberating off his chest and he slid back into his tuck position next to Jim. A deep breath, and then he sighed. "We're sitting ducks, so stay still. I know what this is."

Hiding behind the snow pile on the deck, the scenario was all wrong. Jim was astounded to be on the defense, and he didn't know what to do. Seconds passed, and with each one, frustration mounted. How did the enemy pull this off, and what were they doing?

Suddenly, the helicopters from over the river began their advance and then it was clear there were only two of them. Jim peered over the snow and he saw their flight path merging with the new arrival. The sound waves were aggressive and fast, and as they progressed past the cabin, both men got on their knees and they saw the formation of three perched over the river. They saw the flash and they heard the explosions.

Both men watched, and they were watching the enemy attack Sandpoint, Idaho.

"They're firing at the Long-Bridge," George said. "They'll take out our infrastructure."

Just then, Jim heard another sound and he turned to the south. "Do you hear that?"

The formation of three started moving forward and the volley of rocket-fire was on pause.

"Yeah. I hear it."

In a matter of seconds, the unmistakable sound of rapidly approaching military jets filled the air. The noise came with a distinct and powerful thud, and Jim could hear multiple flight paths arching into the valley.

Looking south for an approximate position, from the corner of his eye he spotted two high speed targets swoosh in front of him and then they climbed aggressively up and over the formation of gunships moving down the river. Heading north, the sound roared as they circled towards the ridge on the other side of the valley.

"Those were Migs, George. Did you get a good look?"

"Yep." He dropped the scope and shook his head. "They were Russian, Jim. I got a clear look—and I was wrong. I was wrong about everything! They're going to hurt us bad!"

Then it came, sudden and immediate. The cabin erupted with a thudding blast of two turbojet fighters arching from the southern ridgeline and then down into the valley. The power was immense, and at about five-miles to the south Jim could see the two fast-movers entering side-by-side over the river.

This is it, he thought. His heart was broken. Russia was the enemy. It was here to finish the job and they were responsible for everything. He knew they'd hit the airport. They'll get our food. They'll take out our weapons and our fuel, and like George said, they'll hurt us bad. His stomach was churning and the jets were approaching fast. We're screwed! We need—.

Before he could finish, the answers came. The unique and distinctive mechanical hum of big bullets launching out of fast guns erupted, and then the unthinkable happened. In slow-motion—two of the three helicopters exploded in mid-air, and then they both started falling. George pointed to the third gunship, but before he got his hand up it broke in-half and it was spiraling.

They saw it all, and when they looked at each other they were both speechless. Just then the jets flew overhead and the cabin rumbled. They were heading north towards Sandpoint, and Jim ran to the edge of the deck to follow. Just above the tree line, he could see both jets in formation as they started to circle the town. They weren't killing any patriots. When the enemy fired, they destroyed the enemy, and George wasn't wrong. He was right!

Now wings level, the two fast-movers were heading back towards the cabin and they flew straight over the three offenders who were now dead. Within seconds the cabin shook as they banked left and then climbed into the moonlit sky. They were heading south and the valley echoed with a sound nobody would forget. The jets were leaving, and again he looked at George.

Panicked, both Sarah and Darleen came running out the door and Sarah wanted answers. "What's happening?" she asked staring at Jim. He took her hand, but he was still speechless and he pointed to George.

"It's okay," he said with a calm voice. George grabbed Darleen's hand and they all four walked to the edge of the deck and stood against the snow-covered rail. Just to the right, the battlefield was in-sight—and George couldn't believe what he'd just seen. He was astonished, and he didn't know what to say.

"They almost got us," he said pointing to the enemy gunships. "It was way too close."

The departing jets were still echoing in the valley and Sarah wanted answers now.

"Was that us?" she said pointing to the south. "Do we have our military back?"

Jim shook his head.

"They were Russians."

CHAPTER 25

A NEW FREEDOM

On Day 122 the war against America became the war against freedom, liberty, and man. Evil thought it had the throne, and it wanted the entire world to stay put while it killed the remaining blasphemers spreading American morals. It was the "Big Day", and after the President's address the enemy couldn't wait any longer. The patriots had to be eliminated and America had to fall. The superpowers would concede. If they launched an air-strike now, nobody would intervene.

While China watched, Russia made the historical choice to say no. The deception had gone too far, and the deceivers were insane, delusional, and un-trustable. In one life-saving event; they defended the patriots and they forced the enemy to be held accountable for its defilement of everything.

While China watched, Russia saved the day, and they embraced the American people as an essential force fighting for liberty. On the night of the attack, they foiled the enemy's tactics over Idaho, Utah, and Arizona, and then they left so that the patriots could fight the inescapable battle. Now one-year later; America was still here—and the patriot's were still fighting.

Following the President's call to war, America's civil defense forces united. Millions assembled, and with brigades from all zones they came forth and they fought for their countrymen. New supply lines were forged, and while the U.S military reconstructed its troops the Civil Air Patrol fulfilled the mission of SafePort defense and forward air support. Rapid expansion ladders were carved into the non-SafePort states and safe-zones provided safe-passage. Forsaken no more were the refugees hiding from slaughter while trapped behind enemy lines. The people of America were an army of one, and evil had lost its special advantage.

Within six weeks following the enemy's failed air-attack; America's air power was back, and on Day 169 the U.S military returned with a vengeance. Where the civil defense forces had already decimated the camouflaged infantry, and where both the invaders and the marauders were in retreat, the Homeland was still divided and the enemy's infrastructure was still here.

The U.S. Government had a crime scene, and its Armed Forces locked the doors. Found inside were several covert air bases, and they all had the same fingerprint. America's EMP attack involved a treasonous agreement. Certain officials had conspired with the government of Iran. Where a high-altitude weather balloon delivered a smaller EMP over the southern states, the new reports were astounding and they added a new twist. America's infrastructures were destroyed by a Super EMP and it's origins point to a foreign satellite. The extent of collaboration is still unknown, but the official reports suggest the following. The Super EMP was likely a product of North Korea. It was likely an unexpected event that immediately followed the weather balloon terrorist attack. There appears to be no traceable alliance, either internally or with the government of Iran.

Found to be well established along the borders of both Canada and Mexico, and with secret bases in Eastern Oregon and California; it was clear that the enemy had been transporting its war machine into key locations since Day One. Had SafePort failed, the enemy would be in full control, but on Day 169—America was revived and the patriots prevailed. Freedom had its muscle back. All enemy bases were destroyed. All conspirators were put on notice and all veils were removed. The mystery was over. The enemy would pay.

With an army of millions, and on Day 402; America was defending the inalienable rights of all humans. The betrayal had run its course and it was time to deal with the damage. The deception was over—and so was the New World Order—but the Muslim faith had evolved and billions were becoming united. They were inheriting the world and the war was unstoppable. It wasn't radical at all. The infidels needed to obey. It was all part of the prophecy and it was Muslim law. There were no alternatives.

Planet Earth was a dangerous place, but mankind was smart and its survival would go to the most diligent, most rational, and fittest. Where many nations were under siege and where terror and civil war was erupting, a new America with a new knowledge was teaching the world how to proceed.

Survival was a right of life—and with every life defended—the good people could survive, communicate, and overcome. It was modern-day war and the enemy wouldn't stop. Defend your family now. Organize your civil defense. Fight as a whole.

In the center of the rear couch, Anne leaned back and kicked up her feet. "I had no idea you actually saw the Migs." Her cast resting on her lap, she was in awe. "And you saw it with the colonel!"

She turned off the recorder and looked at Jim. His story was stunning, and she didn't know where to start. There was so much, and it was so vivid. She could see the marauders and the invaders, and she could see the war in full.

"They had a front row seat," Ken said, stretching his arm over the steering wheel. "They watched it all."

"Did you see 'em?" she asked.

Shaking his head no, Ken was changing lanes and he was still using his blinker.

"Heard 'em when they passed over, but by the time I looked outside they were gone."

In America, the historical moment was still un-documented, and it was still spreading by word of mouth. Like folklore, everybody knew that Russia had stepped in, but few had heard the reports from participating eye-witnesses. Anne was going to change that, and with what she'd heard today she had the details of something incredible. There were unique connections between Ken, Jim, and the colonel, and her heart was pumping. She could thread the needle, and her dad was right. This is the big story.

Anne was getting excited and she could feel her ordeal in Montana slipping away. She had a purpose, and it overshadowed the little voice that said fear everything. Tonight she'd be in Salt Lake City and tomorrow she'd see her new office. She'd get her computer and her printer set up, and she'd set up a coffee pot. She'd go step-by-step and she was fully committed.

Now at fourteen-hours in, Salt Lake City was just over the horizon. The flatlands were over and the hills had a shallow flow. To the east, the rugged mountains were back and they had one-hundred miles to go. The night was dark and her notepad was full.

"So here's what I'm thinking, guys." Scooting forward, she rested her broken arm on the center console.

"We need to slow this interview down. There's something here, and I need deal with it before we go any further."

Anne took a deep breath and then she leaned forward. "My dad knows the colonel well, and he said the expanding supply chains saved millions. At a time when the U.S military couldn't, he said your unorthodox tactics made it possible for thousands of American's to patrol our airspace, defend our new supply chains, and spy on the enemy. He said I'd find a unique connection, and he said the circumstance and timing seamed miraculous. He sent me here to discover the truth, and I think I have."

Fumbling with her cast she could hear her stomach grumbling. "Let me document this, and then we'll explore the battle. We'll go slow and steady. And in reality, the story never ends. I mean, we're in it now, and it's still going."

Again, she could hear her stomach grumbling and she was sure that Jim could hear it too.

"With the airline front—and with the news media—we've got news coming out of our ears. We're stuck with each other."

Cracking a smile, she chuckled. "Plus, I know where you live."

Yawning, Jim stretched out his arms and he smiled back.

"Sounds good, Anne. You tell us when you're ready. Is that your stomach?"

"Yes," she said laughing.

"It's dark, and it's late, and we need some food. I did spot some crackers and salami back there."

Anne reached behind her and she held up a packet of cheese spread she'd pulled from the refrigerator. "We've got this stuff too. Who wants dinner? I can make us crackers."

Both men were nodding and both held up their thumbs.

"Okay then. Let's eat."

Anne gathered all of her supplies and she put them on a cutting board she'd found next to the small refrigerator. At five-foot two, she had plenty of head room and she was getting familiar with the layout. From the miniature galley and around the rear couch, supplies in-hand she returned to her seat with grace.

"So, Ken," she said, struggling with the cracker bag. "I do have a question for you."

With the seal broken, she pulled out a handful. "It's about your daughter."

"Samantha?"

"Yeah."

Leaning sideways, she could see him in the mirror. "When is she due? It sounds soon."

"It is. She's got a month to go."

Ken had a grin emerging and he shook his head. "Her and Pete got married at the Bluff."

"I knew it!"

Anne had been working the puzzle all day and she was thrilled at the news. It had to be Pete, and she was right.

"Way to go Samantha!"

Anne had three crackers with salami and she passed two to Jim. "She married the hero! I need to meet her," she said with her mouth full.

The small talk was good, and the food was spectacular. Anne could see the horizon ahead and her new home was getting closer. It was an important day. She had a strange feeling, and it felt good.

"We'll try this next," she said squeezing the cheese-like product out of its foil packet. "It smells okay."

Waiting patiently for another cracker, Jim was curious. "Have you seen the property yet?"

"Yep. Try these." She passed him the two samples with cheese, and then cautiously, she took a bite. "I saw it with my Dad."

Unimpressed, the salami was far better and she started slicing. "I saw your place too."

Anne paused for a moment and then she looked up. "You guys haven't seen it yet. I just remembered."

Both men laughed and then Jim responded. "Nope. But we know that our wives are happy there and we've got a home. It's kind of exciting."

"You'll love it, Jim. And I promise! You're both at the base of a national forest and you're both on the river. It's an outpost, but it's spectacular!"

With her eyes sincere, she was convincing and it was good to hear. "It's got a distinct quality, guys. You'll like it. It's far enough to be safe, but its close enough to commute and I hear we'll have a train soon. I know for a fact the airport is up-and running."

Anne had three slices cut and she pulled out three more crackers. "Doesn't the FAA have a new airplane waiting for you out there?"

"Yes. They do." Happy with the speed of the government's new project, it seemed everything was coming into place. "I guess we'll see that tomorrow too."

Jim was ready, and his new life was almost here. He was eager, but it was moving fast and it was hard to catch up.

"I talked with Paul last week. He told me he's learning how to be a cattle farmer with your dad."

"Yeah, I heard," she said, passing him two more specials.

"And I know my dad's a general, but he's a cowboy at heart. It's an important project, and it's good he's got a preacher on his side. He seems to like your brother."

"He's got a way," Jim said nodding. "Have you heard his story?"

"Only from my dad. But I'll talk with him next week at the ranch."

Anne grabbed the knife and she started slicing for one more round. Her stomach was happy, but one more would make it a dinner. This time, she'd slice it thick.

"I think the outpost exit is next," Ken said, flipping his high-beams on. "Then it's about two-hours east from there, right?"

"Yeah. I think so," Anne said.

She stowed the knife in her cup holder and started stacking the final slices. "You're both leaving in the morning?"

"First thing." Jim looked over to Ken and then back to Anne. "We haven't seen our wives in three-months. We drop this off, we sleep at the base, and then tomorrow we'll drive out with George."

"Ralph too," Ken said, nodding. "Don't forget about Ralph."

Anne looked up and she started laughing. "He's your dog. My dad didn't tell me, but now it makes sense."

She turned to Jim. "I want to meet him. We'll see Ralphy tonight, right?"

"Yeah. We'll see him."

Everybody loved Ralph, and Jim started to smile. He missed his family, and he'd be home soon. It was happening, and he was ready.

"I see a light," Ken said. "Just showed up."

"I see it." Jim could see a bright light in the middle of the darkness, and from here it looked like a lighted sign. In formation, they had security vehicles at both ends and Roberto had the lead. At one-mile ahead, he was almost there.

"Checkpoint's coming up. It's got to be a road sign." Jim grabbed the paperwork folder and he placed it on the dash.

All three looked into the darkness and the target was approaching fast. It was on the top of a small hill—and coming out of the turn it was clearly a road sign. At any second they'd see the message, and Jim was the first to read.

"Welcome to Salt Lake City. Checkpoint Ahead. Secured Area."

Just then, and as they crested the hill, there were more lights popping out of the darkness. Sporadic, but they were bright, and as Ken took his foot off the gas and coasted down the hill he could see they were industrial.

"These are farms," Ken said slowing down. "Is this the grid?"

"I think it is." Jim pointed to the building a mile ahead. "That's a warehouse and that's a parking lot. And it's bright."

He turned to Anne. "Have you seen this yet? The grid?"

Stunned, she smiled and shook her head. "No. It went on last week." Anne raised her arm and pointed. "Look at that!"

Suddenly, the cab got quiet and all three gazed at the powerful street lights that were approaching fast. They were flooding the entire highway, and on the horizon there were more lights. They were in awe, and they'd forgotten what it was like.

With Roberto only a half-mile ahead and slowing, Ken matched his speed. The highway was fully illuminated, and so was the cab. Jim turned to Anne, and he could see the light hitting her from all sides.

"Trippy," she said handing him two more crackers. "This is cool!"

For the three occupants who hadn't seen modern-day America for over a year, it was a sight to behold. While finishing their makeshift dinner, all three stared out the windows and they could see lights popping up everywhere. There were moving vehicles, and it was more than just a few. From out of the darkness—they were approaching a working city, and it felt good.

"Here's another checkpoint sign," Ken said, flipping on his high-beams and leaning forward.

Jim had the best eyes and it was almost in focus. "Let's see—what do we got here? Checkpoint Area—20 mile zone. All cars and trucks—Right two lanes only. All government vehicles—Left two lanes only. Stay in your lane."

"Okay then," Ken said, putting his blinker on. "Left lane it is."

Just then, Jim saw a trail of moving lights about two-miles ahead. "We've got on-coming. Look at that."

On the next hill and approaching fast, all three could see the long swath of oncoming headlights that were evenly spaced and spanning a good mile.

Anne scooted to the edge of her seat. "Wonder where they're going?"

"They're military." Ken could see the convoy under the streetlights and it was unmistakable.

"That's a troop movement," Jim said.

"Sure is." Ken pointed behind with his thumb. "And we've got company coming-up fast."

Just then, four high-speed vehicles with their orange lights flashing rapidly flew on by. It was almost midnight, and with Salt Lake City just ahead, the darkness was behind them. America was coming alive. It was beautiful, and it was getting better with every mile.

"This is definitely cool," Ken said, slowing to match Roberto. "Forgot what it was like."

Both men had been on the front lines, and from the beginning, they'd only heard about how the SafePort cities were recovering. Tonight, and on Day 402, they were finally seeing it for real. This was the America they'd been fighting for, and America was winning.

Anne tapped Jim on the shoulder and she pointed to the helicopter passing them on the right side. Scanning the sky, Jim found three-more, and they were all heading west into the desert. Everywhere they looked there was something to see, and then they saw another convoy coming around the turn.

"This is a deployment," Ken said, nodding. "Something's going on."

Just then the radio came alive and it was Roberto. "Leader One. Revision. Revision."

Jim picked it up and responded quickly. "What's the change, Rob?"

"I just talked with the colonel. He wants us to divert into a "holding pen" four-miles ahead, and he said he and the general are waiting for us there. He said our destination has been revised."

Looking over to Ken, Jim knew what it meant and he pushed the transmit button. "Roger. We'll follow you."

He put the radio down in its holster and turned to Anne. "It's probably the grid," he said calmly. "I'm guessing it's under attack."

"I wouldn't doubt it," Ken said, reducing his speed. "Something's afoot."

With Roberto slowing down, he could see another set of orange flashers approaching in his rearview mirror. Passing fast on his left, the two vehicles passed Rob's vehicle next and then they assumed the escort position in front of him. It was the U.S Army, and they had a "Follow Me" sign. They had their blinkers on, and they were heading for the exit.

"If my dad's here, that means we're going to the outpost. If we're under attack, it's standard procedure."

The uncertainty was getting to her and she could feel her heart-rate accelerating. She was curious, and she thought about what her dad had told her about the enemy's plan. He said they'd use terrible weapons against our new cities. He said they'd try to extinguish our grids, and he said we needed to defend our technology, or we'd lose. Why is he here? What did he mean by terrible? What's going on, Dad?

Now on the access road and at slow pace, the entrance to the holding pen was just ahead, and it was filled with cargo trucks waiting to get into the checkpoint crossing. There was food, gas, and everything else, and they were all waiting to get into the city. It looked busy, and Ken was thankful to see the lead vehicles pass it by. They were continuing down the access road.

While Roberto followed the escorts in a tight formation, Ken kept his maneuverability distance and they were now paralleling the holding pen.

Looking out the window, Jim was admiring the view and he couldn't take his eyes off of it. He was astonished. This was the supply chain we almost lost, but here it is, and America's technology was coming back. It was happening fast, and he was impressed with the progress.

It looked like a truck stop, but it was bigger. He could see produce, cattle, and refrigeration trucks. He could see hundreds of new cars, and he could see there were three lanes dedicated to auto transport. Now at the front of the line, there was a huge gas station—and there might even be a restaurant over there, but he couldn't tell, and it was time to look forward.

With the holding pen behind them they were crossing the "Do Not Enter" zone now. Ken added a little gas to keep pace and they could see a small building a half-mile down the road. It was well lit, and there were several vehicles, parked and running.

"That's got to be them," Jim said, pointing.

Ken took his foot off the gas and he leaned forward on the steering wheel. The engine went quiet, and so did the cab. Nobody was talking and the uncertainty was rising. Then they saw George.

Standing next to a large SUV, the colonel was waving his hands and it looked like the general was waving too. There was an Army unit surrounding the perimeter and the guards were guiding Rob into the defended area. The two men who were changing things were only five-hundred feet away. Curiosity was building.

While Rob pulled up next to the SUV, Ken stopped where he could still make the turn back onto the access road. He set the brake, turned off his headlights, and then sighed.

"Shall we?" he said unbuckling his seatbelt. He turned to Anne. "Let's go talk with your dad."

Tapping his shoulder, Jim pointed. "Here's George."

Both the colonel and the general were walking fast and they were each heading for opposite sides of the cab. With the windows coming down, George grabbed the handrail on Jim's side and walked up the two steps.

"Hey guys. We're going to the outpost."

From the other side, Ken and the general were shaking hands and Anne wanted answers.

"Hi Dad. What's going on?"

Grabbing the handrail, he bent down.

"It's a precaution, Annie. They got Phoenix with a dirty nuke—and we're under heavy fire near Hoover Dam. We need to scoot. Troops coming in."

He looked at Ken. "It's Summertime. Too hot and the city was abandoned months ago. No casualties. But nobody's going back. Phoenix is gone, and we've got a whole new strategy here."

"We know there's two more," George said nodding. "We're working on it, and we're close, but we've got to be careful with our cities."

Bending down, he squatted on his knees. "It's our southern border. Heavy troops, looters, you name it. We've got us a gold rush here, and they're coming in fast, so we're going to slow this down. We play it safe."

With both men nodding, George stood up.

"We're going home, guys." He let go of the handrail and walked down the two steps. "Follow us," he said pulling out a fresh cigar. Heading for the curb, he pulled out his lighter. "Four hours."

While giving his boss some time with his daughter, George was standing under the lone streetlight thirty-feet away. While Jim watched him light up his cigar he let his mind catch up with the revision—and everything. It was interesting, and he liked safe.

Just then, the lights flickered and he watched George shake his head.

"They can't win," he said puffing out the smoke. "They might knock this down. They might slow us up. But they can't win."

Ken turned to the general. "Safe is good, sir. We'll follow you."

Unbuckling his seatbelt, Jim was ready for the new diversion and it was his turn at the wheel. He'd fill up his coffee cup, he'd drive the final leg home, and he'd see Sarah. They were safe and it was the new way to survive. It felt right.

Again, Jim looked over to George, and when he did the smell coming from his cigar brought good memories. A unique view of his friend, he was a remarkable man and he was unusual. With an army behind him, the smoke was hiding his identity, but Jim knew—and his mind took a snapshot. Then he saw something.

Through the small cloud of billowing smoke he could see a large dog nose sticking out of the SUV parked next to the building. His heart thumped.

"Is that Ralph?" Jim said in an elevated voice.

"Yep. That's him," George replied.

Ralph heard the familiar sound and he started whining out the window. Chuckling, Jim felt the same, but he and his dog would have to wait. First things, first.

"You ready?" the general asked. "We'll merge you in. You're in my unit now."

Nodding, both men watched as the general shifted his attention to his daughter.

"We've got room, Annie. You can ride with us."

Knowing her father was worried sick, Ken turned.

"Later, Anne. We'll continue as planned. Call us."

Looking at her father, she smiled. "Okay. Let's go."

Grabbing her bag, she scooted towards the passenger door. "Wait until you see this, guys. Just follow us."

Jim opened up his door and he held her good hand so she could get out onto the boarding step. With her dad waiting below, she shuttled her belongings and then she leaned in.

"I'll hug your dog for you. See you there."

She stepped back and Jim closed the door. "Thank you both. Thank you for everything!"

The general, the colonel, and Anne, all walked to the large SUV parked next to the building. While George briefed Roberto on the revision, Jim switched seats with Ken and they were ready for another leg. It was all part of the new strategy and America had a backup. Resiliency was the new ingredient. Ready on demand.

With an entire unit making the trip, multiple vehicles departed first, and then George got on the radio and directed Jim and his two security vehicles to enter the formation behind them. From the access road, and then onto the overpass—the caravan was heading north, and it was armed with a new freedom that changed everything.

From now on; America couldn't be killed, weakened, or taken away. It was everywhere. It had an army. It had food, water, and guns. It had everything it needed to survive, communicate, and defend, and today was just another day.

Opening his window, Jim let in some fresh air and it felt good to breathe. They were at ease, and they could feel a new future taking hold. It was sinking in, and with the streetlights bright, they could see the darkness ahead and they could see where the grid ended at the bottom of the long hill. It was all superficial, and in the Safe States it didn't matter. America was underneath and freedom had a brick wall.

"Tomorrow's another day," Jim said, cinching up his seat belt. "It's still on. Maybe it'll stay that way."

"Maybe." Ken tilted his head and turned. "We'll see."

Jim closed his window and the fresh air went away. The road noise was gone and the cab went quiet. Suddenly the lights flickered again—and both men chuckled. Then it flickered hard and everything went dark.

"How about some tunes, Ken? Plug us in. Something good."

While Ken searched the playlist, Jim could see the lights popping on in the distance. They were all dim and they were random, but as the seconds passed, more and more were coming on.

"There's the backup," he said, scanning the valley. Sipping his coffee, he gazed. "It's impressive, Ken. I think George is right. We'll be fine."

Scrolling through the music, Ken felt the same, but he still wondered.

"You know that border's been open for years. Before and after, Jim. It is a gold rush."

Finding his favorite song, he pushed enter and leaned back in his chair. "If you want to kill, steal, and invade, this is the place to be. It's not a civil war, it's ground-zero."

"Yep," Jim said, nodding. He reached for the volume and turned it up. "And we're ready."

THE SAFE STATE CHALLENGE

No Suffering. No Death.

Where SAFE STATES reveals an America that has endured a great deception, herein resides the tangible evidence of a great undermining. In our *real* America, we've endured the catastrophic discrepancy of *real* risk, and our entrenched powers have gone to great lengths to conceal, ignore, and discredit any meaningful mention of it. With a *"smoking gun"* however, the truth about our concealed vulnerability and our concealed defense is easily deduced.

Appropriately, the continuity of our U.S government and its associated agencies are fully defended against the HEMP weapon and the sudden loss of our critical infrastructures. The civilian populace, however, has been left grossly uninformed, lethally vulnerable, and completely undefended. Where the reasons are many, the SAFE STATE Countermeasure provides us with substantial proof that our continued survival has been inappropriately weakened for political benefit.

Herein, an emergency defense solution built for the modern-day war strategy of HEMP is revealed. Implemented by the individual community, it would save millions, it would preserve freedom, and it would inspire unity. As a substitute for NIPP (National Infrastructure Protection Plan) that has failed to deliver and is politically restrained from defending the private sector from HEMP, every American would have a backup supply chain and the people could communicate, organize, and unite. In other words, the American system would work as advertised and the will of the people would be real.

Where the unstoppable collision is now irreversible and approaching fast; the attack on our freedom is inevitable and the deception of risk must stop. SAFE zones are real. We can change our future and our families can live.

Today, the SAFE STATE Project is striving to empower the American people with a new freedom that keeps us alive, gives us hope, and makes us strong. Step-by-step, the countermeasure is maturing, the message is clear, and the patriots can see and hear. The choice is ours and the time is now. This is how we prevail.

Herein, the SAFE STATE Challenge begins. Using the SAFE STATE Countermeasure Manual to restore basic survival, liberty, and freedom; the challenge has three (3) objectives.

1. Civilian Survival: General implementation of SAFE STATE countermeasure. All Americans should secure an emergency private SAFE zone at home—or if required—establish a prearranged escape plan.

2. Patriotic Support: Make your voice known. Organize, donate, and petition your local government to help the SAFE STATE Project grow. Seek peaceful and honest debate. Help NIPP onto the national stage. Help our government agencies do the job they want to do—without political restraints. Demand community shielding be a part of our critical resources and national security.

3. Community-wide/State-wide implementation. SAFE STATES.

A short excerpt from the new SAFE STATE Countermeasure Manual (SSCM) is attached for public review and discussion. Released as part of the SAFE STATE Project, SSCM is a groundbreaking document that merges achievable/high-confidence survival standards for the private individual, community, county, and state.

The countermeasure summary, its purpose, and its structure reveal the consensus of experts in guiding a new industry to defend the people of the United States from HEMP. It is a glimpse of our future. It is a platform where no government platform exists. It is the beginning of a national discussion that must commence.

CHAPTER 1.0

MANUAL INTRODUCTION

Section 1: Alternative to NIPP/Countermeasure (CM) Introduction

Section 2: SAFESTATE CM Assets

Section 3: SAFESTATE Objectives

Section 4: Threat Assessment/Industry Experts/Reference Material

Section 5: Manual Structure/Survival Target Standards (STS)

Section 6: Manual Currency

Important Note: The SAFE STATE Countermeasure Manual (SSCM) supplements the failed execution and incomplete goals of the U.S National Infrastructure Protection Plan (NIPP) in two (2) **critical** ways.

1. Failed Execution: Where NIPP has routinely failed to receive the required funding and political will necessary to execute the hardening of our civilian infrastructures/protection of our key sectors and resources; the standardized SAFE STATE Countermeasure Manual (SSCM) provides the private sector with a rudimentary alternative to defend their families and communities. At its root, and in accordance with all regulatory requirements, including continuing compliance and certification compliance, the SSCM is specifically designed for *private use* (nationally), and *state use* at the local level.

2. Incomplete Goals: Following September 11, 2001, and over a period of many years; NIPP, and its principal agencies (DHS, FEMA) have formulated a comprehensive plan to harden the key sectors of our critical infrastructures, *however*, under its current scope, and if executed, it would **only** defend the American populace from a solar event (solar flare/CME) and cyberwarfare event. Given the worst-case scenario of a now looming, and strategically viable EMP attack, the NIPP plan inherently fails to defend the American populace (the front lines) from this catastrophic risk. In contrast to the mission statement, calls for action, and mandate; NIPP offers no lifeline to the 300 million people that would be stranded on foot with little to no food, few working cars, and potentially no working communication devices. While it references the need for community preparedness, it offers no published plan or set of goals that serve to defend the American people from the elevated EMP threat emerging from N. Korea and Iran.

   - Where a solar flare or CME will **not** destroy our autonomous electronics, communication devices, or cars; hardening our critical infrastructures in accordance with NIPP **will** therefore provide the American people with a functional supply chain to regain/restart following a solar flare/CME event. *However*; if America were to suffer a catastrophic high altitude EMP attack (HEMP), the private sector (300 million people) would likely be stripped of all personal technology (damaged electronics/ appliances, phones and cars), and they'd be trapped and isolated with no way to organize, no way to receive or distribute food, and no way to survive. Massive death tolls would ensue, and the hardened infrastructures would fail to function without a mobilized workforce.

- Where NIPP's plan to harden our critical infrastructures would only defend America from a catastrophic solar flare/ CME/cyberwarfare event, the SAFE STATE countermeasure bridges the EMP gap that separates the American people from a responsible, lifesaving defense. Whether incorporated as an essential supplement to NIPP at some future date, or whether implemented by the populace and states as a stand-alone community defense today, the SSCM defends the American people from both an EMP and solar flare/CME event, respectively, and it provides a high confidence/low-cost alternative to **no defense** at all.

- Given our divided government, diverging political goals, and the elevated EMP threat coming from N. Korea and Iran, a catastrophic recipe for national destruction is present. Therefore, while America resides in this state of no defense, an emergency shielding plan that defends the American people at the local and state level is not only prudent, but rationally required. The combination of a united government, NIPP, and a community shielding plan (SSCM) is the best and most effective defense for modern-day America. SAFE STATES seeks to advance this combined defense, but while America remains terminally **undefended**, this private sector/community shielding countermeasure is published as an emergency supplement.

Summary:

The SAFE STATE Countermeasure (SSCM) Manual is a private instructional guide for individuals, communities, and states seeking to develop and implement the private sector SAFE Zone infrastructure. The manual's primary purpose is to provide the civilian populace of the continental U.S with an effective defense to the escalating wartime threat of a sudden and catastrophic infrastructure collapse. The SSCM is both an emergency *substitute*, and private sector *supplement* to the National Infrastructure Protection Plan (NIPP) that has failed to receive the requisite bipartisan support.

Designed and created as a civilian defense that can withstand the inevitable worst-case scenario of a HEMP attack, whether a cyber-attack on our national power grids, or whether a catastrophic solar flare, the SAFE STATE Countermeasure is a simple 3-step plan that can effectively shield its users from the deadly threats of a long-term grid-down event.

In pursuit of maximum survivability—the SSCM combats the world's most sinister man-made threat with a unique and specialized defense. Not only will it shield our essential survival technology from the damaging forces of weaponized EMP, but it also serves the critical function of empowering our civilian populace with an appropriate framework to survive and defend during a national emergency/grid-down event. The SSCM purpose is two-fold.

- **Civilian Survival:** Through an equivalency system of low-tech electromagnetic defense that mirrors our troops in the modern-day battlefield, Preservation Shielding will protect a standardized set of essential technology for each user (CM Step 1). Through standardized emergency stores, basic survival equipment, and a predetermined Crossover plan (CM Step 2); each user will have met the minimum requirements necessary for long-term/indefinite survival in the post-HEMP/grid-down environment.

- **Civilian Unification:** Through a predetermined civil defense communications infrastructure that has been adopted herein, is well established, and has been specifically designed to survive and operate in the post-HEMP environment, the basic requirements for civilian unification, organization, communication, and command and control have been met. Additionally, through the SSCM's Survival Zone Sharing Program (proposed 2020); the unification and merger of patriots nationwide—regardless of geographical location—can be prearranged to form an emergency coalition when required (CM Step3).

Standardized for immediate implementation, SAFE STATE's step-by-step manual provides the civilian populace with a life-saving countermeasure that can be self-administered and customized to fit the specific needs of each individual. All citizens from high-risk nations who currently rely on civilian infrastructures for daily sustenance and basic survival are now vulnerable, and given the elevating risk for mass suffering, mass death, and an irreversible national collapse, a HEMP proof countermeasure is intrinsically required.

Both the SSCM and its companion novel, SAFE STATES are the essential learning tools of the countermeasure system. In an effort to maximize civilian knowledge and promote a tactical understanding, countermeasure presentation has been delivered along with a fictional experience designed to illuminate the real-world suffering that is produced by HEMP. Unique learning structure builds the appropriate life-changing skills that are needed to perceive our dangerous condition and to survive accordingly. With the relevant information presented herein, and with the practical experience found within the storyline of the novel, readers will find their instincts empowered with the truth of our world, a special survival plan, and a dutiful purpose.

Where the SSCM has a primary function, which is to mitigate the catastrophic risk of an enemy HEMP attack on America and her allies, a secondary function exists. In the SAFESTATE Risk Analysis (Section 1; Chapter 2)—the disturbing conclusion that the American people have been left grossly undefended to the threat of HEMP, solar flare/CME, and cyberwarfare can be made. Furthermore, it can be reasonably deduced that our catastrophic vulnerability has been inappropriately created, facilitated, and enhanced for political benefit.

Urgently, and in an effort to mitigate the deadly consequence of a divided government and nation, herein SAFE STATE delivers the rational response to the reasonable people who are both willing and capable of defending their families, future, and freedom.

Countermeasure (CM) assets are described below.

SECTION 2: SAFESTATE CM Assets

1. HEMP-Proof Grid-Down Survival System: Both enemy induced (EMP, computer hacking, terrorism), and naturally occurring (solar flare, etc.) grid-down supply-chain failure events are responsibly defended.

2. Worst-Case Scenario Advantage: Simplified techniques provide private individuals, families, and communities with functioning technology (essential survival equipment, communications, transportation, etc.) in the post-HEMP environment, and therefore, all grid-down emergencies to include natural disasters, terrorism, or any long-term supply-chain failures are defended appropriately.

3. Self-Administered: SAFE STATE is a personal survival countermeasure that is simple and low-cost. Most individuals/ families can self-implement a private SAFE Zone at a cost similar to the standard health insurance costs for one individual. Advantages are extreme and CM implementation can make the difference between life and death.

4. Protected Survival Infrastructure: Personal transportation, power generators, water harvesting equipment, communications, and modern-day tools can all be defended from HEMP and safely preserved for emergency use.

5. Customized Survival Zone Strategy: Home-base shelter—versus—emergency escape to a more survivable location. Countermeasure can be applied to user's existing residence for long-term shelter—or with protected emergency transportation—countermeasure ensures that an escape function is both available and operational

if required. If desired, long-term food and water acquisition can be extended from most any location—and potentially, long-term survival can be safely managed from a home base that would otherwise be un-survivable due to its physical location.

> **NOTE 1**: In a post-HEMP attack/grid-down failure, most of the undefended populace will be forced to leave their existing residence and seek out a more survivable location. Without an operating survival infrastructure, and without the essential technology that can help manage and transport off-site food and water acquisitions back to the home base, the starving populace will be forced to leave their homes. Within days, most will have to take what they can carry on their backs and then move to an area that is closer to natural food and water sources. In an undefended America, it is expected that the transient refugee populace will grow to the tens of millions within a very short amount of time.

> **NOTE 2**: For those citizens living in a high-density population/high-risk area that is not conducive to long-term survival, escape is inherently required. For those citizens who do not have a survivable location for which to plan an emergency escape and subsequent relocation, the SSCM Survival Sharing Program (proposed 2020) and Relocation Policy apply. It is with this essential program where patriots can help other patriots in maximizing an effective survival plan and maximizing an effective civil defense through strategic arrangements that only apply if a national emergency occurs.

6. Survival Command and Control: Survival zone infrastructure can maintain a strong post-event survival and rescue force. With preserved communications, the operating command and control infrastructures of the SAFE Zone can assist communities and emergency services with life-saving duties.

> **NOTE 1**: The expert consensus declares the following with respect to self-sufficiency in the long-term survival environment.

All self-contained private survival systems (to include the private SAFE Zone infrastructure and the many random survivalists) are woefully insufficient to maintain long-term stability and strength if left to survive isolated from one another and on their own. Without mutual support from other local survivors with complimentary specialty skills, the structural integrity of the private survival zone is compromised to the point where severe weakness and eventual failure is likely. Only with the added support of local participants (neighborhoods and communities) can the private survival zone infrastructure maintain a strong and dependable force that is capable of defending its people and territory.

7. Local Defense/Law and Order: Mobilization of the SAFE Zone populace (organized civilians with functional command and control) creates an effective local defense force.

8. Civil Defense: the SAFE STATE Countermeasure (SAFE Zone) strengthens national security and defends freedom appropriately. In America, and within all towns and all states, civilian command-and-control infrastructures (SAFE Zones) can provide critical assistance to the U.S. government (DHS, FEMA, etc.) during any post-event national emergency.

9. Emergency Services Support: SAFE STATE Countermeasure strengthens local functionality of emergency services (Police, Fire, Hospital, etc.) to operable levels that can benefit the local community. With Preservation Shielding, adequate technology (such as communications and transportation) can provide the necessary infrastructure to aid the local populace with both law and order and emergency services.

NOTE 1: Without sufficient CM defense; following a successful HEMP detonation—all emergency services will experience a sudden and indefinite collapse. As the national suffering commences with no food and no water, the local populace will be left isolated and on their own.

SECTION 3: SAFESTATE Objectives

OBJECTIVE ONE

Provide an effective, low-cost civilian countermeasure to HEMP, solar flare/CME, cyberwarfare, terrorism, that mirrors the national continuity and defense objectives existing within our government and military today:

1. Civilian Equivalent: SSCM provides a simplified 3-step solution which enables a private and secure SAFE Zone. Through standardized Preservation Shielding, standardized emergency stores, and standardized policy, civilian vulnerability is reduced so that high-confidence survivability and civil defense continuity is appropriately obtained.

2. Low-Cost Self Defense: Manual provides private individuals with a step-by-step path to the most cost-effective method of survival. See NOTES below.

> **NOTE 1**: Several methods for defending our civilian infrastructures from HEMP exist, however none, with the exception of the SSCM are both cost-effective and achievable. National hardening of our power and communication grids would require an enormous fiscal investment and it would require bipartisan political support. Regulations requiring manufactures to produce hardened electronics would be insufficient against the threat and it would destabilize the global markets.

> **NOTE 2**: With simplified Preservation Shielding of standardized survival equipment, (see MSHEL; Chapter 3.0), an emergency backup is obtained for each user employing the SSCM. Both home-built and pre-manufactured preservation systems (see Faraday Cage enclosures: Chapter 3.0; Section 1) can reduce EMP vulnerability to sufficient levels if constructed with the proper design and materials.

NOTE 3: To reduce countermeasure costs, manual promotes the cost-effective practice of self-built Faraday Cage enclosures by capable individuals. As shielding effectiveness of the enclosure is critical, the SAFE STATE Countermeasure Manual strives to provide its users with recommended expert resources that can aid in the construction of home-built EMP-proof enclosures. Only those industry sources which provide design and materials that meet the SSCM Certification Standards will be recommended (see Faraday Cage Certification Standards, Chapter 3.0; Section 2).

NOTE 4: Manufactured Shielding Enclosures: Shielding effectiveness is a critical component of the SAFE STATE Countermeasure. Any design error of the enclosure can cause a catastrophic failure in its shielding capability and render it useless in protecting the stored equipment inside. Professionally manufactured enclosures can be the safest and quickest path to CM implementation and compliance; however, it is imperative that all shielding products purchased from manufacturers meet the minimum SSCM Certification Standards. Equivalent to the U.S Military certification standards for electromagnetic shielding defense, only those products meeting these standards will be recommended.

3. National Strength: Ultimately, increased community and state-wide compliance is sought. In its expanded/community form, the SAFE Zone infrastructure complements both FEMA and DHS national security goals, and with the additional war-time strength of a cohesive civil defense—government workloads can be reduced. In times of national emergency, shielded, prepositioned command and control infrastructures which sustain the survival/defense needs of the local populace provides an extreme and inherent national security advantage.

OBJECTIVE TWO

Provide a standardized, step-by-step instruction manual that will not only provide every citizen with an effective method to survive modern-day war, but it will also provide an emergency survival infrastructure that has the capability to sustain life indefinitely for all participants.

1. SAFE STATES is a 3-Step Plan: Manual objective is to help the user implement and manage the SAFE STATE Countermeasure in three (3) simple steps. Standardized minimums and easy-to-understand instructions help the users achieve rapid compliance and the required operational knowledge to maximize the new survival strength and advantage when needed.

2. Standardized System: Methods incorporating Strategic Preservation Shielding (Faraday Cage protection)—merged with strategic food, water, equipment, and medical provisions have been standardized into an organized, long-term national contingency plan that is designed for indefinite grid-down survival. Incorporating the Crossover Plan (CM Step 2)—a backup supply chain can be developed and expanded for indefinite use.

3. Wartime Strength: SAFE STATE Manual seeks to arm the civilian populace with a sufficiently adequate civil defense standard that meets the war-time threats of our modern-day. In addition to the life-saving survival methods described above, Standardized SAFE STATE Operating Procedures (SSOP's) are provided for both pre and post emergency operations.

OBJECTIVE THREE

Provide SSCM users with a Standardized SAFE STATE Operating Procedures Manual (SSOP) for both pre and post emergency operations:

1. Standardized Procedures: SSOP Manual provides a basic survival and defense procedural guide (pre-event/post-event) to be used in times of national emergency (catastrophic). Post-event survival

policies are provided as a recommendation only and are intended to establish a unified standard for all SAFE Zones during times of national supply-chain failure/national communications failure/ war. Further development of the SSOP will expand with increased implementation, industry alliance, and user feedback.

2. Civil Defense Policies and User Guidance: Provide a standardized policy and procedure that can be used as an effective "baseline" guide to help define the survival and defense roles of a civilian populace at war. Issued separately; and designed to be a supplementary manual system that is downloadable on-demand, User Guidance for all areas of CM preparations, CM survival, and CM defense will be provided through multiple resources. Both the SSOP Manual and other valuable industry resources will be recommended.

> **NOTE 1**: CM policies can aid the civilian populace in maximizing civil defense capabilities so that freedom can be defended effectively in a time of war or national tragedy. Hardened SAFE Zone communication infrastructures merged with pre-existing national Ham radio infrastructures (U.S users only) not only enables post-event connectivity, but it promotes an effective post-event command and control. See Chapter 5.0: Section 3; Civil Defense Connectivity.

> **NOTE 2**: Expanded SAFE Zone compliance within the national populace will elevate civil defense capabilities exponentially. Post-event survival policies will therefore expand with increased compliance, implementation, and practical application.

OBJECTIVE FOUR

Provide an effective framework that will not only unify all patriots with CM protection, but it will maximize civil defense through its Survival Zone Sharing Program and its Civil Defense Connectivity.

1. United Survival Force: Given the increasing risk of a HEMP attack

on the American Homeland all the barriers to an effective civil defense force (geographical locations, economical restraints, etc.) must be solved. Where many patriots living in large cities will have to escape and relocate to survivable areas if the national grids go down, and where all patriots nationwide will have to maintain post-event connectivity and command and control, the SAFE STATE CM provides the essential framework that will facilitate both.

2. Survival Zone Sharing Program (proposed 2020; U.S only): The SSCM Survival Zone Sharing Program is a revolutionary method that circumvents the economical barriers of an at-risk populace that has no viable location to survive if the grids go down. By uniting all patriots under an emergency agreement that enables preplanned escape, pre-planned relocation, and pre-planned long-term survival, a unified civil defense force is achieved. For those patriots with various skills and assets who would otherwise be trapped with no predetermined destination for escape and relocation, it is clear that other patriots living in a more survivable location would likely benefit from any arrangement that brings skilled personnel to the vicinity of the SAFE Zone. A critical component of the SSCM, the Survival Zone Sharing Program is an essential tool for uniting all patriots with CM defense. See Chapter 5.0: Section 3; United Survival Force.

3. Civil Defense Connectivity (U.S only): Where each SAFE Zone must have the exclusive ability to communicate effectively with other CM survivors, and where all CM survivors must be able to organize and perform as an effective unified force, a pre-event connectivity plan that establishes a discreet national communications infrastructure for post-event command and control is therefore required. Adopting the existing Ham radio infrastructures already established in the U.S, the SSCM has integrated the ARES (Amateur Radio Emergency Service), the ARRL (Amateur Radio Relay League), and all similar networks as the proposed standard communications infrastructure for post-event connectivity. See Chapter 5.0: Section 3; United Survival Force.

OBJECTIVE FIVE

Provide SAFE STATE users with an Event Analysis and Troubleshooting tool that can be used in the grid-down environment (post-event). Based on user observations (post-event), both the Damage Assessment checklist and the Event Source Analysis (root cause of the grid-down environment) will help identify both the long-term challenges and the associated survival strategies that will be required. Event Analysis and Troubleshooting tools are components of the SSOP and can be downloaded from the SAFESTATE website when made available.

1. Strategic Development and Troubleshooting Flow-Chart: With standardized methods and the most current, up-to-date expert recommendations on best survival practices, the SAFE STATE Manual provides the user with a Damage Assessment/Troubleshooting Flowchart for post-event strategic planning.

    NOTE 1: The Troubleshooting Flowchart is a simple but powerful post-event survival tool built to assist the user in defining an accurate perception of the emerging post-event threat, event magnitude, and associated risk. Additionally—the Troubleshooting Flowchart will help identify tactical challenges and recommend prudent solutions as they evolve in the field.

    NOTE 2: Based on user observations, when measured against the manual's data, the troubleshooting tool will help determine the tactical differences between solar flare damage, hacking damage, and weaponized EMP damage—all of which have varying effects on the survival requirements of the exposed populace.

    NOTE 3: Damage Assessment/Troubleshooting Flowchart and all post-event survival guidance tools to include the SSOP Manual will be provided separately on the SAFE STATE website to assist the user in making knowledgeable post-event SAFE Zone decisions. These additional documents are essential components of the Countermeasure Manual System and are based in scientific principles, expert recommendations, standardized data, and the most current and available information.

SECTION 4: Threat Assessment

See Catastrophic Vulnerability and the SAFE STATE Defense: Chapter 2; Section 1. Threat assessment requires the ongoing measurement of risk. Where an abreviated analysis has been provided herein, as new developments mandate an update or revision—this section will be revised accordingly. Industry experts will play a key role.

Industry Experts

Where the structural integrity of the SAFE Zone is maximized through the standardized shielding of specialty components, high-confidence survivability can only be obtained through the guidance and knowledge of industry experts. In an effort to maximize simplicity and standardization, the Countermeasure Manual itself applies minimal comment on risk/threat analysis and expanded survival methods, theory and tactics.

To maximize high-confidence survivability; the fundamental belief that expanded procedures and comprehensive survival techniques are best left to the respective experts in each field is applicable, and it has been incorporated into this manual. When required, general components within the countermeasure will be listed as a recommended minimum standard (Survival Target Standard)—and users will be directed to an outside source (or multiple sources) for compliance methods.

General survival knowledge is an essential ingredient of a successful SAFE Zone. Having the appropriate reference material on hand and readily available during an emergency is a minimum requirement of responsible CM compliance. Therefore, in addition to complying with the essential Preservation Shielding component (CM Step 1) and Emergency Stores (CM Step 2) of the SSCM—the swift acquisition of key reference materials providing the basic survival knowledge and techniques that can help users stay alive is strongly encouraged.

As with all elements of the SAFE STATE defense, personal delay has a direct effect on risk—and with any deferment the opportunity to survive can be lost forever. To assist users with the acquisition of key documents, Safe States provides the following general recommendations of basic resources required.

REFERENCE MATERIAL RECOMMENDATIONS:

Basic survival and Advanced survival

Survival methods and techniques

Emergency stores/self-sustenance/food acquisition and food storage

Hunting/fishing

Survival medicine/emergency medical

Operating Manuals for all survival equipment

Home defense

NOTE: Countermeasure Manual may reference supplemental information that has either been adopted or is recommended. When outside resources are referred to as a recommended practice, they will be noted as the exterior source for expanded information. Supplemental products and manufacturers found beneficial to SAFE Zone development and CM compliance are recommended on the SAFESTATE website.

SECTION 5: Manual Structure: 3-step Plan

The SAFESTATE Countermeasure Manual has been standardized into a 3-step plan. High confidence survival is obtained through completing steps 1 and 2, whereas step 3 is provided as procedural guidance for post-event survival operations. Herein, Standardized SAFE STATE Operating Procedure's (SSOP) are briefly described within Step-3 (Chapter 5), however, expanded guidance will be provided separately on the SAFESTATE website when made available.

STEP 1: Preservation Shielding of critical equipment— Chapter 3.0

STEP 2: Emergency Stores (food, water, medical, etc.)— Chapter 4.0

STEP 3: Operational Policy and Procedure (SSOP)—Chapter 5.0

Survival Target Standards (STS):

The SSCM is a standardized countermeasure plan that promotes uniform compliance for the benefit of all users. The two (2) key components that form an effective SAFE Zone are Preservation Shielding and Emergency Stores. Within each component are subcomponents which are firstly defined—then followed by an assigned Survival Target Standard (STS). The STS is established for both user planning and user implementation purposes and should be used as the primary tool for measuring the basic needs of each zone.

Source Documents:

The SSCM has integrated the cumulative knowledge, expertise, and data that have been published within the public domain. The following is only a partial listing of the source documents incorporated herein:

Congressional Reports; EMP Commission 2000, 2004, 2008, 2017

Unified Theory of Survivability; DOD

Vulnerability Risk Assessment; Army Research Laboratory

CS116, RS105; Enclosure Resistance to both HEMP and NEMP

U.S Army Corps of Engineers/EP 1110-3-2 EMP Defense/ Protection

SECTION 6: Manual Currency

To meet the escalating needs of evolving standards and improved practices, SSCM Manual incorporates a List of Effective Pages (LEP) and Manual Revision System to ensure up-to-date information and tactical currency. LEP/Manual Revision System is further described below.

List of Effective Pages (LEP; Appendix A), Manual Revision System.

List of Effective Pages (LEP):

The SAFE STATE Manual includes a List of Effective Pages (LEP; Appendix A) which ensures manual currency when revised chapters have been issued. As expanded and improved Policy, Procedures, and Standards become applicable for inclusion or revision to a manual chapter, the LEP chapter will identify the most current chapter revision by date. Constructed for "at-a-glance" reference by the user, the List of Effective Pages is a primary component of the Manual Revision System.

Manual Revision System:

Manual Revision System is an updating system to manage expansion and improvements. When updates are made to a chapter within the Counter-measure manual, to ensure accuracy, a complete chapter revision is issued by date. Revised chapters are tracked by the LEP and each revision is summarized. Manual users requiring updated/revised chapters can download/print from the Revisions tab on the SAFE STATE website.

CATASTROPHIC SUPPLY CHAIN FAILURE

Section 1: Catastrophic Vulnerability and the SAFE STATE Defense

Section 2: Indefinite Survival—The 6-Month Food Contingency

Section 3: SAFE Zone; Survival Area Freedom Enforcement Operational Reach Territory

Section 4: Civil Defense—A National Duty

Section 5: Countermeasure Training—Mental Readiness

1. In America, the "people's" power and strength is a fundamental component of defending freedom. Within the framework of its Constitution, the American people have been duly assigned as the essential final defenders that protect freedom from insidious attack. Through its armed populace, it is the American people who not only ensure that a loyal representation of the people's will is substantially defended, but through a united force of overwhelming strength, deters both oppression and aggression. A successful and effective system, throughout the centuries it has been the "will of the American people" that has carved freedom's path.

2. In all nations; corruption, fanaticism, deceitful politics, and radical religions all appear to be on a deadly and unstoppable collision course with the defenders of freedom. Concurrently, and while the instability of our present-day world continues to escalate, the essential systems of freedom which rely on a well-organized populace to provide an effective defense have been tactically nullified by the advent of modern-day weapons and political malfeasance. With the new war-winning strategy of HEMP, radicalized enemies of America (N. Korea and Iran) are now tactically driven to target our civilian supply chains and infrastructures, and MAD (Mutually Assured Destruction) may not work as rational deterrent. With one nuclear weapon detonated at a high altitude, the war can be won. Ensured victory while diminishing America's ability to retaliate effectively makes the HEMP weapon the most likely war strategy to be used.

3. Hyper-reliant on all national "ready-to-fail" supply chains and while distracted from the induced vulnerability, by political design the general populace remains unaware that our critical infrastructures can be purposely destroyed by a rogue enemy such as North Korea or Iran—or naturally destroyed by our own Sun. Within seconds or less, at any time this life changing event can occur. Through the inevitable forces of nature (catastrophic solar flare),

or a manmade nuclear EMP (high-altitude detonation/HEMP), the supply chain is suddenly removed, and the undefended populace is rendered trapped, helpless, and lethally exposed.

4. Without functioning critical infrastructures to support the fundamental needs of our modern-day society, the people's food, water, communication, and transportation suddenly stops. Expert estimates for the repair of our national grids following a catastrophic HEMP attack range from several years—to never. The estimated national death toll in America ranges from 70 to 90 percent of our populace in the first year.

5. Following a catastrophic HEMP attack in America, the armed populace charged with protecting freedom would be instantly stranded without food, water, transportation or communication. Within days and weeks, the largest army in the world would be starving, impotent, and weak. Our Homeland defense would degrade to near zero. Within weeks to months, the extreme exposure to an undefended overthrow or invasion would end with surrender, submission, and death.

Summary: Catastrophic vulnerability and the SAFE STATE Defense

At its roots, the SAFESTATE Countermeasure is a community survival and defense system that is built for the unique condition emerging in America today. Issued directly to the American people who've been denied critical information, its core mission is to bridge the gap of life and death that our divided government has woefully ignored. If implemented on a national scale, the countermeasure will save millions of lives if attacked by HEMP— and it will empower the populace of our cities and states with an on-demand survival defense that will enforce the peoples will—and freedom—appropriately. If our supply chain's go down—or if our nation is undermined by a criminal element seeking to undo our checks and balances, suppress our free speech, or sever the republic—the American people will prevail.

SECTION 2: Indefinite Survival:

The 6-Month Food Contingency

With adequate countermeasure defense methods applied, the vulnerability to a grid-down starvation event can be advantageously reduced to both survivable levels and defendable levels. In determining the adequate countermeasure response that is both viable and achievable, minimum standards were applied to the HEMP survival scenario. Where both viability and achievability are minimum requirements, effective targets that balanced both elements were identified.

In determining the most effective "baseline" standard for the general populace, the SAFE STATE's civilian defense project first measured attainable levels of survival resilience, then compared optimum countermeasure response with lesser degrees of survival resilience in its search for an effective minimum practical standard. With all variables considered, an achievable and optimized minimum standard for worldwide application was identified.

In determining practical standards for "long-term" survival resilience during an extended grid-down failure, while considering the essential contingency of minimum food stores (a reserve amount sufficient to meet a minimum calendar time frame), the goal of indefinite self-reliance was set as the intended target.

With respect to practical standards, contingency minimums, and pre-arranged supply-chain expansion strategies (Crossover) that promote this intended target (indefinite self-reliance), the following conclusions and Survival Target Standards (STS) were made:

1. 6-month food store contingency is a sufficient STS for supply chain recovery scenarios (if grid repair is a viable option), and additionally, it is a sufficient STS for establishing a local supply-chain infrastructure expansion system that will support continued self-sustaining survival during an indefinite grid-down event. See Crossover Plan—Chapter 5.0.

2. 6-month food reserve (emergency food stores for each person) will conservatively increase to an indefinite self-sustaining food

supply-chain infrastructure when the advantages of a SAFE Zone Crossover Plan is employed to foster expansion. Within 6-months of grid-failure, food/water acquisition techniques are expected to sustain the survival needs of the zone indefinitely.

3. Where a longer food store contingency is optimum, a 6-month-food reserve for each user within each zone constitutes an effective minimum that is conducive to supply chain expansion (Crossover).

SECTION 3: SAFE Zone; Survival Area Freedom Enforcement Operational Reach Territory

1. SAFE Zone (Survival Area Freedom Enforcement Operational Reach Territory) is the operational reach territory of both the private survival zone and/or community's survival zone infrastructure.

2. SAFE Zone infrastructure constitutes a prepared/pre-positioned survival zone to be used in times of national emergency. A ready-to-go "on demand" backup system for individuals, it is formed by uniting three (3) critical survival standards into an organized and effective countermeasure plan:

   • Protected Technology (see MSHEL; Chapter 3.0)

   • Standardized Survival Stores (see Emergency Stores; Chapter 4.0)

   • Standardized SAFE STATE Operating Procedures (see SSOP; Chapter 5.0)

3. Homes, apartments, neighborhoods, communities, and even defended vehicles can all be SAFE Zones depending on the specific circumstances.

4. SAFE Zone construction/development is low cost. Preservation Shielding (Faraday Cage enclosures) can either be owner-built or purchased directly from manufacturers.

5. High-risk areas such as large cities with dense unprepared populations may compel an escape strategy over bunkering down within a localized survival area. For citizens entrenched within an area that is conducive to long-term survival, a fixed SAFE Zone around the home and property in which they reside is recommended. For others anticipating an escape to a more survivable location, a mobile SAFE Zone built for the relocation/escape environment is alternatively recommended.

6. Fixed or mobile, the SAFE Zone is a hardened infrastructure to promote successful survival through intelligent preparation. With an effective shielding enclosure to defend and preserve critical survival technology (see MSHEL; Minimum Shield Hardening Equipment List, chapter 3.0), the survival mission of bunkering down—or escape—can be optimized for high-confidence success.

7. Within the SAFE STATE Countermeasure Manual, strategic considerations will help to refine and optimize the required SAFE Zone structure based on each citizen's unique circumstance. Additionally, the Countermeasure Manual will help identify the required equipment to be preserved in a Faraday Cage enclosure so as to maximize the individual success of each citizen faced with the differing challenges of both the fixed zone and the mobile zone.

Fixed SAFE Zone:

Three (3) key elements

1. CM Step 1; Preservation Shielding of Critical Electronic Equipment (MSHEL)

   - Food/water supply and acquisition equipment (fluid pumps, tools, etc.)

   - Transportation (backup electronics, preserved cars, motorcycles, etc.)

- Communications (HAM/portable hand-held radios)

- Power Generation (backup electronics for power systems)

- Medical (refrigeration, monitors, etc.)

- Miscellaneous (computing device, security device, information device, etc.)

2. CM Step 2; Emergency Stores

- Food

- Water

- Fuel

- Medical Equipment

- Survival Equipment

- Defense Equipment

3. CM Step 3; Standardized SAFE STATE Operating Procedures

- SSOP (post-event operations/command-and-control)

Mobile SAFE Zone: Requires Tactical Considerations (see note below).

NOTE: Whenever possible, all elements required for the implementation of a Fixed SAFE Zone should be considered as a minimum requirement, regardless of whether the survival zone is "fixed" or "mobile." In many circumstances, however, varying conditions will require adjustments in both Preservation Shielding (recommended MSHEL equipment) and Emergency Stores. Determining the best structure for each individual case will require that tactical considerations be made.

EXAMPLE: For geographical areas where both an emergency escape and a Mobile SAFE Zone is required, if three (3) months of stored food, protected radios, and a protected escape vehicle is all that can be managed, a tremendous advantage over the non-defended populace is acquired and the potential for survival success has been maximized.

Customized countermeasure defense will be a required function for many users, and when using the Survival Zone Sharing Program as a tactical advantage—civil defense can be maximized. Accordingly, industry experts will play a large role in redefining the modern-day "Go Bag" that is protected from HEMP and ready for escape should an attack occur.

SECTION 4: Civil Defense—A National Duty

SAFE STATE survival methodology has been uniquely developed to form a cohesive foundation for both the private and the community-based survival zone infrastructure. With the countermeasure manual providing a step by step path to private implementation, it is the inherent plug-and-play design standards that compel our local communities and states to join forces.

As substantially revealed in the companion novel, SAFE STATES—and with an industry-wide consensus of the experts regarding long-term survival—only with the support of a community-based survival infrastructure will survivors organize, thrive, and prevent national collapse. Following a grid-down attack, the self-defenders will undoubtedly live longer than the un-defended, but in the end, and without community support, the marauders will unite and take control.

Therefore, not only is an effective civil defense force inherently required, it is the first and critical step of being a modern-day American. Where our freedom can be removed at any given moment, countermeasure implementation is now a fundamental duty.

Tactical Considerations—The Super EMP

In contrast to many published emergency preparedness plans issued by local/state/federal agencies, SAFE STATE is a hardened survival plan built for the realities of modern-day war. As a shield from catastrophic collapse, it is important to understand the tactical necessity of a hardened (EMP-proof) survival infrastructure as it relates to saving lives.

The fatal destruction of America's supply-chains and national grids can be acquired with one well-placed high-altitude nuclear detonation (HEMP) over the center of the nation. With an immediate post-event internal collapse of the civilian population, the pulse weapon will not only ensure a "total" victory for America's attacker (s), but in the war-time environment, with a successful HEMP detonation it can ensure that America is removed from the battlefield forever. A weapon of submission, for the enemies of freedom who seek dominance and control, who can't win with a nuclear detonation on the ground, and who likely don't care about the consequences of MAD as long as they win, the HEMP weapon fulfills the intended mission on all fronts.

Known as a nation-killing device, the electromagnetic force produced by a nuclear detonation at high altitude has an unclassified damage capacity ranging from nominal to catastrophic. The classified damage capacity of a modern-day HEMP weapon is unknown to the general public; however, for the observer it must be reasonably assumed that if the unclassified damage potential is identified as catastrophic, the classified damage potential must be well beyond catastrophic. Where the destructive powers of these amplified weapons have a classified value, there is no dispute over the damage that they can inflict.

Known as Super-EMPs, it is with these modern-day weapons where a society can be stopped in its tracks and forever destroyed. When detonated from above, the powerful E1 pulse from a high altitude Super-EMP can pierce and destroy all exposed electronics within line-of-sight below. Cars and trains stop, and the modern-day airliners have no choice but to make an emergency landing with little to no control. The food and the water stop, and the people walk home. Within months, hundreds of millions die.

Where the SAFE Zone has incorporated minimum standards designed to withstand the forces of a Super EMP, users are advised to comply with the countermeasure's continuing compliance procedures to ensure high confidence survival at all times.

SECTION 5: Countermeasure Training:

Mental Readiness

Thriller novel, SAFE STATES—is an essential component/companion of the SAFE STATE Countermeasure Manual learning system. Detailing the catastrophic scenario of a surprise HEMP attack on America, the novel describes a nation half protected with SAFE STATE defense, and half not—and it ignites the survival instincts that have been inappropriately obscured by our modern-day politics. Where the impending suffering and death of every American has been intentionally marginalized, discounted, and underreported, the ensuing consequences are clearly depicted in the heart of the storyline. Where many states are well defended, and where many are not, the SAFE STATES novel reveals the details of our personal risk, the suffering and death of the undefended, and why America must overcome the likely scenario of half defended, half not. A "cautionary" tale, it's sole purpose is to expose the core consequence of our divided nation, and to inspire a responsible and united defense.

An essential training scenario created for the general populace, users are encouraged to use the companion novel as a tool to help identify the personal risks that each of us are exposed to as a result of our location and readiness. A fundamental step toward becoming prepared, situational awareness is an essential knowledge and it must be acquired rapidly.

ACKNOWLEDGMENTS

For some, and maybe all, better left unsaid. Acknowledgments are for later. We thank God for the opportunity.